THE PIONEERS

THE PIONEERS

BY

James Fenimore Cooper

INTRODUCTION BY LEON HOWARD

HOLT, RINEHART AND WINSTON
NEW YORK

Fourth Printing, August, 1962

Introduction copyright © 1959 by Leon Howard
Typography Design by Stefan Salter
Printed in the United States of America
Library of Congress Catalog Card Number: 59-6916
23752-0119

James Cooper—the eleventh of his parents' twelve children— was born on September 15, 1789, and died the day before reaching his sixty-second birthday in 1851. Half his life was spent before he became a novelist, but during his last thirty-one years he produced some fifty separate titles of fiction and history, and saw the American novel firmly established on the foundations he had built. By a special act of the New York State Legislature in 1826 he took his mother's family name, Fenimore, as a part of his own and used it for all the books published under his signature. As James Fenimore Cooper he was at the time of his death—and has remained for more than a century since—the most widely read of American novelists. It has taken all the resources of Hollywood, for a generation, to dim the picture of America which he gave to the world.

The first and nonliterary half of his life was a varied and often purposeless one. His father, William Cooper, was one of America's most energetic and successful promoters of new settlements during the eighteenth century; and in 1790 he moved his entire family from their New Jersey home to central New York—according to one story, putting his reluctant wife into a wagon while she sat firmly in her chair holding the infant James in her arms. There the elder Cooper had already established the village of Cooperstown and had built a wooden mansion house on the shore of Lake Otsego for his family's use until the more pretentious brick Otsego Hall was completed a decade later. He was a Quaker by birth, an Episcopalian and a Federalist by later conviction, and a man of firm principles throughout his life. He would not follow the conventional New York version of the Dutch patroon system by settling land with tenants, but sold his holdings outright while maintaining as much paternal interest in the community as was expected of any lord of a manor. He was the village squire, the county judge, and the sometimes district representative in the Federal Congress until he died, in 1809 at the age of fifty-five, of a blow struck from behind by a political opponent at the end of a public meeting.

Before his death, he planned James's life. He sent his son to Albany at the age of eleven to prepare for Yale College under the direction of an Episcopal clergyman, and two years later he saw the boy entered at Yale under the strict paternalistic guidance of President Timothy Dwight—a Congregationalist and a Yankee, but as staunch a Federalist as New England could boast. When the Dwight discipline and the inherited Cooper spirit clashed in 1806 and James was expelled shortly before he was due to graduate, the boy was sent to sea for a year's experience before the mast which qualified him for the midshipman's commission. He grew a queue and served in the United States Navy—mostly in a wilderness headquarters on the shore of Lake Ontario—from January 1, 1809, until May 9, 1810, when he used his father's recent death as an excuse for requesting a year's furlough, during which he courted and married "a fair damsel of eighteen," before resigning his commission and settling down to enjoy the substantial first share of his inheritance.

At first the young couple settled in the home of the bride, Susan DeLancey, whose Tory family had managed to retain large holdings of land in aristocratic Westchester County. They built their own home at Mamaroneck but soon abandoned it to return to the DeLancey mansion on Heathcote Hill, overlooking Long Island Sound, until 1814 when James constructed his own frame house on Fenimore Farm in Cooperstown to use as a temporary residence until a proper stone manor house could be finished. He abandoned the project, however, before the new house was ready for occupancy, and in the spring of 1817 returned to Westchester where he built still another home, Angevine, on Susan's property in Scarsdale. He became an active member of the County Agricultural Society, a Colonel on the Governor's Staff, and paymaster for the Fourth Division of the state militia, but remained restless. A two-thirds interest in a whaling vessel, the *Union,* enabled him to get the smell of tar in his nostrils once more as he took charge of her fitting and manning; and he spent some time in Sag Harbor, reequipping her between voyages and marketing the oil. But he was obviously an unsettled man, subject to some inner rhythm which had compelled him toward a major change of life every third year since he had entered college.

II

None of these changes had directed him in any apparent way toward a literary career, and the ex-naval officer and gentleman farmer has been charged with such indifference to the pen that he could barely be brought to write a letter. But he could and did read, and it was reading, according to the familiar story, which made him a writer. Disgusted with an English novel he was rendering aloud to his family, he swore that he could write a better one himself and was challenged by his wife to do so. The result was *Precaution*—a novel of manners, with an English setting—which he published anonymously in 1820.

It was a poor job, even for apprentice work, but it showed that Cooper had the taste required to select good models from the mass of English popular fiction which surrounded him. For he chose Jane Austen as his example, and when he realized that the characters and manners which so interested the author of *Persuasion* were not suited to his more forthright and masculine disposition he turned to the other outstanding British novelist of his time—Walter Scott, the author of *Waverley,* whose border romances were making history as exciting as Gothic sensationalism.

Cooper's second novel, *The Spy,* was a historical romance of border warfare in the Westchester district of his wife's home; and if his portraits of historical characters were more artificial than Scott's, his freehand representations of common people were almost as natural. Harvey Birch, the yeoman farmer who sacrificed reputation to patriotism in playing the role of the Spy, is a memorable character in fiction, whether or not he is based upon a real character in history. With all his unskilled awkwardness, Cooper could create better than he could copy, and the public recognized the fact by making *The Spy* enough of a literary success to justify its author in taking seriously the profession of authorship.

Cooper's motives in 1822 are not altogether clear. Undoubtedly, in an old journalistic expression, he had got ink on his fingers while writing his first two novels and could not get it off. His discovery that he could write must have been a profoundly satisfying one, because it was not only a realization of unexpected talent, but also a means of release for the inherent energy which was later to overflow the bounds of literature and which certainly could not have been contained forever within the limits of a Westchester farm. It may have been, too, that he felt the need for a remunerative profession, for he had been disappointed in his later expectations from his father's estate and the financial depression of 1819 doubtless affected him as it did almost everybody else. But we can be sure only that he took serious stock of his resources, began a new book, and decided to move his family to New York City, where the Irvings and Pauldings and other members of "the Knickerbocker group" made the literary atmosphere a stimulating one.

The new author's evaluation of his own resources was probably his most important act because it led indirectly to his most memorable literary achievement. His first interest had been in the novel of manners, but *Precaution* had revealed the inadequacy of his acquaintance with the sort of manners which were refined and elevated and, in short, English enough to interest the conventional reading public. He had been happier and more successful with the familiar scenes and local customs of *The Spy,* but he was not at all sure that his native country provided the materials and associations necessary for an American Scott and the professional practice of historical romance. The book most suited to his own interest and knowledge could be neither an imitation of Jane Austen nor of Walter Scott. It would be, instead, an application of the approach of one to the material of the other. It would be a semihistorical novel of manners on the American border, an examination of American life in its most distinctive and peculiar aspects, a story of the pioneers of a new world.

The following of his "humor"—as he put it—to write such a novel was an act of courage in 1822. No one at the time had advanced the notion that realism, in itself, was a major artistic quality. A novel involved some conformity to the truth of everyday life in order to be distinguishable from a romance, but its literary value was determined by some additional quality—

humor, sentiment, or refinement in manners or morals—either inherent in its substance or superimposed upon it by the author. A mere "slice of life," such as came to be admired a century later, would have puzzled the reading public and infuriated the literary critics.

Furthermore, according to the prevailing esthetic theory of the time, the highest excellence of a literary work was determined by the ideas "associated" with it. If an author dealt with material which stimulated a train of fresh and natural associations in his mind, he was supposed to display a vitality of style he could achieve in no other way; but this vitality could not be recognized and appreciated by his readers unless they shared with him these associations. Such a theory created, for American writers, a problem of which Cooper was acutely aware. The scenes of his own pioneer childhood were rich with associations. They could set in motion the imaginative processes by which he had created the character of Harvey Birch, without placing upon him the historical restrictions which had made his portrait of Washington stiffer than anything on canvas and more rigid than marble. Yet pioneer life was crude, outside the experience of most novel readers even in America, and likely to suggest a train of vulgar associations completely antagonistic to sentiment and refinement. Washington Irving had solved the problem by treating American manners humorously, but Cooper was too serious-minded to take that way out. He was a man of consciously elevated sentiments, who felt the need to prove himself "grave" in his writings and saw only an incidental value in humor.

Fortunately, however, he was convinced that the conquest of the wilderness was in no way incompatible with the highest nobility of sentiment. William Cooper's pride in the 40,000 souls who had been settled under his direction was, in the eyes of his son, thoroughly justified. It was the achievement of a man whose faults and foibles and mistakes in judgment did not disguise his essential greatness of character. Pioneers might be rude and sometime uncouth, but they were not—despite the assertions of President Timothy Dwight of Yale, in his recently published *Travels*—ignoble. A novel of unique American manners might fail to achieve popular or critical success, but from the author's literary point of view there was no reason why the experiment should not be attempted. He gave it the distinctively American title *The Pioneers, or The Sources of the Susquehanna,* called it "a Descriptive Tale," and drew its material partly from his imagination and partly from his childhood memories of personal experience and family stories about the settlement on Lake Otsego.

Actually Cooper's experiment, although he could hardly have known it in advance, was well timed. For the United States was going through a period of national myth-making and entering into an era of patriotic enthusiasm which was to transform the adjective "American" from an apology into a boast. George Washington had recently been placed upon a cherry stump pedestal by the Reverend Mason Weems; General Israel Putnam had been transformed into a dashing cavalier by the Honorable David Humphreys; and Captain John Paul Jones was being rescued from the aspersions cast upon him by his first biographer. More important, the old Federalist antagonism toward men in leather aprons and breeches was beginning to fade away in an era of good feeling, and the leather-clad common man was already emerging from the forest as a folk hero. Before his death in 1820 Daniel Boone had been celebrated in an epic poem, and the backwoodsman had become such a familiar type that James Kirke Paulding had used him as the subject for a long humorous poem. But Paulding, for all his literary experience, had dealt with him in the wrong manner. The generation of settlers who had been pouring across the mountains into Kentucky, Tennessee, and the Ohio country had learned to appreciate the qualities of men who had scouted the difficult mountain passes and established primitive settlements in a hostile environment. These were not, until they began to describe themselves as "half horse and half alligator" a few self-confident years later, comic characters. On the contrary, they were on the verge of becoming the heroic symbols of a new buckskin democracy.

Cooper was to do more than any other single person to fix this symbol in the popular mind, but when he began *The Pioneers* he could hardly have intended to do more than give a fair picture of life in a new settlement. The sustaining interest in his book would have to be borrowed from romance—a mystery to be solved, an old wrong to be righted, and a young love to blossom despite the temporary blight of misunderstandings. This he could draw from an imagination which was always more ingenious than plausible, and the Temple-Effingham plot was his concession to artificial unity and the demands of popular romance. Otherwise he insisted that his tale was in "keeping" with human nature and advised anyone who picked up the book "with the expectation of meeting gods and goddesses, spooks or witches, or of feeling that strong excitement that is produced by battles and murders, to throw it aside at once, for no such interest will be found in any of its pages."

What a reader could and can still find in its pages is a genuine insight into the social conditions of American expansion during the early years of the republic. Some of them are peculiar to Lake Otsego. Relatively few frontier communities developed under the supervision of a resident squire who had sold the land outright to its settlers and yet tried to keep them under his own benevolent control. Marmaduke Temple is a softened portrait of William Cooper, and his efforts to establish an Episcopal church upon a community of nonconformists are a part of the early history of Cooperstown. His determination to introduce law for its own sake into the wilderness was perhaps more representative of other districts, for the regions opened to settlement by investment, rather than by squatters or—in a later period—by homesteading, were generally planned as law-abiding communities. In any case, Judge Temple was the squire of a district which contained a representation of the various peoples who had earlier given St. John de Crèvecoeur the idea of America as a melting pot and inspired his essay "What is an American?" It included the refugee French storekeeper M. Le Quoi, the German Major Hartmann, the English Ben Pump, the African Agamemnon, and a variety of New England Yankees in addition to the middle colonists who obviously—as Cooper saw it—provided the respectable backbone of the settlement. Some of these have been identified as real people, drawn from the author's memory, and they are all representative. Like the hostess of the tavern, the half-educated and envious lawyer, the ill-trained doctor, the stubborn carpenter, and the professional wood chopper, they were a part of the social scene which Cooper had in mind when he selected four lines of Paulding's verse for his title page

> Extremes of habits, manners, time and space,
> Brought close together, here stood face to face,
> And gave at once a contrast to the view,
> That other lands and ages never knew.

This was the subject of his "descriptive tale"—a novel of manners which would make him the Maria Edgeworth, if not the Jane Austen, of the American frontier.

III

The greatest contrast Cooper had in view, however, was not that of the extremes of habit and manners brought face to face in the settlement, but the contrast between the settlement and the wilderness. Implicit in his basic conception of the book was a conflict which had bothered many Americans ever since John Winthrop, in 1645, had made a distinction between "natural" and "civil" liberty—the liberty to do as one pleased, and the liberty to do only that which was right, just, and honest. The Declaration of Independence had taken Americans far away from the Puritan attitude of contempt toward natural liberty, but the social and political problems which led to the adoption of the Constitution had tended to revive it. After the French Revolution, Timothy Dwight had given a national application to Winthrop's belief that "civil" liberty was the only liberty proper to New England; and Judge William Cooper, in his political activities, had been a forceful representative of the same point of view. As time was to show, James Cooper's mind was biased in that direction; but in 1822 he was still too restless and unsettled to feel a greater instinctive concern for his "civil" than for his "natural" rights. Furthermore, all his childhood associations with the Otsego country probably included ideas of freedom and antagonism toward restraint.

In any case, he displayed a stronger emotional attachment than he may have realized to the two characters he used as representatives of wilderness manners. One was the lone "Indian John," familiar to almost every settlement usually as an outcast both of his own people and of the whites from whom he begged support. The other was the buckskin-clad hunter with his long rifle and solitary disposition, who was known in the settlements only through his occasional appearances for lead and gunpowder and whiskey. Cooper kept them both around throughout his entire story, partly because they were essential to his major design of contrasting manners and partly because they were needed in the romantic Effingham-Temple plot; and perhaps for those reasons, too, he assigned them more dignity than such characters ordinarily possessed in reality. Chingach-gook was not a begging outcast but the last survivor of a great tribe who had returned to his native region to die in surroundings through which he had once bounded like a roe and which he could still view with a chastened and subdued pleasure. Natty Bumppo was a hunter who had settled down in a less Wordsworthian spirit for reasons of loyalty which did not become clear until the end of the book.

Chingachgook may have been, in Cooper's mind, as realistic a figure as Judge Temple. For he belongs less to the tradition of the noble savage in European romanticism than he does to that of the American historians who—from Thomas Jefferson in his *Notes on Virginia* to Samuel Williams in his *History of Vermont*—had been collecting evidence that Buffon and other European philosophers were wrong in their contention that "the man of America" was a degenerate specimen of humanity. Cooper was very sensitive to "scientific" observations on America, as he was to show clearly by his treatment of Dr. Obed Batt in *The Prairie* and by his explicit comments in later books, and his first portrait of an Indian may have been his first contribution to what was in his day a thriving controversy over the alleged "degenerative effects" of the American climate. John Heckewelder's often-noted influence upon Cooper came later as he developed his distinction between the Delawares and the Iroquois. But the hunter was, from the beginning, half man and half myth—the uncouth Nathaniel Bumppo and the romantic Leatherstocking.

Cooper's original visualization of Bumppo was certainly anything but romantic. As scrawny as Irving's Ichabod Crane, he cut almost as ridiculous a figure with his scraggy neck surmounted by a head of lank sandy hair, shaggy gray brows, and an enormous mouth which opened to expose a single tusk of yellow bone. Even his nicknames were ironic. A foxskin cap, a hairy deerskin coat belted with colored worsted, and a pair of "tarnished" buckskin breeches all belied the implications of "Natty"; and Cooper took pains to point out that he was called "Leatherstocking" despite the fact that his legs were protected beneath his leggings "by thick garments of woolen, duly made of good blue yarn." There was little in his first sullen appearance to indicate that he was going to become the most widely admired romantic hero in American literature.

But he had one characteristic which associated him with romantic rather than comic myth: he was a hunter, not a schoolmaster. As a hunter, he possessed the rugged endurance, the accomplished skill, and the self-reliant shrewdness which were the necessary attributes of his profession; and these were qualities which Cooper himself genuinely admired. His ruggedness was noted and his skill celebrated in his introductory scene. His self-reliance increased and his shrewdness ripened into wisdom as the book progressed, and his character developed as did none of the others. In his protest against the new game laws he was the spokesman for his kind against what they considered civilization's arbitrary restrictions upon natural liberty, and Cooper sympathized with his point of view even if he could not share it. But in his protest against the wanton massacre of passenger pigeons in the name of sport, he was the spokesman for Cooper's own sentiments toward the blind, irrational destructiveness of men who could not subdue nature without destroying it. Far removed though he was from his creator's position and personality, Natty Bumppo took on some of Cooper's own waverings between impulse and reason, became human, and acquired such dignity that the reader forgets his grotesque entrance into the book and follows his exit into the western forest sympathetically and perhaps a little wistfully.

The human qualities of Natty Bumppo may have captured the sympathies of Cooper's contemporary readers, but what they recognized in him was a type. A publishing convention of the time was to advertise a book by releasing a portion of it in advance to the newspapers, and the section chosen for this purpose from *The Pioneers* was the account of Elizabeth's rescue from the panther. In it appeared the Leatherstocking who caught the public fancy, self-portrayed in a single sentence: "I wonder if I had aimed at the varmint's eye, if I shouldn't have touched the life sooner than in the forehead? but they are hard-lived animals, and it was a good shot, consid'ring that I could see nothing but the head and the peak of its tail." Here was the quick and accurate shooting which made possible America's individualistic advance into the wilderness. Here was Daniel Boone and the conquest of the Dark and Bloody Ground. Here was one of Andy Jackson's hunters of Kentucky whose marksmanship was credited with the recent victory over the British in New Orleans. Here was the distinctive American —a new folk hero, casually cradling his rifle as he slouched toward glory.

The sale of 3,500 copies of *The Pioneers* on the morning of its publication, February 1, 1823, has been attributed to the publication of this extract; and, in any event, the book surely owed its success to Leatherstocking. Reviewers at home and abroad singled him out for praise, whatever they may have thought or said about Cooper's plot or style or the "manners" with which he had been primarily concerned. Natty Bumppo was the first genuinely original character to be recognized in American fiction.

IV

Leatherstocking was also to linger long in the mind of his creator. Cooper's next novel, conceived and composed after his removal to New York in 1822, was *The Pilot*—another historical tale of the American Revolution, designed, it is said, to give readers of Scott some needed lessons in seamanship. In it the major character was not John Paul Jones, whose disguise gave the book its title, but Long Tom Coffin, who was a common sailor with most of the personal qualities of Natty Bumppo but without the mythological attachments which enabled the hunter to catch the public fancy. After Cooper had settled firmly into the profession of authorship and before he went abroad in 1826, he returned to Natty Bumppo and gave him more heroic stature and greater symbolic meaning.

The Last of the Mohicans, the second book in what came to be a series of Leatherstocking Tales, is the best known of

Cooper's works. It supplied a background, suggested in *The Pioneers,* for Natty Bumppo and Chingachgook by presenting them in the full glory of their maturity. The Indian became the noble representative of a disappearing race when his son Uncas, the last potential leader of the tribe, was killed and the father left with memories which made his death scene in *The Pioneers* plausible. Natty, as Hawkeye, became the representative of the triumphant whites who had learned to meet the Indians on their own terms, master their woodcraft, and improve on their marksmanship until the "varmints" among them were destroyed and the good Indians were ready for some happier hunting ground. In *The Last of the Mohicans* Cooper abandoned his interest in the novel of manners and made it frankly a tale of exciting incident, battles and pursuits, escapes from danger, and demonstrations of woodcraft. It was Cooper's closest approach to the popular novel of sensationalism.

In Paris, while completing the third Leatherstocking Tale, Cooper brought Natty's life to an end on the distant western prairies which Lewis and Clark had explored but Cooper himself had never seen. At this distance and without the complicating factors of memory and personal associations, Cooper's perspective was better and his view of the social forces involved in the advancing frontier was clearer than it had been in *The Pioneers*. The plot of *The Prairie* was sillier than anything he had yet invented, but the characters in it were a realistic lot of honest settlers, adventurers, and ruffians of the sort who were actually beginning to pour across the plains. They were a self-selected group, wilder and more violent than the chosen landowners in Cooperstown, and Cooper allowed them the "one or two hangings" which he recognized as being of manifest advantage to new settlements but which he had kept out of *The Pioneers* on the grounds that they "would have been out of 'keeping' with the humane laws of this compassionate country." Among these rougher characters Leatherstocking, now a "trapper," fell for the first time into his own proper perspective as a shadowy figure who was most at home among the Indians. He might be regarded as the advance agent of a race whose progress he made possible, but with whom he had almost nothing in common.

In Europe Cooper was to become preoccupied with his "gleanings" of observation and with his aggressive defense of American democracy; and out of his observation, reading, and argument came three novels—*The Bravo, The Heidenmauer,* and *The Headsman*—which reflected his view of the European social history that Scott had neglected. He had written and was to continue to write throughout his life other historical novels of the American land and sea. But his major achievements were the results of strong bursts of feeling, such as his feeling about the fictional neglect of European social history and his violent reaction to social change in America when he returned home in 1833, and discovered that Jeffersonian democracy had been transformed into the Jacksonian kind and that the Bumppos had grown bumptious in their attitude toward their betters. He became engaged in a long series of personal quarrels, enlarged them to include the whole country in two novels called *Homeward Bound* and *Home as Found,* and carried a chip on his shoulder when he wrote a *History of the Navy.* None of these improved his public reputation, but in them he worked off the violence he had to get rid of before he could manage his many lawsuits with one part of his mind and with the other manage the extraordinary professional achievement of his last decade.

Of the sixteen novels he published between 1840 and the time of his death the most remarkable are those of the "Littlepage" series or the "Rent-War" trilogy—*Satanstoe, The Chainbearer,* and *The Redskins.* Of these, only the last deals directly with the conflict between landlords and tenants which marked the breaking up of the Dutch patroon system and the breaking down of the old political parties in New York State during the turbulent 'forties. The others provide historical background, and *Satanstoe* is the finest of Cooper's attempts to combine social fiction and history. Although its period is the mid-eighteenth century, its tone and richness of detail have the warm suggestion of memory found in *The Pioneers;* and its analytic comments upon the effects of different modes of settlement, its representation of the relationship between English and Dutch, and its frequently amusing reflection of different human points of view reveal a better social perspective than

Cooper had shown in *The Prairie*. It is one of Cooper's major successes.

Perhaps he could not have felt his way so successfully back into the past, had he not started his own professional revival with a revival of Leatherstocking. For the first book of his later period was *The Pathfinder*, a romance which showed Natty Bumppo in love and made him a man of sentiment and sacrifice as well as of rugged independence. It was followed immediately by *The Deerslayer*, in which the youthful Natty drew his first blood and achieved manhood. Both of these stories were skilfully managed on a high plane of sentiment, implicitly contradicting the new, extravagant, and comic version of the frontiersman as represented by Davy Crockett, and reasserting the original heroic myth for a new age of somewhat finer sentiment. In these two novels the Leatherstocking saga—and the myth—was made complete.

Cooper's myth has been the one which prevailed. Leatherstocking has affected the popular imagination of the world as has no other single character in American fiction, and, in America, even Davy Crockett has been made over into an image closer to that of Natty Bumppo than to the hero of Crockett's own *Autobiography*. Readers of the Leatherstocking Tales can approach them in either of two ways. They can absorb the complete myth, as most of them do, by beginning with the youthful Deerslayer and following the chronology of Natty Bumppo's own life, as Cooper finally imagined it. Or they can observe in the Tales the phenomenon of a myth developing from reality to romance, the pattern of Cooper's development from an amateur to a professional novelist, and the beginnings of American fiction. For those whose curiosity leads them beneath the surface of literature and into the complex world of experience, from which books grow into a creative life of their own, the first of Cooper's novels—and the first genuinely original novel in the history of American literature—is the book in which he stood on the threshold of remembered experience, cast aside his English models, and boldly followed his own "humor" along a new path which led him through the conflicts and emerging dreams of his own age to a creation he did not entirely anticipate. This book is *The Pioneers*.

· *Bibliographical Note* ·

The text of this edition of *The Pioneers* has been set from the edition of 1825, which is a reprint of the first edition of 1823 with a few minor corrections, especially of eccentricities of punctuation that may be attributed to the original printer. Cooper himself later revised the text which was used for the collected edition of his works.

The most modern biography of Cooper is by James Grossman in the *American Men of Letters* series (New York, 1949), and an interesting earlier work is the illustrated biography by Mary E. Phillips (New York, 1913). Maurice Clavel's *Fenimore Cooper: sa vie et son oeuvre* (*Aix-en-Provence*, 1938) is a pioneer work which remains a valuable source of information, and the same author's *Fenimore Cooper and His Critics*, of the same place and date, is the standard work on Cooper's contemporary reception. Selections from Cooper's letters have been published in *The Correspondence of James Fenimore Cooper* (2 vols., New Haven, 1922), but a more complete edition by James F. Beard, Jr., is in preparation. The standard bibliography is Robert E. Spiller and Philip C. Blackburn's *A Descriptive Bibliography of James Fenimore Cooper* (New York, 1934). Among the special studies the most valuable are R. E. Spiller's *James Fenimore Cooper: Critic of His Times* (New York, 1931) and the several excellent essays in *James Fenimore Cooper: A Re-Appraisal* (New York Historical Association: Cooperstown, 1954).

THE

PIONEERS,

OR THE

SOURCES OF THE SUSQUEHANNA:

A Descriptive Tale

BY THE AUTHOR OF "PRECAUTION."

"Extremes of habits, manners, time and space,
Brought close together, here stood face to face,
And gave at once a contrast to the view,
That other lands and ages never knew."
Paulding

TO MR. CHARLES WILEY, Bookseller.

Every man is, more or less, the sport of accident; nor do I know that authors are at all exempted from this humiliating influence. This is the third of my novels, and it depends on two very uncertain contingencies, whether it will not be the last:—the one being the public opinion, and the other mine own humour. The first book was written, because I was told that I could not write a grave tale; so, to prove that the world did not know me, I wrote one that was so grave nobody would read it; wherein I think that I had much the best of the argument. The second was written to see if I could not overcome this neglect of the reading world. How far I have succeeded, MR. CHARLES WILEY, must ever remain a secret between ourselves. The third has been written, exclusively, to please myself: so it would be no wonder if it displeased every body else; for what two ever thought alike, on a subject of the imagination?

I should think criticism to be the perfection of human acquirements, did there not exist this discrepancy in taste. Just as I have made up my mind to adopt the very sagacious hints of one learned Reviewer, a pamphlet is put into my hands, containing the remarks of another, who condemns all that his rival praises, and praises all that his rival condemns. There I am, left like an ass between two locks of hay; so that I have determined to relinquish my animate nature, and remain stationary, like a lock of hay between two asses.

It is now a long time, say the wise ones, since the world has been told all that is new and novel. But the Reviewers (the cunning wights!) have adopted an ingenious expedient, to give a freshness to the most trite idea. They clothe it in a language so obscure and metaphysical, that the reader is not about to comprehend their pages without some labour. This is called a great "range of thought;" and not improperly, as I can testify; for, in my own case, I have frequently ranged the universe of ideas, and come back again in as perfect ignorance of their meaning as when I set out. It is delightful, to see the literati of a circulating library get hold of one of these difficult periods! Their praise of the performance is exactly commensurate with its obscurity. Every body knows, that to seem wise is the first requisite in a great man.

A common word in the mouths of all Reviewers, readers of magazines, and young ladies, when speaking of novels, is *"keeping;"* and yet there are but few who attach the same meaning to it. I belong, myself, to the old school, in this particular, and think that it applies more to the subject in hand, than to any use of terms, or of cant expressions. As a man might just as well be out of the world as out of "keeping," I have endeavoured to confine myself, in this tale, strictly to its observance. This is a formidable curb to the imagination, as, doubtless, the reader will very soon discover; but under its influence I have come to the conclusion, that the writer of a tale, who takes the earth for the scene of his story, is in some degree bound to respect human nature. Therefore I would advise any one, who may take up this book, with the expectation of meeting gods and goddesses, spooks or witches, or of feeling that strong excitement that is produced by battles and murders, to throw it aside at once, for no such interest will be found in any of its pages.

I have already said, that it was mine own humour that suggested this tale; but it is a humour that is deeply connected with feeling. Happier periods, more interesting events, and, possibly, more beauteous scenes, might have been selected, to exemplify my subject; but none of either that would be so dear to me. I wish, therefore, to be judged more by what I have done, than by my sins of omission. I have introduced one battle, but it is not of the most Homeric kind. As for murders, the population of a new country will not admit of such a waste of human life. There might possibly have been one or two hangings, to the manifest advantage of the "settlement;" but then it would have been out of "keeping" with the humane laws of this compassionate country.

The "Pioneers" is now before the world, MR. WILEY, and I shall look to you for the only true account of its reception. The critics may write as obscurely as they please, and look much wiser than they are; the papers may puff or abuse, as their changeful humours dictate; but if you meet me with a smiling face, I shall at once know that all is essentially well.

If you should ever have occasion for a preface, I beg you will let me hear from you in reply.

Yours, truly,

THE AUTHOR.

New York, January 1st, 1823.

· Chapter I ·

See, Winter comes, to rule the varied year,
Sullen and sad, with all his rising train;
Vapours, and clouds, and storms—

THOMSON

Near the centre of the great State of New-York lies an extensive district of country, whose surface is a succession of hills and dales, or, to speak with greater deference to geographical definitions, of mountains and valleys. It is among these hills that the Delaware takes its rise; and flowing from the limpid lakes and thousand springs of this country, the numerous sources of the mighty Susquehanna meander through the valleys, until, uniting, they form one of the proudest streams of which the old United States could boast. The mountains are generally arable to the top, although instances are not wanting, where their sides are jutted with rocks, that aid greatly in giving that romantic character to the country, which it so eminently possesses. The vales are narrow, rich, and cultivated; with a stream uniformly winding through each, now gliding peacefully under the brow of one of the hills, and then suddenly shooting across the plain, to wash the feet of its opposite rival. Beautiful and thriving villages are found interspersed along the margins of the small lakes, or situated at those points of the streams which are favourable to manufacturing; and neat and comfortable farms, with every indication of wealth about them, are scattered profusely through the vales, and even to the mountain tops. Roads diverge in every direction, from the even and graceful bottoms of the valleys, to the most rugged and intricate passes of the hills. Academies, and minor edifices for the encouragement of learning, meet the eye of the stranger, at every few miles, as he winds his way through this uneven territory; and places for the public worship of God abound with that frequency which characterizes a moral and reflecting people, and with that variety of exterior and canonical government which flows from unfettered liberty of conscience. In short, the whole district is hourly exhibiting how much can be done, in even a rugged country, and with a severe climate, under the dominion of mild laws, and where every man feels a direct interest in the prosperity of a commonwealth, of which he knows himself to form a distinct and independent part. The expedients of the pioneers who first broke ground in the settlement of this country, are succeeded by the permanent improvements of the yeoman, who intends to leave his remains to moulder under the sod which he tills, or, perhaps, of the son, who, born in the land, piously wishes to linger around the grave of his father. Only forty years have passed since this whole territory was a wilderness.

Very soon after the establishment of the independence of the States by the peace of 1783, the enterprise of their citizens was directed to a developement of the natural advantages of their widely extended dominions. Before the war of the revolution the inhabited parts of the colony of New-York were limited to less than a tenth of her possessions. A narrow belt of country, extending for a short distance on either side of the Hudson, with a similar occupation of fifty miles on the banks of the Mohawk, together with the islands of Nassau and Staten, and a few insulated settlements on chosen land along the margins of streams, composed the country that was then inhabited by less than two hundred thousand souls. Within the short period we have mentioned, her population has spread itself over five degrees of latitude and seven of longitude, and has swelled to the powerful number of nearly a million and a half, who are maintained in abundance, and can look forward to ages before the evil day must arrive, when their possessions will become unequal to their wants.

Our tale begins in 1793, about seven years after the commencement of one of the earliest of those settlements, which have conduced to effect that magical change in the power and condition of the state, to which we have alluded.

It was near the setting of the sun, on a clear, cold day in December of that year, when a sleigh was moving slowly up one of the mountains in the district which we have described. The day had been fine for the season, and but two or three large clouds, whose colour seemed brightened by the light reflected from the mass of snow that covered the earth, floated in a sky of the purest blue. The road wound along the brow of a precipice, and on one side was upheld by a foundation of logs, piled for many feet, one upon the other, while a narrow excavation in the mountain, in the opposite direction, had made a passage of sufficient width for the ordinary travelling of that day. But logs, excavation, and every thing that did not reach for several feet above the earth, lay promiscuously buried under the snow. A single track, barely wide enough to receive the sleigh, denoted the route of the highway, and this was sunken near two feet below the surrounding surface. In the vale, which lay at a distance of several hundred feet beneath them, there was what in the language of the country was called a *clearing*, and all the usual improvements of a new settlement; these even extended up the hill to the point where the road turned short and ran across the level land, which lay on the summit of the mountain; but the summit itself yet remained a forest. There was a littering in the atmosphere, as if it were filled with innumerable shining particles, and the noble bay horses that drew the sleigh were covered, in many parts, with a coat of frost. The vapour from their nostrils was seen to issue like smoke; and every object in the view, as well as every arrangement of the travellers, denoted the depth of a winter in the mountains. The harness, which was of a deep dull black, differing from the glossy varnishing of the present day, was ornamented with enormous plates and buckles of brass that shone like gold in the transient beams of the sun, which found their way obliquely through the tops of the trees. Huge saddles, studded with nails of the same material, and fitted with cloth that admirably served as blankets to the shoulders of the animals, supported four high, square-topped turrets, through which the stout reins led from the mouths of the horses to the hands of the driver, who was a negro, of apparently twenty years of age. His face, which nature had coloured with a glistening black, was now mottled with the cold, and his large shining eyes were moistened with a liquid that flowed from the same cause; still there was a smiling expression of good humour in his happy countenance, that was created by the thoughts of his home, and a Christmas fire-side, with its Christmas frolics. The sleigh was one of those large, comfortable, old-fashioned conveyances, which would admit a whole family within its bosom, but which now contained only two passengers besides the driver. Its outside was a modest green, and its inside of a fiery red, that was intended to convey the idea of heat in that cold climate. Large buffalo skins, trimmed around the edges with red cloth, cut into festoons, covered the back of the sleigh, and were spread over its bottom, and drawn up around the feet of the travellers—one of whom was a man of middle age, and the other a female, just entering upon womanhood. The former was of a large stature; but the precautions he had taken to guard against the cold, left but little of his person exposed to view. A great-coat, that was abundantly ornamented, if it were not made more com fortable, by a profusion of furs, enveloped the whole of his figure, excepting the head, which was covered with a cap of martin skins, lined with morocco, the sides of which were made to fall, if necessary, and were now drawn close over the ears, and were fastened beneath his chin with a black riband; its top was surmounted with the tail of the animal whose skin had furnished the materials for the cap, which fell back not ungracefully, a few inches behind the head. From beneath this masque were to be seen part of a fine manly face, and particularly a pair of expressive, large blue eyes, that promised extraordinary intellect, covert humour, and great benevolence. The form of his companion was literally hid beneath the multitude and variety of garments which she wore. There were furs and silks peeping from under a large camlet cloak, with a thick flannel lining, that, by its cut and size, was evidently intended for a masculine wearer. A hugh hood of black silk, that was quilted with down, concealed the whole of her head, except at a small opening in front for breath, through which occasionally sparkled a pair of animated eyes of the deepest black.

Both the father and daughter (for such was the connexion

between the travellers) were too much occupied with their different reflections to break the stillness, that received little or no interruption from the easy gliding of the sleigh, by the sound of their voices. The former was thinking of the wife that had held this their only child fondly to her bosom, when, four years before, she had reluctantly consented to relinquish the society of her daughter, in order that the latter might enjoy the advantages which the city could afford to her education. A few months afterward death had deprived him of the remaining companion of his solitude; but still he had enough of real regard for his child, not to bring her into the comparative wilderness in which he dwelt, until the full period had expired, to which he had limited her juvenile labours. The reflections of the daughter were less melancholy, and mingled with a pleased astonishment at the novel scenery that she met at every turn in the road.

The mountain on which they were journeying was covered with pines, that rose without a branch seventy or eighty feet, and which frequently towered to an additional height, that more than equalled that elevation. Through the innumerable vistas that opened beneath the lofty trees the eye could penetrate, until it was met by a distant inequality in the ground, or was stopped by a view of the summit of the mountain which lay on the opposite side of the valley to which they were hastening. The dark trunks of the trees rose from the pure white of the snow, in regularly formed shafts, until, at a great height, their branches shot forth their horizontal limbs, that were covered with the meager foliage of an evergreen, affording a melancholy contrast to the torpor of nature below. To the travellers there seemed to be no wind; but these pines waved majestically at their topmost boughs, sending forth a dull, sighing sound, that was quite in consonance with the scene.

The sleigh had glided for some distance along the even surface, and the gaze of the female was bent in inquisitive, and, perhaps, timid glances, into the recesses of the forest, which were lighted by the unsullied covering of the earth, when a loud and continued howling was heard, pealing under the long arches of the woods, like the cry of a numerous pack of hounds. The instant the sounds reached the ears of the gentleman, whatever might have been the subject of his meditations, he forgot it; for he cried aloud to the black—

"Hold up, Aggy; there is old Hector; I should know his bay among ten thousand. The Leather-stocking has put his hounds into the hills this clear day, and they have started their game, you hear. There is a deer-track a few rods ahead;—and now, Bess, if thou canst muster courage enough to stand fire, I will give thee a saddle for thy Christmas dinner."

The black drew up, with a cheerful grin upon his chilled features, and began thrashing his arms together, in order to restore the circulation to his fingers, while the speaker stood erect, and, throwing aside his outer covering, stept from the sleigh upon a bank of snow, which sustained his weight without yielding more than an inch or two. A storm of sleet had fallen and frozen upon the surface a few days before, and but a slight snow had occurred since to purify, without weakening its covering.

In a few moments the speaker succeeded in extricating a double-barrelled fowling-piece from among a multitude of trunks and bandboxes. After throwing aside the thick mittens which had encased his hands, that now appeared in a pair of leather gloves tipped with fur, he examined his priming, and was about to move forward, when the light bounding noise of an animal plunging through the woods was heard, and directly a fine buck darted into the path, a short distance ahead of him. The appearance of the animal was sudden, and his flight inconceivably rapid; but the traveller appeared to be too keen a sportsman to be disconcerted by either. As it came first into view he raised the fowling-piece to his shoulder, and, with a practised eye and steady hand, drew a trigger; but the deer dashed forward undaunted, and apparently unhurt. Without lowering his piece, the traveller turned its muzzle towards his intended victim, and fired again. Neither discharge, however, seemed to have taken effect.

The whole scene had passed with a rapidity, that confused the female, who was unconsciously rejoicing in the escape of the buck, as he rather darted like a meteor, than ran across the road before her, when a sharp, quick sound struck her ear, quite different from the full, round reports of her father's gun, but still sufficiently distinct to be known as the concussion produced by fire arms. At the same instant that she heard this unexpected report, the buck sprang from the snow, to a great height in the air, and directly a second discharge, similar in sound to the first, followed, when the animal came to the earth, falling headlong, and rolling over on the crust once or twice with its own velocity. A loud shout was given by the unseen marksman, as triumphing in his better aim; and a couple of men instantly appeared from behind the trunks of two of the pines, where they had evidently placed themselves in expectation of the passage of the deer.

"Ha! Natty, had I known you were in ambush, I would not have fired," cried the traveller, moving towards the spot where the deer lay—near to which he was followed by the delighted black, with the sleigh; "but the sound of old Hector was too exhilarating to let me be quiet; though I hardly think I struck him either."

"No—no—Judge," returned the hunter, with an inward chuckle, and with that look of exultation, that indicates a consciousness of superior skill; "you burnt your powder, only to warm your nose this cold evening. Did ye think to stop a full grown buck, with Hector and the slut open upon him, within sound, with that robin pop-gun in your hand? There's plenty of pheasants among the swamps; and the snow birds are flying round your own door, where you may feed them with crumbs, and shoot enough for a potpie, any day; but if you're for a buck, or a little bear's meat, Judge, you'll have to take the long rifle, with a greased wadding, or you'll waste more powder than you'll fill stomachs, I'm thinking."

As the speaker concluded, he drew his bare hand across the bottom of his nose, and again opened his enormous mouth with a kind of inward laugh.

"The gun scatters well, Natty, and has killed a deer before now," said the traveller, smiling good humouredly. "One barrel was charged with buck shot; but the other was loaded for birds only. Here are two hurts that he has received; one through his neck, and the other directly through his heart. It is by no means certain, Natty, but I gave him one of the two."

"Let who will kill him," said the hunter, rather surlily, "I suppose the cretur is to be eaten." So saying, he drew a large knife from a leathern sheath, which was stuck through his girdle or sash, and cut the throat of the animal. "If there is two balls through the deer, I want to know if there wasn't two rifles fired—besides, who ever saw such a ragged hole from a smooth-bore, as this is through the neck?—and you will own yourself, Judge, that the buck fell at the last shot, which was sent from a truer and a younger hand, than your'n or mine 'ither; but for my part, although I am a poor man, I can live without the venison, but I don't love to give up my lawful dues in a free country. Though, for the matter of that, might often makes right here, as well as in the old country, for what I can see."

An air of sullen dissatisfaction pervaded the manner of the hunter during the whole of this speech; yet he thought it prudent to utter the close of the sentence in such an under tone, as to leave nothing audible but the grumbling sounds of his voice.

"Nay, Natty," rejoined the traveller, with undisturbed good humour, "it is for the honour that I contend. A few dollars will pay for the venison; but what will requite me for the lost honour of a buck's tail in my cap? Think, Natty, how I should triumph over that quizzing dog, Dick Jones, who has failed seven times this season already, and has only brought in one wood-chuck and a few gray squirrels."

"Ah! the game is becoming hard to find, indeed, Judge, with your clearings and betterments," said the old hunter, with a kind of disdainful resignation. "The time has been, when I have shot thirteen deer, without counting the fa'ns, standing in the door of my own hut!—and for bear's meat, if one wanted a ham or so from the cretur, he had only to watch a-nights, and he could shoot one by moonlight, through the cracks of the logs; no fear of his over-sleeping himself, n'ither, for the howling of the wolves was sartin to keep his eyes open. There's old Hector,"—patting with affection a tall hound, of black and yellow spots, with white belly and legs, that just then came in on the scent, accompanied by the slut he had mentioned; "see where the wolves bit his throat, the night I druve them from the venison I was smoking on the chimbly top—that dog is more to be trusted nor many a Christian man; for he never forgets a friend, and loves the hand that gives him bread."

There was a peculiarity in the manner of the hunter, that struck the notice of the young female, who had been a close and interested observer of his appearance and equipments, from the moment he first came into view. He was tall, and so meagre as to make him seem above even the six feet that he actually stood in his stockings. On his head, which was thinly covered with lank, sandy hair, he wore a cap made of fox-skin, resembling in shape the one we have already described, although much inferior in finish and ornaments. His face was skinny, and thin almost to emaciation; but yet bore no signs of disease;—on the contrary, it had every indication of the most robust and enduring health. The cold and the exposure had, together, given it a colour of uniform red; his gray eyes were glancing under a pair of shaggy brows, that overhung them in long hairs of gray mingled with their natural hue; his scraggy neck was bare, and burnt to the same tint with his face; though a small part of a shirt collar, made of the country check, was to be seen above the over-dress he wore. A kind of coat, made of dressed deer-skin, with the hair on, was belted close to his lank body, by a girdle of coloured worsted. On his feet were deer-skin moccasins, ornamented with porcupines' quills, after the manner of the Indians, and his limbs were guarded with long leggings of the same material as the moccasins, which, gartering over the knees of his tarnished buck-skin breeches, had obtained for him, among the settlers, the nick-name of Leather-stocking, notwithstanding his legs were protected beneath, in winter, by thick garments of woollen, duly made of good blue yarn. Over his left shoulder was slung a belt of deer-skin, from which depended an enormous ox horn, so thinly scraped, as to discover the dark powder that it contained. The larger end was fitted ingeniously and securely with a wooden bottom, and the other was stopped tight by a little plug. A leathern pouch hung before him, from which, as he concluded his last speech, he took a small measure, and, filling it accurately with powder, he commenced reloading the rifle, which, as its butt rested on the snow before him, reached nearly to the top of his fox-skin cap.

The traveller had been closely examining the wounds during these movements, and now, without heeding the ill-humour of the hunger's manner, exclaimed—

"I would fain establish a right, Natty, to the honour of this capture; and surely if the hit in the neck be mine, it is enough; for the shot in the heart was unnecessary—what we call an act of supererogation, Leather-stocking."

"You may call it by what larned name you please, Judge," said the hunter, throwing his rifle across his left arm, and knocking up a brass lid in the breech, from which he took a small piece of greased leather, and wrapping a ball in it, forced them down by main strength on the powder, where he continued to pound them while speaking. "It's far easier to call names, than to shoot a buck on the spring; but the cretur come by his end from a younger hand than 'ither your'n or mine, as I said before."

"What say you, my friend," cried the traveller, turning pleasantly to Natty's companion; "shall we toss up this dollar for the honour, and you keep the silver if you lose; what say you, friend?"

"That I killed the deer," answered the young man, with a little haughtiness, as he leaned on another long rifle, similar to that of Natty's.

"Here are two to one, indeed," replied the Judge, with a smile; "I am outvoted—overruled, as we say on the bench. There is Aggy, he can't vote, being a slave; and Bess is a minor—so I must even make the best of it. But you'll sell me the venison; and the deuce is in it, but I make a good story about its death."

"The meat is none of mine to sell," said Leather-stocking, adopting a little of his companion's hauteur; "for my part, I have known animals travel days with shots in the neck, and I'm none of them who'll rob a man of his rightful dues."

"You are tenacious of your rights, this cold evening, Natty," returned the Judge, with unconquerable good nature; "but what say you, young man, will three dollars pay you for the buck?"

"First let us determine the question of right to the satisfaction of us both," said the youth, firmly but respectfully, and with a pronunciation and language vastly superior to his appearance; "with how many shot did you load your gun?"

"With five, sir," said the Judge, gravely, a little struck with the other's manner; "are they not enough to slay a buck like this?"

"One would do it; but," moving to the tree from behind which he had appeared, "you know, sir, you fired in this direction—here are four of the bullets in the tree."

The Judge examined the fresh marks in the rough bark of the pine, and, shaking his head, said with a laugh—

"You are making out the case against yourself, my young advocate—where is the fifth?"

"Here," said the youth, throwing aside the rough over-coat that he wore, and exhibiting a hole in his under garment, through which large drops of blood were oozing.

"Good God!" exclaimed the Judge, with horror; "have I been trifling here about an empty distinction, and a fellow-creature suffering from my hands without a murmur? But hasten—quick—get into my sleigh—it is about a mile to the village, where surgical aid can be obtained;—all shall be done at my expense, and thou shalt live with me until thy wound is healed—ay, and for ever afterwards, too."

"I thank you, sir, for your good intentions, but must decline your offer. I have a friend who would be uneasy were he to hear that I am hurt and away from him. The injury is but slight, and the bullet has missed the bones; but I believe, sir, you will now admit my title to the venison."

"Admit it!" repeated the agitated Judge; "I here give thee a right to shoot deer, or bears, or any thing thou pleasest in my woods, for ever. Leather-stocking is the only other man that I have granted the same privilege to; and the time is coming when it will be of value. But I buy your deer—here this bill will pay thee, both for thy shot and my own."

The old hunter gathered his tall person up into an air of pride, during this dialogue, and now muttered in an under tone—

"There's them living who say, that Nathaniel Bumppo's

right to shoot in these hills, is of older date than Marmaduke Temple's right to forbid him. But if there's a law about it at all, though who ever heard tell of a law, that a man shouldn't kill deer where he pleased!—but if there is a law at all, it should be to keep people from the use of them smooth-bores. A body never knows where his lead will fly; when he pulls the trigger of one of them fancified fire-arms."

Without attending to the soliloquy of Natty, the youth bowed his head silently to the offer of the bank note, and replied—

"Excuse me, sir, I have need of the venison."

"But this will buy you many deer," said the Judge; "take it, I entreat you," and lowering his voice to nearly a whisper, he added—"it is for a hundred dollars."

For an instant only, the youth seemed to hesitate, and then, blushing even through the high colour that the cold had given to his cheeks, as if with inward shame at his own weakness, he again proudly declined the offer.

During the scene the female arose, and, regardless of the cold air, she threw back the hood which concealed her features, and now spoke, with great earnestness—

"Surely, surely—young man—sir—you would not pain my father so much, as to have him think that he leaves a fellow-creature in this wilderness, whom his own hand has injured. I entreat you will go with us and receive medical aid for your hurts."

Whether his wound became more painful, or, there was something irresistible in the voice and manner of the fair pleader for her father's feelings, we know not, but the haughty distance of the young man's manner was sensibly softened by this appeal, and he stood, in apparent doubt, as if reluctant to comply with, and yet unwilling to refuse her request. The Judge, for such being his office, must in future, be his title, watched, with no little interest, the display of this singular contention in the feelings of the youth, and advancing, kindly took his head, and, as he pulled him gently towards the sleigh, urged him to enter it.

"There is no human aid nearer than Templeton," he said; "and the hut of Natty is full three miles from this;—come—

come, my young friend, go with us, and let the new doctor look to this shoulder of thine. Here is Natty will take the tidings of thy welfare to thy friend; and should'st thou require it, thou shalt be returned to thy home in the morning."

The young man succeeded in extricating his hand from the warm grasp of the Judge, but continued to gaze on the face of the female, who, regardless of the cold, was still standing with her fine features exposed, which expressed feelings that eloquently seconded the request of her father. Leather-stocking stood, in the mean time, leaning upon his long rifle, with his head turned a little to one side, as if engaged in deep and sagacious musing; when, having apparently satisfied his doubts, by revolving the subject in his mind, he broke silence—

"It may be best to go, lad, after all; for if the shot hangs under the skin, my hand is getting too old to be cutting into human flesh, as I once used to could. Though some thirty years agone, in the old war, when I was out under Sir William, I travelled seventy miles alone in the howling wilderness, with a rifle bullet in my thigh, and then cut it out, with my own jack-knife. Old Indian John knows the time well. I met him with a party of the Delawares, on the trail of the Iroquois, who had been down and taken five scalps on the Schoharie. But I made a mark on the red-skin that I'll warrant he carried to his grave. I took him on his posteerum, saving the lady's presence, as he got up from the amboosh, and rattled three buck shot into his naked hide, so close, that you might have laid a broad joe upon them all—" here Natty stretched out his long neck, and straightened his body, as he opened his mouth, which exposed a single tusk of yellow bone, while his eyes, his face, even his whole frame, seemed to laugh, although no sound was emitted, except a kind of thick hissing, as he inhaled his breath in quavers. "I had lost my bullet mould in crossing the Oneida outlet, and so had to make shift with the buck shot; but the rifle was true, and didn't scatter like your two-legged thing there, Judge, which don't do, I find, to hunt in company with."

Natty's apology to the delicacy of the young lady was unnecessary, for, while he was speaking, she was too much employed in helping her father to remove certain articles of their baggage to hear him. Unable to resist the kind urgency of the travellers any longer, the youth, though still with an un-accountable reluctance expressed in his manner, suffered him-self to be persuaded to enter the sleigh. The black with the aid of his master threw the buck across the baggage, and enter-ing the vehicle themselves, the Judge invited the hunter to do likewise.

"No—no—" said the old man, shaking his head; "I have work to do at home this Christmas eve—drive on with the boy, and let your doctor look to the shoulder; though if he will only cut out the shot, I have yarbs that will heal the wound quicker nor all his foreign 'intments." He turned and was about to move off, when, suddenly recollecting himself, he again faced the party, and added—"If you see any thing of Indian John about the foot of the lake, you had better take him with you, and let him lend the doctor a hand; for old as he is, he is curous at cuts and bruises, and it's likelier than not he'll be in with brooms to sweep your Christmas ha'arths."

"Stop—stop," cried the youth, catching the arm of the black as he prepared to urge his horses forward; "Natty—you need say nothing of the shot, nor of where I am going—remember, Natty, as you love me."

"Trust old Leather-stocking," returned the hunter, signifi-cantly; "he hasn't lived forty years in the wilderness, and not larnt from the savages how to hold his tongue—trust to me, lad; and remember old Indian John."

"And, Natty," said the youth eagerly, still holding the black by the arm, "I will just get the shot extracted, and bring you up, to-night, a quarter of the buck, for the Christmas dinner."

He was interrupted by the hunter, who held up his finger with an expressive gesture for silence, and moved softly along the margin of the road, keeping his eyes steadfastly fixed on the branches of a pine near him. When he had obtained such a position as he wished, he stopped, and cocking his rifle, threw one leg far behind him, and stretching his left arm to its ut-most extent along the barrel of his piece, he began slowly to raise its muzzle in a line with the straight trunk of the tree. The eyes of the group in the sleigh naturally preceded the movement of the rifle, and they soon discovered the object of

Natty's aim. On a small dead branch of the pine, which, at the distance of seventy feet from the ground, shot out horizontally, immediately beneath the living members of the tree, sat a bird, that in the vulgar language of the country, was indiscriminately called a pheasant or a partridge. In size, it was but little smaller than a common barn-yard fowl. The baying of the dogs, and the conversation that had passed near the root of the tree on which it was perched, had alarmed the bird, which was now drawn up near the body of the pine, with a head and neck erect, that formed nearly a straight line with its legs. So soon as the rifle bore on the victim, Natty drew his trigger, and the partridge fell from its height with a force that buried it in the snow.

"Lie down, you old villain," exclaimed Leather-stocking, shaking his ramrod at Hector as he bounded towards the foot of the tree, "lie down, I say." The dog obeyed, and Natty proceeded with great rapidity, though with the nicest accuracy, to re-load his piece. When this was ended, he took up his game, and showing it to the party without a head, he cried—"Here is a nice tit-bit for an old man's Christmas—never mind the venison, boy, and remember Indian John; his yarbs are better nor all the foreign 'intments. Here, Judge," holding up the bird again, "do you think a smooth-bore would pick game off their roost, and not ruffle a feather?" The old man gave another of his remarkable laughs, which partook so largely of exultation, mirth, and irony, and shaking his head, he turned, with his rifle at a trail, and moved into the forest with short and quick steps, that were between a walk and a trot. At each movement that he made his body lowered several inches, his knees yielding with an inclination inward; but as the sleigh turned at a bend in the road, the youth cast his eyes in quest of his old companion, and he saw that he was already nearly concealed by the trunks of the trees, while his dogs were following quietly in his footsteps, occasionally scenting the deer track, that they seemed to know instinctively was now of no farther use to them. Another jerk was given to the sleigh, and Leather-stocking was hidden from view.

Chapter II

All places that the eye of Heaven visits,
Are to a wise man ports and happy havens:—
Think not the king did banish thee:
But thou the king.—

RICHARD II

An ancestor of Marmaduke Temple had, about one hundred and twenty years before the commencement of our tale, come to the colony of Pennsylvania, a friend and co-religionist of its great patron. Old Marmaduke, for this formidable prenomen was a kind of appellative to the race, brought with him to that asylum of the persecuted, an abundance of the good things of his life. He became the master of many thousands of acres of uninhabited territory, and the supporter of many a score of dependants. He lived greatly respected for his piety, and not a little distinguished as a sectary: was intrusted by his associates with many important political stations; and died, just in time to escape the knowledge of his own poverty. It was his lot to share the fortune of most of those who brought wealth with them into the new settlements of the middle colonies.

The consequence of an emigrant into these provinces was generally to be ascertained by the number of his white servants or dependants, and the nature of the public situations that he held. Taking this rule as a guide, the ancestor of our Judge must have been a man of no little note.

It is, however, a subject of curious inquiry at the present day, to look into the brief records of that early period, and observe how regular, and with few exceptions how inevitable, were the gradations, on the one hand, of the masters to poverty, and on the other, of their servants to wealth. Accustomed to ease, and unequal to the struggles incident to an infant society, the affluent emigrant was barely enabled to maintain his own rank, by the weight of his personal superiority and acquirements; but the moment that his head was laid in the grave, his indolent, and comparatively uneducated offspring, were compelled to yield precedency to the more active energies of a class, whose exertions had been stimulated by necessity. This is a very common course of things, even in the present state of the Union; but it was peculiarly the fortunes of the two extremes of society, in the peaceful and unenterprising colonies of Pennsylvania and New Jersey.

The posterity of Marmaduke did not escape the common lot of those, who depended rather on their hereditary possessions than on their own powers; and in the third generation, they had descended to a point, below which, in this happy country, it is barely possible for honesty, intellect and sobriety, to fall. The same pride of family, that had, by its self-satisfied indolence, conduced to aid their fall, now became a principle to stimulate them to endeavour to rise again. The feeling, from being morbid, was changed to a healthful and active desire to emulate the character, the condition, and peradventure, the wealth, of their ancestors also. It was the father of our new acquaintance, the Judge, who first began to re-ascend the scale of society: and in this undertaking he was not a little assisted by a marriage that he formed, which aided greatly in furnishing the means of educating his only son, in a rather better manner than the low state of the common schools in Pennsylvania could promise; or than had been the practice in the family, for the two or three preceding generations.

At the school where the reviving prosperity of his father was enabled to maintain him, young Marmaduke formed an intimacy with a youth, whose years were about equal to his own. This was a fortunate connexion for our judge, and paved the way to most of his future elevation in life, when the early inclination for each other in the boys, was matured into friendship.

There was not only great wealth, but high court interest, among the connexions of Edward Effingham. They were one of the very few families, then resident in the colonies, who thought it a degradation to its members to descend to the pursuits of commerce; and who never emerged from the privacy of their domestic life, unless to preside in the councils of the colony, or to bear arms in her defence. The latter had, from youth to approaching age, been the only employment of Edward's father. Military rank, under the crown of Great Britain, was, sixty years ago, attained with much longer probation, and by much more toilsome services, than at the present time. Years were passed without murmuring, in the subordinate grades of the service; and those soldiers who were stationed in the colonies, felt, when they obtained the command of a company, that they were entitled to receive the greatest deference from the peaceful occupants of the soil. Any one of our readers, who in a visit to the falls, has occasion to cross Niagara, by spending a day at Newark, may easily observe, not only the self-importance, but the real estimation enjoyed by the humblest representative of the crown, even in that polar region of royal sunshine. Such, and at no very distant period, was the respect paid to the military in these States, where now, happily, no symbol of war is ever seen, unless at the free and fearless voice of their people. When, therefore, the father of Marmaduke's friend, after forty years' service, retired with the rank of Major, maintaining in his domestic establishment a comparative splendour, it is not to be doubted but that he became a man of the first consideration in his native colony—which was that of New-York. He had served with fidelity and courage, and having been, according to the custom of the provinces, intrusted with commands much superior to those to which he was entitled by rank, with reputation also. When Major Effingham yielded to the claims of age, he retired with dignity, refusing his half-pay or any other compensation for services, that he felt he could no longer perform.

The ministry proffered to his acceptance various civil offices, which yielded not only honour but profit; but he declined them all, with the chivalrous independence and loyalty that had marked his character through life. The veteran soon caused this act of patriotic disinterestedness to be followed by another of private munificence, that, however little it accorded with prudence, was in perfect conformity with the simple integrity of his own views.

The friend of Marmaduke was his only child; and to this son, on his marriage with a lady to whom the father was particularly partial, the Major gave a complete conveyance of his whole estate, consisting of moneys in the funds, a town and country residence, sundry valuable farms in the old parts of the colony, and large tracts of wild land in the new—in this manner throwing himself upon the filial piety of his child for his own future maintenance. Major Effingham, in declining the liberal offers of the British ministry, had subjected himself to the suspicion of having attained his dotage, by all those who throng the avenues to court patronage, even in the remotest corners of that vast empire; but, when he thus voluntarily stript himself of his great personal wealth, the remainder of the community seemed instinctively to adopt the conclusion also, that he had reached a second childhood. This may explain the fact of his importance rapidly declining; and, if privacy was his object, the veteran had soon a free indulgence of his wishes. Whatever views the world might entertain of this act of the Major, to himself and to his child, it seemed no more than a natural gift by a father, of those immunities which he could no longer enjoy or improve, to a son, who was formed, both by nature and education, to do both. The younger Effingham did not object to the amount of the donation; for he felt, that while his parent reserved a moral control over his actions, he was relieving himself from a fatiguing burthen: such, indeed, was the confidence existing between them, that to neither did it seem any thing more, than removing money from one pocket to another.

One of the first acts of the young man, on coming into possession of his wealth, was to seek his early friend, with a view to offer any assistance, that it was now in his power to bestow.

The death of Marmaduke's father, and the consequent division of his small estate, rendered such an offer extremely acceptable to the young Pennsylvanian: he felt his own powers, and saw, not only the excellences, but the foibles, in the character of his friend. Effingham was by nature indolent, confiding, and at times impetuous and indiscreet; but Marmaduke was uniformly equable, penetrating, and full of activity and enterprise. To the latter, therefore, the assistance, or rather connexion, that was proffered to him, seemed to promise a mutual advantage. It was cheerfully accepted, and the arrangement of its conditions left entirely to the dictates of his own judgment. A mercantile house was established in the metropolis of Pennsylvania, with the avails of Mr. Effingham's personal property; all, or nearly all, of which was put into the possession of Temple, who was the only ostensible proprietor in the concern, while in secret, the other was entitled to an equal participation in the profits. This connexion was thus kept private for two reasons; one of which, in the freedom of their intercourse, was frankly avowed to Marmaduke, while the other continued profoundly hid in the bosom of his friend. The last was nothing more than pride. To the descendant of a line of soldiers, commerce, even in that indirect manner, seemed a degrading pursuit; and every sentiment of young Effingham was opposed to the acknowledgement of an arrangement, which he only reconciled to his private feelings, by a knowledge of his own motives—but an insurperable obstacle to the disclosure existed in the prejudices of his father.

We have already said that Major Effingham had served as a soldier, with reputation. On one occasion, while in command on the western frontier of Pennsylvania, against a league of the French and Indians, not only his glory, but the safety of himself and his troops were jeoparded, by the peaceful policy of that colony. To the soldier, this was an unpardonable offence. He was fighting in their defence only—he knew that the mild principles of this little nation of practical Christians would be disregarded by their subtle and malignant enemies; and he felt the injury the more deeply; because he saw that the avowed object of the colonists, in withholding their succours, would only have a tendency to expose his command, without preserving the peace. The gallant soldier succeeded, after a desperate conflict, in extricating himself with a handful of his men, from their murderous enemy; but he never forgave the people who had exposed him to a danger, which they left him to combat alone. It was in vain to tell him, that they had no agency in his being placed on their frontier at all; it was evidently for their benefit that he had been so placed, and it was their "religious duty," so the Major always expressed it; "it was their religious duty to have supported him."

At no time was the old soldier an admirer of the peaceful disciples of Fox. Their disciplined habits, both of mind and body, had endowed them with great physical perfection; and the eye of the veteran was apt to scan the fair proportions and athletic frames of the colonists, with a look that seemed to utter volumes of contempt for their moral imbecility. He was also a little addicted to the expression of a belief, that, where there was so great an observance of the externals of religion, there could not be much of the substance.—It is not our task to explain what is, or ought to be, the substance of Christianity, but merely to record in this place the opinions of Major Effingham.

Knowing the sentiments of the father, in relation to this people, it was no wonder that the son hesitated to avow his connexion with nay, even his dependence on the inegrity of, a quaker.

It has been seen that Marmaduke deduced his origin from the contemporaries and friends of Penn. His father had married without the pale of the church to which he belonged, and had, in this manner, forfeited some of the privileges of his offspring. Still, as young Marmaduke was educated in a colony and society, where even the ordinary intercourse between friends was tinctured with the aspect of this mild religion, his habits and language were somewhat marked by its peculiarities. His own marriage at a future day with a lady without, not only the pale, but the influence of this sect of religionists, had a tendency, it is true, to weaken his early impressions; still he retained them, in some degree, to the hour of his death, and was observed uniformly, when much interested or agitated, to speak in the language of his youth— But this is anticipating our tale.

When Marmaduke first became the partner of young Effingham, he was quite the quaker in externals; and it was too dangerous an experiment for the son to think of encountering the prejudices of the father on this subject. The connexion, therefore, remained a profound secret to all but those who were interested in it.

For a few years, Marmaduke directed the commercial operations of his house with a prudence and sagacity, that afforded rich returns for the labour and hazard incurred. He married the lady we have mentioned, who was the mother of Elizabeth, and the visits of his friend were becoming more frequent; and there was a speedy prospect of removing the veil from their intercourse, as its advantages became each hour more apparent to Mr. Effingham, when the troubles that preceded the war of the revolution, extended themselves to an alarming degree.

Educated in the most dependent loyalty by his father, Mr. Effingham had, from the commencement of the disputes between the colonists and the crown, warmly maintained, what he believed to be, the just prerogatives of his prince; while on the other hand, the clear head and independent mind of Temple had induced him to espouse the cause of the people. Both might have been influenced by early impressions; for, if the son of the loyal and gallant soldier bowed in implicit obedience to the will of his sovereign, the descendant of the persecuted follower of Penn, looked back, with a little bitterness, to the unmerited wrongs that had been heaped upon his ancestors.

This difference in opinion had long been a subject of amicable dispute between them, but, latterly, the contest was getting to be too important to admit of trivial discussions on the part of Marmaduke, whose acute discernment was already catching faint glimmerings of the important events that were in embryo. The sparks of dissension soon kindled into a blaze; and the colonies, or rather, as they quickly declared themselves, THE STATES, became a scene of strife and bloodshed for years.

A short time before the battle of Lexington, Mr. Effingham, already a widower, transmitted to Marmaduke for safekeeping, all his valuable effects and papers; and left the colony without his father. The war had, however, scarcely commenced in earnest, when he re-appeared in New-York, wearing the livery of his king, and in a short time, he took the field at the head of a provincial corps. In the mean time, Marmaduke had completely committed himself in the cause, as it was then called, of the rebellion: of course, all intercourse between the friends ceased—on the part of Col. Effingham, it was unsought, and on that of Marmaduke, there was a cautious reserve. It soon became necessary for the latter to abandon the capital of Philadelphia; but he had taken the precaution to remove to the interior the whole of his effects, beyond the reach of the loyal forces, including the papers of his friend also. There he continued serving his country during the struggle, in various civil capacities, and always with dignity and usefulness. While, however, he discharged his functions with credit and fidelity, Marmaduke never seemed to lose sight of his own interests; for, when the estates of the adherents of the crown fell under the hammer, by the acts of confiscation, he appeared in New-York, and became the purchaser of extensive possessions at, comparatively, very low prices.

It is true that Marmaduke, by thus purchasing estates that had been wrested by violence from others, rendered himself obnoxious to the censures of that sect, which, at the same time that it discards its children from a full participation in the family union, seems ever unwilling to abandon them entirely to the world. But either his success, or the frequency of the transgression in others, soon wiped off this slight stain from his character: and although there were a few, who, dissatisfied with their own fortunes, or conscious of their own demerits, would make dark hints concerning the sudden prosperity of the unportioned quaker, yet his services, and possibly his wealth, soon drove the recollection of these vague conjectures from men's minds.

When the war was ended, and the independence of the states acknowledged, Mr. Temple turned his attention from the pursuit of commerce, which was then fluctuating and uncertain, to the settlement of those tracts of land which he had purchased. Aided by a good deal of money, and directed by the suggestions of a strong and practical reason, his enterprises throve to a degree, that the climate and rugged face of the country which he selected, would seem to forbid. His property increased in a tenfold ratio, and he was already to be ranked among the most wealthy and important of his countrymen. To inherit this wealth, he had but one child—the daughter whom we have introduced to the reader, and whom he was now conveying from school, to preside over a household that had too long wanted a mistress.

When the district in which his estates lay, had become sufficiently populous to be set off as a country, Mr. Temple had, according to the custom of the new settlements, been selected to fill its highest judicial station. This might make a Templar smile, but in addition to the apology of necessity, there is ever a dignity in talents and experience, that is commonly sufficient, in any station, for the protection of its possessor; and Marmaduke, more fortunate in his native clearness of mind, than the judge of King Charles, not only decided right, but was generally able to give a very good reason for it. At all events, such was the universal practice of the country and the times; and Judge Temple, so far from ranking among the lowest of his judicial contemporaries in the courts of the new counties, felt himself, and was unanimously acknowledged to be, among the first.

We shall here close this brief explanation of the history and character of some of our personages, leaving them in future to speak and act for themselves.

· *Chapter III* ·

All that thou see'st, is nature's handy-work:
Those rocks that upward throw their mossy brows,
Like castled pinnacles of the elder times!
These venerable stems, that slowly rock
Their tow'ring branches in the wintry gale!
That field of frost, which glitters in the sun,
Mocking the whiteness of a marble breast!—
Yet man can mar such works with his rude taste,
Like some sad spoiler of a virgin's fame.

DUO

Some little while elapsed, after the horses had resumed their journey, ere Marmaduke Temple was sufficiently recovered from his agitation, to scan the person of his new companion. He now observed, that he was a youth of some two or three and twenty years of age; and rather above the middle height. Further observation was prevented by the rough over-coat, which was belted close to his form by a worsted sash, much like the one worn by the old hunter. The eyes of the Judge, after resting a moment on the figure of the stranger, were raised to a scrutiny of his countenance. There had been a contraction of the brows, and a look of care, visible in the features of the youth, when he first entered the sleigh, that had not only attracted the notice of Elizabeth, but which she had been much puzzled to interpret. The passion seemed the strongest when he was enjoining his old companion to secrecy; and when he had decided, and was, rather passively, suffering himself to be conveyed to the village, the expression of the young man's eyes by no means indicated any great degree of self-satisfaction at the step. But the lines of an uncommonly prepossessing countenance were gradually becoming composed; and he now sat in silent, and apparently abstracted musing.

The Judge gazed at him for some time with earnestness, and then smiling as if at his own forgetfulness, he spoke—

"I believe, my young friend, that terror has driven your name from my recollection—your face is very familiar to me, and yet for the honour of a score of buck's-tails in my cap, I could not tell your name."

"I came into the country but three weeks since, sir," returned the youth coldly, "and, I understand you have been absent more than that time."

"It will be five to-morrow. Yet your face is one that I have seen; though it would not be strange, such has been my affright, should I see thee in thy winding-sheet, walking by my bed-side, to-night. What say'st thou, Bess? Am I compos mentis or not?—Fit to charge a grand jury, or, what is just now of more pressing necessity, able to do the honours of a Christmas-eve, in the hall of Templeton?"

"More able to do either, my dear father," said a playful voice from under the ample enclosures of the hood, "than to kill deer with a smoothbore." A short pause followed; and the same voice, but in a different accent continued—"We shall have good reasons for our thanksgiving to-night, on more accounts than one.'"

A slightly scornful smile passed over the features of the youth, at the archness of the first part of this speech; but it instantly vanished, as he listened to the tremulous tones in which it was concluded. The Judge, also, seemed to be affected with the consciousness of how narrowly he had escaped taking the life of a fellow-creature, and, for some time, there was a dead silence in the sleigh.

The horses soon reached a point, where they seemed to know by instinct that their journey was nearly ended, and, bearing on the bits, as they tossed their heads, uneasily, up and down, they rapidly drew the sleigh over the level land, which lay on the top of the mountain, and soon came to the point where the road descended suddenly, but circuitously, into the valley.

The Judge was roused from his reflections, when he saw the four columns of dense smoke, which floated along the air from his own chimneys. As house, village, and valley burst on his sight, he exclaimed cheerfully to his daughter—

"See, Bess, there is thy resting-place for life! And thine too, young man, if thou wilt consent to dwell with us."

The eyes of the youth and maiden involuntarily met, as the Judge, in the warmth of his feelings, thus included them in an association which was to endure so long; and if the deepening colour, that, notwithstanding her hood, might be seen gathering over the face even to the forehead of Elizabeth, was contradicted in its language by the proud expression of her eye, the scornful but covert smile that again played about the lips of the stranger, seemed equally to deny the probability of his consenting to form one of this family group. The scene was one, however, which might easily warm a heart less given to philanthropy than that of Marmaduke Temple.

The side of the mountain, on which our travellers were journeying, though not absolutely perpendicular, was yet so steep as to render great care necessary in descending the rude and narrow path, which, in that early day, wound along the precipices. The negro reined in his impatient steeds, and time was given to Elizabeth to dwell on a scene which was so rapidly altering under the hands of man, that it only resembled, in its outlines, the picture she had so often studied, with delight, in her childhood. On the right, and stretching for several miles to the north, lay a narrow plain, buried among mountains, which, falling occasionally, jutted in long low points, that were covered with tall trees, into the valley; and then again, for miles, stretched their lofty brows perpendicularly along its margin, nourishing in the crags that formed their sides, pines and hemlocks thinly interspersed with chestnut and beech, which grew in lines nearly parallel to the mountains themselves. The dark foliage of the evergreens was brilliantly contrasted by the glittering whiteness of the plain, which exhibited, over the tops of the trees, and through the vistas formed by the advancing points of the hills, a single sheet of unspotted snow, relieved occasionally by a few small dark objects that were discovered, as they were passing directly beneath the feet of the travellers, to be sleighs moving in various directions. On the western border of the plain, the mountains, though equally high, were less precipitous, and as they receded, opened into irregular valleys and glens, and were formed into terraces and hollows that admitted of cultivation. Although the evergreens still held dominion over many of the hills that rose on this side of the valley, yet the undulating outlines of the distant mountains, covered with forests of beech and maple, gave a relief to the eye, and the promise of a kinder soil. Occasionally, spots of white were discoverable amidst the forests of the opposite hills, that announced, by the smoke which curled over the tops of the trees, the habitations of man, and the commencement of agriculture. These spots were sometimes, by the aid of united labour, enlarged into what were called settlements; but more frequently were small and insulated; though so rapid were the changes, and so persevering the labours of those who had cast their fortunes on the success of the enterprise, that it was not difficult for the imagination of Elizabeth to conceive they were enlarging under her eye, while she was gazing, in mute wonder, at the alterations that a few short years had made in the aspect of the country. The points on the western side of the plain were both larger and more numerous than those on its eastern, and one in particular thrust itself forward in such a manner, as to form beautifully curved bays of snow on either side. On its extreme end a mighty oak stretched forward, as if to overshadow, with its branches, a spot which its roots were forbidden to enter. It had released itself from the thraldom, that a growth of centuries had imposed on the branches of the surrounding forest-trees, and threw its gnarled and fantastic arms abroad, in all the wildness of unrestrained liberty. A dark spot of a few acres in extent at the southern extremity of this beautiful flat, and immediately under the feet of our travellers, alone showed, by its rippling surface, and the vapours which exhaled from it, that what at first might seem a plain, was one of the mountain lakes, locked in the frosts of winter. A narrow current rushed impetuously from its bosom at the open place we have mentioned, and might be traced for a few miles, as it wound its way towards the south through the real valley, by its borders of hemlock and pine, and by the vapour which arose from its warmer surface into the chill atmosphere of the hills. The banks of this lovely basin, at its outlet, or southern end, were steep but not high; and in that direction the land continued for many miles a narrow but level plain, along which the settlers had scattered their humble habitations, with a profusion that bespoke the quality of the soil, and the comparative facilities of intercourse. Immediately on the bank of the lake, stood the village of Templeton. It consisted of about fifty buildings, including those of every description, chiefly built of wood, and which, in their architecture, bore not only strong marks of the absence of taste, but also, by the slovenly and unfinished appearance of most of the dwellings, indicated the hasty manner of their construction. To the eye, they presented a variety of colours. A few were white in both front and rear, but more bore that expensive colour on their fronts only, while their economical but ambitious owners had covered the remaining sides of their edifices with a dingy red. One or two were slowly assuming the russet of age; while the uncovered beams that were to be seen through the broken windows of their second stories, showed, that either the taste, or the vanity of their proprietors, had led them to undertake a task which they were unable to accomplish. The whole were grouped together in a manner that aped the streets of a city, and were evidently so arranged, by the directions of one, who looked far ahead to the wants of posterity, rather than to the convenience of the present incumbents. Some three or four of the better sort of building, in addition to the uniformity of their colour, were fitted with green blinds, that were strangely contrasted to the chill aspect of the lake, the mountains, the forests, and the wide fields of snow. Before the doors of these pretending dwellings, were placed a few saplings, either without branches, or possessing only the feeble shoots of one or two summer's growth, that looked not unlike tall grenadiers on post, near the threshold of princes. In truth, the occupants of these favoured habitations were the nobles of Templeton, as Marmaduke was its king. They were the dwelling of two young men who were cunning in the law; an equal number of that class who chaffered to supply the wants of the community, under the significant title of store-keepers; and a disciple of Æsculapius, who, for a novelty, brought more subjects into the world than he sent out of it. In the midst of this incongruous group of dwellings, rose the mansion of the Judge, towering proudly above all its neighbours. It stood in the centre of an enclosure that included several acres, which were covered with fruit-trees. Some of these were of Indian origin, and began already to assume the moss and inclination of age, therein forming a very marked contrast to the infant plantations that peered over most of the picketed fences in the village. In addition to this show of cultivation, were two rows of young poplars, a tree but lately introduced into America, formally lining either side of a pathway, which led from a gate, that opened on the principal street, to the front door of the building. The house itself had been built entirely under the superintendence of a Mr. Richard Jones, whom we have already mentioned, and who, from a certain cleverness in small matters, and his willingness to exert his talents, added to the circumstance of their being sisters' children, ordinarily superintended all the minor concerns of Marmaduke Temple's business. Richard was fond of saying, that this child of his invention consisted of nothing more nor less, than what should form the ground-work of a clergyman's discourse; viz. a firstly, and a lastly. He had commenced his labours in the first year of their residence, by erecting a tall, gaunt edifice of wood, with its gable towards the highway. In this shelter, for it was but little more, the family resided for three years. By the end of that period, Richard had completed his design. He had availed himself, in this heavy undertaking, of the experience of a certain wandering, eastern mechanic, who, by exhibiting a few solid plates of English architecture, and talking learnedly of friezes, entablatures, and particularly of the composite order, had obtained a very undue influence over Richard's taste, in every thing that pertained to that branch of the fine arts. Not but that Mr. Jones affected to consider Mr. Hiram Doolittle a perfect empyric in his profession; being in the constant habit of listening to his treatises on architecture, with a kind of indulgent smile, yet, either from an inability to oppose them by any thing plausible from his own stores of learning, or from a secret admiration of their truth, Richard generally submitted to the arguments of his coadjutor. Together, they had not only erected a dwelling for Marmaduke, but had given a fashion to the architecture of the country. The composite order, Mr. Doolittle would contend, was an order composed of many others, and was intended to be the most useful, for it admitted into its construction such alterations as convenience or circumstances might require. To this proposition Richard very gravely assented; and it was by this unison in sentiment that the composite order, or a style of architecture that emanated from the carpenter's own genius, with a few suggestions from the other, became the fashion of the new county.

The house itself, or the "lastly," was of stone; large, square, formal, and far from uncomfortable. These were four requisites, on which Marmaduke had insisted with a little more than his ordinary pertinacity. But every thing else was peaceably resigned to Richard and his associate. These worthies found but little opportunity for the display of their talents on a stone edifice, excepting in the roof and in the porch. The former, it was soon decided, should be made with four faces and a platform, in order to hide a part of the building that all writers agreed was an object that ought to be concealed. To this arrangement, Marmaduke objected the heavy snows that lay for months, frequently covering the earth to a depth of three or four feet. Happily, the facilities of the composite order presented themselves to effect a compromise, and the rafters were lengthened, so as to give a descent that should carry off the frozen element. But unluckily, some mistake was made in the admeasurement of these material parts of the fabric, and as one of the greatest recommendations of Hiram, was his ability to work by the "square rule," no opportunity was found of discovering the effect that was to be produced by this offspring of compound genius, until the massive timbers were raised, with much labour, on the four walls of the building. Then, indeed, it was soon seen, that, in defiance of all rule, the roof was by far the most conspicuous part of the edifice. Richard and his associate consoled themselves with the belief, that the covering would aid in concealing this unnatural elevation; but every shingle that was laid, was only multiplying objects to look at. Richard essayed to remedy the evil with paint, and four different colours were laid on by his own hands. The first was a sky-blue, in the vain expectation that the eye might be cheated into the belief, it was the heavens themselves that hung so imposingly over Marmaduke's dwelling; the second was, what he called, a "cloud-colour," being nothing more nor less than an imitation of light smoke; the third was what Richard termed an invisible green, which he laid on with a belief, that the deformity might be blended with the background of pines, that rose, in tall grandeur, but a short distance in the rear of the mansion-house. But all these ingenious expedients entirely failed, and our artists relinquished the desire to conceal, and attempted to ornament, the offensive member. The last colour that Richard bestowed on the luckless roof, was a "sun-shiny yellow;" so called, both from its resemblance to, and its powers to resist, the rays of the great luminary. The platform, as well as the eaves of the house, were surmounted by gaudily painted railings, and the genius of Hiram was exerted in the fabrication of divers urns and mouldings, that were scattered profusely around this part of their labours. Richard had originally a cunning expedient, by which the chimneys were intended to be so low, and so situated, as to resemble ornaments on the balustrades; but comfort required that the chimneys should rise with the roof, in order that the smoke might be carried off, and they thus became four extremely conspicuous objects in the view.

As this was much the most important undertaking in which Mr. Jones was ever engaged, his failure produced a correspondent degree of mortification. At first, he whispered among his acquaintances, that it all proceeded from ignorance of the square rule on the part of Hiram, but as his eye became gradually accustomed to the object, he grew better satisfied with his labours, and instead of apologizing for the defects, he commenced praising the beauties of the mansion-house. He soon found hearers; and, as wealth and comfort are at all times attractive, it was made a model for imitation on a small scale. In less than two years from its erection, he had the pleasure of standing on the elevated platform, and of looking down on three humble imitators of its beauty.—Thus it is ever with fashion, which even renders the faults of the great subjects of admiration.

Marmaduke bore this deformity in his dwelling with great good nature, and soon contrived, by his own improvements, to give an air both of respectability and comfort to his place of residence; still there was much of incongruity, even immediately about the mansion-house. Although poplars had been brought from Europe to ornament the grounds, and willows and other trees were gradually springing up nigh the dwelling, yet many a pile of snow betrayed the presence of the stump of a mighty pine; and even, in one or two instances, unsightly remnants of trees that had been partly destroyed by fire, were seen rearing their black and glistening columns, for twenty or thirty feet above the pure white of the snow. These, which in the language of the country are termed stubs, abounded in the open fields adjacent to the village, and were accompanied, occasionally, by the ruin of a pine or a hemlock that had been stripped of its bark, and which waved in melancholy grandeur its naked limbs to the blast, a skeleton of its former glory. But these unpleasant additions to the view were unnoticed by the delighted Elizabeth, who, as the horses slowly moved down the side of the mountain, saw only in gross, the cluster of houses that lay like a map at her feet; the fifty smokes, that were diagonally curling from the valley to the clouds; the frozen lake, as it lay embedded in mountains of evergreen, with the long shadows of the pines on its white surface, lengthening in the setting sun; the dark riband of water, that gushed from the outlet, and was winding its way already, towards the far distant Chesapeake—the altered, though still remembered, scenes of her childhood and of joy!

Five years had here wrought greater changes, than a century would produce in older countries, where time and labour have given permanency to the works of man. To the young hunter and the Judge the scene had less of novelty; though none ever emerge from the dark forests of that mountain, and witness the glorious scenery of that beauteous valley, as it bursts unexpectedly upon them, without a feeling of delight. The former cast one admiring glance from north to south, and then sunk his face again beneath the folds of his coat; while the latter contemplated, with philanthropic pleasure, the prospect of affluence and comfort, that was expanding around him; the result of his own enterprise, and much of it, the fruits of his own industry.

The cheerful sound of sleigh-bells, however, soon attracted the attention of the whole party, as they came jingling up the sides of the mountain, at a rate that announced both a powerful team and a hard driver. The bushes which lined the highway interrupted the view, and they were close upon this vehicle, before they discovered who were its occupants.

· *Chapter IV* ·

How now? whose mare's dead? what's the matter?

FALSTAFF

A few minutes resolved whatever doubts our travellers entertained, as to the description of those who were approaching them with such exhilarating sounds. A large lumber-sleigh, drawn by four horses, was soon seen dashing through the leafless bushes, which fringed the road that was here, as on the other side of the mountain, cut into the hill. The leaders were of gray, and the pole-horses of a jet black. Bells, innumerable, were suspended from every part of the harness, where one of those tinkling balls could be placed; while the rapid movement of the equipage, in defiance of the steep ascent, announced the desire of the driver to ring them to the utmost. The first glance at this singular arrangement, satisfied the Judge as to the character of those in the sleigh. It contained four male figures. On one of those stools that are used at writing-desks, lashed firmly to the sides of the vehicle, was seated a little man, enveloped in a great coat fringed with fur, in such a manner that no part of him was visible excepting a face, of an unvarying red colour. There was a habitual upward look about the head of this gentleman, as if it were dissatisfied with the proximity to the earth that nature had decreed in his stature, and the expression of his countenance was that of busy care. He was the charioteer, and he guided the mettled animals that he drove along the precipice, with a fearless eye, and a steady hand. Immediately behind him, with his face toward the other two, was a tall figure, to whose appearance not even the duplicate over-coats which he wore, aided by the corner of a horse-blanket, could give the appearance of strength. His face was protruding from beneath a woollen night-cap; and when he turned to the vehicle of Marmaduke as the sleighs approached each other, it seemed formed by nature to cut the atmosphere with the least possible resistance. The eyes alone appeared to create an obstacle, as from either side of his forehead their light, blue, glassy balls projected. The sallow of his countenance was a colour too permanent to be affected even by the intense cold of the evening. Opposite to this personage, sat a square figure of large proportions. No part of his form was to be discovered through his over-dress, but a full face with an agreeable expression, that was illuminated by a pair of animated black eyes of a lurking look, that gave the lie to every demure feature in his countenance. A fair, jolly wig furnished a neat and rounded outline to his visage, and he, as well as the other two, wore martin-skin caps as outward coverings for their heads. The fourth, was a meek-looking, long-visaged man, without any other protection from the cold than that which was furnished by a black surtout, made with some little formality, but which was rather thread-bare and rusty. He wore a hat of extremely decent proportions, though frequent brushing had quite destroyed its nap. His face was pale, with a little melancholy, but so slightly expressed, as to leave the beholder in doubt, whether it proceeded from mental or bodily ailment. The air had given it, just now, a slight and somewhat feverish flush. The character of his whole appearance, especially contrasted to the air of humour in his next companion, was that of a habitual, but subdued dejection. No sooner had the two sleighs approached within speaking distance, than the driver of this fantastic equipage shouted aloud—

"Draw up in the quarry—draw up, thou king of the Greeks; draw into the quarry, Agamemnon, or I shall never be able to pass you. Welcome home, cousin 'duke—welcome, welcome, my black-eyed Bess. Thou seest, Marmaduke, that I have taken the field with an assorted cargo, to do thee honour. Monsieur Le Quoi has come out with only one cap; Old Fitz would not stay to finish the bottle; and Mr. Grant has got to put the 'lastly' to his sermon, yet. Even all the horses would come—by-the-by, Judge, I must sell these blacks for you, immediately; they both interfere, and then the nigh one is a bad goer in double harness. I can get rid of them to——"

"Sell what thou wilt, Dickon," interrupted the cheerful

voice of the Judge, "so that thou leavest me my daughter and my lands. Ah! Fritz, my old friend, this is a kind compliment, indeed, for seventy to pay to five and forty. Monsieur Le Quoi, I am your servant. Mr. Grant," lifting his cap, "I feel indebted to your attention. Gentlemen, I make you acquainted with my child.—Yours are names with which she is very familiar."

"Velcome, velcome, Tchooge," said the elder of the party, with a strong German accent. "Miss Petsy vilt owe me a kiss."

"And cheerfully will I pay it, my good sir," cried the soft voice of Elizabeth; which sounded in the clear air of the hills, like tones of silver, amid the loud cries of Richard, and the manly greetings of the gentleman. "I have always a kiss for my old friend, Major Hartmann."

By this time the gentleman on the front seat, who had been addressed as Monsieur Le Quoi, rose with some difficulty, owing to the impediment of his over coats, and steadying himself by placing one hand on the stool of the charioteer, with the other, he removed his cap, and bowing politely to the Judge, and profoundly to Elizabeth, he said with a smile that opened a mouth of no common dimensions—

"Ver velcome home, Monsieur Templ'. Ah! Mam'selle Liz'bet, you ver humble sairvant."

"Cover thy poll, Gaul, cover thy poll," cried the driver, who was Mr. Richard Jones; "cover thy poll, or the frost will pluck out the remnant of thy locks. Had the hairs on the head of Absalom been as scarce as on this crown of thine, he might have been living to this day." The jokes of Richard never failed of exciting risibility, for if others were unbending, he uniformly did honour to his own wit; and he enjoyed a hearty laugh on the present occasion, while Mr. Le Quoi resumed his seat with a polite reciprocation in his mirth. The clergyman, for such was the office of Mr. Grant, modestly, though quite affectionately, exchanged his greetings with the travellers also, when Richard prepared to turn the heads of his horses homeward.

It was in the quarry alone that he could effect this object, without ascending to the summit of the mountain. A very considerable excavation had been made into the side of the hill, at the point where Richard had succeeded in stopping the sleighs, from which the stones used for building in the village, were ordinarily quarried, and in which he now attempted to turn his team. Passing itself, was a task of difficulty and frequently of danger, in that narrow road; but Richard had to meet the additional risk of turning his four-in-hand. The black very civilly volunteered his services to take off the leaders, and the Judge very earnestly seconded the measure, with his advice. Richard treated the proposals with great disdain.—

"Why, and wherefore, cousin 'duke," he exclaimed a little angrily; the horses are as gentle as lambs. You know that I broke the leaders myself, and the pole-horses are too near my whip to be restive. Here is Mr. Le Quoi, now, who must know something about driving, because he has rode out so often with me; I will leave it to Mr. Le Quoi whether there is any danger."

Thus appealed to, it was not in the nature of the Frenchman to disappoint expectations that were so confidently formed; although he sat looking down the precipice which fronted him, as Richard turned his leaders into the quarry, with a pair of eyes that stood at least half-an-inch from his visage. The German's muscles were unmoved, but his quick sight scanned each movement with an understanding expression, that blended amusement at Richard's dilemma, with anxiety at their situation. Mr. Grant placed his hands on the side of the sleigh, in preparation for a spring, but moral timidity deterred him from taking the leap, that bodily apprehension strongly urged him to attempt.

Richard, by a sudden application of his whip, succeeded in forcing his leaders into the snow-bank that covered the quarry; but the instant that the impatient animals suffered by the crust, through which they broke at each step, they positively refused to move an inch further in that direction. On the contrary, finding that the cries and blows of their driver were redoubled at this junction, the leaders backed upon the pole-horses, who, in their turn, backed the sleigh. Only a single log lay above the pile which upheld the road, on the side toward the valley, which was now buried in the snow. The sleigh was easily forced across this slight impediment; and before Richard became conscious of his danger, one half of the vehicle was projected over a precipice, which fell, nearly perpendicularly, more than a hundred feet. The Frenchman, who, by his position, had a full view of their threatened flight, instinctively threw his body as far forward as possible in the sleigh, and cried, "Ah! Mon cher monsieur Deeck! mon dieu! prenez gardez vous!"

"Donner and blitzen, Richart," exclaimed the veteran German, looking over the side of the sleigh with unusual emotion, "put you will preak ter sleigh and kilt ter horses."

"Good Mr. Jones," said the clergyman, losing the slight flush that cold had given to his cheeks, "be prudent, good sir—be careful."

"Get up, you obstinate devils!" cried Richard, catching a bird's eye view of his situation, applying his whip with new vigour, and unconsciously kicking the stool on which he sat, as if inclined to urge the inanimate wood forward; "Get up, I say—Cousin 'duke, I shall have to sell the grays too; they are the worst broken horses—Mr. Le Quaw!" Richard was too much agitated to regard his pronunciation, of which he was commonly a little vain; "Monsieur Le Quaw, pray get off my leg; you hold my leg so tight that it's no wonder I can't guide the horses."

"Merciful Providence!" exclaimed the Judge, they will be all killed!"

Elizabeth gave a piercing shriek, and the black of Agamemnon's face changed to a muddy white.

At this critical moment, the young hunter, who, during the salutations of the parties, had sat in rather sullen silence, sprang from the sleigh of Marmaduke to the heads of the refactory leaders. The horses, who were yet suffering under the injudicious and somewhat random blows from Richard, were dancing up and down with that ominous movement, that threatens a sudden and uncontrollable start, and pressing backward instead of going into the quarry. The youth gave the leaders a powerful jerk, and they plunged aside, by the path they had themselves trodden, and re-entered the road in the position in which they were first halted. The sleigh was whirled from its dangerous position, and upset with its runners outwards. The German and the divine were thrown rather unceremoniously into the highway, but without danger to their bones. Richard appeared in the air, for a moment, describing the segment of a circle, of which the reins were the radii, and was landed at the distance of some fifteen feet, in that snowbank which the horses had dreaded, right end uppermost. Here, as he instinctively grasped the reins, as drowning men seize at straws, he admirably served the purpose of an anchor, to check the further career of his steeds. The Frenchman, who was on his legs in the act of springing from the sleigh, took an aerial flight also, much in that attitude which boys assume when they play leap-frog, and flying off in a tangent to the curvature of his course, came into the snow-bank head-foremost, where he remained, exhibiting two lathy legs on high, like scarecrows waving in a corn field. Major Hartmann, whose self-possession had been admirably preserved during the whole evolution, was the first of the party that gained his feet and his voice.

"Ter deyvel, Richart!" he exclaimed, in a voice half serious, half comical, "put you unloat your sleigh very hantily."

It may be doubtful, whether the attitude in which Mr. Grant continued for an instant after his overthrow, was the one into which he had been thrown, or was assumed, in humbling himself before the power that he reverenced, in thanksgiving at his escape. When he rose from his knees, he began to gaze about him, with anxious looks, after the welfare of his companions, while every joint in his body was trembling with nervous agitation. There was also a slight confusion in the faculties of Mr. Jones, that continued for some little time; but as the mist gradually cleared from before his eyes, he saw that all was safe, and with an air of great self-satisfaction, he cried "Well—that was neatly saved, any how—it was a lucky thought in me to hold on the reins, or the fiery devils would have been over the mountain by this time. How well I recovered myself, cousin 'duke! Another moment would have been too late; but I know just the spot where to touch the off-leader

that blow under his right flank, and the sudden jerk I gave
with the reins, brought them round quite handsomely, I must
own myself."

"Thou jerk! thou recover thyself, Dickon!" cried the Judge,
whose fears were all vanished in mirth at the discomfiture of
the party; "but for that brave lad yonder, thou and thy horses,
or rather mine, would have assuredly been dashed to pieces—
But where is Monsieur Le Quoi?"

"Oh! mon cher Juge! Mon ami!" cried a smothered voice,
"praise be God I live; vill-a you, Mister Agamemnon, be
pleased come down ici, and help-a me on my foot?"

The divine and the negro seized the incarcerated Gaul by
his legs, and extricated him from a snowbank of three feet in
depth, whence his voice had sounded as from the tombs. The
thoughts of Mr. Le Quoi, immediately on his liberation, were
not extremely collected; and when he reached the light, he
threw his eyes upwards, in order to examine the distance he
had fallen. His good humour returned, however, with a knowledge of his safety, though it was some little time before he
clearly comprehended the case.

"What, monsieur," said Richard, who was busily assisting
the black in taking off the leaders; "are you there? I thought
I saw you flying up towards the top of the mountain but just
now."

"Praise be God, I no fly down into de lake," returned the
Frenchman, with a visage that was divided between pain, occasioned by a few large scratches that he had received in forcing his head through the crust, and the look of complaisance
that seemed natural to his pliable features: "ah! mon cher
Mister Deeck, vat you do next?—dere be noting you no try."

"The next thing, I trust, will be to learn to drive," said the
Judge, who had busied himself in throwing the buck, together
with several articles of his baggage, from his own sleigh into
the snow; "here are seats for you all, gentlemen; the evening
grows piercingly cold, and the hour approaches for the service
of Mr. Grant: we will leave friend Jones to repair the damages, with the assistance of Agamemnon, and hasten to a warm
fire. Here, Dickon, are a few articles of Bess's trumpery, that

you can throw into your sleigh when ready, and there is also a deer of my taking, that I will thank you to bring—Aggy! remember there will be a visit from Santaclaus to your stocking to-night, if you are smart and careful about the buck, and get in, in season."

The black grinned with the consciousness of the bribe that was thus offered him for his silence on the subject of the deer, while Richard, without, in the least, waiting for the termination of his cousin's speech, at once began his reply—

"Learn to drive, sayest thou, cousin 'duke? Is there a man in the county who knows more of horseflesh than myself? Who broke in the filly, that no one else dare mount? though your coachman did pretend that he had tamed her before I took her in hand, but anybody could see that he lied—he was a great liar, that John—what's that, a buck?"—Richard abandoned the horses, and ran to the spot where Marmaduke had thrown the deer: "It is a buck indeed! I am amazed! Yes, here are two holes in him; he has fired both barrels, and hit him each time. Ecod! how Marmaduke will brag! he is a prodigious bragger about any small matter like this now; well, well, to think that 'duke has killed a buck before Christmas! There will be no such thing as living with him—they are both bad shots though, mere chance—mere chance;—now, I never fired twice at a cloven hoof in my life;—it is hit or miss with me—dead or runaway:—had it been a bear, or a wild-cat, a man might have wanted both barrels. Here! you Aggy! how far off was the Judge when this buck was shot?"

"Eh! Massa Richard, may be a ten rod," cried the black, bending under one of the horses, with the pretence of fastening a buckle, but in reality to conceal the broad grin that opened a mouth from ear to ear.

"Ten rod!" echoed the other; "why, Aggy, the deer I killed last winter was at twenty—yes! if any thing it was nearer thirty than twenty. I wouldn't shoot at a deer at ten rod: besides, you may remember, Aggy, I only fired once."

"Yes, Massa Richard, I 'member 'em! Natty Bumppo fire t'oder gun. You know, sir, the folk say, Natty kill 'em."

"The folks lie, you black devil!" exclaimed Richard in great heat. "I have not shot even a gray squirrel these four years, to which that old rascal has not laid claim, or some one for him. This is a damn'd envious world that we live in—people are always for dividing the credit of a thing, in order to bring down merit to their own level. Now they have a story about the Patent, that Hiram Doolittle helped to plan the steeple to St. Paul's; when Hiram knows that it is entirely mine; a little taken from a print of its namesake in London, I own; but all the rest is mine."

"I don't know where he come from," said the black, losing every mark of humour in an expression of deep admiration, "but eb'ry body say, he wonnerful hansome."

"And well they may say so, Aggy," cried Richard, leaving the buck and walking up to the negro with the air of a man who has new interest awakened within him. "I think I may say, without bragging, that it is the handsomest and the most scientific country church in America. I know that the Connecticut settlers talk about their Weathersfield meeting-house; but I never believe more than half of what they say, they are such unconscionable braggers. Just as you have got a thing done, if they see it likely to be successful, they are always for interfering; and then its ten to one but they lay claim to half, or even all of the credit. You may remember, Aggy, when I painted the sign of the bold dragoon for Capt. Hollister, there was that fellow, who was about town laying brick dust on the house, came one day and offered to mix what I call the streaky black, for the tail and mane, and then, because it looks just like horse hair, he tell every body that the sign was painted by himself and Squire Jones. If Marmaduke don't send that fellow off the Patent, he may ornament his village with his own hands, for me." Here Richard paused a moment, and cleared his throat by a loud hem, while the negro, who was all this time busily engaged in preparing their sleigh, proceeded with his work in respectful silence. Owing to the religious scruples of the Judge, Aggy was the servant of Richard, who had his services for a *time,* and who, of course, commanded a legal claim to the respect of the young negro. But when any dispute between his lawful master and his real benefactor occurred, the black felt too much deference for both to express any opinion. In the mean while, Richard continued watching the negro as he fastened buckle after buckle, until, stealing a look of consciousness toward the other, he continued, "Now, if that young man, who was in your sleigh, is a real Connecticut settler, he will be telling every body how he saved my horses, when, if he had just let them alone for one half a minute longer, I would have brought them in much better, without upsetting, with the whip and rein—it spoils a horse to give him his head. I should not wonder if I had to sell the whole team, just for that one jerk that he gave them." Richard again paused, and again hemmed; for his conscience smote him a little, for censuring a man who had just saved his life—"Who is the lad, Aggy—I don't remember to have seen him before?"

The black recollected the hint about Santaclaus; and while he briefly explained how they had taken him on the top of the mountain, he forbore to add any thing concerning the accident of the wound, only saying, that he believed the youth was a stranger. It was so usual for men of the first rank to take into their sleighs any one whom they found toiling through the snow, that Richard was perfectly satisfied with this explanation. He heard Aggy, with great attention, and then remarked, "Well, if the lad has not been spoiled by the people in Templeton, he may be a modest young man, and as he certainly meant well, I shall take some notice of him—perhaps he is land-hunting— I say, Aggy—may be he is out hunting."

"Eh! yes, massa Richard," said the black, a little confused; for as Richard did all the flogging, he stood in great terror of his master, in the main—"yes, sir, I b'lieve he be."

"Had he a pack and an ax?"

"No, sir, only he rifle."

"Rifle?" exclaimed Richard, observing the confusion of the negro, which now amounted to terror.

"By Jove! he killed the deer. I knew that Marmaduke couldn't kill a buck on the jump— How was it, Aggy? tell me all about it, and I'll roast 'duke quicker than he can roast his saddle— How was it, Aggy? the lad shot the buck, and the Judge bought it, ha! and is taking him down to get the pay?"

The pleasure of this discovery had put Richard in such a good humour, that the negro's fears in some measure vanished, and he remembered the stocking. After a gulp or two, he made out to reply—

"You forgit a two shot, sir?"

"Don't lie, you black rascal!" cried Richard, stepping on the snowbank to measure the distance from his long lash to the negro's back; "speak the truth, or I'll trounce you." While speaking, the stock was slowly rising in Richard's right hand, and the lash drawing through his left, in the scientific manner with which drummers apply the cat, and Agamemnon, after turning each side of himself towards his master, and finding all equally unwilling to remain there, forgetful of his great name, fairly gave in. In a very few words he made his master acquainted with the truth, at the same time earnestly conjuring Richard to protect him from the displeasure of the Judge.

"I'll do it, boy, I'll do it," cried the other, rubbing his hands with delight; "say nothing, but leave me to manage 'duke— I have a damn'd great mind to leave the deer on the hill, and to make the fellow send for his own carcass: but no, I will let Marmaduke tell a few bouncers about it before I come out upon him. Come, hurry in, Aggy, I must help to dress the lad's wound; this Yankee doctor knows nothing of surgery— I had to hold old Milligan's leg for him, while he cut it off."
—Richard was now seated on the stool again, and the black taking the hind seat, the steeds were put in motion towards home. As they dashed down the hill, on a fast trot, the driver occasionally turned his face to Aggy, and continued speaking; for notwithstanding their recent rupture, the most perfect cordiality was again existing between them. "This goes to prove that I turned the horses with the reins, for no man who is shot in the right shoulder, can have strength enough to bring round such obstinate devils. I knew I did it from the first; but I did not want to multiply words with Marmaduke about it— Will you bite, you villain?—hip, boys, hip! Old Natty too, that is the best of it— Well, well,—'duke will say no more about my deer—and the Judge fired both barrels, and hit nothing but a poor lad, who was behind a pine-tree. I must help that quack to take out the buck-shot for the poor fellow." In this manner

Richard descended the mountain; the bells ringing, and his tongue going, until they entered the village, when the whole attention of the driver was devoted to a display of his horsemanship, to the admiration of all the gaping women and children, who thronged the windows, to witness the arrival of their landlord and his daughter.

Chapter V

Nathaniel's coat, sir, was not fully made,
And Gabriel's pumps were all unfinish'd i' th' heel;
There was no link to colour Peter's hat,
And Walter's dagger was not come from sheathing:
There were none fine, but Adam, Ralph, and Gregory.

SHAKSPEARE

After winding along the side of the mountain, the road, on reaching the gentle declivity which lay at the base of the hill, turned at a right angle to its former course, and shot down an inclined plain, directly into the village of Templeton. The rapid little stream, that we have already mentioned, was crossed by a bridge of hewn timber, which manifested by its rude construction, and the unnecessary size of its frame-work, both the value of labour and the abundance of materials. This little torrent, whose dark waters gushed in mimic turbulence over the limestones that lined its bottom, was nothing less than one of the many sources of the Susquehanna; a river, to which the Atlantic herself has extended her right arm, to welcome into her bosom. It was at this point, that the powerful team of Mr. Jones brought him up to the more sober steeds of our travellers. A small hill was risen, and the astonished Elizabeth found herself, at once, amid the incongruous dwellings of the village. The street was laid out of the width of an ordinary avenue to a city, notwithstanding that the eye might embrace in one view, thousands, and tens of thousands of acres, that were yet tenanted only by the beasts of the forest. But such had been the will of her father, and such had also met the wishes of his followers. To them, the road, that made the most rapid approaches to the condition of the old, or, as they expressed it, the *down* countries, was the most pleasant; and surely nothing could look more like civilization, than a city.

even if it lay in a wilderness! The width of the street, for so it was called, might have been one hundred feet; but the track for the sleighs was much more limited. On either side of the highway were piled before the houses huge heaps of logs, that were daily increasing rather than diminishing in size, notwithstanding the enormous fires that might be seen lighting every window through the dusk of the evening.

The last object at which Elizabeth had gazed when they renewed their journey, after the rencontre with Richard, was the sun, as it expanded in the refraction of the horizon, and over whose disk the dark umbrage of a pine was stealing, while it slowly sunk behind the western hills. But his setting rays darted along the openings of the mountain she was on, and lighted the shining covering of the birches, until their smooth and glossy coats nearly rivalled the mountain-sides in colour. The outline of each dark pine was delineated far in the depths of the forest; and the rocks, too smooth and too perpendicular to retain the snow that had fallen, brightened, as if smiling in scorn at the changes in the season. But at each step, as they descended, Elizabeth observed that they were leaving the day behind them. Even the heartless, but bright rays of a December sun were missed, as they glided into the cold gloom of the valley. Along the summits of the mountains in the eastern range, it is true, that the light still lingered, receding step by step from the earth into the few clouds that were gathering, with the evening mist, about the limited horizon; but the frozen lake lay without a shadow on its chill bosom; the dwellings were becoming already gloomy and indistinct; and the wood-cutters were shouldering their axes, and preparing to enjoy, throughout the long evening before them, the comforts of those exhilarating fires that their labour had been supplying with fuel. They paused only to gaze at the passing sleighs, to lift their caps to Marmaduke, to exchange familiar nods with Richard, and each disappeared in his dwelling. The paper curtains dropped behind our travellers in every window, shutting from the air even the fire-light of their cheerful apartments; and when the horses of her father turned, with a rapid whirl, into the open gate of the mansion-house, and nothing stood before her but the cold, dreary stone-walls of the building, as she approached them through an avenue of young and leafless poplars, Elizabeth felt as if all the loveliness of the mountain-view had vanished like the fancies of a dream. Marmaduke retained so much of his early habits as to reject the use of bells, but the equipage of Mr. Jones came dashing through the gate after them, sending its jingling sounds through every cranny in the building, and in a moment the dwelling was in an uproar.

On a stone platform, of rather small proportions, considering the size of the building, Richard and Hiram had, conjointly, reared four little columns of wood, which in their turn supported the shingled roofs of the portico—this was the name that Mr. Jones had thought proper to give to a very plain, covered, entrance to the mansion. The ascent to the platform was by five or six stone steps, somewhat hastily laid together, and which the frost had already begun to move from their symmetrical positions. But the evils of a cold climate, and a superficial construction, did not end here. As the steps lowered, the platform necessarily fell also, and the foundations actually left the superstructure suspended in the air, leaving an open space of a foot from the base of the pillars to the bases on which they had originally been placed. It was lucky for the whole fabric, that the carpenter, who did the manual part of the labour, had fastened the canopy of this classic entrance so firmly to the side of the house, that, when the base deserted the superstructure in the manner we have described, and the pillars, for the want of a foundation, were no longer of service to support the roof, the roof was able to uphold the pillars. Here was indeed an unfortunate gap left in the ornamental part of Richard's column; but like the window in Aladdin's palace, it seemed only left in order to prove the fertility of its master's resources. The composite order again offered its advantages, and a second edition of the base was given, as the booksellers say, with additions and improvements. It was necessarily larger, and it was properly ornamented with mouldings: still the steps continued to yield, and, at the moment when Elizabeth returned to her father's door, a few rough wedges were driven under the pillars to keep them steady, and to prevent their weight from separating them from the pediment which they ought to have supported.

From the great door, which opened into the porch, emerged two or three female domestics, and one male. The latter was bare-headed, but evidently more dressed than usual, and in the whole, was of so singular a formation and attire, as to deserve a more minute description. He was about five feet in height, of a square and athletic frame, with a pair of shoulders that would have fitted a grenadier. His low stature was rendered the more striking by a bend forward that he was in the habit of assuming, for no apparent reason, unless it might be in order to give a greater freedom to his arms, in a particularly sweeping swing, that they constantly practised when their master was in motion. His face was long, of a fair complexion, burnt to a fiery red; with a snub nose, cocked into an inveterate pug; a mouth of enormous dimensions, filled with fine teeth; and a pair of blue eyes, that seemed to look about them, on surrounding objects, with vast contempt. His head composed full one-fourth of his whole length, and the queue that depended from its rear occupied another. He wore a coat of very light drab cloth, with buttons as large as dollars, bearing the impression of a "foul anchor." The skirts were extremely long, reaching quite to the calf, and were broad in proportion. Beneath, there were a vest and breeches of red plush, somewhat worn and soiled. He had shoes with large buckles, and stockings of blue and white stripes.

This odd-looking figure reported himself to be a native of the county of Cornwall, in the island of Great Britain. His boyhood had passed in the neighbourhood of the tin mines, and his youth as the cabin-boy of a smuggler, between Falmouth and Guernsey. From this trade he was impressed into the service of his king, and, for the want of a better, had been taken into the cabin, first as a servant, and finally as steward to the captain. Here he acquired the art of making chowder, lobskous, and one or two other sea-dishes, and, as he was fond of saying, had an opportunity of seeing the world. With the exception of one or two outports in France, and an occasional visit to Portsmouth, Plymouth, and Deal, he had in reality seen no more of mankind, however, than if he had been riding a donkey in one of his native mines. But, being discharged from the navy at the peace of '83, he declared, that, as he had seen all the civilized parts of the world, he was inclined to a trip to the wilds of America. We will not trace him in his brief wanderings, under the influence of that spirit of emigration, that sometimes induces a dapper Cockney to quit home, and lands him, before the sound of Bow bells is fairly out of his ears, within the roar of the cataract of Niagara, but shall only add, that, at a very early day, even before Elizabeth had been sent to school, he had found his way into the family of Marmaduke Temple, where, owing to a combination of qualities, he held, under Mr. Jones, the office of major-domo. The name of this worthy was Benjamin Penguillan, according to his own pronunciation; but, owing to a marvellous tale that he was in the habit of relating, concerning the length of time he had to labour to keep his ship from sinking after Rodney's victory, he had universally acquired the nickname of Ben Pump.

By the side of Benjamin, and pressing forward as if a little jealous of her station, stood a middle-aged woman, dressed in calico, rather violently contrasted in colour, with a tall, meager, shapeless figure, sharp features, and a somewhat acute expression in her physiognomy. Her teeth were mostly gone, and what did remain were of a light yellow. The skin of her nose was drawn tightly over the member, and then suffered to hang in large wrinkles in her cheeks and about her mouth. She took snuff in such large quantities, as to create the impression, that she owed the saffron of her lips and the adjacent parts, to this circumstance; but it was the unvarying colour of her whole face. She presided over the female part of the domestic arrangements, in the capacity of housekeeper; was a spinster, and bore the name of Remarkable Pettibone. To Elizabeth she was an entire stranger, having been introduced into the family since the death of her mother.

In addition to these, were three or four subordinate menials, mostly black, some appearing at the principal door, and some running from the end of the building where stood the entrance to the cellar-kitchen.

Besides these, there was a general rush from Richard's kennel, accompanied with every canine tone, from the howl of the wolf-dog to the petulant bark of the terrier. The master received their boisterous salutations with a variety of imitations from his own throat, when the dogs, probably from shame at being outdone, ceased their outcry. One stately, powerful mastiff, who wore around his neck a brass collar, with "M. T." engraved in large letters on the rim, alone was silent. He walked majestically, amid the confusion, to the side of the Judge, where, receiving a kind pat or two, he turned to Elizabeth, who even stooped to kiss him, as she called him kindly by the name of "Old Brave." The animal seemed to know her, as she ascended the steps, supported by Monsieur Le Quoi and her father, in order to protect her from falling on the ice, with which they were covered. He looked wistfully after her figure, and when the door closed on the whole party, he laid himself in a kennel that was placed nigh by, as if conscious that the house contained something of additional value to guard.

Elizabeth followed her father, who paused a moment to whisper a message to one of his domestics, into a large hall, that was dimly lighted by two candles, placed in high, old-fashioned, brass candlesticks. The door closed, and the party were at once removed from an atmosphere that was nearly at zero, to one of sixty degrees above. In the centre of the hall stood an enormous stove, the sides of which appeared to be quivering with the heat it emitted; from which a large, straight pipe, leading through the ceiling above, carried off the smoke. An iron basin, containing water, was placed on this furnace, for such only it could be called, in order to preserve a proper humidity in the apartment. The room was carpeted, and furnished with convenient, substantial furniture, of a great variety in its appearane and materials; some of which was brought from the city, and the remainder manufactured by the mechanics of Templeton. There was a sideboard of mahogany, inlaid with ivory, and bearing enormous handles of glittering brass, and groaning under piles of silver plate. Near it stood a set of prodigious tables, made of the wild cherry, to imitate the imported wood of the sideboard, but plain, and without ornament of any kind. Opposite to these stood a smaller table, formed from a lighter coloured wood, through the grains of which the wavy lines of the curled-maple of the mountains were undulating in precise regularity. Near to this, in a corner, stood a heavy, old-fashioned, brass-faced clock, encased in a high box, with the dark hue of the black-walnut from the seashore. An enormous settee, or sofa, covered with light chintz, stretched along the walls for near twenty feet on one side of the hall, and chairs of wood, painted a light yellow, with black lines that were drawn by no very steady hand, were ranged opposite, and in the intervals between the other pieces of furniture. A Fahrenheit's thermometer, in a mahogany case, and with a barometer annexed, was hung against the wall, at some little distance from the stove, which Benjamin consulted, every half-hour, with prodigious veneration. Two small glass chandeliers were suspended at equal distances between the stove and the outer doors, one of which opened at either end of the hall, and gilt lustres were affixed to the framework of the numerous side doors that led from the apartment. Some little display in architecture had been made in constructing these frames and casings, which were surmounted with pediments, that bore each a little pedestal in its centre. On these pedestals were small busts in blacked plaster of Paris. The style of the pedestals, as well as the selection of the busts, had been executed under the auspices of Mr. Jones. On one stood Homer, a most striking likeness, Richard affirmed, "as any one might see, for it was blind." Another bore the image of a smooth visaged gentleman, with a pointed beard, whom he called Shakspeare. A third ornament was an urn, which, from its shape, Richard was accustomed to say, intended to represent itself as holding the ashes of Dido. A fourth was certainly old Franklin, in his cap and spectacles. A fifth as surely bore the dignified composure of the face of Washington. A sixth was a non descript, representing "a man with a shirt-collar open," to use the language of Richard, "with a laurel on his head;—it was Julius Caesar or Dr. Faustus; there were good reasons for believing either."

The walls were hung with a dark, lead-coloured English

paper, that represented Britannia weeping over the tomb of Wolfe. The hero himself stood at a little distance from the mourning goddess, at the edge of the paper. Each width contained the figure, with the slight exception of one arm of the General running over on to the next piece, so that when Richard essayed, with his own hands, to put together this delicate outline, some difficulties occurred, that prevented a nice conjunction, and Britannia had reason to lament, in addition to the loss of her favourite's life, numberless cruel amputations of his right arm.

The luckless cause of these unnatural divisions announced his presence in the hall by a loud crack of his whip, that startled the party, and his voice was first heard, exclaiming—

"Why, Benjamin! you Ben Pump! is this the manner in which you receive the heiress? Excuse him, cousin Elizabeth. The arrangements were too delicate and nice to be trusted to every one; but now I am here, things will go on better. Come, light up, Mr. Penguillan, light up, light up, and let us see one another's faces. Well, 'duke, I have brought home your deer; what is to be done with it, ha?"

"By the lord, Squire," commenced Benjamin in reply, first giving his mouth a wipe with the back of his hand, "if this here thing had been ordered sum'at earlier in the day, it might have been got up, d'ye see, to your liking. I had mustered all hands, and was exercising candles, when you hove in sight; but when the women heard your bells, they started an end, as if they were riding the boatswain's colt; and, if-so-be there is that man in the house, who can bring up a parcel of women when they have got headway on them, until they've run out the end of their rope, his name is not Benjamin Pump. But Miss Betsy here must have altered more than a privateer in disguise, since she has got on her woman's duds, if she will go to take offence with an old fellow, for the small matter of lighting a few candles."

Elizabeth and her father continued silent, for both experienced the same sensations on entering the hall. The former had resided one year in the building before she left home for the school, and the figure of its late lamented mistress was missed by both the husband and the child.

But candles had been placed in the chandeliers and lustres, and the attendants were so far recovered from their surprise as to recollect their use: the oversight was immediately remedied, and in a minute the apartment was in a blaze of light.

The slight melancholy of our heroine and her father was banished by this brilliant interruption; and the whole party began to lay aside the numberless garments that they had worn in the air.

During this operation, Richard kept up a desultory dialogue with the different domestics, occasionally throwing out a remark to the Judge concerning the deer; but as his conversation at such moments was much like an accompaniment on a piano, a thing that is heard without being attended to, we will not undertake the task of recording his wonderfully diffuse discourse.

The instant that Remarkable Pettibone had executed her portion of the labour in illuminating, she returned to a position near Elizabeth, with the apparent motive of receiving the clothes that the other threw aside, but in reality to examine, with an air of mingled curiosity and jealousy, the appearance of the lady who was to supplant her in the administration of their domestic economy. The housekeeper felt a little appalled, when, after cloak, coats, shawls, and socks had been taken off in succession, the large black hood was removed, and the dark ringlets, shining like the raven's wing, fell from her head, and left the sweet but commanding features of the young lady exposed to view. Nothing could be fairer and more spotless than the forehead of Elizabeth, and preserve the appearance of life and health. Her nose would have been called Grecian, but for a softly rounded swell, that gave in character to the feature what it lost in beauty. Her mouth, at first sight, seemed only made for love; but the instant that its muscles moved, every expression that womanly dignity could utter, played round it, with the flexibility of female grace. It spoke not only to the ear, but to the eye. So much, added to a form of exquisite proportions, rather full and rounded for her years, and of the tallest medium height, she inherited from her mother. Even the colour of her eye, the arched brows, and the long silken lashes, came from the same source; but its expression was her father's. Inert and composed, it was soft, benevolent, and attractive; but it could be roused, and that without much difficulty. At such moments it was still beautiful, though it was beauty in its grandeur. As the last shawl fell aside, and she stood, dressed in a rich blue riding-habit, that fitted her form with the nicest exactness; her cheeks burning with roses, that bloomed the richer for the heat of the hall, and her eyes slightly suffused with moisture, that rendered their ordinary beauty more dazzling, and with every feature of her speaking countenance illuminated by the lights that flared around her, Remarkable felt that her own power had ended.

The business of unrobing had been simultaneous. Marmaduke appeared in a suit of plain neat black; Monsieur Le Quoi, in a coat of snuff colour, covering a vest of embroidery, with breeches, and silk stockings, and buckles—that were commonly thought to be of paste. Major Hartmann wore a coat of sky-blue, with large brass buttons, a club wig, and boots; and Mr. Richard Jones had set off his dapper little form in a frock of bottle-green, with bullet buttons; by one of which the sides were united over his well-rounded waist, opening above, so as to show a jacket of red cloth, with an under vest of flannel faced with green velvet, and below, so as to exhibit a pair of buckskin breeches, with long, soiled, white-top boots, and spurs; one of the latter a little bent, from its recent attacks on the unfortunate stool.

When the young lady had extricated herself from the duresse of her garments, she was at liberty to gaze about her and to examine not only the household over which she was to preside, but also the air and manner in which their domestic arrangements were conducted. Although there was much incongruity in the furniture and appearance of the hall, there was nothing mean. The floor was carpeted, even in its remote corners. The brass candlesticks, the gilt lustres, and the glass chandeliers, whatever might be their *keeping* as to propriety and taste, were admirably kept as to all the purposes of use and comfort. They were all clean, and each glittering, in the strong light of the apartment, with its peculiar lustre. Compared with the chill aspect of the December night without, the warmth and brilliancy of the apartment produced an effect that was not unlike enchantment. Her eye had not time to detect in detail the little errors, which, in truth, existed, but was glancing around her in delight, when an object arrested her view, that was strongly contrasted to the smiling faces and neatly attired personages who had thus assembled to do honour to the heiress of Templeton.

In a corner of the hall, near to the grand entrance, stood the young hunter, unnoticed, and for the moment apparently forgotten. But even the forgetfulness of the Judge, which, under the influence of strong emotion, had banished the recollection of the wound of this stranger, seemed surpassed by the absence of mind in the youth himself. On entering the apartment he had mechanically lifted his cap, and exposed a head, covered with hair that rivalled in colour and gloss the locks of Elizabeth. Nothing could have wrought a greater transformation, than the single act of removing the rough fox-skin cap. If there was much that was prepossessing in the countenance of the young hunter, there was something noble in the rounded outlines of his head and brow. The very air and manner with which the member haughtily maintained itself over the coarse, and even wild attire, in which the rest of his frame was clad, bespoke not only familiarity with a splendour that in those new settlements was thought to be unequalled, but something very like contempt also.

The hand that held the cap, rested lightly on the little ivory-mounted piano of Elizabeth, with neither rustic restraint, nor obtrusive vulgarity. A single finger touched the instrument, as if accustomed to dwell on such places. His other arm was extended to its utmost length, and the hand grasped the barrel of his long rifle, with something like convulsive energy. The act and the attitude were both involuntary, and evidently proceeded from a feeling much deeper than that of vulgar surprise. His appearance, connected as it was with the rough exterior of his dress, rendered him entirely distinct from the busy group that were moving across the other end of the long hall, occupied in receiving the travellers, and exchanging their welcomes; and Elizabeth, herself as much an object to be looked at by the others, continued to gaze at him in a kind of stupid wonder. The contraction of the stranger's brows increased, as his eyes moved slowly from one object to another. For moments of expression of his countenance was fierce, and then again it seemed to pass away in some painful emotion. The arm, that was extended, bent, and brought the hand nigh to his face, when his head dropped upon it, and concealed the wonderfully speaking lineaments of his features.

"We forget, dear sir, the strange gentleman," (for her life Elizabeth could not call him otherwise,) "whom we have brought here for assistance, and to whom we owe every attention."

All eyes were instantly turned in the direction of those of the speaker, and the youth, rather proudly, elevated his head again, while he answered—

"My wound is trifling, and I believe that Judge Temple sent for a physician the moment we arrived."

"Certainly," said Marmaduke; "I have not forgotten the object of thy visit, young man, nor the nature of my debt to thee."

"Oh!" exclaimed Richard, with something of a waggish leer, "thou owest the lad for the venison, I suppose, that thou killed, cousin 'duke! Marmaduke! Marmaduke! That was a marvellous tale of thine about the buck! Here, young man, are two dollars for the deer, and Judge Temple can do no less than pay the doctor. I shall charge you nothing for my services, but you shall not fare the worse for that. Come, come, 'duke don't be down-hearted about it; if you missed the buck, you contrived to shoot this poor fellow through a pine-tree. Now I own that you have beat me; I never did such a thing in all my life."

"And I hope never will," returned the Judge, "if you are to experience the uneasiness that I have suffered. But be of good cheer, my young friend, the injury must be but small, as thou movest thy arm with apparent freedom."

"Don't make the matter worse, 'duke, by pretending to talk about surgery," interrupted Mr. Jones, with a contemptuous wave of the hand; "it is a science that can only be learnt by practice. You know that my grandfather was a doctor, but you haven't got a drop of medical blood in your veins; these kind of things run in families. All my family by the father's side had a knack at physic. There was my uncle that was killed at Brandywine, he died twice as easy as any other man in the regiment, only from knowing how to do the thing as it ought to be done."

"I doubt not, Dickon," returned the Judge playfully, after meeting the bright smile, which, in spite of himself, stole over the stranger's features, "that thy family understood the art of letting a life slip through their fingers with great facility."

Richard heard him quite coolly, and, putting a hand in either pocket of his surtout, so as to press forward the skirts with an air of vast disdain, began to whistle a tune; but the desire to reply overcame his philosophy, and with great heat he exclaimed—

"You may affect to smile, Judge Temple, at hereditary virtues, if you please; but there is not a man on your Patent who don't know better. Here, even this young man, who has never seen anything but bears, and deers, and wood-chucks, knows better, than not to believe in virtues being transmitted down in families. Don't you, friend?"

"I believe that vice is not," said the stranger abruptly, his eye glancing keenly from the father to the daughter.

"The Squire is right, Judge," observed Benjamin, with a knowing nod of his head towards Richard, that bespoke of the cordiality between them. "Now, in the old country, the King's Majesty touches for the evil, and that is a disorder that the greatest doctor in the fleet, or, for the matter of that, admiral either, can't cure; only the King's Majesty, or a man that's been hung. Oh! yes, the Squire is right, for if-so-be that he isn't, how is it that the seventh son always is a doctor, whether he ships for the cock-pit or not? Now, when we fell in with the mounsheers, under De Grasse, d'ye see, we had aboard of us a doctor——"

"Very well, Benjamin," interrupted Elizabeth, glancing her eyes from the hunter to Monsieur Le Quoi, who was most politely attending to what fell from each individual in succession, "you shall tell me of that, and all your entertaining adventures together; just now, a room must be prepared, in which the arm of the gentleman can be dressed."

"I will attend to that myself, cousin Elizabeth," observed Richard, somewhat haughtily. "The young man shall not suffer, because Marmaduke chooses to be a little obstinate. Follow me, my friend, and I will examine the hurt myself."

"It will be well to wait for the physician," said the hunter coldly; "he cannot be distant; I will save you the trouble."

Richard paused, and looked earnestly at the speaker, a little astonished at the language, and a good deal appalled at the refusal. He instantly construed the latter into an act of hostility, and placing his hands in the pockets again, he walked up to Mr. Grant, and putting his face close to the countenance of the divine, he said in an under tone—

"Now mark my words: there will be a story among the settlers, that all our necks would have been broken, but for that fellow there—as if I did not know how to drive. Why, you might have turned the horses yourself, sir; nothing was easier; it was only pulling hard on the nigh rein, and touching the off flank of the leader. I hope, my dear sir, you are not at all hurt by the upset the lad gave us?"

The reply was interrupted by the entrance of the village physician.

· *Chapter VI* ·

And about his shelves,
A beggarly account of empty boxes,
Green earthen pots, bladders, and musty seeds,
Remnants of pack-thread, and old cakes of roses,
Were thinly scattered to make up a show.

SHAKSPEARE

Doctor Elnathan Todd, for such was the unworthy name of the man of physic, was commonly thought to be, among the settlers, a gentleman of great mental endowments; and he was assuredly of rare personal proportions. In height he measured, without his shoes, exactly six feet and four inches. His hands, feet and knees, corresponded in every respect with this formidable stature; but every other part of his frame appeared to have been intended for a man several sizes smaller, if we except the length of the limbs. His shoulders were square, in one sense at least, being in a right line from one side to the other; but they were so narrow, that the long, dangling arms that they supported, seemed to issue out of his back. His neck possessed, in an eminent degree, the property of length to which we have alluded, and it was topped by a small bullet-head, that exhibited, on one side, a bush of bristling brown hair, and on the other, a short, twinkling visage, that appeared to maintain a constant struggle with itself in order to look wise. He was the youngest son of a farmer in the western part of Massachusetts, who, being in somewhat easy circumstances, had allowed this boy to shoot up to the height we have mentioned, without the ordinary interruptions of field-labour, wood-chopping, and such other toils as were imposed on his brothers. Elnathan was indebted for this exemption from labour, in some measure, to his extraordinary growth, which, leaving him pale, inanimate and listless, induced his tender mother to pronounce him "a sickly boy, and one that was not equal to work, but who might earn a living, comfortably enough, by taking to pleading law, or turning minister, or doctoring, or some sitch-like easy calling." Still there was a great uncertainty which of these vocations the youth was best endowed to fill with credit and profit; but, having no other employment, the stripling was constantly lounging about the "homestead" munching green apples, and hunting for sorrel; when the same sagacious eye, that had brought to light his latent talents, seized upon this circumstance, as a clue to direct his future path through the turmoils of the world. "Elnathan was cut out for a doctor," she knew, "for he was forever digging for yarbs, and tasting all kinds of things that grow'd about the lots. Then again he had a nateral love for doctor-stuff, for when she had left the bilious pills out for her man, all nicely covered with maple sugar, just ready to take, Nathan had come in, and swallowed them, for all the world as if they were nothing, while Ichabod (her husband) could never get one down without making sitch desperate faces, that it was awful to look on."

This discovery decided the matter. Elnathan, then about fifteen, was, much like a wild colt, caught and trimmed, by clipping his bushy locks; dressed in a suit of homespun, died in the butternut bark; furnished with a "New Testament," and a "Webster's Spelling-Book," and sent to school. As the boy was by nature quite shrewd enough, and had previously, at odd times, laid the foundations of reading, writing, and arithmetic, he was soon conspicuous in the school for his learning. The delighted mother had the gratification of hearing, from the lips of the master, that her son was a "prodigious boy, and far above all his class." He also thought that "the youth had a natural love for doctoring, as he had known him frequently advise the smaller children against eating too much; and once or twice, when the ignorant little things had persevered in opposition to Elnathan's advice, he had known her son to empty the school-baskets with his own mouth, to prevent the consequences."

Soon after this comfortable declaration from his schoolmaster, the lad was removed to the house of the village doctor, a gentleman whose early career had not been unlike that of our hero, where he was to be seen, sometimes watering a horse, at others watering medicines, blue, yellow, and red; then again he might be noticed, lolling under an appletree, with Ruddiman's Latin Grammar in his hand, and a corner of Denman's Midwifery sticking out of the pocket of his coat;—for his instructor held it absurd to teach his pupil how to despatch a patient regularly from this world, before he knew how to bring him into it.

This kind of life continued for a twelvemonth, when he suddenly appeared at meeting in a long coat (and well did it deserve the name!) of black homespun, with little bootees, bound with uncoloured calf-skin, for the want of red morocco.

Soon after, he was seen shaving with a dull razor; and but three or four months elapsed before several elderly ladies were observed hastening towards the house of a poor woman in the village, while others were running to and fro in great apparent distress. One or two boys were mounted, bareback, on horses, and sent off at speed in various directions. Several indirect questions were put concerning where the physician was last observed; but all would not do; and at length Elnathan was seen issuing from his door, with a very grave air, preceded by a little white-headed boy, who, out of breath, was trotting before him. The following day the youth appeared in the street, as the highway was called, and the neighbourhood was astonished in observing how much he had grown lately. The same week he bought a new razor; and the succeeding Sunday he entered the meeting-house with a red silk handkerchief in his hand, and with an extremely demure countenance. In the evening he called upon a young woman of his own class in life, for there were no others to be found, and, when he was left alone with the fair, he was called for the first time in his life, Doctor Todd, by her prudent mother. The ice once broken in this manner, Elnathan was greeted from every mouth with his official appellation.

Another year was passed under the superintendence of the same master, during which the young physician had the credit of "riding with the old doctor," although they were generally observed to travel different roads. At the end of that period, Dr. Todd attained his legal majority. He then took a jaunt to Boston, to purchase medicines, and, as some intimated, to walk the hospital; we know not how the latter might have been, but if true, he soon walked through it, for he returned within a fortnight, bringing with him a suspiciously looking box, that smelled powerfully of brimstone.

The next Sunday he was married; and the following morning he entered a one-horse sleigh with his bride, having before him the box we have mentioned, and another filled with home-made household linen, a paper-covered trunk, with a red umbrella lashed to it, a pair of quite new saddle-bags, and a bandbox. The next intelligence that his friends received of the bride and bridegroom was, that the latter was "settled in the new countries, and well to do as a doctor, in Templeton, in York state."

If a Templar would smile at the qualifications of Marmaduke to fill the judicial seat that he occupied, we are certain that a graduate of Leyden or Edinburgh would be extremely amused with this true narration of the servitude of Elnathan in the temple of Æsculapius. But the same consolation was afforded to both the jurist and the leech; for Dr. Todd was quite as much on a level with his compeers in profession in that country, as was Marmaduke with his brethren on the bench.

Time and practice did wonders for the physician. He was naturally humane, but possessed no small share of moral courage; or, in other words, he was chary of the lives of his patients, and never tried uncertain experiments on such members of society as were considered useful; but once or twice, when a luckless vagrant had come under his care, he was a little addicted to trying the effects of every vial in his saddle-bags on the stranger's constitution. Happily their number was small, and in most cases their natures innocent. By these means Elnathan had acquired a certain degree of knowledge in fevers and agues, and could talk with much judgement concerning intermittents, remittents, tertains, quotidians, &c. In certain cutaneous disorders, very prevalent in new settlements, he was considered to be infallible; and there was no woman on the Patent, but would as soon think of becoming a mother without a husband, as without the assistance of Dr. Todd. In short, he was rearing, on this foundation of sand, a superstructure, cemented by practice, though composed of somewhat brittle materials. He, however, occasionally renewed his elementary studies, and, with the observation of a shrewd mind, was applying his practice to his theory.

In surgery, having the least experience, and it being a business that spoke directly to the senses, he was most apt to distrust his own powers; but he had applied oils to several burns, cut round the roots of sundry defective teeth, and sewed up the wounds of numberless wood-choppers, with considerable eclat, when an unfortunate jobber suffered a fracture of his leg, by the tree that he had been felling. It was on this occasion that our hero encountered the greatest trial that his nerves and moral feeling had ever sustained. In the hour of need he was, however, not found wanting!—Most of the amputations in the new settlements, and they were quite frequent, were performed by some one practitioner, who, possessing originally a reputation, was enabled by this circumstance to acquire an experience that rendered him deserving of it; and Elnathan had been present at one or two of these operations. But on the present occasion the man of practice was not to be obtained, and the duty fell, as a matter of course, to the share of Mr. Todd. He went to work with a kind of blind desperation, observing, at the same time, all the externals of decent gravity and great skill. The sufferer's name was Milligan, and it was to this event that Richard alluded, when he spoke of assisting the Doctor, at an amputation—by holding the leg! The limb was certainly cut off, and the patient survived the operation. It was, however, two years before poor Milligan ceased to complain that they had buried the leg in so narrow a box, that it was straitened for room; he knew this to be true, for he could feel the pain shooting up from the inhumed fragment into his living members. Marmaduke suggested that the fault might lie in the living arteries and nerves; but Richard, considering the amputation as part of his own handy-work, strongly repelled the insinuation, at the same time declaring, that he had often heard of men who could tell when it was about to rain, by the toes of amputated limbs. After two or three years, notwithstanding that Milligan's complaints gradually diminished, the leg was dug up, and a larger box furnished, and from that hour no one had heard the sufferer utter another complaint on the subject. This gave the public great confidence in Doctor Todd, whose reputation was hourly increasing, and luckily for his patients, his information also.

Notwithstanding Mr. Todd's six years' practice, and his success with the leg, he was not a little appalled, on entering the hall of the Mansion-house. It was glaring with the light of day; it looked so splendid and imposing, compared with the hastily built and scantily furnished apartments which he frequented in his ordinary practice, and contained so many well-dressed persons, and anxiously looking-faces, that his usually firm nerves were a good deal discomposed. He had heard from the messenger who summoned him, that it was a gun-shot wound, and had come from his own home, wading through the snow, with his saddle-bags thrown over his arm, while separated arteries, penetrated lungs, and injured vitals, were whirling through his brain, as if he were stalking over a field of battle, instead of Judge temple's peaceful enclosure.

The first object that met his eye, as he moved into the room, was Elizabeth, in her riding-habit, richly laced with gold cord, her fine form bending towards him, with her face expressing deep anxiety in every one of its beautiful features. The enormous bony knees of the physician struck each other with a noise that was audible; for in the absent state of his mind, he mistook her for a general officer, perforated with bullets, hastening from the field of battle to implore his assistance. The delusion, however, was but momentary, and his eye glanced rapidly from the daughter to the earnest dignity of the father's countenance; thence to the busy strut of Richard, who was cooling his impatience at the hunter's indifference to his offered assistance, by pacing the hall and cracking his whip; from him to the Frenchman, who had stood for several minutes unheeded with a chair for the lady; thence to Major Hartmann, who was very coolly lighting a pipe three feet long by a candle in one of the chandeliers; thence to Mr. Grant, who was turning over a manuscript with much earnestness at one of the lustres; thence too. Remarkable, who stood, with arms demurely folded before her, surveying with a look of admiration and envy the dress and beauty of the young lady; and from her to Benjamin, who, with his feet standing wide apart, and his arms a-kimbo, was balancing his square little body, with the indifference of one who was accustomed to wounds and bloodshed. All of these seemed to be unhurt, and the operator began to breathe more freely; but before he had time to take a second look, the Judge, advancing, shook him kindly by the hand, and spoke.

"Thou art welcome, my good sir, quite welcome, indeed; here is a youth, whom I have unfortunately wounded in shooting a deer this evening, and who requires some of thy assistance."

"Shooting at a deer, 'duke," interrupted Richard, abruptly—"Shooting at a deer. Who do you think can prescribe, unless he knows the truth of the case? It is always so, with some people; they think a doctor can be deceived, with the same impunity as another man."

"Shooting at a deer truly," returned the Judge, with a smile, "although it is by no means certain that I did not aid in destroying the buck; but the youth is injured by my hand, be that as it may; and it is thy skill, that must cure him, and my pocket, that shall amply reward thee for it."

"Two ver good tings to depend on," observed Monsieur De Quoi, bowing politely, with a sweep of his head, to the Judge and the practitioner.

"I thank you, Monsieur," returned the Judge; "but we keep the young man in pain. Remarkable, thou wilt please to provide linen, for lint and bandages."

This remark caused a cessation of the compliments, and induced the physician to turn an inquiring eye in the direction of his patient. During the dialogue, the young hunter had thrown aside his over coat, and now stood clad in a plain suit of the common, light-coloured, homespun of the country, that was evidently but recently made. His hand was on the lapels of his coat, in the attitude of removing the garment, when he suddenly suspended the movement, and looked towards the commiserating Elizabeth, who was standing in an unchanged posture, too much absorbed with her anxious feelings to heed his actions. A slight colour appeared passing over the brow of the youth, as he spoke.

"Possibly the sight of blood may alarm the lady; I will retire to another room, while the wound is dressing."

"By no means," said Doctor Todd, who, having discovered that his patient was far from being a man of importance, felt wonderfully emboldened to perform his duty.—"The strong light of these candles is favourable to the operation, and it is seldom that we hard students enjoy good eyesight."

While speaking, Elnathan placed a pair of large iron-rimmed spectacles on his face, where they dropped, as it were by long practice, to the extremity of his slim, pug nose; and if they were of no service as assistants to his eyes, neither were they any impediment to his vision; for his little, gray organs were twinkling above them, like two stars emerging from the cover of an envious cloud. The action was unheeded by all but Remarkable, who observed to Benjamin—

"Doctor Todd is a comely man to look on, and a disp'ut pretty spoken one too. How well he seems in spectacles. I declare, they give a grand look to a body's face. I have quite a great mind to try them myself."

The speech of the stranger recalled the recollection of Miss Temple, who started, as if from deep abstraction, and, colouring excessively, she motioned to a young woman, who served in the capacity of a maid, and retired, with an air of womanly reserve.

The field was now left to the physician and his patient, while the different personages who remained, gathered around the latter, with faces expressing the various degrees of interest, that each one felt in his condition. Major Hartmann alone retained his seat, where he continued to throw out vast quantities of smoke, now rolling his eyes up to the ceiling, as if musing on the uncertainty of life, and now bending them on the wounded man, with an expression, that bespoke some consciousness of his situation.

In the mean time, Elnathan, to whom the sight of a gun-shot wound was a perfect novelty, commenced his peparations, with a solemnity and care that were worthy of the occasion. An old shirt was procured by Benjamin, and placed in the hands of the other, who tore divers bandages from it, with an exactitude, that marked both his own skill, and the importance of the operation.

The moment Richard heard the sound that was produced by rending the linen, he stepped up to the group, with the air of one who well understood the business in hand. When this preparatory measure was taken, Dr. Todd selected a piece of the shirt with great care, and handing it to Mr. Jones, without moving a muscle, said—

"Here, Squire Jones, you are well acquainted with these things; will you please to scrape the lint? It should be fine, and soft, you know, my dear sir; and be cautious that no cotton gets in, or it may p'ison the wound. The shirt has been made with cotton thread, but you can easily pick it out."

Richard assumed the office, with a nod at his cousin, that said, quite plainly, "You see, this fellow can't get along without me;" and began to scrape the piece of linen on his knee, with great diligence.

A table was now spread, by the practitioner, with vials, boxes of salve, and divers surgical instruments. As the latter appeared, in succession, from a case of red morocco, their owner held up each implement to the strong light of the chandelier, near to which he stood, and examined it, with the nicest care and precision. A red silk handkerchief was frequently applied to the glittering steel, as if to remove from the polished surfaces, the least impediment, which might exist, to the most delicate operation. After the rather scantily furnished pocket-case, which contained these instruments, was exhausted, the physician turned to his saddle-bags, and produced various vials, filled with liquids, of the most radiant colours. These were arranged, in due order, by the side of the murderous saws, knives, and scissors, when Elnathan stretched his long body to its utmost elevation, placing his hand on the small of his back, as if for support, and looked about him to discover what effect this display of his professional skill, was likely to produce on the spectators.

"Upon my word, toctor," observed Major Hartmann, with a roguish roll of his little black eyes, but with every other feature of his face in a state of perfect rest, "put you have a very pretty pocket-pook of tools tere, and your toctor-stuff glitters, as if it was petter for ter eyes as for ter pelly."

Elnathan gave a somewhat equivocal hem, before he replied—one that might have been equally taken, for that kind of noise, which cowards are said to make, in order to awaken their dormant courage, or for a natural effort, to clear the throat: if for the latter, it was successful; for, turning his face to the veteran German, he said—

"Very true, Major Hartmann, very true, sir; a prudent man will always strive to make his remedies agreeable to the eyes, though they may not altogether suit the stomach. It is no small part of our art, sir," and he now spoke with the confidence of a man who understood his subject, "to reconcile the patient to what is for his own good, though, at the same time, it may be unpalatable."

"Sartain! Doctor Todd is right," said Remarkable, "and has Scripter for what he says. The Bible tells us, how things mought be sweet to the mouth, and bitter to the inwards."

"True, true," interrupted the Judge, a little impatiently; "but here is a youth who needs no deception to lure him to his own benefit. I see, by his eye, that he fears nothing more than delay."

The stranger had, without assistance, bared his own shoulder, when the slight perforation, produced by the passage of the buck-shot, was plainly visible. The intense cold of the evening had stopped the bleeding, and Dr. Todd, casting a furtive glance at the wound, thought it by no means so formidable an affair as he had anticipated. Thus encouraged, he approached his patient, and made some indication of an intention to trace the route that had been taken by the lead.

Remarkable often found occasions, in after days, to recount the minutiae of that celebrated operation: and when she arrived at this point, she commonly proceeded as follows: —"And then the Doctor tuck out of the pocket-book a long thing, like a knitting-needle, with a button fastened to the end on't; and then he pushed it into the wownd; and then the young man looked awful; and then I thought I should have swaned away—I felt in sitch a disp'ut taking; and then the Doctor had run it right through his shoulder, and shoved the bullet out on t'other side; and so Doctor Todd cured the young man—of a ball that the Judge had shot into him, for all the world, as easy as I could pick out a splinter, with my darning-needle."

Such were the impressions of Remarkable on the subject; and such, doubtless, were the opinions of most of those, who felt it necessary to entertain a species of religious veneration for the abilities and skill of Elnathan; but such was far from the truth.

When the physician attempted to introduce the instrument, described by Remarkable, he was repulsed by the stranger, with a good deal of decision, and some little contempt, in his manner.

"I believe, sir," he said, "that a probe is not necessary; the shot has missed the bone, and has passed directly through the arm, to the opposite side, where it remains, but skin-deep, and whence, I should think, it might be easily extracted."

"The gentleman knows best," said Dr. Todd, laying down the probe, with the air of a man who had assumed it merely in compliance with forms; and, turning to Richard, he fingered the lint, with the appearance of great care and foresight. "Admirably well scraped, squire Jones! it is about the best lint I have ever seen. I want your assistance, my good sir, to hold the patient's arm, while I make an incision for the ball. Now, I rather guess, there is not another gentleman present, who could scrape the lint so well as Squire Jones."

"Such things run in families," observed Richard, rising with alacrity, to render the desired assistance. "My father, and my grandfather before him, were both celebrated for their knowledge of surgery; they were not, like Marmaduke here, puffed up with an accidental thing, such as the time when he drew in the hip-joint of the man who was thrown from his horse: that was the fall before you came into the settlement, Doctor; but they were men who were taught the thing regularly, spending half their lives in learning those little niceties; though, for the matter of that, my grandfather was a college-bred physician, and the best in the colony, too—that is, in his neighbourhood."

"So it goes with the world, Squire," cried Benjamin; "if-so-be that a man wants to walk the quarter-deck with credit, d'ye see, and with regular built swabs on his shoulders, he musn't think to do it, by getting in at the cabin-windows. There are two ways to get into a top, besides the lubber-holes. The true way to walk aft, is to begin forrard; tho'f it be only in an humble way, like myself, d'ye see, which was, from being only a hander of top-gallant-sails, and a stower of the flying-jib, to keeping the key of the Captain's locker."

"Benjamin speaks quite to the purpose," continued Richard, with a benevolent smile, directed to the Doctor. "I dare say, that he has often seen shot extracted, in the different ships in which he has served; suppose we get him to hold the basin; he must be used to the sight of blood."

"That he is, Squire, that he is," interrupted the ci-devant steward: "many's the good shot, round, double-headed, and grape, that I've seen the doctors at work on. For the matter of that, I was in a boat, alongside the ship, when they cut out the twelve-pound shot from the thigh of the Captain of the Foody-rong, one of Mounsheer Ler Quaw's countrymen, there!"

"A twelve-pound ball, from the thigh of a human being!" exclaimed Mr. Grant, with great simplicity, dropping the sermon he was again reading, and raising his spectacles, from before his eyes, to the top of his forehead.

"A twelve-pounder!" echoed Benjamin, staring around him, with much confidence; "a twelve-pounder! ay! a twenty-four pound shot can easily be taken from a man's body, if-so-be a doctor only knows how. There's Squire Jones, now, ask him, sir; he reads all the books; ask him, if he never fell in with a page, that keeps the reckoning of such things."

"Certainly, more important operations than that have been performed," observed Richard; "the Encyclopaedia mentions much more incredible circumstances than that, as, I dare say, you know, Doctor Todd."

"Certainly, there are incredible tales told of such matters," returned Elnathan, "though I cannot say, that I have ever seen, myself, any thing larger than a musket-bullet extracted."

During this discourse, an incision had been made through the skin of the young hunter's shoulder, and the lead was laid bare. Elnathan now took into his hand, with a solemn air, a pair of glittering forceps, and was in the act of applying them to the wound, when a sudden motion of the patient caused the shot to fall out of itself. The long arm and broad hand of the operator were now of singular service; for the latter expanded itself, and caught the lead, while at the same time, an extremely ambiguous motion was made, by its brother, so as to leave it doubtful to the spectator, how great was its agency in releasing the shot. Richard, however, put the matter at rest, by exclaiming—

"Very neatly done, Doctor! I have never seen a shot more neatly extracted; and, I dare say, Benjamin will say the same."

"Why, considering," returned Benjamin, "I must say, that it was ship-shape, and Brister-fashion.—Now all that the Doctor has to do, is to clap a couple of plugs in the shot-holes, and the lad will float in any gale, that blows in these here hills."

"I thank you, sir, for what you have done," said the youth, with a little distance: But here is a man, who will take me under his care, and spare you all, gentlemen, any further trouble on my account."

The whole group turned their heads, in surprise, and beheld, standing at one of the distant doors of the hall, the person of Indian John.

· *Chapter VII* ·

From Susquehanna's utmost springs,
Where savage tribes pursue their game,
His blanket tied with yellow strings,
The shepherd of the forest came.

FRENEAU

Before the Europeans, or, to use a more significant term, the Christians, dispossessed the original owners of the soil, all that section of country, which contains the New-England States, and those of the Middle, which lie east of the mountains, was occupied by two great nations of Indians, from whom numberless tribes had descended. But, as the original distinctions between these nations were marked by a difference in language, as well as by repeated and bloody wars, they never were known to amalgamate, until after the power and inroads of the whites had reduced some of the tribes to a state of dependence, that rendered not only their political, but, considering the wants and habits of a savage, their animal existence also, extremely precarious.

These two great divisions consisted, on the one side, of the Five, or, as they were afterward called, the Six Nations, and their allies; and, on the other, of the Lenni Lenape, or Delawares, with the numerous and powerful tribes, that owned that nation as their Grandfather. The former were generally called, by the Anglo-Americans, Iroquois, or the Six Nations, and sometimes Mingoes. Their appellation, among their rivals, seems generally to have been the Mengwe, or Maqua. They consisted of the tribes, or, as their allies were fond of asserting, in order to raise their consequence, of the several nations, of the Mohawks, the Oneidas, the Onondagas, Cayugas, and Senecas; who ranked, in the confederation, in the order with which they are named. The Tuscaroras were admitted to this union, near a century after its formation, and thus completed the number to six.

Of the Lenni Lenape, or as they were called by the whites, from the circumstance of their holding their great council-fire on the banks of that river, the Delaware nation, the principal tribes, besides that which bore the generic name, were, the Mahicanni, Mohicans or Mohegans, and the Nanticokes, or Nentigoes. Of these, the latter held the country along the waters of the Chesapeake, and the seashore; while the Mohegans occupied the district between the Hudson and the ocean, including most of New-England. Of course, these two tribes were the first who were dispossessed of their land by the Europeans.

The wars of a portion of the latter, are celebrated among us, as the wars of King Philip; but the peaceful policy of William Penn, or Miquon, as he was termed by the natives, effected its object, with less difficulty, though not with less certainty. As the natives gradually disappeared from the country of the Mohegans, some scattering families sought a refuge around the council-fire of the mother tribe, or the Delawares.

This people had been induced to suffer themselves to be called *women* by their old enemies, the Mingoes, or Iroquois, after the latter, having in vain tried the effects of hostility, had recourse to artifice, in order to circumvent their rivals. According to this declaration, the Delawares were to cultivate the arts of peace, and to intrust their defence, entirely, to the *men,* or warlike tribes of the Six Nations.

This state of things continued until the war of the revolution, when the Lenni Lenape formally asserted their independence, and fearlessly declared, that they were again men. But, in a government, so peculiarly republican as the Indian polity, it was not, at all times, an easy task, to restrain their members within the rules of their nation. Several fierce and renowned warriors of the Mohegans, finding the conflict with the whites to be in vain, sought a refuge with their Grandfather, and brought with them the feelings and principles, that had so long distinguished them in their own tribe. These chieftains kept alive, in some measure, the martial spirit of the Delawares; and would, at times, lead small parties against their ancient enemies, or such other foes as incurred their resentment.

Among these warriors, was one race, particularly famous for their prowess, and for those qualities that render an Indian hero celebrated. But time, disease, and want, had conspired to thin their number; and the sole representative of this once renowned family now stood in the hall of Marmaduke Temple. He had, for a long time, been an associate of the white men, particularly in their wars; and, having been, at a season when his services were of importance, much noticed and flattered, he had turned Christian, and was baptized by the name of John. He had suffered severely in his family, during the recent war, having had every soul to whom he was allied cut off by an inroad of the enemy; and when the last, lingering remnant of his nation extinguished their fires, among the hills of the Delaware, he alone had remained, with a determination of laying his bones in that country, where his fathers had so long lived and governed.

It was only, however, within a few months, that he had appeared among the mountains that surrounded Templeton. To the hut of the old hunter, he seemed peculiarly welcome; and, as the habits of the "Leather-Stocking" were so nearly assimilated to those of the savages, the conjuction of their interests excited no surprise. They resided in the same cabin, ate of the same food, and were chiefly occupied in the same pursuits.

We have already mentioned the baptismal name of this ancient chief; but in his conversation with Natty, held in the language of the Delawares, he was heard uniformly to call himself Chingachgook, which, interpreted, means the "Great Snake." This was a name that he had attained in his youth, by his skill and prowess in the art of war; but when his brows began to wrinkle with time, and he stood alone, the last of his family, and his particular tribe, the few Delawares, who yet continued about the head-waters of their river, gave him the expressive appellation of Mohegan. Perhaps there was something of deep feeling excited in the bosom of this inhabitant of the forest by the sound of a name, that recalled the idea of his nation in ruins, for he seldom used it himself—never indeed, excepting on the most solemn occasions; but the settlers had united, according to the Christian custom, his baptismal with his national name, and to them, he was generally known as John Mohegan, or, more familiarly, as Indian John.

From his long association with the white men, the habits of Mohegan were a mixture of the civilized and savage states, though there was certainly a strong preponderance in favour of the latter. In common with all his people, who dwelt within the influence of the Anglo-Americans, he had acquired new wants, and his dress was a mixture of his native fashions with European manufactures. Notwithstanding the intense cold of the atmosphere without, his head was uncovered; but a profusion of long, black, course hair, concealed his forehead, his crown, and even hung about his cheeks, so as to convey the idea, to one who knew his present and former conditions, that he encouraged its abundance, as a willing veil, to hide the shame of a noble soul, mourning for a glory that it had once known. His forehead, when it could be seen, appeared lofty, broad, and noble. His nose was high, and of the kind called Roman, with nostrils, that expanded, in his seventieth year, with the air of freedom that had distinguished them when a youth. His mouth was large, but compressed, and possessing a great share of expression and character, and, when opened, discovered a perfect set of short, strong and regular teeth. His chin was full, though not prominent; and his face bore the infallible mark of his people, in its square, high cheekbones. The eyes were not large, but their black orbs glittered in the rays of the candles, as he gazed intently down the hall, like two balls of fire.

The instant that Mohegan observed himself to be noticed by the group around the young stranger, he dropped the blanket, which covered the upper part of his frame, from his shoulders, suffering it to fall over his leggins, of untanned deer-skin, where it was retained by a belt of bark, that confined it to his waist, and moved forward.

As he walked slowly down the long hall, the unusually dignified and deliberate tread of the Indian surprised the spectators. His shoulders, and body to his waist, were entirely bare, with the exception of a silver medallion of Washington, that was suspended from his neck by a thong of buck-skin, and rested on his high chest, amidst the scars of many wounds. His shoulders were rather broad and full; but the arms, though straight and graceful, wanted the muscular appearance that labour alone can give to a race of men. The medallion was the only ornament he wore, although enormous slits in the rim of either ear, which suffered the cartilages to fall for two inches below the members, were evidently used for the purpose of decoration, in other days. In his hand he held a small basket, of the ash-wood slips, coloured in divers fantastical conceits, with red and black paints mingled with the white of the wood.

As this child of the forest approached them the whole party stood aside, and allowed him to confront the evident object of his visit. He did not speak, however, but stood, fixing his glowing eyes on the shoulder of the young hunter, and then turning them intently on the countenance of the Judge. The latter was a good deal astonished at this unusual departure from the ordinary subdued and quiet manner of the Indian; but soon recovering himself, he extended his hand, and said—

"Thou art welcome, John. This youth entertains a high opinion of thy skill, it seems, for he prefers thee, to dress his wound, even to our good friend Dr. Todd."

Mohegan now spoke, in tolerable English, but in a low monotonous, guttural tone:—

"The children of Miquon do not love the sight of blood; and yet, the young eagle has been struck by the hand that should do no evil!"

"Mohegan! old John!" exclaimed the Judge, in horror, and turning his fine, manly, open countenance to the other; "thinkest thou, that my hand has ever drawn human blood willingly? For shame! for shame, old John! thy religion should have taught thee better."

"The evil spirit sometimes lives in the best heart," returned John, impressively, as he tried to study the countenance of the Judge; "but my brother speaks the truth; his hand has never taken life, when awake; no not even when the children of the great English Father, were making the waters red with the blood of his people."

"Surely, John," said Mr. Grant, with much earnestness,

"you remember the divine command of our Saviour, 'judge not, lest ye be judged.' What motive could Judge Temple have for injuring a youth like this; one to whom he is unknown, and from whom he can receive neither injury nor favour?"

John listened respectfully to the divine, and when he had concluded, the Indian stretched out his arm, and said with energy—

"He is innocent—my brother has not done this wrong."

Marmaduke received the offered hand of the other, with a benevolent smile, that showed, however he might be astonished at his suspicion, he had ceased to resent it; while the wounded youth stood, gazing from his red friend to his host, with an expression of scornful pity powerfully delineated to his countenance. No sooner was this act of pacification exchanged, than John proceeded to discharge the duty, to perform which he had come. Dr. Todd was far from manifesting any displeasure at this invasion of his rights, but made way for the new leech, with an air that expressed a willingness to gratify the humours of his patient, now that the all-important part of the business was so successfully performed, and nothing remained to be done, but what any child might effect. Indeed, he whispered as much to Monsieur Le Quoi, when he said—

"It was fortunate that the ball was extracted before this Indian came in; but any old woman can dress the wound now. The young man, I hear, lives with John and Natty Bumppo, and it's always best to humour a patient, when it can be done discreetly—I say, discreetly, Monsieur."

"Certainement," returned the Frenchman; "you seem ver happy, Mister Todd, in your practeece. I should tink de elderly lady might ver well finish, vat you so skeelfully begin."

But Richard had, at the bottom, a great deal of veneration for the knowledge of Mohegan, especially in external wounds; and retaining all his desire for a participation in glory, he advanced nigh to the Indian and said—

"Sago, sago, Mohegan! sago, my good fellow! I am right glad you have come; give me a regular physician, like Dr. Todd, to cut into flesh, and a native to heal the wound. Do you remember, John, the time when I and you set the bone of Natty Bumppo's little finger, after he broke it by falling from the rock, when he was trying to get the partridge down, that fell on the cliffs. I never could tell yet, whether it was I or Natty, who killed that bird: he fired first, and the bird stooped, but then it was rising again, just as I pulled the trigger. I should have claimed it, for a certainty, but Natty said the hole was too big for shot, and he fired a single ball from his rifle; but the piece I carried then didn't scatter, and I have known it to bore a hole through a board, when I've been shooting at the mark, very much like rifle-bullets. Shall I help you, John? You know that I have a nack at these things."

Mohegan heard this disquisition quite patiently, and when Richard concluded, he held out the basket, which contained his specifics, indicating, by a gesture, that he might hold it. Mr. Jones was quite satisfied with this commission; and, ever after, in speaking of the event, was used to say, that "Doctor Todd and I cut out the bullet, and I and Indian John dressed the wound."

The patient was much more deserving of that epithet, while under the hands of Mohegan, than while suffering under the practice of the true physician. Indeed, the Indian gave him but little opportunity for the exercise of a forebearing temper, as he had come prepared for the occasion. His dressings were soon applied, and consisted only of some pounded bark, moistened with a fluid that he had expressed from some of the simples of the woods.

Among the native tribes of the forest, there were always two kinds of leeches to be met with. The one placed its whole dependence on the exercise of a supernatural power, and was held in greater veneration than their practice could at all justify; but the other was really endowed with great skill, in the ordinary complaints of the human body, and were, more particularly, as Natty had intimated, "curous in cuts and burises."

When John and Richard were placing the dressings on the wound, Elnathan was acutely eyeing the contents of Mohegan's basket, which Mr. Jones, in his physical ardour, had transferred to the Doctor, in order to hold, himself, one end of the bandages. Here he was soon enabled to detect sundry fragments of wood and bark, of which he, quite coolly, took possession, very possibly without any intention of speaking at all upon the subject; but when he beheld the full, blue eye of Marmaduke, watching his movements, he whispered to the Judge—

"It is not to be denied, Judge Temple, but what the savages are knowing, in small matters of physic. They hand these things down in their traditions. Now in cancers, and hydrophoby, they are quite ingenious. I will just take this bark home, and analyze it; for, though it can't be worth sixpence to the young man's shoulder, it may be good for the toothache, or rheumatis, or some of them complaints. A man should never be above learning, even if it be from an Indian."

It was fortunate for Dr. Todd, that his principles were so liberal, as, coupled with his practice, they were the means by which he acquired all his knowledge, and by which he was gradually qualifying himself for the duties of his profession. The process to which he subjected the specific, differed, however, greatly from the ordinary rules of chymistry; for, instead of separating, he afterward united the component parts of Mohegan's remedy, and thus was able to discover the tree whence the Indian had taken it.

Some ten years after this event, when civilization and its refinements had crept, or rather rushed, into the settlements among these wild hills, an affair of honour occurred, and Elnathan was seen to apply a salve to the wound that was received by one of the parties, which had the flavour that was peculiar to the tree, or root, that Mohegan had used. Ten years later still, when England and the United States were again engaged in war, and the hordes of the western parts of the state of New-York were rushing to the field, Elnathan, presuming on the reputation obtained by these two operations, followed in the rear of a brigade of militia, as its surgeon!

When Mohegan had applied the bark, he freely relinquished to Richard the needle and thread, that were used in sewing the bandages, for these were implements of which the native but little understood the use; and, stepping back, with decent gravity, awaited the completion of the business by the other.

"Reach me the scissors," said Mr. Jones, when he had finished, and finished for the second time, after tying the linen in every shape and form that it could be placed; "reach me the scissors, for here is a thread that must be cut off, or it might get under the dressings, and inflame the wound. See, John, I have put the lint I scraped, between two layers of the linen; for though the bark is certainly best for the flesh, yet the lint will serve to keep the cold air from the wound. If any lint will do it good, it is this lint; for I scraped it myself, and I will not turn my back at scraping lint, to any man on the Patent. But I ought to know how, if any body ought, for my grandfather was a doctor, and my father had a natural turn that way."

"Here, Squire, is the scissors," said Remarkable, producing from beneath her petticoat of green moreen, a pair of dull-looking shears; "well, upon my say so, you *have* sewed on the rags, as well as a woman."

"As well as a woman!" echoed Richard, with indignation; "what do women know of such matters? and you are proof of the truth of what I say. Who ever saw such a pair of shears used about a wound? Dr. Todd, I will thank you for the scissors from the case. Now, young man, I think you'll do. The shot has been very neatly taken out, although, perhaps, seeing I had a hand in it, I ought not to say so; and the wound is most admirably dressed. You will soon be well again; though the jerk you gave my leaders, must have a tendency to inflame the shoulder, yet, you will do, you will do. You were rather flurried, I suppose, and not used to horses; but I forgive the accident, for the motive:—no doubt, you had the best of motives;—yes, yes, now you will do."

"Then, gentlemen," said the wounded stranger, rising, and resuming his clothes, "it will be unnecessary for me to trespass longer on your time and patience. There remains but one thing more to be settled, and that is, our respective rights to the deer, Judge Temple."

"I acknowledge it to be thine," said Marmaduke; "and much more deeply am I indebted to thee, than for this piece of venison. But in the morning thou wilt call here, and we can adjust this, as well as more important matters. Elizabeth," —for the young lady, being apprised that the wound was dressed, had re-entered the hall,—"thou wilt order a repast, for this youth, before we proceed to the church; and Aggy will have a sleigh prepared, to convey him to his friend."

"But, sir, I cannot go without a part of the deer," returned the youth, seemingly struggling with his own feelings; "I have already told you, that I needed the venison for myself."

"Oh! we will not be particular," exclaimed Richard; "the Judge will pay you, in the morning, for the whole deer; and, Remarkable, give the lad all of the animal excepting the saddle: so, on the whole, I think, you may consider yourself as a very lucky young man;—you have been shot, without being disabled; have had the wound dressed in the best possible manner, here in the woods, as well as it would have been done in the Philadelphia hospital, if not better; have sold your deer at a high price, and yet can keep most of the carcass, with the skin in the bargain. 'Marky, tell Tom to give him the skin too; and in the morning, bring the skin to me, and I will give you half-a-dollar for it, or at least, three-and-six-pence. I want just such a skin, to cover the pillion that I am making for cousin Bess."

"I thank you, sir, for your liberality, and, I trust, am also thankful for my escape," returned the stranger; "but you reserve the very part of the animal that I wished for my own use. I must have the saddle myself."

"Must!" echoed Richard; "must is harder to be swallowed than the horns of the buck."

"Yes, must," repeated the youth; when, turning his head proudly around him, as if to see who would dare to controvert his rights, he met the astonished gaze of Elizabeth, and proceeded more mildly—"that is, if a man is allowed the possession of that which his hand hath killed, and the law will protect him in the enjoyment of his own."

"The law will do so," said Judge Temple, with an air of mortification, mingled with surprise. "Benjamin, see that the whole deer is placed in the sleigh; and have this youth conveyed to the hut of Leather-stocking. But, young man, thou hast a name, and I shall see you again, in order to compensate thee for the wrong I have done thee?"

"I am called Edwards," returned the hunter, "Oliver Edwards. I am easily to be seen, sir, for I live nigh by, and am not afraid to show my face, having never injured any man."

"It is we who have injured you, sir," said Elizabeth; "and the knowledge that you decline our assistance, would give my father great pain. He would gladly see you in the morning."

The young hunter gazed at the fair speaker, until his earnest look brought the blood to her very temples; when, recollecting himself, he bent his head, dropping his eyes to the carpet, and replied—

"In the morning, then, will I return, and see Judge Temple; and I will accept his offer of the sleigh, in token of our amity."

"Amity!" repeated Marmaduke; "there was no malice in the act that injured thee, young man; there should be none in the feelings which it may engender."

"Forgive our trespasses, as we forgive those who trespass against us," observed Mr. Grant, "is the language of prayer, used by our Divine Master himself, and it should be the golden rule of us, his humble followers."

The stranger stood a moment, lost in thought, and then, glancing his dark eyes, rather wildly, around the hall, he bowed low to the divine, and moved from the apartment, with an air that would not admit of detention.

" 'Tis strange, that one so young should harbour such feelings of resentment," said Marmaduke, when the door closed behind the stranger; "but while the pain is recent, and the sense of the injury is so fresh, he must feel more strongly than in his cooler moments. I doubt not, we shall see him, in the morning more tractable."

Elizabeth, to whom this speech was addressed, did not reply, but moved slowly up the hall, by herself, fixing her eyes on the little figure of the English ingrained carpet, that covered the floor; while, on the other hand, Richard gave a loud crack with his whip, as the stranger disappeared, and cried.

"Well, 'duke, you are your own master, but I would have tried law for the saddle, before I would have given it to the fellow. Do you not own the mountains, as well as the valleys? are not the woods your own? what right has this chap, or the

Leather-stocking, to shoot in your woods, without your permission? Now, I have known a farmer, in Pennsylvania, order a sportsman off his farm, with as little ceremony as I would order Benjamin to put a log in the stove. By-the-by, Benjamin, see how the thermometer stands. Now, if a man has a right to do this on a farm of a hundred acres, what power must a landlord have, who owns sixty thousand—ay! for the matter of that, including the late purchases, a hundred thousand? There is Mohegan, to-be-sure, he may have some right, being a native; but it's little the poor fellow can do now with his rifle. How is this managed in France, Monsieur Le Quoi? do you let every body run over your land, in that country, helter-skelter, as they do here, shooting the game, so that a gentleman has but little or no chance with his gun?"

"Bah! diable, no, Meester Deeck," replied the Frenchman; "we give, in France, no liberty, except to de ladi."

"Yes, yes, to the women, I know," said Richard; "that is your Sallick law. I read, sir, all kinds of books; of France, as well as England; of Greece, as well as Rome. But if I were in 'duke's place, I would stick up advertisements to-morrow morning, forbidding all persons to shoot, or trespass, in any manner, on my woods. I could write such an advertisement myself, in an hour, as would put a stop to the thing at once."

"Richart," said Major Hartmann, very coolly, knocking the ashes from his pipe into the spitting-box by his side, "now listen: I have livet seventy-five years on ter Mohawk, and in ter woots.—You hat petter mettle as mit ter deyvel, as mit ter hunters. Tey live mit ter gun, and a rifle is petter as ter law."

"A'nt Marmaduke a Judge?" said Richard, indignantly. "Where is the use of being a Judge, or having a Judge, if there is no law? Damn the fellow! I have a great mind to sue him in the morning myself, before Squire Doolittle, for meddling with my leaders. I am not afraid of his rifle. I can shoot too. I have hit a dollar, many a time, at fifty rods."

"Thou hast missed more dollars than ever thou hast hit, Dickon," exclaimed the cheerful voice of the Judge again.— "But we will now take our evening's repast, which, I perceive by Remarkable's physiognomy, is in the next room. Monsieur Le Quoi, Miss Temple has a fair hand at your service. Will you lead the way, my child?"

"Ah! ma chere Mam'selle, but too happy to do so," said the polite Frenchman, while he offered his hand; "it is de consolashong, in my baneesh to meet a smile from de fair ladi."

Mr. Grant and Mohegan continued in the hall, while the remainder of the party withdrew to an eating parlour, if we except Benjamin, who civilly remained, to close the rear after the divine, and to open the front door for the exit of the Indian.

"John, said the divine, when the figure of Judge Temple disappeared, the last of the group, "to-morrow is the festival of the nativity of our blessed Redeemer, when the church has appointed prayers and thanksgivings, to be offered up by her children, and when all are invited to partake of the mystical elements. As you have taken up the cross, and become a follower of good, and an eschewer of evil, John, I trust I shall see you before the altar, with a contrite heart and a meek spirit."

"John will come," said the Indian, betraying no surprise; though he did not understand all the terms used by the other.

"Yes," continued Mr. Grant, laying his hand gently on the tawny shoulder of the aged chief; "but it is not enough to be there in the body only; you must come in the spirit, and in truth. The Redeemer died for all, for the poor Indian, as well as for the white man. Heaven knows no difference in colour; nor must earth witness a separation of the church. It is good and profitable, John, to freshen the understanding, and support the wavering, by the observance of our holy festivals; but all form is but stench in the nostrils of the Holy One, unless it be accompanied by a devout and humble spirit."

The Indian stepped back a little, and, raising his body to its utmost powers of erection, he stretched his right arm on high, and dropped his fore-finger downward, as if pointing from the heavens, and striking his other hand on his naked breast, he said, with energy—

"The eye of the Great Spirit can see from the clouds;—the bosom of Mohegan is bare!"

"It is well, John, and I hope you will receive profit and consolation from the performance of this duty. The Great Spirit overlooks none of his children; and the man of the woods is as much an object of his care, as he who dwells in a palace. I wish you a good night, and pray God to bless you."

The Indian bent his head, and they separated—the one to seek his hut, and the other to join the party at the supper-table. While Benjamin was opening the door for the passage of the chief, he cried, in a tone that was meant to be quite consoling—

"The parson says the word that is true, John. If-so-be that they took count of the colour of a skin in heaven, why, they might refuse to muster on their books a Christian-born, like myself, just for the matter of a little tan, from cruising in warm latitudes; though, for the matter of that, this damned nor-wester is enough to whiten the skin of a blackamoor. Let the reefs out of your blanket, man, or your red hide will hardly weather the night, without a touch from the frost."

· *Chapter VIII* ·

For here the exile met from every clime,
And spoke, in friendship, every distant tongue.
                                    CAMPBELL

We have made our readers acquainted with some variety in character and nations, in introducing the most important personages of this legend to their notice: but, in order to establish the fidelity of our narrative, we will briefly attempt to explain the "why and wherefore" of so motely a dramatic personae.

Europe was, at the period of our tale, in the commencement of that mighty commotion which afterward shook her political institutions to their centre. Louis the Sixteenth had been beheaded, and a nation, once esteemed the most refined among the civilized people of the world, was changing her character, and substituting cruelty for mercy, and subtlety and ferocity for magnanimity and courage. Thousands of Frenchmen were compelled to seek protection in distant lands. Among the crowds who fled from France and her islands, to the United States of America, was the gentleman whom we have already mentioned as Monsieur Le Quoi. He had been recommended to the favour of Judge Temple, by the head of an eminent mercantile house in New-York, with whom Marmaduke was in habits of intimacy, and accustomed to an exchange of good offices. At his first interview with the Frenchman, our Judge had discovered him to be a man of breeding, and one who had seen much more prosperous days in his own country. From certain hints that had escaped him, Monsieur Le Quoi was suspected of having been a West-India planter, great numbers of whom had fled from St. Domingo and other islands, and were now living in the Union, in a state of comparative poverty, and some in absolute want. The latter was not, however, the lot of Monsieur Le Quoi. He had bu tlittle, he acknowledged, but that little was enough to furnish, in the language of the country, an assortment for a store.

The knowledge of Marmaduke was eminently practical, and there was no part of a *settler's* life with which he was not familiar. Under his direction, Monsieur Le Quoi made some purchases, consisting of a few cloths; some groceries, with a good deal of tea and tobacco; a quantity of iron-ware, among which was a large proportion of Barlow's jack-knives, potash-kettles, and spiders; a very formidable collection of crockery, of the coarsest quality, and most uncouth forms; together with every other common article that the art of man has devised for his wants, not forgetting the luxuries of looking-glasses and Jew's-harps. With this collection of valuables, Monsieur Le Quoi had stepped behind a counter, and, with a wonderful pliability of temperament, had dropped into his assumed character as gracefully as he had ever moved in any other. The gentleness and suavity of his manners rendered him extremely popular; besides this, the women soon discovered that he had a taste. His calicoes were the finest, or, in other words, the most showy, of any that were brought into the country; and it were impossible to look at the prices asked for his goods, by "so pretty a spoken man." Through those conjoint means, the affairs of Monsieur Le Quoi were again in a prosperous condition, and he was looked up to by the settlers as the second best man on the "Patent."

This term, Patent, which we have already used, and for which we may have further occasion, meant the district of country that had been originally granted to old Major Effingham, by the "King's letters patent," and which had now become, by purchase under the act of confiscation, the property of Marmaduke Temple. It was a term in common use, throughout the *new* parts of the state, and was usually annexed to the landlord's name, as "Temple's or Effingham's Patent."

Major Hartmann was the descendant of a man, who, in company with a number of his countrymen, had migrated, with their families, from the banks of the Rhine, to those of the Mohawk. This transmigration had occurred as far back as the reign of Queen Anne; and their descendants were now living, in great peace and plenty, on the fertile borders of that beautiful stream.

The Germans or "High Dutchers," as they were called, to distinguish them from the original, or Low Dutch colonists, were a very peculiar people. They possessed all the gravity of the latter, without any of their phlegm; and, like them, the "High Dutchers" were industrious, honest, and economical.

Fritz, or Frederick Hartmann, was an epitome of all the vices and virtues, foibles and excellencies, of his race. He was passionate, though silent, obstinate, and a good deal suspicious of strangers; of immoveable courage, inflexible honesty, and undeviating in his friendships. Indeed, there was no change about him, unless it were from grave to gay. He was serious by months, and jolly by weeks. He had early in their acquaintance, formed an attachment for Marmaduke Temple, who was the only man, that could not talk High Dutch, that ever gained his entire confidence. Four times in each year, at periods equidistant, he left his low stone dwelling, on the banks of the Mohawk, and travelled the thirty miles, through the hills, to the door of the mansion-house in Templeton. Here he generally staid a week, and was reputed to spend much of that time in riotous living, countenanced by Mr. Richard Jones. But every one loved him, even to Remarkable Pettibone, to whom he occasioned some additional trouble; he was so frank, so sincere, and, at times, so mirthful. He was now in his regular Christmas visit, and had not been in the village an hour, when Richard summoned him to fill a seat in the sleigh, to meet the landlord and his daughter.

Before explaining the character and situation of Mr. Grant, it will be necessary to recur to times far back in the brief history of the settlement.

There seems to be a tendency in human nature to endeavour to provide for the wants of this world, before our attention is turned to the business of the other. Religion was a quality but little cultivated amid the stumps of Temple's Patent, for the first few years of its settlement; but, as most of its inhabitants were from the moral states of Connecticut and Massachusetts, when the wants of nature were satisfied, they began seriously to turn their attention to the introduction of those customs and observances, which had been the principal care of their fore-fathers. There was certainly a great variety of opinions, on the subject of grace and free-will among the tenantry of Marma-duke; and, when we take into consideration the variety of the religious instruction which they received, it can easily be seen, that it could not well be otherwise.

Soon after the village had been formally laid out into the streets and *blocks* that resembled a city, a meeting of its in-habitants had been convened, to take into consideration the propriety of establishing an Academy! This measure ori-ginated with Richard, who, in truth, was much disposed to have the institution designated a University, or at least a Col-lege. Meeting after meeting was held, for this purpose, year after year. The *resolutions* of these assemblages appeared in the most conspicuous columns of a little, blue looking news-paper, that was already issued weekly from the garret of a dwelling-house in the village, and which the traveller might as often see, stuck into the fissure of a stake, that had been erected, at the point where the footpath from the log cabin of some settler entered the highway, as a post-office for an in-dividual. Sometimes the stake supported a small box, and a whole neighbourhood received a weekly supply, for their literary wants, at this point, where the man who "rides post," regularly deposited a bundle of the precious commodity. To these flourishing resolutions, which briefly recounted the gen-eral utility of education, the political and geographical rights of the village of Templeton, to a participation in the favours of the regents of the university, and the salubrity of the air, and wholesomeness of the water, together with the cheapness of food, and the superior state of morals in the neighbourhood, were uniformly annexed, in large Roman capitals, the names of Marmaduke Temple, as chairman, and Richard Jones, as secretary.

Happily for the success of this undertaking, the regents were not accustomed to resist these appeals to their generosity, whenever there was the prospect of a donation to second the request. Eventually, Judge Temple concluded to bestow the necessary land, and to erect the required edifice chiefly at his own expense. The skill of Mr., or, as he was now called, from the circumstance of his having received the commission of a justice of the peace, Squire Doolittle, was again put in requisition, and the science of Mr. Jones was once more restored to.

We shall not recount the different devices of these architects on the occasion; nor would it be decorous so to do, seeing that there was a convocation of the society of the ancient and honourable fraternity "of the free and accepted masons," at the head of whom was Richard, in the capacity of master, doubtless to approve or reject such of the plans as, in their wisdom, they deemed to be for the best. The knotty point was, however, soon decided; and, on the appointed day, the brotherhood marched, in great state, displaying sundry banners and mysterious symbols, each man with a little mimic apron before him, from a most cunningly contrived apartment in the garret of the "Bold Dragoon," an inn kept by one Captain Hollister, to the site of the intended edifice. Here Richard laid the corner-stone, with great state, amidst an assemblage of more than half the men, and all the women, within ten miles of Templeton.

In the course of the succeeding week, there was another meeting of the people, not omitting swarms of the gentler sex, when the abilities of Hiram, at the "square rule," were put to the test of experiment. The frame fitted well; and the skeleton of the fabric was reared without a single accident, if we except a few falls from horses, while the labourers were returning home in the dusk of the evening. From this time, the work advanced with great rapidity, and in the course of the season in all its beauty and proportions, the boast of the village, the study of the young aspirants for architectural fame, and the admiration of every settler on the Patent.

It was a long, narrow house, of wood, painted white, and more than half windows; and when the observer stood at the western side of the building, the edifice offered but a small obstacle to a full view of the rising sun. It was, in truth, but a very comfortless, open place, through which the daylight shone with prodigious facility. On its front were divers ornaments, in wood, designed by Richard, and executed by Hiram; but a window in the centre of the second story, immediately over the door, or grand entrance, and the "steeple," were the pride of the building. The former was, we believe, of the composite order, for it included in its composition a multitude of ornaments, and a great variety of figure. It consisted of an arched compartment in the centre, with a square, and smaller division on either side, the whole encased in heavy frames, deeply and laboriously moulded in pine wood, and lighted with a vast number of blurred and green-looking glass, of those dimensions which are commonly called "eight by ten." Blinds, that were intended to be painted green, kept the window in a state of preservation, and probably might have contibuted to the effect of the whole, had not the failure in the public funds, which seems always to be incidental to any undertaking of this kind, left them in the sombre coat of lead colour with which they had been originally clothed. The "steeple" was a little cupola, reared on the very centre of the roof, on four tall pillars of pine, that were fluted with a gouge, and loaded with mouldings. On the tops of the columns was reared a dome, or cupola, resembling in shape an inverted tea-cup without its bottom, from the centre of which projected a spire, or shaft of wood, transfixed with two iron rods, that bore on their ends the letters N. S. E. and W., in the same metal. The whole was surmounted by an imitation of one of the finny tribe, carved in wood, by the hands of Richard, and painted, what he called, a "scale-colour." The animal Mr. Jones affirmed to be an admirable resemblance of a great favourite of the epicures in that country, which bore the title of "lake-fish;" and doubtless the assertion was true; for, although intended to answer the purposes of a weathercock, the fish was observed invariably to look, with a longing eye, in the direction of the beautiful sheet of water that lay imbedded in the mountains of Templeton.

For a short time after the charter of the regents was received, the trustees of this institution employed a graduate of one of the eastern colleges, to instruct such youth as aspired to knowledge, within the walls of the edifice which we have described. The upper part of the building was in one apartment, and was intended for gala-days and exhibitions; and the lower contained two, that were intended for the great divisions of education, viz. the Latin and the English scholars. The former were never very numerous; though the sounds of "nominative, *pennaa;* genitive, *penny,*" were soon heard to issue from the windows of the room, to the great delight and manifest edification of the passenger.

Only one labourer in this temple of Minerva, however, was known to get so far as to attempt a translation of Virgil. He, indeed, appeared at the annual exhibition, to the prodigious exhultation of all his relatives, a farmer's family in the vicinity, and repeated the whole of the first eclogue from memory, observing the intonations of the dialogue with much judgement and effect. The sounds, as they proceeded from his mouth, of

"Titty-ree too patty-lee ree-coo-bans sub teg-mi-nee faa-gy
Syl-ves-trem ten-oo-i moo-sam med-i-taa-ris aa-ve-ny"—

were the last that had been heard in the building, as probably they were the first that had ever been heard, in the same language, there or any where else. For by this time the trustees had discovered, that they had anticipated the age, and the *instructor, or principal,* was superseded by a *master,* who went on to teach the more humble lesson of "the more haste the worse speed," in good, plain English.

From this time, until the date of our incidents, the Academy was a common country school; and the great room of the building was sometimes used as a court-room, on extraordinary trials; sometimes for conferences of the religious, and the morally disposed in the evening; at others for a ball in the afternoon, given under the auspices of Richard; and on Sundays, invariably, as a place of public worship.

When an itinerant priest, of the persuasion of the Methodists, Baptists, Universalists, or of the more numerous sect of the Presbyterians, was accidently in the neighbourhood, he was ordinarily invited to officiate, and was commonly rewarded for his services by a collection in a hat, before the congregation separated. When no such regular minister offered, a kind of colloquial prayer or two was made, by some of the more gifted members, and a sermon was usually read, from Sterne, by Mr. Richard Jones.

The consequence of this desultory kind of priesthood was, as we have already intimated, a great diversity in opinion, on the more abstruse points of our faith. Each sect had its adherents, though neither was regularly organized and disciplined. Of the religious education of Marmaduke, we have already written, nor was the doubtful character of his faith completely removed by his marriage. The mother of Elizabeth was an Episcopalian, as, indeed, was the mother of the Judge himself; and the good taste of Marmaduke revolted at the familiar colloquies which the leaders of the conferences held with the Deity, in their nightly meetings. In form, he was certainly an Episcopalian, though not a sectary of that denomination. On the other hand, Richard was as rigid in the observance of the canons of his church, as he was inflexible in his opinions. Indeed, he had once or twice essayed to introduce the Episcopal form of service, on the Sundays that their pulpit was vacant; but Richard was a good deal addicted to carrying all things to an excess, and then there was something so papal in his air, that the greater part of his hearers deserted him on the second Sabbath—on the third, his only auditor was Ben Pump!

Before the war of the revolution, the English church was supported, in their colonies, with much interest, by some of its adherents, in the mother country, and a few of the congregations were very amply endowed. But, for a season, after the independence of the states was established, this sect of Christians languished, for the want of the highest order of its priesthood. Pious and suitable divines were at length selected, and sent to the mother country, to receive that authority, which, it is understood, can only be transmitted directly from one to the other, and thus obtain, in order to preserve, that unity in their churches, which properly belonged to a people of the same nation. But unexpected difficulties presented themselves, in the oaths with which the policy of England had fettered their establishment; and much time was spent, before a conscientious sense of duty would permit the prelates of Britain to delegate the authority which was so earnestly sought. Time, patience, and zeal, however, removed every impediment; and the venerable men, who had been set apart by the American churches, at length returned to their expecting dioceses, endowed with the most elevated functions of their earthly church. Priests and deacons were ordained; and missionaries provided, to keep alive the expiring flame of devotion in such members as were deprived of the ordinary ministrations, by dwelling in new and unorganized districts.

Of this number was Mr. Grant. He had been sent into the country of which Templeton was the capital, and had been kindly invited by Marmaduke, and officiously pressed by Richard, to take up his abode in the village itself. A small and humble dwelling was prepared for his family, and the divine had made his appearance in the place, but a few days previously to the time of his introduction to the reader. As his forms were entirely new to most of the inhabitants, and a clergyman of another denomination had previously occupied the field, by engaging the academy, the first Sunday after his arrival was suffered to pass in silence; but now that his rival had passed on, like a meteor, filling the air with the light of his wisdom, Richard was empowered to give notice, that "Public worship, after the forms of the Protestant Episcopal Church, would be held on the night before Christmas, in the long-room of the academy in Templeton, by the Rev. Mr. Grant."

This annunciation excited great commotion among the sectaries to whom it was made. Some wondered as to the nature of the exhibition; others sneered; but a far greater part, recollecting the essays of Richard in that way, and mindful of the liberality, or rather laxity, of Marmaduke's notions on the subject of sectarianism, thought it most prudent to be silent.

The expected evening was, however, the wonder of the hour; nor was the curiosity at all diminished, when Richard and Benjamin, on the morning of the eventful day, were seen to issue from the woods in the neighbourhood of the village, each bearing on his shoulders a large bunch of evergreens. This worthy pair was observed to enter the academy, and carefully to fasten the door, after which their proceedings remained a profound secret to the rest of the village; Mr. Jones, before he commenced this mysterious business, having informed the schoolmaster, to the great delight of the white-headed flock he governed, that there could be no school that day. Marma-duke was apprised of all these preparations, by letter, and it was especially arranged, that he and Elizabeth should arrive in season, to participate in the solemnities of the evening.

After this digression, we shall return to our narrative.

Chapter IX

Now all admire, in each high-flavour'd dish,
The capabilities of flesh—fowl—fish;
In order due each guest assumes his station.
Throbs high his breast with fond anticipation,
And prelibates the joys of mastication.

HELIOGABALIAD

The apartment to which Monsieur Le Quoi handed Elizabeth, communicated with the hall, through the door that led under the urn which was supposed to contain the ashes of Dido. The room was spacious, and of very just proportions; but in its ornaments and furniture, the same diversity of taste, and imperfection of execution, were to be observed, as existed in the hall. Of furniture, there were a dozen green, wooden arm-chairs, with cushions of moreen, taken from the same piece as the petticoat of Remarkable. The tables were spread, and their materials and workmanship could not be seen; but they were heavy, and of great size. There was an enormous glass, in a gilt frame, hung against the wall, and a cheerful fire, of the hard or sugar-maple, burning on the hearth. The latter was the first object that struck the attention of the Judge, who, on be-holding it, exclaimed, rather angrily, to Richard—

"How often have I forbidden the use of the sugar-maple for fires, in my dwelling. The sight of that sap, as it exudes with the heat from the ends of those logs, is painful to me, Richard. Really, it behooves the owner of woods so extensive as mine, to be cautious what example he sets to his people, who are already felling the forests, as if no end could be found to their treasures, nor any limits to their extent. If we go on this way, twenty years hence we shall want fuel."

"Fuel in these hills, cousin 'duke!" exclaimed Richard, in

derision—"fuel for our fires! why you might as well predict, that the fish will die, for the want of water in the lake, because I intend, when the frost gets out of the ground, to lead one or two of the springs, through logs, into the village. But you are always a little wild on such subjects, Marmaduke."

"Is it wildness," returned the Judge, earnestly, "to condemn a practice, which devotes these jewels of the forest, these precious gifts of nature, these mines of comfort and wealth, to the common uses of a fire-place? But I must, and will, the instant that the snow is off the earth, send out a party into the mountains to explore for coal."

"Coal!" echoed Richard; "who the devil do you think will dig for coal, when in hunting for a bushel, he would have to rip up more roots of trees, than would keep him in fuel for a twelve-month? Poh! poh! Marmaduke, you should leave the management of these things to me, who have a natural turn that way. It was I that ordered this fire, and a noble one it is, to warm the blood in the veins of my pretty cousin Bess."

"The motive, then, must be your apology, Dickon," said the Judge.—"But, gentlemen, we are waiting. Elizabeth, my child, take the head of the table; Richard, I see, means to spare me the trouble of carving, by sitting opposite to you."

"To be sure I do," cried Richard; "here is a turkey to carve; and I flatter myself that I understand carving a turkey, or, for that matter, a goose, as well as any man alive. Mr. Grant! where's Mr. Grant? will you please to say grace, sir? Every thing is getting cold. Take a thing from the fire, this cold weather, and it will freeze in five minutes, Mr. Grant! we want you to say grace. 'For what we are about to receive, the Lord make us thankful.' Come, sit down, sit down. Do you eat wing or breast, cousin Bess?"

But Elizabeth had not taken her seat, nor was she in readiness to receive either the wing or breast. Her laughing dark eyes, were glancing at the arrangements of the table, and the quantity and selection of the food. The eyes of her father soon met the wondering looks of his daughter, and he said, with a smile—

"You perceive, my child, how much we are indebted to Remarkable, for her skill in housewifery; she has indeed provided a noble repast; such as well might stop the cravings of hunger."

"Law!" said Remarkable. "I'm glad if the Judge is pleased; but I'm notional that you'll find the sa'ce overdone. I thought, as Elizabeth was coming home, that a body could do no less than make things agreeable."

"My daughter has now grown to woman's estate, and is from this moment mistress of my house," said the Judge, sternly; "it is proper that all who live with me, address her as Miss Temple."

"*Do* tell!" exclaimed Remarkable, a little aghast; "well, who ever heerd of a young woman's being called Miss? If the Judge had a wife now, I shouldn't think of calling her any thing but Miss Temple; but——"

"Having nothing but a daughter, you will observe that style to her, if you please, in future," interrupted Marmaduke.

As the Judge looked seriously displeased, and, at such moments, carried a particularly commanding air with him, the wary housekeeper made no reply; and Mr. Grant entering the room, the whole party were soon seated at the table. As the arrangements of this repast were much in the prevailing taste of that period and country, we shall endeavour to give a short description of the appearance of the banquet.

The table-linen was of the most beautiful damask, and the plates and dishes of real china, an article of great luxury at this early period in American commerce. The knives and forks were of exquisitely polished steel, and were set in unclouded ivory. So much being furnished by the wealth of Marmaduke, was not only comfortable, but even elegant. The contents of the several dishes, and their positions, however, were the result of the sole judgement of Remarkable. Before Elizabeth, was placed an enormous roasted turkey, and before Richard, one boiled. In the centre of the table, stood a pair of heavy silver castors, surrounded by four dishes; one a fricassee, that consisted of gray squirrels; another of fish fried; a third of fish boiled; the last was a venison steak. Between these dishes and the turkeys, stood, on one side, a prodigious chine of roasted bear's meat, and on the other a boiled leg of delicious mutton.

Interspersed among this load of meats, was every species of vegetables that the season and country afforded. The four corners were garnished with plates of cake. On one was piled certain curiously twisted and complicated figures, called "nut-cakes." On another were heaps of a black-looking substance, which, receiving its hue from molasses, was properly termed "sweet-cake;" a wonderful favourite in the coterie of Remarkable. A third was filled, to use the language of the house-keeper, with "cards of gingerbread;" and the last held a "plum-cake," so called from the number of large raisins that were showing their black heads, in a substance of a wonderfully similar colour. At each corner of the table, stood saucers, filled with a thick fluid, of somewhat equivocal colour and consistence, variegated with small dark lumps of a substance that resembled nothing but itself, which Remarkable termed her "sweet-meats." At the side of each plate, which was placed bottom upwards, with its knife and fork most accurately crossed above it, stood another, of smaller size, containing a motley-looking pie, composed of triangular slices of apple, mince, pumpkin, craneberry, and *custard,* so arranged as to form an entire whole. Decanters of brandy, rum, gin and wine, with sundry pitchers of cider, beer, and one hissing vessel of "flip," were put wherever an opening would admit of their introduction. Notwithstanding the size of the tables, there was scarcely a spot where the rich damask could be seen, so crowded were the dishes, and their associated bottles, plates, and saucers. The object seemed to be profusion, and it was obtained entirely at the expense of order and elegance.

All the guests, as well as the Judge himself, seemed perfectly familiar with this description of fare, for each one commenced eating, with an appetite that promised to do great honour to Remarkable's taste and skill. What rendered this attention to the repast a little surprising, was the fact that both the German and Richard had been summoned from another table, to meet the Judge; but Major Hartmann both ate and drank without any rule, when on his excursions; and Mr. Jones invariably made it a point to participate in the business in hand, let it be what it would. The host seemed to think some apology necessary, for the warmth he had betrayed on the subject of the fire-wood, and when the party were comfortably seated, and engaged with their knives and forks, he observed—

"The wastefulness of the settlers, with the noble trees of this country, is shocking, Monsieur Le Quoi, as doubtless you have noticed. I have seen a man fell a pine, when he has been in want of fencing-stuff, and roll its first cuts into the gap, where he left it to rot, though its top would have made rails enough to answer his purpose, and it but would have sold in the Philadelphia market for twenty dollars."

"And how the devil—I beg your pardon, Mr. Grant," interrupted Richard; "but how is the poor devil to get his logs to the Philadelphia market, pray? put them in his pocket, ha! as you would a handful of chestnuts, or a bunch of chicker-berries? I should like to see you walking up High-street, with a pine log in each pocket!—Poh! poh!, cousin 'duke, there are trees enough for us all, and some to spare. Why I can hardly tell which way the wind blows, when I'm out in the clearings, they are so thick, and so tall;—I couldn't at all, if it wasn't for the clouds, and I happen to know all the points of the compass as it were, by heart."

"Ay! ay! Squire," cried Benjamin, who had now entered, and taken his place behind the Judge's chair, a little aside withal, in order to be ready for any observation like the present; "look aloft, sir, look aloft. The old seamen say, 'that the devil wouldn't make a sailor, unless he look'd aloft.' As for the compass, why, there is no such thing as steering without one. I'm sure I never lose sight of the maintop, as I call the Squire's look-out, but I set my compass, d'ye see, and take the bearings and distance of things, in order to work out my course, if-so-be that it should cloud up, or the tops of the trees should shut out the light of heaven. The steeple of St. Paul's, now that we have got it on end, is a great help to the navigation of the woods, for, by the lord Harry, as I was"——

"It is well, Benjamin," interrupted Marmaduke, observing his daughter, who manifested evident displeasure at the major-domo's familiarity; "but you forget there is a lady in company, and the women love to do most of the talking themselves."

"The Judge says the true word," cried Benjamin, with one of his discordant laughs: "now here is Mistress Remarkable

Prettybones; just take the stopper off her tongue, and you'll hear a gabbling, worse like than if you should happen to fall to leeward, in crossing a French privateer, or some such thing, mayhap, as a dozen monkeys stowed in one bag."

It were impossible to say, how perfect an illustration of the truth of Benjamin's assertion the house-keeper would have furnised, if she dare; but the Judge looked sternly at her, and, unwilling to incur his resentment, yet unable to contain her anger, she threw herself out of the room, with a toss of her body, that nearly separated her frail form in the centre.

"Richard," said Marmaduke, observing that his displeasure had produced the desired effect, "can you inform me of any thing concerning the youth, whom I so unfortunately wounded? I found him on the mountain, hunting in company with the Leather-stocking, as if they were of the same family; but there is a manifest difference in their manners. The youth delivers himself in chosen language; such as is seldom heard in these hills, and such as occasions great surprise to me, how one so meanly clad, and following so lowly a pursuit, could attain. Mohegan also knew him. Doubtless he is a tenant of Natty's hut. Did you notice the language of the lad, Monsieur Le Quoi?"

"Certainement, Monsieur Templ'," returned the Frenchman, "he deed conevairse in de most excellent Anglaise."

"The boy is not a miracle," exclaimed Richard; "I've known children that were sent to school early, talk much better, before they were twelve years old. There was Zareed Coe, old Nehemiah's son, who first settled on the beaverdam meadow, he could write almost as good a hand as myself, when he was fourteen; though it's true, I helped to teach him a little, in the long evenings. But this shooting gentleman ought to be put in the stocks, if he ever takes a rein in his hand again. He is the most arkward fellow about a horse I ever met with. I dare say, he never drove any thing but oxen in his life."

"There I think, Dickon, you do the lad injustice," said the Judge; "he uses much discretion in critical moments.—Dost thou not think so, Bess?"

There was nothing in this question particularly to excite the blushes of a maiden, but Elizabeth started from the reverie into which she had fallen, and coloured to her forehead, as she answered—

"To me, my dear sir, he appeared extremely skilful, and prompt, and courageous; but perhaps cousin Richard will say I am as ignorant as the gentleman himself."

"Gentleman!" echoed Richard; "do you call such chaps gentleman, at school, Elizabeth?"

"Every man is a gentleman, who knows how to treat a woman with respect and consideration," returned the young lady, promptly, and with an air of a little dignity.

"So much for hesitating to appear before the heiress in his shirt sleeves," cried Richard, winking at Monsieur Le Quoi, who returned the hint with one eye, while he rolled the other, with an expression of great sympathy, towards the young lady. —"Well, well, to me he seemed anything but a gentleman. I must say, however, for the lad, that he draws a good trigger, and has a true aim. He's good at shooting a buck, ha! Marmaduke?"

"Richart," said Major Hartmann, turning his grave countenance towards the gentleman he addressed, with much earnestness, "ter poy is goot. He savet your life, and my life, and ter life of Tominie Grant, and ter life of ter Frenchman; and Richart, he shall never vant a pet to sleep in vile olt Fritz Hartmann hast a shingle to cover his bet mit."

"Well, well, as you please, old gentleman," returned Mr. Jones, endeavouring to look excessively indifferent; "put him into your own stone house, if you will, Major. I dare say the lad never slept in anything better than a bark shanty in his life, unless it was some such hut as the cabin of Leatherstocking. I prophesy you will soon spoil him; any one can see how proud he grew, in a short time, just because he stood by my horses' heads, while I turned them into the highway."

"No, no, my old friend," cried Marmaduke, "it shall be my task, to provide in some manner for the youth: I owe him a debt of my own, besides the service he has done me, through my friends. And yet I anticipate some little trouble, in inducing him to accept of my services. He showed a marked dislike, I thought, Bess, to my offer of a residence within these walls for life."

"Really, dear sir," said Elizabeth, projecting her beautiful under-lip, "I have not studied the gentleman so closely, as to read his feelings in his countenance. I thought he might very naturally feel pain from his wound, and therefore pitied him; but"—and as she spoke, she glanced her eye, with a conscious timidity, towards the major-domo—"I dare say, sir, that Benjamin can tell you something about him. He cannot have been in the village, and Benjamin not have seen him often."

"Ay! I have seen the boy before," said Benjamin, who wanted no other encouragement to speak: "he has been backing and filling in the wake of Natty Bumppo, through the mountains, after deer, like a Dutch long-boat in tow of an Albany sloop. He carries a good rifle too. The Leather-stocking said, in my hearing, before Betty Hollister's bar-room fire, no later than the Tuesday night, that the younker was certain death to the wild beasts. If-so-be he can kill the wild cat, that has been beard moaning on the lake side, since the hard frosts and deep snows have driven the deer to her, he will be doing the thing that is good. Your wild-cat is a bad ship-mate, and should be made to cruise out of the track of all Christian men."

"Lives he in the hut of Bumppo?" asked Marmaduke, with some interest; and the full black eyes of Elizabeth resting intently on the scorched visage of the steward, while she waited his reply.

"Cheek by jowl," said Benjamin; "the Wednesday will be three weeks since he first hove in sight, in company with Leather-stocking. They had captured a wolf between them, and had brought in his scalp for the bounty. That Mister Bump-ho has a handy turn with him, in taking off a scalp; and there's them, in this here village, who say he larnt the trade by working on Christian men. If-so-be that there is truth in the saying, and I commanded along shore here, as your honour does, why, d'ye see, I'd bring him to the gangway for it, yet. There's a very pretty post rigged alongside of the stocks, and for the matter of a cat, I can fit one with my own hands; ay! and use it too, for the want of a better."

"You are not to credit all the idle tales, sir, that you hear of Natty," said the Judge: "he has a kind of natural right to gain a livelihood in these mountains; and if the idlers in the village take it into their heads to annoy him, as they sometimes do reputed rogues, they shall find him protected by the strong arm of the law."

"Ter rifle is petter as ter law," said the Major, sententiously.

"That for his rifle!" exclaimed Richard, snapping his fingers; "ben is right, and I"——He was stopped by the sounds of a common shipbell, that had been elevated to the belfry of the academy, which now announced, by its incessant ringing, that the hour for the appointed service had arrived, " 'For this, and every other instance of his goodness'—I beg pardon, Mr. Grant; will you please to return thanks, sir? it is time we should be moving, as we are the only Episcopalians in the neighborhood; that is, I, and Benjamin, and Elizabeth."

The divine arose, and performed the office, meekly and fervently, and the whole party instantly prepared themselves for the church—or rather academy.

· *Chapter X* ·

And calling sinful man to pray,
Loud, long, and deep the bell had toll'd.
SCOTT'S BURGHER

While Richard and Monsieur Le Quoi attended by Benjamin, proceeded to the academy, by a foot-path that was trodden in the snow, across the grounds of the Mansion-house, the Judge, his daughter, the Divine, and the Major, took a more circuitous route to the same place, through the streets of the village.

The moon had risen, during the time that our travellers were housed, and its orb was shedding a flood of light over the dark outline of pines, which crowned the eastern mountain. In other climates, the sky would have been thought clear and lucid for a noon-tide. The stars twinkled in the heavens, like the last faint glimmerings of distant fire, so much were they obscured by the overwhelming radiance of the atmosphere; the rays from the moon striking upon the smooth white surfaces of the lake and fields, reflecting upwards a light that was brightened by the spotless colour of the immense bodies of snow, which covered the earth.

Elizabeth employed herself with reading the signs, one of which appeared over almost every door, while the sleigh moved, steadily and at an easy gait, along the principal street. Not only new occupations, but names that were strangers to her ears, met her bewildered gaze, at every step they proceeded. The very houses seemed changed. This had been altered by an addition; that had been painted; another had been erected on the site of an old acquaintance, which had been banished from the earth almost as soon as it made its appearance on it. All were, however, pouring forth their inmates, who uniformly held their way towards the point where the expected exhibition, of the taste of Richard and Benjamin, was to be made.

After viewing the buildings, which really appeared to some advantage, under the bright but mellow light of the moon, our heroine turned her eyes to a scrutiny of the different figures that they passed, in search of any form that she knew. But all seemed alike, as muffled in cloaks, hoods, coats, or tippets, they glided along the narrow passages in the snow, which led under the houses, half hid by the bank that had been thrown up in excavating the deep path in which they trod. Once or twice she thought there was a stature, or a gait, that she recollected, but the person who owned it instantly disappeared behind one of those enormous piles of wood, that lay before most of the doors. It was only as they turned from the main street into another that intersected it at right angles, and which led directly to the place of meeting, that she recognised a face and building that she knew.

The house stood at one of the principal corners in the village, and, by its well-trodden doorway, as well as the sign, that was swinging, with a kind of doleful sound, in the blasts that occasionally swept down the lake, was clearly one of the most frequented inns in the place. The building was only of one story, but the dormant windows in the roof, the paint, the window-shutters, and cheerful fire that shone through the open door, gave it an air of comfort, that was not possessed by many of its neighbours. The sign was suspended from a common ale-house post, and represented the figure of a horseman, armed with sabre and pistols, and surmounted by a bear-skin cap, with a fiery animal that he bestrode "rampant." All these particulars were easily to be seen, by the aid of the moon, together with a row of somewhat illegible writing, in black paint, but in which Elizabeth, to whom the whole was familiar, read with facility "The Bold Dragoon."

A man and a woman were issuing from the door of this habitation, as the sleigh was passing. The former moved with a stiff, military step, that was a good deal heightened by a limp that he had in one leg; but the woman advanced with a measure and an air, that seemed not particularly regardful of what she might encounter. The light of the moon fell directly upon

her full, broad, and red visage; exhibiting her masculine countenance, under the mockery of a ruffled cap, that was intended,
evidently, to soften the lineaments of her features. A small
bonnet, of black silk, and of a slightly formal cut, was placed
on the back of her head, but so as not to shade her visage in
the least. Her face, as it encountered the rays of the moon from
the east, seemed not unlike a sun rising in the west. She advanced, with masculine strides, to intercept the sleigh, and the
Judge, directing the namesake of the Grecian king, who held
the lines, to check his horses, the parties were soon near to
each other.

"Good luck to ye, and a wilcome home, Jooge!" cried the
female, with a strong Irish accent; "and I'm sure it's to me
that ye'r always wilcome. Sure! and there's Miss 'Lizzy, and
a fine young woman is she grown. What a heartache would she
be giving the young men now, if there was sich a thing as a
rigiment in the town. Och! but it's idle to talk of sich vanities,
while the bell is calling us to mateing jist as we shall be call'd
away unexpictedly, some day, when we are the laist calkilating
on it. Good even, Major; will I make the bowl of gin-toddy
the night?—or it's likely ye'll stay at the big house, the Christmas eve, and the very night of ye'r getting there?"

"I am glad to see you, Mrs. Hollister," returned the voice
of Elizabeth. "I have been trying to find a face that I knew,
since we left the door of the mansion-house, but none have
I seen except your own. Your house, too, is unaltered, while
all the others are so changed, that, but for the places where
they stand, they would be utter strangers. I observe you keep
also the dear sign, that I saw cousin Richard paint, and even
the name at the bottom, about which, you may remember, you
had the disagreement."

"Is it the bould dragoon ye mane? and what name would ye
have, who niver was known by any other, as my husband here,
the Captain, can testify to. He was a pleasure to wait upon,
and was iver the foremost in the hour of need. Och! but he had
a sudden ind! But it's to be hoped, that he was justified by the
cause. And it's not Parson Grant there, who'll gainsay that
same.—Yes, yes—the Squire would paint, and so I thought
that we might have *his* face up there, who had so often shared

good and evil wid us. The eyes is no so large nor so fiery as the Captain's own, but the whiskers and the cap is as like as two peas.—Well, well—I'll not keep ye in the cowld, talking, but will drop in, the morrow, after sarvice, and jist ask ye how ye do. It's our bounden duty to make the most of this present, and to go to the house which is open to all: so God bless ye, and keep ye from evil.—Will I make the gin-twist the night, or no, Major?

To this question the German replied, very sententiously, in the affirmative; and, after a few words had passed between the husband of this fiery-faced hostess and the Judge, the sleigh moved on. It soon reached the door of the academy, where the party alighted and entered the building.

In the mean time, Mr. Jones and his two companions having a much shorter distance to journey, had arrived before the appointed place several minutes sooner than the party in the sleigh. Instead of hastening into the room, in order to enjoy the astonishment of the settlers, Richard placed a hand in either pocket of his surtout, and affected to walk about, in front of the academy, with great indifference.

The villagers proceeded uniformly into the building, with a decorum and gravity that nothing could move, on such occasions; but with a haste, that was probably a little heightened by curiosity. Those who came in from the adjacent country, spent some little time in placing certain blue and white blankets over their horses, before they proceeded to indulge their desire to view the interior of the house. Most of these men Richard approached, and inquired after the health and condition of their families. The readiness with which he mentioned the names of even the children, showed how very familiarly acquainted he was with their circumstances; and the nature of the answers he received, proved that he was a general favourite.

At length one of the pedestrians from the village stopped also, and fixed an earnest gaze at a new brick edifice, that was throwing a long shadow across the fields of snow, as it rose, with a beautiful gradation of light and shade, under the rays of a full moon. In front of the academy was a vacant piece of ground, that was intended for a public square. On the side op-

posite to where stood Mr. Jones, the new and as yet unfinished, church of St. Paul's was erected. This edifice had
been reared, during the preceding summer, by the aid of what
was called a subscription; though all, or nearly all, of
the money it had cost, came from the pocket of the landlord.
It had been built under the strong conviction of the necessity
of a more seemly place of worship than "the long-room of the
academy," and under an implied agreement, that, after its
completion, the question should be fairly put to the people,
that they might decide to what denomination it should belong.
Of course, this expectation kept alive a strong excitement, in
some few of the sectaries who were interested in its decision;
though but little was said openly on the subject. Had Judge
Temple espoused the cause of any particular sect, the question would have been immediately put at rest; for his
influence was too powerful to be opposed; but he declined all
interference in the matter, positively refusing to lend even the
weight of his name on the side of Richard, who had secretly
given an assurance to his Diocesan, that both the building and
the congregation would cheerfully come within the pale of the
Protestant Episcopal Church. But when the neutrality of the
Judge was clearly ascertained, Mr. Jones discovered that he
had to contend with a stiff-necked people. His first measure
was to go among them, and commence a course of reasoning,
in order to bring them around to his own way of thinking.
They all heard him patiently, and not a man uttered a word
in reply, in the way of argument: and Richard thought, by the
time that he had gone through the settlement, the thing was
to be conclusively decided in his favour. Willing to strike while
the iron was hot, he called a meeting, through the newspaper,
with a view to decide the question, by a vote, at once. Not a
soul attended; and one of the most anxious afternoons that
he had ever known, was spent by Richard in a vain discussion with Mrs. Hollister, who strongly contended that the
Methodist (her own) church was the best entitled to, and
most deserving of the possession of the new tabernacle. Richard
now perceived that he had been too sanguine, and had fallen
into the error of all those who, ignorantly, deal with that
wary and sagacious people. He assumed a disguise himself,

that is, as well as he knew how, and proceeded step by step to advance his purpose.

The task of erecting the building had been unanimously transferred to Mr. Jones and Hiram Doolittle. Together they had built the mansion-house, the academy, and the jail; and they alone knew how to plan and rear such a structure as was now required. Early in the day, these architects had made an equitable division of their duties. To the former was assigned the duty of making all the plans, and to the latter, the labour of superintending the execution.

Availing himself of this advantage, Richard silently determined that the windows should have the Roman arch, as the first positive step he would take in effecting his wishes. As the building was made of bricks, he was enabled to conceal his design, until the moment arrived for placing the frames: then, indeed, it became necessary to act. He communicated his wishes to Hiram with great caution; and without in the least adverting to the spiritual part of his project, he pressed the point a little warmly, on the score of architectural beauty. Hiram heard him patiently, and without contradiction; but still Richard was unable to discover the views of his coadjutor, on this interesting subject. As the right to plan was duly delegated to Mr. Jones, no direct objection was made in words, but numberless unexpected difficulties arose in the execution. At first, there was a scarcity in the right kind of material necessary to form the frames; but this objection was instantly silenced by Richard running his pencil through two feet of their length at one stroke. Then the expense was mentioned; but Richard reminded Hiram that his cousin paid, and that *he* was his treasurer. This last intimation had great weight, and after a silent and protracted, but fruitless opposition, the work was suffered to proceed on the original plan.

The next difficulty occurred in the steeple, which Richard had modelled after one of the smaller of those spires that adorn the great London Cathedral. The imitation was somewhat lame, it is true, the proportions being but indifferently observed; but, after much difficulty, Mr. Jones had the satisfaction of seeing an object reared, that bore, in its outlines, a prodigious resemblance to an old-fashioned vinegar-cruet. There was no less opposition to this model than to the windows, for the settlers were fond of novelty, and their steeple was without a precedent.

Here the labour had ceased for the season, and the difficult question of the interior remained for further deliberation. Richard well knew, that when he came to propose a reading-desk and a chancel, he must unmask; for these were arrangements, known to no church in the country, but his own. Presuming, however, on the advantages he had already obtained, he boldly styled the building St. Paul's, and Hiram prudently acquiesced in this appellation, making, however, the slight addition of calling it "*New* St. Paul's," feeling less aversion to a name taken from the English Cathedral, than from the saint.

The pedestrian, whom we have already mentioned, as pausing to contemplate this edifice, was no other than the gentleman so frequently named as Mr., or Squire Doolittle. He was of a tall, gaunt formation, with sharp features, and a face that expressed formal propriety, mingled with low cunning. Richard approached him, followed by Monsieur Le Quoi and the Major Domo.

"Good evening, Squire," said Richard, bobbing his head, but without moving his hands from his pockets.

"Good evening, Squire," echoed Hiram, turning his body, in order to turn his head also.

"A cold night, Mr. Doolittle, a cold night, sir."

"Coolish," said Hiram: "a tedious spell on't."

"What, looking at our church, ha! it looks well by moon-light; how the tin of the cupola glistens. I warrant you, the dome of the other St. Paul's never shines so in the smoke of London."

"It is a pretty meeting-house to look on," returned Hiram, "and I believe that Monshure Ler Quow and Mr. Penguilliam will allow it."

"Sairtainlee!" exclaimed the complaisant Frenchman, "it ees ver fine."

"I thought the Monshure would say so," observed Hiram. "Them last molasses that we had was excellent good. It isn't likely that you have any more of it on hand?"

"Ah! oui; ess, sair," returned Monsieur Le Quoi, with a

slight shrug of his shoulder, and a trifling grimace, "dere is more. I feel ver happi dat you love eet. I hope dat Madame Dooleet' is in good 'ealth."

"Why, so as to be stirring," said Hiram.—"The Squire hasn't finished the plans for the inside of the meeting house yet?"

"No—no—no," returned Richard, speaking quickly, but making a significant pause between each negative—"it requires reflection. There is a great deal of room to fill up, and I am afraid we shall not know how to dispose of it to advantage. There will be a large vacant spot around the pulpit, which I do not mean to place against the wall, like a sentry-box stuck up on the side of a fort."

"It is ruleable to put the deacon's box under the pulpit," said Hiram; and then, as if he had ventured too much, he added, "but there's different fashions in different countries."

"That there is," cried Benjamin; "now, in running down the coast of Spain and Portingall, you may see a nunnery stuck out of every headland, with more steeples and outriggers, such as dog-vanes and weather-cocks, than you'll find aboard of a three-masted schooner. If-so-be that a well built church is wanting, Old England, after all, is the country to go to, after your models and fashion-pieces. As to Paul's thof I've never seen it, being that it's a long way up town from Radcliff-highway and the docks, yet every body knows that it's the grandest place in the world. Now, I've no opinion but this here church over there, is as like one end of it, as a grampus is to a whale; and that's only a small difference in bulk. Mounsheer Ler Quaw here, has been in foreign parts, and thof that is not the same as having been at home, yet he must have seen churches in France, too, and can form a small idee of what a church should be: now, I ask the Mounsheer to his face, if it is not a clever little thing, taking it by and large.

"It ees ver apropos to saircumstonce," said the Frenchman —"ver judgement—but it is in de catholique country dat dey build de—vat you call—ah a ah-ha—la grande cathedrale— de big church. St. Paul Londre, is ver fine; ver bootiful; ver grand—vat you call beeg; but, Monsieur en, pardonnez moi, it is no vort so much as Notre Dame"—

"Ha! Monsheer, what is that you say?" cried Benjamin—
"St. Paul's Church not worth so much as a damn! Mayhap
you may be thinking too, that the Royal Billy isn't as good a
ship as the Billy de Paris; but she would have lick'd two of
her, any day, and in all weathers."

As Benjamin had assumed a very threatening kind of attitude, flourishing an arm, with a bunch at the end of it, that
was half as big as Monsieur Le Quoi's head, Richard thought
it time to interpose his authority.

"Hush, Benjamin, hush," he said; "you both misunder-
stand Monsieur Le Quoi, and forget yourself.—But here comes
Mr. Grant, and the service will commence. Let us go in."

The Frenchman, who received Benjamin's reply with a well-
bred good humour, that would not admit of any feeling but
pity for the other's ignorance, bowed in acquiescence, and followed his companion.

Hiram and the Major-Domo brought up the rear, the latter
grumbling, as he entered the building—

"If-so-be that the King of France had so much as a house
to live in, that would lay along-side of Paul's, one might put
up with their jaw. It's more than flesh and blood can bear, to
hear a Frenchman run down an English church in this manner.
Why, Squire Doolittle, I've been at the whipping of two of
them in one day—clean built, snug frigates, with standing-
royals, and them new-fashioned cannonades on their quarters
—such as, if they had only Englishmen aboard of them, would
have fout the devil."

With this ominous word in his mouth Benjamin entered the
church!

Chapter XI

And fools, who came to scoff, remain'd to pray.
GOLDSMITH

Notwithstanding the united labours of Richard and Benjamin, the "long-room" was but an extremely plain and inartificial temple. Benches, made in the coarsest manner, and entirely with a view to usefulness, were arranged in rows, for the reception of the congregation; while a rough, unpainted box, was placed against the wall, in the centre of the length of the apartment, as an apology for a pulpit. Something like a reading-desk was in front of this rostrum, and a small mahogany table, from the Mansion-house, covered with a spotless damask cloth, stood a little on one side, by the way of an altar. Branches of pines and hemlocks were stuck in each of the fissures that offered, in the unseasoned, and hastily completed wood-work, of both the building and its furniture; while festoons and hieroglyphics met the eye, in vast profusion, along the brown sides of the scratch-coated walls. As the room was only lighted by some ten or fifteen miserable candles, and the windows were without shutters, it would have been but a dreary, cheerless place for the solemnities of a Christmas-eve, had not the large fire, that was crackling at each end of the apartment, given an air of cheerfulness to the scene, by throwing an occasional glare of light through the vistas of bushes and faces.

The two sexes were separated by an area in the centre of the room, immediately before the pulpit, and a few benches lined this space, that were occupied by the principal personages of the village and its vicinity. This distinction was rather a gratuitous concession, made by the poorer and less polished part of the population, than a right claimed by the favoured few. One bench was occupied by the party of Judge Temple, including his daughter, and, with the exception of Dr. Todd, no one else appeared willing to incur the imputation of pride, by taking a seat in what was, literally, the high place of the tabernacle.

Richard filled a chair, that was placed behind another table, in the capacity of clerk; while Benjamin, after heaping sundry logs on the fires, posted himself nigh by, in reserve for any movement that might require his co-operation.

It would be greatly exceeding our limits, to attempt a description of the congregation, for their dresses were as various as there were individuals. Some one article, of more than usual finery, and perhaps the relic of other days, was to be seen about most of the females, in connexion with the course attire of the woods. This, wore a faded silk, that had gone through at least three generations, over coarse, woollen, black stockings; that, a shawl, whose dies were as numerous as those of the rainbow, over an awkwardly fitting gown, of rough, brown "woman's wear." In short, each one exhibited some favourite article, and all appeared in their best, both men and women; while the ground-works in dress, in either sex, were the coarse fabrics manufactured within their own dwellings. One man appeared in the dress of a volunteer company of artillery, of which he had been a member, in the "down-countries," precisely for no other reason, than because it was the best suit he had. Several, particularly of the younger men, displayed pantaloons of blue, edged with red cloth down the seams, part of the equipments of the "Templeton Light Infantry," from a little vanity to be seen in "boughten clothes." There was also one man in a "rifle frock," with its fringes and folds of spotless white, striking a chill to the heart with the idea of its coolness; although the thick coat of brown "home made," that was concealed beneath, preserved to the wearer a proper degree of warmth.

There was a marked uniformity of expression in countenance, especially in that half of the congregation, who did not enjoy the advantages of the polish of the village. A sallow skin, that indicated nothing but exposure, was common to all, as was an air of great decency and attention, mingled, generally, with an expression of shrewdness, and in the present instance, of active curiosity. Now and then a face and dress were to be seen, among the congregation, that differed entirely from this description. If pock-marked and florid, with gaitered legs, and a coat that snugly fitted the person of the wearer, it was surely an English emigrant, who had bent his steps to this retired quarter of the globe. If hard featured, and without colour, with high cheek-bones, it was a native of Scotland, in similar circumstances. The short, black-eyed man, with a cast of the swarthy Spaniard in his face, who rose repeatedly, to make room for the belles of the village, as they entered, was a son of Erin, who had lately left off his pack, and become a stationary trader in Templeton. In short, half the nations in the north of Europe had their representatives in this assembly, though all had closely assimilated themselves to the Americans, in dress and appearance, except the Englishman. He, indeed, not only adhered to his native customs, in attire and living, but usually drove his plough, among the stumps, in the same manner as he had before done, on the plains of Norfolk, until dear-bought experience taught him the useful lesson, that a sagacious people knew what was suited to their circumstances, better than a casual observer; or a sojourner, who was, perhaps, too much prejudiced to compare, and, peradventure, too conceited to learn.

Elizabeth soon discovered that she divided the attention of the congregation, equally with Mr. Grant. Timidity, therefore, confined her observation of the appearances which we have described, to stolen glances; but, as the stamping of feet was now becoming less frequent, and even the coughing, and other little preliminaries of a congregation settling themselves down into reverential attention, were ceasing, she felt emboldened to look around her. Gradually all noises diminished, until the suppressed cough denoted that it was necessary to avoid singularity, and the most profound stillness pervaded the apartment. The snapping of the fires, as they threw a powerful heat into the room, was alone heard, and each face, and every eye, were turned in expectation on the divine.

At this moment, a heavy stamping of feet was heard in the passage below, as if a new comer was releasing his limbs from the snow, that was necessarily clinging to the legs of a pedestrian. It was succeeded by no audible tread; but directly Mohegan, followed by the Leather-stocking and the young hunter, made his appearance. Their footsteps would not have been heard, as they trod the apartment in their moccasins, but for the silence which prevailed.

The Indian moved with great gravity across the floor, and, observing a vacant seat next to the Judge, he took it, in a manner that manifested his sense of his own dignity. Here, drawing his blanket closely around him, so as partly to conceal his countenance, he remained during the service, immovable, but deeply attentive. Natty passed the place, that was so freely taken by his red companion, and seated himself on one end of a log that was lying near the fire, where he continued, with his rifle standing between his legs, absorbed in reflections, seemingly, of no very pleasing nature. The youth found a seat among the congregation, and another dead silence prevailed.

Mr. Grant now arose, and commenced the service, with the sublime declaration of the Hebrew prophet—"The Lord is in his holy temple; let all the earth keep silence before him." The example of Mr. Jones was unnecessary, to teach the congregation to rise; the solemnity of the manner of the divine, effected this as by magic. After a short pause, Mr. Grant proceeded with the solemn and winning exhortation of his service. Nothing was heard but the deep, though affectionate, tones of the reader, as he slowly went through this exordium; until, something unfortunately striking the mind of Richard as incomplete, he left his place, and walked on tip-toe from the room.

When the clergyman bent his knees in prayer and confession, the congregation so far imitated his example, as to resume their seats; whence no succeeding effort of the divine, during the evening, was able to remove them in a body. Some rose, at times, but by far the larger part continued unbending; observant, it is true, but it was the kind of observation that regarded the ceremony as a spectacle, rather than a worship in which all were to participate. Thus deserted by his clerk, Mr. Grant continued to read; but no response was audible.

The short and solemn pause, that succeeded each petition, was made; still no voice repeated the eloquent language of the prayer.

The lips of Elizabeth moved, but they moved in vain; and, accustomed as she was to the service in the churches of the metropolis, she was beginning to feel the awkwardness of the circumstance most painfully, when a soft, low, female voice repeated after the priest, "We have left undone those things which we ought to have done." Startled at finding one of her own sex in that place, who could rise superior to their natural timidity, Miss Temple turned her eyes in the direction of the humble penitent. She observed a young female, on her knees, but a short distance from her, with her meek face humbly bent over her book. The appearance of this stranger, for such she was, entirely, to Elizabeth, was light and fragile. Her dress, without being either rich or fashionable, was neat and becoming; and her countenance, though pale, and slightly agitated, excited deep interest, by its sweet, and perhaps melancholy expression. A second and third response were made by this juvenile assistant, when the rich, manly sounds of a youthful, male voice, proceeded from the opposite part of the room. Miss Temple knew the tones of the young hunter instantly, and struggling to overcome her own diffidence, she added her low voice to the number.

All this time, Benjamin stood thumbing the leaves of a prayer-book with great industry, but some unexpected difficulties prevented his finding the place. Before the divine reached the close of the confession, however, Richard reappeared at the door, and, as he moved lightly across the room he took up the response, in a voice that betrayed no other concern than that of not being heard. In his hand he carried a small open box, with the figures of "8 by 10" written in black paint, on one of its sides; which having placed in the pulpit, apparently as a footstool for the divine, he returned to his station in time to say, most sonorously, "amen." The eyes of the congregation, very naturally, were turned to the windows, as Mr. Jones entered with this singular load, and then, as if accustomed to his "general agency," were again bent on the priest, in close and curious attention.

The long experience of Mr. Grant had admirably qualified him to perform with success his present duty. He well understood the character of his listeners, who were mostly a primitive people in their habits; and who, being a good deal addicted to subtleties and nice distinctions in their religious opinions, viewed the introduction into their spiritual worship by any such temporal assistance as form, not only with jealousy, but frequently with disgust. He had acquired much of his knowledge from studying the great book of human nature, as it lay open in the world; and, knowing how dangerous it was to contend with ignorance, uniformly endeavoured to avoid dictating, where his better reason taught him it was the most prudent to attempt to lead. His orthodoxy had no dependence on his cassock; he could pray, with fervour and with faith, if circumstances required it, without the assistance of his clerk; and he had even been known to preach a most evangelical sermon, in the winning manner of native eloquence, without the aid of a cambric handkerchief!

In the present instance he yielded, in many places, to the prejudices of his congregation; and when he had ended, there was not one of his new hearers, who did not think the ceremonies less papal and offensive, and more conformant to his or her own notions of devout worship, than they had been led to expect from a service of forms. Truly, Richard found in the divine, during the evening, a most powerful co-operator in his religious schemes. In preaching, Mr. Grant endeavoured to steer a middle course, between the mystical doctrines of those sublimated creeds, which daily involve their professors in the most absurd contradictions, and those fluent rules for moral government, which would reduce the Saviour to a level with the teacher of a school of ethics. Doctrine it was necessary for him to preach, for nothing less would have satisfied the disputatious people who were his listeners, and who would have interpreted silence on his part, into a tacit acknowledgement of either the superficial nature of his creed, or his own inability to defend it. We have already said that among the endless variety of their religious instructors, the settlers were accustomed to hear every denomination urge its own distinctive precepts; and to have found one indifferent to this interesting subject would have been destructive to his influence. But Mr. Grant so happily blended the universally received opinions of the Christian faith, with the dogmas of his own church, that, although none were entirely exempt from the influence of his reasons, very few took any alarm at the innovation.

"When we consider the great diversity of the human character, influenced as it is by education, by opportunity, and by physical and moral conditions of the creature, my dear hearers," he earnestly concluded, "it can excite no surprise, that creeds, so very different in their tendencies, should grow out of a religion, revealed, it is true, but whose revelations are obscured by the lapse of ages, and whose doctrines were, after the fashion of the countries in which they were first promulgated, frequently delivered in parables, and in a language abounding in metaphors, and loaded with figures. On points where the learned have, in purity of heart, been compelled to differ, the unlettered will necessarily be at variance. But, happily for us, my brethren, the fountain of divine love flows from a source too pure to admit of pollution in its course; it extends, to those who drink of its vivifying waters, the peace of the righteous, and life everlasting; it endures through all time, and it pervades creation. If there be mystery in its workings, it is the mystery of a Divinity. With a clear knowledge of the nature, the might, and majesty of God, there might be conviction, but there could be no faith. If we are required to believe in doctrines that seem not in conformity with the deductions of human wisdom, let us never forget, that such is the mandate of a wisdom that is infinite. It is sufficient for us, that enough is developed to point out path aright, and to direct our wandering steps to that portal, which shall open on the light of an eternal day. Then, indeed, it may be humbly hoped, that the film, which has been spread by the subtleties of earthly arguments, will be dissipated by the spiritual light of heaven; and that our hour of probation, by the aid of divine grace, being once passed in triumph, will be followed by an eternity of intelligence, and endless ages of fruition. All that is now obscure, shall become plain to our expanded faculties;

and what, to our present senses, may seem irreconcileable to our limited notions of mercy, of justice, and of love, shall stand, irradiated by the light of truth, confessedly the suggestions of Omniscience, and the acts of an All-powerful Benevolence.

"What a lesson of humility, my brethren, might not each of us obtain, from a review of his infant hours, and the recollection of his juvenile passions! How differently do the same acts of parental rigour appear, in the eyes of the suffering child, and of the chastened man! When the sophist would supplant with the wild theories of his worldly wisdom, the positive mandates of inspiration, let him remember the expansion of his own feeble intellects, and pause—let him feel the wisdom of God, in what is partially concealed, as well as in that which is revealed;—in short, let him substitute humility for pride of reason—let him have faith, and live!

"The consideration of this subject is full of consolation, my hearers, and does not fail to bring with it lessons of humility and of profit, that, duly improved, would both chasten the heart, and strengthen the febble-minded man in his course. It is a blessed consolation, to be able to lay misdoubtings of our arrogant nature at the threshold of the dwelling place of the Diety, from whence they shall be swept away, at the great opening of the portal, like the mists of the morning before the rising sun. It teaches us a lesson of humility, by impressing us with the imperfection of human powers, and by warning us of the many weak points where we are open to the attacks of the great enemy of our race; it proves to us, that we are in danger of being weak, when our vanity would fain soothe us into the belief that we are most strong; it forcibly points out to us the vain-glory of intellect, and shows us the vast difference between a saving faith, and the corollaries of a philosophical theology; and it teaches us to reduce our self-examination to the test of good works. By good works, must be understood the fruits of repentance, the chiefest of which is charity. Not that charity only, which causes us to help the needy and comfort the suffering, but that feeling of universal philanthropy, which, by teaching us to love, causes us to judge with lenity, all men; striking at the root of self-righteousness, and warning us to be sparing of our condemnation of others, while our own salvation is not yet secure.

"The lesson of expediency, my brethren, which I would gather from the consideration of this subject, is most strongly inculcated by our humility. On the leading and essential points of our faith, there is but little difference, among those classes of Christians who acknowledge the attributes of the Saviour, and depend on his mediation. But heresies have polluted every church, and schisms are the fruits of disputation. In order to arrest these dangers, and to ensure the union of his followers, it would seem that Christ had established his visible church, and delegated the ministry. Wise and holy men, the fathers of our religion, have expended their labours in clearing what was revealed from the obscurities of language and the results of their experience and researches have been embodied in the form of evangelical discipline. That this discipline must be salutary, is evident from the view of the weakness of human nature that we have already taken: and that it may be profitable to us, and all who listen to its precepts and its liturgy, may God, in his infinite wisdom, grant.—And now to," &c.

With this ingenious reference to his own forms and ministry, Mr. Grant concluded his discourse. The most profound attention had been paid to the sermon during the whole of its delivery, although the prayers had not been received with such a perfect demonstration of respect. This was by no means an intended slight of that liturgy, to which the divine had alluded, but was the habit of a people, who owed their very existence, as a distinct nation, to the doctrinal character of their ancestors. Sundry looks of private dissatisfaction were exchanged between Hiram and one or two of the leading members of the *conference,* but the feeling went no farther at that time; and the congregation, after receiving the blessing of Mr. Grant, dispersed in silence, and with great decorum.

· *Chapter XII* ·

Your creeds and dogmas of a learned church,
May build a fabric, fair with moral beauty;
But it would seem, that the strong hand of God
Can, only, 'rase the devil from the heart.

DEO

While the congregation was separating, Mr. Grant approached the place where Elizabeth and her father were seated, leading the youthful female, whom we have mentioned in the prededing chapter, and presented her as his daughter. Her reception was as cordial and frank as the manners of the country, and the value of good society, could render it; the two young women feeling, instantly, that they were necessary to the comfort of each other. The Judge, to whom the clergyman's daughter was also a stranger, was pleased to find one, who, from habits, sex, and years, could probably contribute largely to the pleasures of his own child, during her first privations, in her removal from the associations of a city to the solitude of Templeton; while Elizabeth, who had been forcibly struck with the sweetness and devotion of the youthful suppliant, removed the slight embarrassment of the timid stranger, by the ease and finish of her own manners. They were at once acquainted, and, during the ten minutes that the "academy" was clearing, engagements were made between the young people, not only for their pursuits during the succeeding day, after the service, but they would probably have embraced in their arrangements half of the winter, had not the divine interrupted them, by saying—

"Gently, gently, my dear Miss Temple, or you will make my girl too dissipated. You forget that she is my housekeeper, and that my domestic affairs must remain unattended to, should Louisa accept of half the kind offers that you are so good as to make her."

"And why should they not be neglected entirely, sir?" interrupted Elizabeth. "There are but two of you; and certain I am that my father's house will not only contain you both, but will open its door spontaneously, to receive such guests. Society is a good, not to be rejected on account of cold forms, in this wilderness, sir; and I have often heard my father say, that hospitality is not a virtue in a new country, the favour being conferred on the host by the guest."

"The manner in which Judge Temple exercises its rites, would confirm this opinion," said the divine; "but we must not trespass too freely. Doubt not that you will see us often; my child particularly, during the frequent visits that I shall be compelled to make to the distant parts of the country. But to obtain an influence with such a people," he continued, glancing his eyes towards the few, who were still lingering, as curious observers of the interview, "a clergyman must not awaken envy or distrust, by dwelling under so splendid a roof as that of Judge Temple."

"You like the roof, then, Mr. Grant," said Richard, who had been directing the extinguishment of the fires, and other little necessary duties, and who now approached, so as to hear the close of the divine's speech—"I am glad to find one man of taste at last. Here's 'duke now, pretends to call it by every abusive name he can invent; but though 'duke is a very tolerable Judge, sir, he is a very poor carpenter, let me tell him. Well, sir, well, I think we may say, without boasting, that the service was as well performed this evening as you often see; I think, quite as well as I ever knew it to be done in old Trinity —that is, if we except the organ. But there is the schoolmaster leads a psalm with a very good air. I used to lead myself, but latterly I have sung nothing but bass, and it affords a fine opportunity to show off a full, deep voice. Benjamin, too, sings a good bass, though he is often out in the words. Did you ever hear Benjamin sing the 'Bay of Biscay, O?' "

"I believe he gave us part of it this evening," said Marmaduke, laughing. "There was, now and then, a fearful quaver in his voice, and it seems that Mr. Penguillian, like most

others who do one thing particularly well, he knows nothing
else. He has, certainly, a wonderful partiality to one tune,
and he has a prodigious self-confidence in that one, for he
delivers himself like a north-wester sweeping across the lake.
But come, gentlemen, our way is clear, and the sleigh waits.
—Good evening, Mr. Grant. Good night, young lady. Remember that you dine beneath the Corinthian roof to-morrow, with
Elizabeth."

The parties separated, Richard holding a close dissertation
with Mr. Le Quoi, as they descended the stairs, on the subject
of psalmody, which he closed by a violent eulogium on the
air of the "Bay of Biscay O," as particularly connected with
his friend Benjamin's execution.

During the preceding dialogue, Mohegan had retained his
seat, with his head shrouded in his blanket, as seemingly in-
attentive to surrounding objects, as the departing congregation
was, itself, to the presence of the aged chief. Natty, also, continued on the log, where he had first placed himself, with his
head resting on one of his hands, while the other held the rifle,
which was thrown carelessly across his lap. His countenance
expressed extraordinary uneasiness, and the occasional un-
quiet glances that he had thrown around him during the service, plainly indicated some unusual causes for unhappiness.
His continuing seated was, however, from respect to the Indian chief, to whom he paid the utmost deference, on all occasions, although it was mingled with the rough manner of a
hunter.

The young companion of these two ancient inhabitants of
the forest, remained also, standing before the extinguished
brands, probably from an unwillingness to depart without his
comrades. The room was now deserted by all but this group,
the divine and his daughter. As the party from the Mansion-
house disappeared, John arose, and dropping the blanket from
his head, he shook back the mass of black hair from his face,
and approaching Mr. Grant, he extended his hand, and said
solemnly—

"Father, I thank you. The words that have been said, since
the rising moon, have gone upward, and the Great Spirit is
glad. What you have told your children, they will remember,

and be good." He paused a moment, and then elevating himself to all the grandeur of an Indian chief, he added—"If Chingachgook lives to travel towards the setting sun, after his tribe, and the Great Spirit carries him over the lakes and mountains, with the breath in his body, he will tell his people the good talk he has heard; and they will believe him; for who can say that Mohegan has ever lied?"

"Let him place his dependence on the goodness of Divine mercy," said Mr. Grant, to whom the proud consciousness of the Indian sounded a little heterodox, "and it never will desert him. When the heart is filled with love to God, there is no room left for sin.—But, young man, to you I owe not only an obligation, in common with those you saved this evening, on the mountain, but my thanks, for your respectful and pious manner, in assisting in the service, at a most embarrassing moment. I should be happy to see you sometimes at my dwelling, when, perhaps, my conversation may strengthen you in the path which you appear to have chosen. It is so unusual to find one of your age and appearance, in these woods, at all acquainted with our holy liturgy, that it lessens at once the distance between us, and I feel that we are no longer strangers. You seem quite at home in the service: I did not perceive that you had even a book, although good Mr. Jones had laid several in different parts of the room."

"It would be strange, if I were ignorant of the service of our church, sir," returned the youth, modestly, for I was baptized in its communion, and I have never yet attended public worship elsewhere. For me, to use the forms of any other denomination, would be as singular as our own have proved to the people here this evening."

"You give me great pleasure to hear you, my dear sir," cried the divine, seizing the other by the hand, and shaking it cordially.—"You will go home with me now—indeed you must—my child has yet to thank you for saving my life. I will listen to no apologies. This worthy Indian, and your friend there, will accompany us.—Bless me! to think that he has arrived at manhood, in this country, without entering a dissenting meeting-house!"

"No, no," interrupted the Leather-stocking, "I must away

to the wigwam: there's work there, that mus'nt be forgotten, for all your churchings and merry-makings. Let the lad go with you in welcome; he is used to keeping company with ministers, and talking of such matters; so is old John, who was Christianized by the Moravians, about the time of the old war. But I am a plain, unlarned man, that has sarved the king and his country, in his day, ag'in the French and savages, but never so much as looked into a book, or larnt a letter of scholarship, in my born days. I've never seen the use of sitch in-door kind of work, though I have lived to be partly bald, and in my time, have killed two hundred beaver in a season, and that without counting the other game.—If you mistrust what I am telling you, you can ask Chingachgook there, for I did it in the heart of the Delaware country, and the old man is knowing to the truth of every word I say."

"I doubt not, my friend, that you have been both a valiant soldier and skilful hunter, in your day," said the divine; "but more is wanting, to prepare you for that end which approaches. You may have heard the maxim, that 'young men *may* die, but that old men *must*.' "

"I'm sure I never was so great a fool as to expect to live for ever," said Natty, giving one of his silent laughs: "no man need do that, who trails the savages through the woods, as I have done, and lives for the hot months, on the lake streams. I've a strong constitution, I must say that for myself, as is plain to be seen, for I've drank the Onondaga water a hundred times, while I've been watching the deer-licks, when the fever-an-agy seeds was to be seen in it, as plain and as plenty as you can see the rattle-snakes on old Crumhorn. But then, I never expected to hold out for ever; though there's them living, who have seen the Garman Flats a wilderness, ay! and them that's larned and acquainted with religion too; though you might look a week now and not find even the stump of a pine on them; and that's a wood that lasts in the ground the better part of a hundred years."

"This is but time, my good friend," returned Mr. Grant, who began to take an interest in the welfare of his new acquaintance, "but it is for eternity that I would have you prepare. It is incumbent on you to attend places of public worship, as I am pleased to see that you have done this evening. Would it not be heedless in you to start on a day's toil of hard hunting, and leave your ramrod and flint behind you?"

"It must be a young hand in the woods," interrupted Natty, with another laugh, "that didn't know how to dress a rod out of an ash sapling, or find a fire-stone in the mountains. No, no, I never expected to live for ever; but I see, times be altering in these mountains from what they was thirty years ago, or for that matter, ten years. But might makes right, and the law is stronger than an old man, whether he is one that has much larning, or only one like me, that is better now at standing at the passes than in following the hounds, as I once used to could. Heigh-ho! I never know'd preaching come into a settlement, but it made game scearce, and raised the price of gun-powder; and that's a thing that's not as easily made as a ramrod, or an Indian flint."

The divine, perceiving that he had given his opponent an argument, by his own unfortunate selection of a comparison, very prudently relinquished the controversy, for the present; although he was fully determined to resume it at a more happy moment. Repeating his request to the young hunter, with great earnestness, the youth and Indian consented to accompany him and his daughter to the dwelling, that the care of Mr. Jones had provided for their temporary residence. Leather-stocking perservered in his intention of returning to the hut, and at the door of the building they separated.

After following the course of one of the streets of the village, for a short distance, Mr. Grant, who led the way, turned into a field, through a pair of open bars, and entered a foot-path, of but sufficient width to admit of only one person to walk in it, at a time. The moon had gained a height that enabled her to throw her rays nearly perpendicularly on the valley; and the distinct shadows of the party flitted along on the banks of the silver snow, like the presence of aerial figures, gliding to their appointed place of meeting. The night still continued intensely cold, although not a breath of wind was to be felt. The path was beaten so hard, that the gentle female, who made one of the party, moved with ease along its windings; though the frost emitted a low creaking, at the impression of even her light footsteps.

The clergyman in his dark dress of broad cloth, with his mild, benevolent countenance occasionally turned towards his companions, expressing that look of subdued care, that was its characteristic, presented the first object of this singularly constituted group. Next to him moved the Indian, with his hair falling about his face, his head uncovered, and the rest of his form concealed beneath his blanket. As his swarthy visage, with its muscles fixed in rigid composure, was seen under the light of the moon, which struck his face obliquely, he seemed a picture of resigned old age, on whom the storms of winter had beaten in vain, for the greater part of a century; but when in turning his head, the rays fell directly on his dark, fiery eyes, they told a tale of passions unrestrained, and of thoughts free as the air he breathed. The slight person of Miss Grant, which followed next, and which was but too thinly clad for the severity of the season, formed a marked contrast to the wild attire, and uneasy glances of the Delaware chief; and more than once, during their walk, the young hunter, himself no insignificant figure in the group, was led to consider the difference in the human form, as the face of Mohegan, and the gentle countenance of Miss Grant, with eyes that rivalled the soft hue of the sky in colour, met his view, at the instant that each turned, to throw a glance at the splendid orb, that lighted their path. Their way, which led through fields, that lay at some distance in the rear of the houses, was cheered by a conversation, that flagged or became animated with the subject. The first to speak was the divine.

"Really," he said, "it is so singular a circumstance to meet with one of your age that has not been induced by an idle curiosity, to visit any other church than the one in which he has been educated, that I feel a strong curiosity to know the history of a life so fortunately regulated.—Your education must have been an excellent one; as indeed is evident from your manners and language. Of which of the states are you a native, Mr. Edwards? for such, I believe, was the name that you gave to Judge Temple."

"Of this——"

"Of this! I was at a loss to conjecture, from your dialect, which does not partake, particularly, of the peculiarities of any country with which I am acquainted. You have, then, resided much in the cities, for no other part of this country is so fortunate as to possess the constant enjoyment of our excellent liturgy."

The young hunter smiled, as he listened to the divine while he so clearly betrayed from what part of the country he had come himself; but, for reasons, probably connected with his present situation, he made no answer.

"I am delighted to meet with you, my young friend, for I think an ingenuous mind, such as I doubt not yours must be, will exhibit all the advantages of a settled doctrine and devout liturgy. You perceive how I was compelled to bend to the humours of my hearers this evening. Good Mr. Jones wished me to read the communion, and, in fact, all the morning service; but, happily, the canons do not require this in an evening. It would have wearied a new congregation; but to-morrow I purpose administering the sacrament—do you commune, my young friend?"

"I believe not, sir," returned the youth, with a little embarrassment, that was not at all diminished by Miss Grant's pausing involuntarily, and turning her eyes on him in evident surprise—"I fear that I am not qualified; I have never yet approached the altar; neither would I wish to do it, while I find so much of the world clinging to my heart, as I now experience."

"Each must judge for himself," said Mr. Grant; "though I should think that a youth who had never been blown about by the wind of false doctrines, and who has enjoyed the advantages of our liturgy for so many years in its purity, might safely come. Yet, sir, it is a solemn festival, which none should celebrate, until there is reason to hope it is not mockery. I observed this evening in your manner to Judge Temple, a resentment, that bordered on one of the worst of human passions.—We will cross this brook on the ice: it must bear us all, I think, in safety.—Be careful not to slip my child." While speaking, he descended a little bank by the path, and crossed one of the small streams that poured their waters into the lake; and turning to see his daughter pass, observed that the youth had advanced, and was kindly directing her footsteps. When all were safely over, he moved up the opposite bank, and continued his discourse:—"It was wrong, my dear sir, very wrong, to suffer such feelings to rise, under any circumstances, and especially in the present, where the evil was not intended."

"There is good in the talk of my father," said Mohegan, stopping short, and causing those who were behind him to pause also; "It is the talk of Miquon. The white man may do as his fathers have told him; but the 'Young Eagle' has the blood of a Delaware chief in his veins: it is red, and the stain it makes can only be washed out with the blood of a Mingo."*

Mr. Grant was surprised by the interruption of the Indian, and stopping, faced the speaker. His mild features were confronted to the fierce and determined looks of the chief, and expressed all the horror that he felt at hearing such sentiments from one who professed the religion of his Saviour. Raising his hands to a level with his head, he exclaimed—

"John, John! is this the religion you have learned from the Moravians? But no—I will not be so uncharitable as to suppose it. They are a pious, a gentle, and a mild people, and could never tolerate these passions. Listen to the language of the Redeemer—'But I say unto you, love your enemies, bless them that curse you; do good to them that hate you; and pray for them that despitefully use you and persecute you.'—This is the command of God, John, and without striving to cultivate such feelings, no man can see him."

The Indian heard the exclamation of the divine with attention; the unusual fire of his eye gradually softened, and his muscles relaxed into their ordinary composure; but, slightly shaking his head, he motioned with dignity for Mr. Grant to resume his walk, and followed himself again in silence. The agitation of the divine caused him to move with unusual rapidity along the deep path, and the Indian, without any apparent exertion, kept an equal pace; but the young hunter

* His enemy.

observed the female to linger in her steps, until a trifling distance intervened between the two former and the latter. Struck by the circumstance, and not perceiving any new impediment to retard her footsteps, the youth made a tender of his assistance, by saying—

"You are fatigued Miss Grant; the snow yields to the foot, and you are unequal to the strides of us men. Step on the crust, I entreat you, and take the help of my arm. Yonder light is, I believe, the house of your father; but it seems yet at some distance."

"I am quite equal to the walk," returned a low, tremulous voice; "but I am startled by the manner of that Indian chief. Oh! his eye was horrid, as he turned to the moon, in speaking to my father. But I forget, sir; he is your friend, and, by his language may be your relative; and yet, of you I do not feel afraid."

The young man stepped on the bank of the snow, which firmly sustained his weight, and by a gentle effort, induced his companion to follow him. Drawing her arm through his own, he lifted his cap from his head allowing his dark locks to flow in rich curls over his open brow, and walked by her side, with an air of conscious pride as if inviting an examination of his inmost thoughts.—Louisa took but a furtive glance at his person, and moved quietly along, at a rate that was greatly quickened by the aid of his arm.

"You are but little acquainted with this peculiar people, Miss Grant," he said, "or you would know that revenge is a virtue with an Indian. They are taught from infancy upward, to believe it a duty, never to allow an injury to pass unresisted; and nothing but the stronger claims of hospitality, can guard one against their resentments, where they have power to act their will."

"Surely, sir," said Miss Grant, involuntarily withdrawing her arm from his, "you have not been educated with such unholy sentiments."

"It might be a sufficient answer to your excellent father, to say, that I was educated in the church," he returned; "but to you I will add, that I have been taught deep and practical lessons of forgiveness. I believe that, on this subject, I have but little cause to reproach myself; but it shall be my endeavour, that there yet be less."

While speaking, he stopped, and stood with his arm again proffered to her assistance. As he ended, she quietly accepted his offer, and they resumed their walk.

Mr. Grant and Mohegan had reached the door of the former's residence, and stood waiting near its threshold for the arrival of their young companions. The former was earnestly occupied, in endeavouring to correct, by his precepts, the evil propensities that he had discovered in the Indian, during their conversation; which the latter heard in profound, but respectful attention. On the arrival of the young hunter and the lady, they entered the building.

The house stood at some distance from the village, in the centre of a field, surrounded by stumps, that were peering above the snow, bearing caps of pure white nearly two feet in thickness. Not a tree or a shrub was nigh it; but the house, externally, exhibited that cheerless, unfinished aspect, which is so common to the hastily-erected dwellings of a new country. The uninviting character of its outside was, however, happily contrasted by the exquisite neatness, and comfortable warmth, within.

They entered an apartment that was fitted as a parlour, though the large fire-place, with its culinary arrangements, betrayed the domestic uses to which it was occasionally applied. The bright blaze from the hearth, rendered the light that proceeded from the candle that Louisa produced, unnecessary; for the scanty furniture of the room was easily seen and examined, by the former. The floor was covered, in the centre, by a carpet made of rags, a species of manufacture that was, then, and yet continues to be, much in use, in the interior; while its edges, that were exposed to view, were of unspotted cleanliness. There was a trifling air of better life, in a tea-table and work stand, as well as in an old-fashioned mahogany book-case; but the chairs, the dining table, and the rest of the furniture, were of the plainest and cheapest construction. Against the walls were hung a few specimens of needlework and drawing, the former executed with great neatness, though of somewhat equivocal merit in their designs, while the latter were strikingly deficient in both.

One of the former represented a tomb, with a youthful female weeping over it, exhibiting a church with arched windows, in the background. On the tomb were the names, with the dates of the births and deaths, of several individuals all of whom bore the name of Grant. An extremely cursory glance at this record, was sufficient to discover to the young hunter the domestic state of the divine. He there read, that he was a widower, and that the innocent and timid maiden, who had been his companion, was the only surviver of six children. The knowledge of the dependence, which each of these meek Christians had on the other, for happiness, threw an additional charm around the gentle, but kind attentions, which the daughter paid to the father.

These observations occurred while the party were seating themselves before the cheerful fire, during which time, there was a suspension of their discourse. But when each was comfortably arranged, and Louisa, after laying aside a thin coat of faded silk, and a Gypsy hat, that was more becoming to her modest, ingenuous countenance than appropriate to the season, had taken a chair between her father and the youth, the former resumed the conversation.

"I trust, my young friend," he said, "that the education which you have received has eradicated most of those revengeful principles, which you may have inherited by descent; for I understand from the expressions of John, that you have some of the blood of the Delaware tribe. Do not mistake me, I beg, for it is not colour, nor lineage, that constitutes merit; and I know not that he who claims affinity to the proper owners of this soil, has not the best right to tread these hills with the lightest conscience."

Mohegan turned solemnly to the speaker, and, with the peculiarly significant gestures of an Indian, he spoke:—

"Father, you are not yet past the summer of life; your limbs are young. Go to the highest hill, and look around you. All that you see, from the rising to the setting sun, from the head waters of the great spring, to where the 'crooked river' is hid by the hills, is his. He has Delaware blood, and his right is strong. But the brother of Miquon is just: he will cut the country in two parts, as the river cuts the low-lands, and will say to the 'Young Eagle,' Child of the Delawares! take it—keep it—and be a chief in the land of your fathers."

"Never!" exclaimed the young hunter, with a vehemence that destroyed the rapt attention with which the divine and his daughter were listening to the earnest manner of the Indian— "The wolf of the forest is not more rapacious for his prey, than that man is greedy for gold; and yet his glidings into wealth are as subtle as the movements of a serpent."

"Forbear, forbear, my son, forbear," interrupted Mr. Grant. —"These angry passions must be subdued. The accidental injury you have received from Judge Temple has heightened the sense of your hereditary wrongs. But remember that the one was unintentional and that the other is the effect of political changes, which have, in their course, greatly lowered the pride of kings, and swept mighty nations from the face of the earth. Where now are the Philistines, who so often held the children of Israel in bondage! or that city of Babylon, which rioted in luxury and vice, and who styled herself the Queen of Nations, in the drunkenness of her pride? Remember the prayer of our holy litany, where we implore the Divine power—'That it may please thee to forgive our enemies, persecutors, and slanderers, and to turn their hearts.' The sin of the wrongs which have been done to the natives is shared by Judge Temple, only, in common with a whole people, and your arm will speedily be restored to its strength."

"This arm!" repeated the youth, scornfully, pacing the floor in violent agitation; "think you, sir, that I believe the man a murderer!—oh, no! he is too wily, too cowardly, for such a crime. But let him and his daughter riot in their wealth— there will a day of retribution come. No, no, no," he continued as he trod the floor more calmly—"it is for Mohegan to suspect him of such a crime, as an intent to injure me: but the trifle is not worth a second thought."

He seated himself, and hid his face between his hands, as they rested on his knees.

"It is the hereditary violence of a native's passion, my

child," said Mr. Grant, in a low tone, to his affrighted daughter, who was clinging in terror, to his arm. "He is mixed with the blood of the Indians, you have heard; and neither the refinements of education, nor the advantages of our excellent liturgy, have been able entirely to eradicate the evil. But care and time will do much for him yet."

Although the divine spoke in a low tone, yet what he uttered was heard by the youth, who raised his head, with a smile of indefinite expression and spoke more calmly.

"Be not alarmed, Miss Grant, at either the wildness of my manner, or that of my dress. I have been carried away by passions, that I should struggle to repress. I must attribute it, with your father to the blood in my veins, although I would not impeach my lineage willingly; for it is all that is left me to boast of. Yes! I am proud of my descent from a Delaware chief, who was a warrior that ennobled human nature. Old Mohegan was his friend, and will vouch for his virtues."

Mr. Grant here took up the discourse, and, finding the young man more calm, and the aged chief attentive, he entered into a full and theological discussion of the duty of forgiveness. The discussion lasted for more than an hour, when the visiters arose, and, after exchanging good wishes with their entertainers, they departed. At the door they separated, Mohegan taking the direct route to the village, while the youth moved towards the lake. The divine stood at the entrance of his dwelling, regarding the figure of the aged chief as it glided at an astonishing gait, for his years, along the deep path; his black, straight hair, just visible over the bundle formed by his blanket, which was sometimes blended with the snow, under the silvery light of the moon. From the rear of the house was a window, that overlooked the lake; and here Louisa was found by her father, when he entered, gazing intently on some object, in the direction of the eastern mountain. He approached the spot, and saw the tall figure of the young hunter, at the distance of half a mile, walking with prodigious steps across the wide fields of frozen snow, that covered the ice, towards the point where he knew the hut that was inhabited by the Leather-stocking was situated on the margin of the lake, under a rock, that was crowned by pines and hemlocks. At the next instant, the wildly looking form entered the dark shadow, that was cast from the overhanging trees, and was lost to view.

"It is marvellous, how long the propensities of the savage, continue in that remarkable race," said the good divine; "but if he perseveres, as he has commenced, his triumph shall yet be complete. Remember me, my child, to lend him the homily 'against peril of idolatry,' at his next visit."

"Surely, father," cried the maiden, "you do not think him in danger of relapsing into the worship of his ancestors!"

"No, my child," returned the clergyman, laying his hand affectionately on her flaxen locks, and smiling, "his white blood would prevent it; but there is such a thing as the idolatry of our passions."

Chapter XIII

And I'll drink out of the quart pot,
Here's a health to the barley mow.
                    DRINKING SONG

On one of the corners, where the two principal streets of Templeton intersected each other, stood, as we have already mentioned, the inn, that was called the "Bold Dragoon." In the original plan, it was ordained that the village should stretch along the little stream, that rushed down the valley, and the street which led from the lake to the academy, was intended to be its western boundry. But convenience frequently frustrates the best regulated plans. The house of Mr.; or as, in consequence of commanding the militia of that vicinity, he was called Captain Hollister, had, at an early day, been erected directly facing the main street, and ostensibly interposed a barrier to its further progress. Horsemen and subsequently teamsters, however, availed themselves of an opening, at the end of the building, to shorten their passage westward, until in time, the regular highway was laid out along this course, and houses were gradually built on either side, so as effectually to prevent any subsequent correction of the evil.

There were two material consequences which followed this insidious change in the regular plans of Marmaduke. The one, that the main street, after running about half its length, was suddenly reduced to precisely that difference in its width; and the other, that the "Bold Dragoon" become next to the Mansion-house, by far the most conspicuous edifice in the place.

This conspicuousness, aided by the characters of the host and hostess, gave the tavern an advantage over all its future competitors, that no circumstances could conquer. An effort was, however, made to do so; and at the corner diagonally opposite, stood a new building, that was intended by its occu-

pants, to look down all opposition. It was a house of wood, ornamented in the prevailing style of architecture, and about
the roof and balustrades, was one of the three imitators of the
Mansion-house. The upper windows were filled with rough
boards, secured by nails, to keep out the cold air; for the edifice was far from finished, although glass was to be seen in
the lower apartments, and the light of the powerful fires
within, denoted that it was already inhabited. The exterior
was painted white, on the front and on the end which was exposed to the street; but in the rear, and on the side which was
intended to join the neighbouring house, it was coarsely
smeared with Spanish brown. Before the door stood two lofty
posts, connected at the top by a beam, from which was suspended an enormous sign, ornamented around its edges, with
certain curious carvings in pine boards on its faces, loaded
with masonic emblems. Over these mysterious figures, was
written, in large letters, "The Templeton Coffee-House, and
Traveller's Hotel," and beneath them, "By Habakkuk Foote
and Joshua Knapp." This was a fearful rival to the "Bold
Dragoon," as our readers will the more readily perceive, when
we add, that the same sonorous names were to be seen over
the door of a newly erected store in the village, a hatter's-shop,
and the gates of a tanyard. But, either because too much was
attempted to be well executed, or that the "Bold Dragoon"
had established a reputation which could not be easily shaken,
not only Judge Temple and his friends, but most of the villagers also, who were not in debt to the powerful firm we have
named, frequented the inn of Captain Hollister, on all occasions where such a house was necessary.

On the present evening, the limping veteran, and his con-
sort, were hardly housed, after their return from the academy,
when the sounds of stamping feet at their threshold announced
the approach of visitors, who were probably assembling, with
a view to compare opinions, on the subject of the ceremonies
they had witnessed.

The "public," or, as it was called, the "bar-room," of the
"Bold Dragoon," was a spacious apartment, lined on three
sides with benches, and on the fourth by fire-places. Of the
latter, there were two, of such size as to occupy, with their

enormous jambs, the whole of that side of the apartment where they were placed, excepting room enough for a door or two, and a little apartment in one corner, which was protected by miniature pallisadoes, and profusely garnished with bottles and glasses. In the entrance to this sanctuary, Mrs. Hollister was seated with great gravity in her air, while her husband occupied himself with stirring the fires; moving the logs with a large stake, burnt to a point at one end.

"There, Sargeant dear," said the landlady, after she thought the veteran had got the logs arranged in the most judicious manner, "give over poking the fires, for it's no good yee'l be doing, now that they burn so convaniently. There's the glasses on the table there, and the mug that the Doctor was taking his cider and ginger in, before the fire here,—jist put them in the bar, will ye? for we'll be having the Joodge and the Major, and Mr. Jones down the night, widout reckoning Benjamin Poomp, and the Lawyers: so ye'll be fixing the room tidy; and put both flip-irons in the coals; and tell Jude, the lazy black baste, that of she's no be claneing up the kitchen, I'll jist turn her out of the house, and she may live wid the jontlmen that kape the 'Coffee-house,' good luck to 'em. Och! Sargeant, sure it's a great privilege to go to a mateing, where a body can sit asy, widout joomping up and down so often, as this Mr. Grant is doing the same."

"It's a privilege at all times, Mistress Hollister, whether we stand or be seated; or, as good Mr. Whitefield used to do, after he made a wearisome day's march, get on our knees and pray, like Moses of old, with a flanker to the right and left, to lift his hands to heaven," returned her husband, who composedly performed what she had directed to be done. "It was a very pretty fight, Betty, that the Israelites had, on that day, with the Amalekites. It seems that they fout on a plain, for Moses is mentioned, as having gone on to the heights, to overlook the battle, and wrestle in prayer; and if I should judge, with my little larning, the Israelites depended mainly on their horse, for it is written, that Joshua cut up the enemy with the edge of the *sword:* from which I infer, not only that they were horse, but well disciplyn'd troops. Indeed, it says as much, as that they were chosen men; quite likely volunteers; but raw dragoons seldom strike with the *edge* of their swords, particularly if the weapon be any way crooked."

"Pshaw! why do ye bother yourself wid taxts, man, about so small a matter," interrupted the landlady; "sure it was the Lord who was wid 'em; for he always sided with the Jews, at first, before they fell away; and it's but little matter what kind of men Joshua commanded, so that he was doing the right bidding. Aven them cursed millaishy, the Lord forgi'e me for swearing, that was the death of him, wid their cowardice, would have carried the day in old times. There's no rason to be thinking that the soldiers was used to the drill."

"I must say, Mrs. Hollister," rejoined her husband, "that I have not often seen raw troops fight better than the left flank of the militia, at the time you mention. They rallied very handsomely, and that without beat of drum, which is no easy thing to do under fire, and were very steady till he fell. But the Scriptures contain no unnecessary words; and I will maintain, that horse, who know how to strike with the *edge* of the sword, must be well disciplyn'd. Many a good sarmon has been preached about smaller matters than that one word! If the text was not meant to be particular, why wasn't it written, with the sword, and not with the edge? Now, a back-handed stroke, on the edge, takes long practice. Goodness! what an argument would Mr. Whitefield make of that word edge! As to the Captain, if he had only called up the guard of dragoons, when he rallied the foot, they would have shown the inimy what the edge of a sword was; for, although there was no commissioned officer with them, yet I think I may say,"—the veteran continued, stiffening his cravat about the throat, and raising himself up, with the air of a drill-sergeant, "they were led by a man, who know'd how to bring them on, in spite of the ravine."

"Is it lade on ye would?" cried the landlady, "when ye know yourself, Mr. Hollister, that the baste he rode was but little able to joomp from one rock to another, and the animal was as spry as a squirrel? Och! but it's useless to talk, for he's gone this many a long year. I would that he had lived to see the true light; but there's mercy for a brave sowl, that died in the saddle, fighting for the liberty. It's a poor tomb-stone they have given him, any way, and many a good one that died like himself; but the sign is very like, and I will be kapeing it up, while the blacksmith can make a hook for it to swing on, for all the 'coffee-houses' betwane this and Albany."

There is no saying where this desultory conversation would have led the worthy couple, had not the men who were stamping the snow off their feet, on the little platform before the door, suddenly ceased their occupation, and entered the bar-room.

For ten or fifteen minutes, the different individuals, who intended either to bestow or receive edification before the fires of the "Bold Dragoon," on that evening, were collecting, until the benches were nearly filled with men of different occupations. Dr. Todd, and a slovenly-looking, half-genteel young man, who took tobacco profusely, wore a coat of imported cloth, cut with something like a fashionable air, frequently exhibited a large French silver watch, with a chain of woven hair, and who, altogether, seemed as much above the artisans around him as he was inferior to the real gentleman, occupied a high-back, wooden settee, in the most comfortable corner in the apartment.

Sundry brown mugs, containing cider or beer, were placed between the heavy andirons, and little groups were formed among the guests, as subjects arose, or the liquor was passed from one to the other. No man was seen to drink by himself, nor in any instance was more than one vessel considered necessary, for the same beverage; but the glass, or the mug, was passed from hand to hand, until a chasm in the line, or a regard to the rights of ownership, would restore the dregs of the potation to him who defrayed the cost.

Toasts were uniformly drank; and occasionally some one, who conceived himself peculiarly endowed by nature to shine in the way of wit, would attempt some such sentiment as "hoping that he" who treated "might make a better man than his father;" or, "live till all his friends wished him dead;" while the more humble pot-companion contented himself by saying, with a most imposing gravity in his air, "come, here's luck," or by expressing some other equally comprehensive desire. In every instance, the veteran landlord was requested to imitate the custom of the cup-bearers to kings, and taste the liquor he

presented, by the significant invitation of "after you is manners;" with which request he ordinarily complied, by wetting
his lips, first expressing the wish of "here's hoping," leaving it
to the imagination of the hearers to fill the vacuum of whatever good each thought most desirable. During these movements, the landlady was busily occupied with mixing the various compounds required by their customers, with her own
hands, and occasionally exchanging greetings and inquiries
concerning the conditions of their respective families, with
such of the villagers as approached "the bar."

At length the common thirst being in some measure as-
suaged, conversation of a more general nature became the order of the hour. The physician, and his companion, who was
one of the two lawyers of the village, being considered the best
qualified to maintain a public discourse with credit, were the
principal speakers, though a remark was hazarded, now and
then, by Mr. Doolittle, who was thought to be their inferior,
only in the enviable point of education. A general silence was
produced on all but the two speakers, by the following observation from the practitioner of the law:—

"So, Dr. Todd, I understand that you have been performing
an important operation, this evening, by cutting a charge of
buck-shot from the shoulder of the son of Leather-stocking?"

"Yes, sir," returned the other, elevating his little head, with
an air of great importance, "I had a small job up at the Judge's
in that way: it was, however, but a trifle to what it might have
been, had it gone through the body. The shoulder is not a very
vital part; and I think the young man will soon be well. But
I did not know that the patient was a son of Leather-stocking;
it is news to me, to hear that Natty had a wife."

"It is by no means a necessary consequence," returned the
other, winking with a shrewd look around the bar-room;
"there is such a thing, I suppose you know, in law, as a 'filius
nulius.' "

"Spake it out, man," exclaimed the landlady; 'spake it out
in king's English; what for should ye be talking Indian, in a
room full of Christian folks, though it is about a poor hunter,
who is but a little better in his ways than the wild savages
themselves? Och! it's to be hoped that the missionaries will,

in his own time, make a convarsion of the poor divils; and then it will matter but little, of what colour is the skin, or wedder there be wool or hair on the head."

"Oh! It is Latin, not Indian, Mrs. Hollister," returned the lawyer, repeating his winks and shrewd looks; "and Dr. Todd understands Latin, or how would he read the labels on his gallipots and drawers; no, no, Miss Hollister, the Doctor understands me; don't you Doctor?"

"Hem—why I guess I am not far out of the way," returned Elnathan, endeavouring to imitate the expression of the other's countenance, by looking jocular; "Latin is a queer language, gentlemen;—now, I rather guess there is no one in the room, except Squire Lippet, who can believe that 'Far.Av.' means oatmeal, in English."

The lawyer, in his turn, was a good deal embarrassed by this display of learning, for although he actually had taken his first degree at one of the eastern universities, he was somewhat puzzled with the terms used by his companion. It was dangerous, however, to appear to be outdone in learning in a public bar-room, and before so many of his clients; he therefore, put the best face on the matter, and laughed knowingly, as if there were a good joke concealed under it, that was understood only by the physician and himself. All this was attentively observed by the listeners, who exchanged looks of approbation; and the expressions of "tonguey man," and "I guess Squire Lippet knows, if any body does," were heard in different parts of the room, as vouchers for the admiration of his auditors. Thus encouraged, the lawyer rose from his chair, and turning his back to the fire, facing the company, he continued—

"The son of Natty, or the son of nobody, I hope the young man is not going to let the matter drop. This is a country of laws; and I should like to see it fairly tried, whether a man who owns, or says he owns, a hundred thousand acres of land, has any more right to shoot a body, than another. What do you think of it, Dr. Todd?"

"Oh! sir, I am of opinion that the gentleman will soon be well, as I said before; the wound isn't in a vital part; and as the ball was extracted so soon, and the shoulder was what I call well attended to, I do not think there is as much danger as there might have been."

"I say Squire Doolittle," continued the angry attorney, "you are a magistrate, and know what is law, and what is not law. I ask you, sir, if shooting a man is a thing that is to be settled so very easily? Suppose, sir, that the young man had a wife and family; and suppose that he was a mechanic, like yourself, sir; and suppose that his family depended on him for bread; and suppose that the ball, instead of merely going through the flesh, had broken the shoulder-blade, and crippled him for ever;—I ask you all, gentlemen, supposing this to be the case, whether a jury wouldn't give what I call handsome damages?"

As the close of this supposititious case was addressed to the company, generally, Hiram did not, at first, consider himself called on for a reply; but finding the eyes of the listeners bent on him in expectation, he remembered his character for judicial discrimination, and spoke, observing a due degree of deliberation and dignity in his manner.

"Why, if a man should shoot another," he said, "and if he should do it on purpose, and if the law took notice on't, and if a jury should find him guilty, it would be likely to turn out a state-prison matter."

"It would so, sir," returned the attorney.—"The law, gentlemen, is no respecter of persons, in a free country. It is one of the great blessings that has been handed down to us from our ancestors, that all men are equal in the eye of the law, as they are by nater. Though some may get property, no one knows how, yet they are not privileged to transgress the laws, any more than the poorest citizen in the state. This is my notion gentlemen; and I think that if a man had a mind to bring this matter up, something might be made out of it, that would help pay for the salve—ha! Doctor?"

"Why, sir," returned the physician, who appeared a little uneasy at the turn the conversation was taking, "I have the promise of Judge Temple, before men—not but what I would take his word as soon as his note of hand—but it was before men. Let me see—there was Mounshier Ler Quow, and Squire Jones, and Major Hartmann, and Miss Pettibone, and one or two of the blacks by, when he said that his pocket would am‐ply reward me for what I did."

"Was the promise made before or after the service was per‐formed?" asked the attorney.

"It might have been both," returned the discreet physician; "though I'm certain he said so, before I undertook the dress‐ing."

"But it seems that he said his pocket should reward you, Doctor," observed Hiram; "Now I don't know that the law will hold a man to such a promise; he might give you his pocket with sixpence in't, and tell you to take your pay out on't."

"That would not be a reward in the eye of the law," inter‐rupted the attorney—"not what is called a 'quid pro quo;' nor is the pocket to be considered as an agent, but as part of a man's own person, that is, in this particular. I am of opinion that an action would lie on that promise, and I will undertake to bear him out, free of costs, if he don't recover."

To this proposition the physician made no reply, but he was observed to cast his eyes around him, as if to enumerate the witnesses, in order to substantiate this promise also, at a fu‐ture day, should it prove necessary. A subject so momentous, as that of suing Judge Temple, was not very palatable to the present company, in so public a place; and a short silence en‐sued, that was only interrupted by the opening of the door, and the entrance of Natty himself.

The old hunter carried in his hand his never-failing compan‐ion, his rifle; and although all of the company were uncovered, excepting the lawyer, who wore his hat on one side, with a certain knowing air, Natty moved to the front of one of the fires, without in the least altering any part of his dress or ap‐pearance. Several questions were addressed to him, on the sub‐ject of the game he had killed, which he answered readily, and with some little interest; and the land-lord, between whom and Natty there existed much cordiality, on account of their both having been soldiers in their youth, offered him a glass of a liquid, which, if we might judge from its reception, was no unwelcome guest. When the forester had gotten his potation also, he quietly took his seat on the end of one of the logs, that lay nigh to the fires, and the slight interruption, produced by his entrance, seemed to be forgotten.

"The testimony of the blacks could not be taken, sir," continued the lawyer, "for they are all the property of Mr. Jones, who owns their time. But there is a way by which Judge Temple, or any other man, might be made to pay for shooting another, and for the cure in the bargain.—There is a way, I say, and that without going into the 'court of errors' too."

"And a mighty big error ye would make of it, Mister Todd," cried the landlady, "should ye be putting the matter into the law at all, with Joodge Temple, who has a purse as long as one of them pines on the hill, and who is an asy man to dale wid, if yees but mind the humour of him. He's a good man is Joodge Temple, and a kind one, and one who will be no the likelier to do the pratty thing, bekaase ye would wish to tarrify him with the law. I know of but one objection to the same, which is an over carelessness about his sowl. It's nather a Methodie, nor a Papish, nor Prasbetyrian, that he is, but jist nothing at all: and it's hard to think that he, 'who will not fight the good fight, under the banners of a rig'lar church, in this world, will be mustered among the chosen in heaven,' as my husband, the Captain there, as ye call him, says—though there is but one captain that I know, who desaarves the name. I hopes, Lather-stocking, ye'll no be foolish, and putting the boy up to try the law in the matter; for 'twill be an evil day to ye both, when ye first turn the skin of so paceable an animal as a sheep into a bone of contention. The lad is wilcome to his drink for nothing, until his shouther will bear the rifle ag'in."

"Well, that's gin'rous," was heard from several mouths at once, at this liberal offer of the landlady; while the hunter, instead of expressing any of that indignation which he might be supposed to feel, at hearing the hurt of his young companion alluded to, opened his mouth, with the silent laugh for which he was so remarkable; and after he had indulged his humour, made this reply—

"I know'd the Judge would do nothing with his smooth-bore, when he got out of his sleigh. I never see'd but one smooth-bore, that would carry at all, and that was a French duckingpiece, upon the big lakes: it had a barrel half as long ag'in as my rifle, and would throw fine shot into a goose, at a hundred yards; but it made dreadful work with the game, and you wanted a boat to carry it about in. When I went with Sir William ag'in the French, at Fort Niagara, all the rangers used the rifle; and a dreadful weapon it is, in the hands of one who knows how to charge it, and keeps a steady aim. The Captain knows, for he says he was a soldier in Shirley's, and though they were nothing but baggonet-men, he must know how we cut up the French and Iroquois in the skirmmages, in that war. Chingachgook, which means 'Big Sarpent' in English, old John Mohegan, who lives up at the hut with me, was a great warrior then, and was out with us; he can tell all about it, too; though he was an overhand for the tomahawk, never firing more than once or twice, before he was running in for the scalps. Ah! hum! times is dreadfully altered since then. Why, Doctor, there was nothing but a footpath, or at the most a track for pack-horses, along the Mohawk, from the Garman flats clean up to the forts. Now, they say, they talk of running one of them wide roads with gates on't along the river; first making a road, and then fencing it up! I hunted one season back of the Kaatskills, nigh-hand to the settlements, and the dogs often lost the scent, when they com'd to them highways, there was so much travel on them; though I can't say that the brutes was of a very good breed.—Old Hector will wind a deer in the fall of the year, across the broadest place in the Otsego, and that is a mile and a half, for I paced it myself on the ice, when the tract was first surveyed under the Indian grant."

"It sames to me, Natty, but a sorry compliment, to call your comrad after the evil one," said the landlady; "and it's no much like a snake that old John is looking now. Nimrood would be a more besaming name for the lad, and a more christian too, seeing that it comes from the Bible. The Sargeant read me the chapter about him, the night before my christening, and a mighty asement it was, to listen to any thing from the book."

"Old John and Chingachgook were very different men to

look on," returned the hunter, shaking his head at his melancholy recollections.—"In the 'fifty-eighth war' he was in the middle of manhood, and was taller than now by three inches. If you had seen him, as I did, the morning we beat Dieskau, from behind our log walls, you would have called him as comely a red-skin as ye ever set eyes on. He was naked, all to his breech-cloth and leggens; and you never seed a creater so handsomely painted. One side of his face was red, and the other black. His head was shaved clean, all to a few hairs on the crown, where he wore a tuft of eagle's feathers, as bright as if they had come from a peacock's tail. He had coloured his sides so that they looked just like an atomy, ribs and all; for Chingachgook had a great notion in such things: so that, what with his bold, fiery countenance, his knife, and his tomahawk, I have never seed a fiercer warrior on the ground. He played his part, too, like a man; for I seen him next day, with thirteen scalps on his pole. And I will say that for the 'Big Snake,' that he always dealt fair, and never scalped any that he didn't kill with his own hands."

"Well, well," cried the landlady; "fighting is fighting any way, and there is different fashions in the thing; though I can't say that I relish mangling a body after the breath is out of it; neither do I think it can be uphild by doctrine. I hopes, Sargeant, ye niver was helping in sitch evil worrek."

"It was my duty to keep my ranks, and to stand or fall by the baggonet or lead," returned the veteran. "I was then in the fort, and seldom leaving my place, saw but little of the savages, who kept on the flanks, or in front, skrimmaging. I remember, howsomever, to have heard mention made of the 'Great Snake,' as he was called, for he was a chief of renown; but little did I ever expect to see him enlisted in the cause of Christianity, and civilized like old John."

"Oh! he was Christianized by the Moravians, who was always over intimate with the Delawares," said Leatherstocking. "It's my opinion, that had they been left to themselves, there would be no such doings now, about the head waters of the two rivers, and that these hills mought have been kept as good hunting-ground, by their right owner, who is not too old to carry a rifle, and whose sight is as true as a fish-hawk, hovering——"

He was interrupted by more stamping at the door, and presently the party from the Mansion-house entered, followed by the Indian himself.

· *Chapter XIV* ·

There's quart-pot, pint-pot, half-pint,
Gill pot, half-gill, nipperkin,
     And the brown bowl—
Here's a health to the barley mow,
     My brave boys,
Here's a health to the barley mow.

DRINKING SONG

Some little commotion was produced by the appearance of the new guests, during which the lawyer disappeared from the room. Most of the men approached Marmaduke, and shook his offered hand, hoping "that the judge was well;" while Major Hartmann, having laid aside his hat and wig, and substituted for the latter a warm, peaked, woolen night-cap, took his seat very quietly, on one end of the settee, which was relinquished by its former occupants. His tobacco-box was next produced, and a clean pipe was handed him by the landlord. When he had succeeded in raising a smoke, the Major gave a long whiff, and turning his head towards the bar, he said—

"Petty, pring in ter toddy."

In the mean time, the Judge had exchanged his salutations with most of the company, and taken a place by the side of the Major, and Richard had bustled himself into the most comfortable seat in the room. Mr. Le Quoi was the last seated, nor did he venture to place his chair finally, until, by frequent removals, he had ascertained that he could not possibly intercept a ray of heat from any individual present. Mohegan found a place on an end of one of the benches, and somewhat approximated to the bar. When these movements had subsided, the Judge remarked, pleasantly—

"Well, Betty, I find you retain your popularity, through all weathers, against all rivals, and among all religions.—How liked you the sermon?"

"Is it the sarmon?" exclaimed the landlady; "I can't say but it was rasonable; but the prayers is mighty unasy. It's no so small a matter for a body, in their fifty-nint' year, to be moving so much in church. Mr. Grant sames a godly man, any way, and his garrel is a hoomble one, and a devout.— Here, John, is a mug of cider lac'd with whisky. An Indian will drink cider, though he niver be athirst."

"I must say," observed Hiram, with due deliberation, "that it was a tonguey thing; and I rather guess that it gave considerable satisfaction. There was one part, though, which might have been left out, or something else put in; but then, I s'pose that, as it was written discourse, it is not so easily altered, as where a minister preaches without notes."

"Ay! there's the rub, Joodge," cried the landlady; "how can a man stand up and be praching his word, when all that he is saying is written down, and he is as much tied to it as iver a thaving dragoon was to the pickets?"

"Well, well," cried Marmaduke, waving his hand for silence, "there is enough said; as Mr. Grant told us, there are different sentiments on such subjects, and in my opinion he spoke most sensibly. So, Jotham, I am told you have sold your betterments to a new settler, and have moved into the village and opened a school. Was it cash or dicker?"

The man who was thus addressed, occupied a seat immediately behind Marmaduke; and one who was ignorant of the extent of the Judge's observation, might have thought he would have escaped notice.—He was of a thin, shapeless figure, with a discontented expression of countenance, and with something extremely shiftless in his whole air. Thus spoken to after turning and twisting a little, by way of preparation, he made a reply.

"Why, part cash, and part dicker. I sold out to a Pumfretman, who was so'thin forehanded. He was to give me ten dollars an acre for the clearin, and one dollar an acre over the first cost, on the wood-land; and we agreed to leave the buildins to men. So I tuck Asa Mountagu, and he tuck Absalom Bement, and they two tuck old Squire Naphtali Green. And so they had a meetin, and made out a vardict of eighty dollars for the buildins. There was twelve acres of clearin, at ten dollars, and eighty-eight at one, and the whull came to jist two hundred and eighty-six dollars and a half, after paying the men."

"Hum," said Marmaduke: "what did you give for the place?"

"Why, besides what's comin to the Judge, I gi'n my brother Tim, a hundred dollars for his bargain; but then there's a new house on't, that cost me sixty more, and I paid Moses a hundred dollars, for choppin, and loggin, and sowin; so that the whull stood me in about two hundred and sixty dollars. But then I had a great crop off on't, and as I got jist twenty-six dollars and a half more than it cost, I conclude I made a pretty good trade on't."

"Yes, but you forgot that the crop was yours without the trade, and you have turned yourself out of doors for twenty-six dollars."

"Oh! the Judge is clean out," said the man, with a look of sagacious calculation; "he turned out a span of horses, that is wuth a hundred and fifty dollars of any man's money, with a bran new wagon; fifty dollars in cash; and a good note for eighty more; and a side-saddle, that was valood at seven and a half—so there was jist twelve shillings betwixt us. I wanted him to turn out a set of harness, and take the cow and the saptroughs. He wouldn't—but I saw through it; he thought I should have to buy the tacklin afore I could use the wagon and horses; but I know'd a thing or two myself; I should like to know of what use is the tacklin to him! I offered him to trade back ag'in, for one hundred and fifty-five. But my woman said she wanted a churn, so I tuck a churn for the change."

"And what do you mean to do with your time this winter? you must remember that time is money."

"Why, as the master is gone down country, to see his mother, who, they say, is going to make a die on't, I agreed to take the school in hand, till he comes back. If times doosn't get wuss in the spring, I've some notion of going into trade, or maybe I may move off to the Genessee; they say they are carryin on a great stroke of business that-a-way. If the wust comes to the wust, I can but work at my trade, for I was brought up in a shoe manufactory."

It would seem, that Marmaduke did not think his society of sufficient value, to attempt inducing him to remain where he was; for he addressed no further discourse to the man, but turned his attention to other subjects.—After a short pause, Hiram ventured a question:—

"What news does the Judge bring us from the legislater? it's not likely that congress has done much this session; or maybe the French haven't fit any more battles lately?"

"The French, since they have beheaded their king, have done nothing but fight," returned the judge.—"The character of the nation seems changed. I knew many French gentlemen, during our war, and they all appeared to me to be men of great humanity and goodness of heart; but these Jacobins are as blood-thirsty as bull-dogs."

"There was one Roshambow wid us, down at Yorrek-town," cried the landlady; "a might pratty man he was, too; and their horse was the very same. It was there that the Sargeant got the hurt in the leg from the English batteries, bad luck to 'em."

"Ah! mon pauvre Roi!" murmured Monsieur Le Quoi.

"The legislature have been passing laws," continued Marmaduke, "that the country much required. Among others, there is an act, prohibiting the drawing of seines, at any other than proper seasons, in certain of our streams and small lakes; and another, to prohibit the killing of deer in the teeming months. These are laws that were loudly called for, by judicious men; nor do I despair of getting an act, to make the unlawful felling of timber a criminal offence."

The hunter listened to this detail with breathless attention, and when the Judge had ended, he laughed in open derision for a moment, before he made this reply:—

"You may make your laws, Judge, but who will you find to watch the mountains through the long summer days, or the lakes at night? Game is game, and he who finds may kill; that has been the law in these mountains for forty years, to my sartain knowledge; and I think one old law is worth two new ones. None but a green-one would wish to kill a doe with a fa'n by its side, unless his moccasins was gettin old, or his leggins ragged, for the flesh is lean and coarse. But a rifle rings among them rocks along the lake shore, sometimes, as if fifty pieces were fired at once:—it would be hard to tell where the man stood who pulled the trigger."

"Armed with the dignity of the law, Mr. Bumppo," returned the Judge, gravely, "a vigilant magistrate can prevent much of the evil that has hitherto prevailed, and which is already rendering the game scarce. I hope to live to see the day, when a man's rights in his game shall be as much respected as his title to his farm."

"Your titles and your farms are all new together," cried Natty; "but laws should be equal, and not more for one than another. I shot a deer, last Wednesday was a fortnight, and it floundered through the snow-banks till it got over a brush fence; I catch'd the lock of my rifle in the twigs, in following, and was kept back, until finally the creater got off. Now I want to know who is to pay me for that deer; and a fine buck it was. If there hadn't been a fence, I should have gotten another shot into it; and I never draw'd upon any thing that hadn't wings three times running, in my born days.—No, no, Judge, it's the farmers that makes the game scearce, and not the hunters."

"Ter teer is not so plenty as in ter old war, Pumppo," said the Major, who had been an attentive listener, amidst clouds of smoke; "put ter lant is not mate, as for ter teer to live on, put for Christians."

"Why, Major, I believe you're a friend to justice and the right, though you go so often to the grand house; but it's a hard case to a man, to have his honest calling for a livelihood stopt by sitch laws, and that too when, if right was done, he mought hunt or fish on any day in the week, or on the best flat in the Patent, if he was so minded."

"I understand you, Letter-stockint," returned the Major, fixing his black eyes, with a look of peculiar meaning, on the hunter; "put you tidn't use to be so prutent, as to look ahet mit so much care."

"Maybe there wasn't so much 'casion," said the hunter, a little sulkily; when he sunk into a profound silence, from which he was not roused for some time.

"The Judge was saying so'thin about the French," Hiram observed, when the pause in the conversation had continued a decent time.

"Yes, sir," returned Marmaduke, "the Jacobins of France seem rushing from one act of licentiousness to another. They continue those murders, which are dignified by the name of executions. You have heard, that they have added the death of their Queen to the long list of their crimes."

"Les Bêtes!" again murmured Monsieur Le Quoi, turning himself suddenly in his chair, with a convulsive start.

"The province of La Vendée is laid waste by the troops of the republic, and hundreds of its inhabitants, who are royalists in their sentiments, are shot at a time.—La Vendée is a district in the southwest of France, that continues yet much attached to the family of the Bourbons: doubtless Monsieur Le Quoi is acquainted with it, and can describe it more faithfully."

"Non, non, non, mon cher ami," returned the Frenchman, in a suppressed voice, but speaking rapidly, and gesticulating with his right hand, as if for mercy, while with his left he concealed his eyes.

"There have been many battles fought lately," continued Marmaduke, "and the infuriated republicans are too often victorious. I cannot say, however, that I am sorry they have captured Toulon from the English, for it is a place to which they seem to have a just right."

"Ah—ha!" exclaimed Monsieur Le Quoi, springing on his feet, and flourishing both arms with great animation; "ces Anglais! dey be vipt! De French be one gallant peop', if dere vas gen'ral. Ah—ha! Toulon take! c'est bon! I do vish dat dey take Londre—pardonnez moi; mais, it ees bon!"

The Frenchman continued to move about the room with great alacrity for a few minutes, repeating his exclamations to himself; when, overcome by the contradictory nature of his emotions, he suddenly burst out of the house, and was seen wading through the snow towards his little shop, waving his arms on high, as if to pluck down honour from the moon. His departure excited but little surprise, for the villagers were used to his manner; but Major Hartmann laughed outright, for the first time during his visit, as he lifted the mug, and observed—

"Ter Frenchman is mat—put he is goot as for notting to trink; he is trunk mit joy."

"The French are good soldiers," said Captain Hollister; "they stood us in hand a good turn, down at York-town; nor do I think, although I am an ignorant man about the great movements of the army, that his Excellency would have been able to match against Cornwallis, without their reinforcements."

"Ye spake the trut', Sargeant," interrupted his wife, "and I would iver have ye be doing the same. It's varry pratty men is the French; and jist when I stopt the cart, the time when ye was pushing on in front it was, to kape the rig'lers in, a rigiment of the jontlemen marched by, and so I dealt them out to their liking. Was it pay I got? sure did I, and in good, solid crowns: the devil a bit of continental could they muster among them all, for love nor money. Och! the Lord forgive me for swearing and spakeing of sich vanities: but this I will say for the French, that they paid in good silver; and one glass would go a great way wid 'em, for the gin'rally handed it back wid a drop in the cup; and that's a brisk trade, Joodge, where the pay is good, and the men not ovar partic'lar."

"A thriving trade, Mrs. Hollister," said Marmaduke. "But what has become of Richard? he jumped up as soon as seated, and has been absent so long that I am fearful he has frozen."

"No fear of that, cousin 'duke," cried the gentleman himself, "business will sometimes keep a man warm, the coldest night that ever snapt in the mountains. Betty, your husband told me, as we came out of church, that your hogs were getting mangy, so I have been out to take a look at them, and found it true. I stepped across, Doctor, and got your boy to weigh me out a pound of salts, and have been mixing it with their swill. I'll bet a saddle of venison against a gray squirrel, that they are better in a week. And now, Mrs. Hollister, I'm ready for a hissing mug of flip."

"Sure, I know'd yee'd be wanting that same," said the landlady; it's mixt and ready to the boiling. Sargeant dear, jist be handing up the iron, will ye?—no, the one in the far fire, it's black, ye will see.—Ah! you've the thing now; look if it's not as red as a cherry?"

The beverage was heated, and Richard took that kind of draught which men are apt to indulge in, who think that they have just executed a clever thing, especially when they like the liquor.

"Oh! you have a hand, Betty, that was formed to mix flip," cried Richard when he paused for breath. "The very iron has a flavour in it. Here, John; drink, man, drink. I and you and Dr. Todd, have done a good thing with the shoulder of that lad this very night. 'Duke I made a song while you were gone; one day when I had nothing to do; so I'll sing you a verse or two, though I haven't really determined on the tune yet.

> What is life but a scene of care,
>   Where each one must toil in his way?
> Then let us be jolly, and prove that we are
> A set of good fellows, who seem very rare,
>   And can laugh and sing all the day.
>   Then let us be jolly,
>   And cast away folly
> For grief turns a black head to gray.

"There, 'duke, what do you think of that? There is another verse of it, all but the last line. I haven't got a rhyme for the last line yet.—Well, old John, what do you think of the music? as good as one of your war songs, ha!"

"Good," said Mohegan, who had been sharing too deeply in the potations of the landlady, besides paying a proper respect to the passing mugs of the major and Marmaduke.

"Pravo! pravo! Richart," cried the Major, whose black eyes were beginning to swim in moisture; "pravissimo! it is a goot song; but Natty Pumppo hast a petter. Letter-stockint, vilt sing? say, olt poy, vilt sing ter song, as apout the woots?"

"No, no, Major," returned the hunter, with a melancholy shake of the head, "I have lived to see what I thought eyes could never behold in these hills, and I have no heart left for singing. If he, that has a right to be master and ruler here, is forced to squinch his thirst, when a-dry, with snow-water, it ill becomes them that have lived by his bounty to be making merry, as if there was nothing in the world but sunshine and summer."

When he had spoken, Leather-stocking again dropped his head on his knees, and concealed his hard and wrinkled features with his hands. The change from the excessive cold without to the heat of the bar-room, coupled with the depth and frequency of Richard's draughts, had already levelled whatever inequality there might have existed between him and the other guests, on the score of spirits; and he now held out a pair of swimming mugs of foaming flip towards the hunter, as he cried—

"Merry! ay! merry Christmas to you, old boy! Sunshine and summer! no! your are blind, Leather-stocking, 'tis moonshine and winter;—take these spectacles, and open your eyes—

> So let us be jolly,
> And cast away folly,
> For grief turns a black head to gray.

"Hear how old John turns his quavers. What damned dull music an Indian song is, after all, Major. I wonder if they ever sing by note?"

While Richard was singing and talking, Mohegan was uttering dull, monotonous tones, keeping time by a gentle motion of his head and body. He made use of but few words, and such as he did utter were in his native language, and consequently, only understood by himself and Natty. Without heeding Richard, he continued to sing a kind of wild, melancholy air, that rose, at times, in sudden and quite elevated notes, and then fell again into the low, quavering sounds, that seemed to compose the character of his music.

The attention of the company was now much divided, the men in the rear having formed themselves into little groups, where they were discussing various matters; among the principal of which were, the treatment of mangy hogs, and Parson Grant's preaching; while Dr. Todd was endeavouring to explain to Marmaduke the nature of the hurt received by the young hunter. Mohegan continued to sing, while his countenance was becoming vacant, though, coupled with his thick bushy hair, it was assuming an expression very much like brutal ferocity. His notes were gradually growing louder, and soon rose to a height that caused a general cessation in the discourse. The hunter now raised his head again, and addressed the old warrior, warmly, in the Delaware language, which, for the benefit of our readers, we shall render freely into English.

"Why do you sing of your battles, Chingachgook, and of the warriors you have slain, when the worst enemy of all is near you, and keeps the Young Eagle from his rights? I have fought in as many battles as any warrior in your tribe, but cannot boast of my deeds at such a time as this."

"Hawk-eye," said the Indian, tottering with a doubtful step from his place, "I am the Great Snake of the Delawares; I can track the Mingoes, like an adder that is stealing on the whip-poor-will's eggs, and strike them, like the rattlesnake, dead at a blow. The white man made the tomahawk of Chingachgook bright as the waters of Otsego, when the last sun is shining; but it is red with the blood of the Maquas."

"And why have you slain the Mingo warriors? was it not to keep these hunting grounds and lakes to your father's children? and were they not given in solemn council to the Fire-eater? and does not the blood of a warrior run in the veins of a young chief, who should speak aloud, where his voice is now too low to be heard."

"The appeal of the hunter seemed, in some measure, to recall the confused faculties of the Indian, who turned his face towards the listeners, and gazed intently on the Judge. He shook his head, throwing his hair back from his countenance, and exposed his eyes, that were glaring with a fierce expression of wild resentment. But the man was not himself. His hand seemed to make a fruitless effort to release his tomahawk, which was confined by its handle to his belt, while his eyes gradually became again vacant. Richard at that instant thrusting a mug before him, his features changed to the grin of idiocy, and seizing the vessel with both hands, he sunk backward on the bench, and drank until satiated, when he made an effort to lay aside the mug, with the helplessness of total inebriety.

"Shed not blood!" exclaimed the hunter, as he watched the

countenance of the Indian in its moment of ferocity—"but he is drunk, and do no harm. This is the way with all the savages; give them liquor, and they make dogs of themselves. Well, well—the time will come when right will be done, and we must have patience."

Natty still spoke in the Delaware language, and of course was not understood. He had hardly concluded, before Richard cried—

"Well, old John is soon sowed up. Give him a berth, Captain, in the barn, and I will pay for it. I am rich to-night, ten times richer than 'duke, with all his lands, and military lots, and funded debts, and bonds, and mortages.

> Come let us be jolly,
> And cast away folly,
> For grief——

Drink, King Hiram—drink, Mr. Doo-nothing—drink, sir, I say. This is a Christmas eve, which comes, you know but once a year."

"He! he! he! the squire is quite moosical to-night," said Hiram, whose visage began to give marvellous signs of relaxation. "I rather guess we shall make a church on't yet, Squire?"

"A church, Mr. Doolittle! we will make a cathedral of it! bishops, priests, deacons, wardens, vestry, and choir; organ, organist, and bellows! By the lord Harry, as Benjamin says, we will clap a steeple on the other end of it, and make two churches of it. What say you, 'duke, will you pay? ha! my cousin Judge wilt pay?"

"Thou makest such a noise, Dickon," returned Marmaduke, "it is impossible that I can hear what Dr. Todd is saying. I think thou observed, it is probable that the wound will fester, so as to occasion danger to the limb, in this cold weather?"

"Out of nater, sir, quite out of nater;" said Elnathan, attempting to expectorate, but succeeding only in throwing a light, frothy substance, like a flake of snow, in the fire—"quite out of nater, that a wownd so well dressed, and with the ball in my pocket, should fester. I s'pose, as the Judge talks of taking the young man into his house, it will be most convenient if I make but one charge on't."

"I should think one would do," returned Marmaduke, with that arch smile that so often beamed on his face; leaving the beholder in doubt whether he most enjoyed the character of his companion, or his own covert humour.

The landlord had succeeded in placing the Indian on some straw, in one of his out-buildings, where, covered with his own blanket, John continued for the remainder of the night.

In the mean time, Major Hartmann began to grow noisy and jocular; glass succeeded glass, and mug after mug was introduced, until the carousal had run deep into the night, or rather morning; when the veteran German expressed an inclination to return to the Mansion-house. Most of the party had already retired, but Marmaduke knew the habits of his friend too well to suggest an earlier adjournment. So soon, however, as the proposal was made, the Judge eagerly availed himself of it, and the trio prepared to depart; Mrs. Hollister attended them to the door in person, cautioning her guests as to the safest manner of leaving her premises.

"Lane on Mister Jones, Major," said she, "he's young and will be a support to ye. Well, it's a charming sight to see ye, any way, at the Bould Dragoon: and sure it's no harm to be kaping a Christmas-eve wid a light heart, for it's no telling when we may have sorrow come upon us. So good night, Joodge, and a merry Christmas to ye all, to-morrow morning."

The gentlemen made their adieus as well as they could, and taking the middle of the road, which was a fine, wide, and well-beaten path, they did tolerably well until they reached the gate of the Mansion-house; but on entering the Judge's domains, they encountered some slight difficulties. We shall not stop to relate them, but will just mention that, in the morning, sundry diverging paths were to be seen in the snow; and that once during their progress to the door, Marmaduke, missing his companions, was enabled to trace them by one of these paths to a spot, where he discovered them with nothing visible but their heads; Richard singing in a most vivacious strain,

"Come, let us be jolly,
And cast away folly,
For grief turns a black head to gray."

Chapter XV

As she lay, on that day, in the Bay of Biscay, O!

Previously to the occurrence of the scene at the "Bold Dragoon," Elizabeth had been safely reconducted to the Mansion-house, where she was left, as its mistress, either to amuse or employ herelf during the evening, as best suited her own inclination.—Most of the lights were extinguished; but as Benjamin adjusted, with great care and regularity, four large candles, in as many massive candlesticks of brass, in a row on the sideboard, the hall possessed a peculiar air of comfort and warmth, contrasted with the cheerless aspect of the room she had left, in the academy.

Remarkable had been one of the listeners to Mr. Grant, and returned with her resentment, which had been not a little excited by the language of the Judge, somewhat softened by reflection and the worship. She recollected the youth of Elizabeth, and thought it no difficult task, under present appearances, to exercise that power indirectly, which hitherto she had enjoyed undisputed. The idea of being governed, or of being compelled to pay the deference of servitude, was absolutely intolerable; and she had already determined within herself, some half-dozen times, to make an effort, that should at once bring to an issue the delicate point of her domestic condition. But as often as she met the dark, proud eye of Elizabeth, who was walking up and down the apartment, musing on the scenes of her youth, and the change in her condition, and perhaps the events of the day, the housekeeper experienced an awe, that she would not own to herself could be excited by any thing mortal. It, however, checked her advances, and for some time held her tongue-tied. At length she determined to commence the discourse, by entering on a subject that was apt to level all human distinctions, and in which she might display her own abilities.

"It was quite a wordy sarmont that Parson Grant give us to-night," said Remarkable.—"Them church ministers be commonly smart sarmonizers: but they write down their idees, which is a great privilege.—I don't think that by nater they are sitch tonguey speakers for an off-hand discourse, as the standing-order ministers be."

"And what denomination do you distinguish as the standing-order?" inquired Miss Temple, with some surprise.

"Why, the Presbyter'ans, and the Congregationals, and Baptists too, for-ti-'now; and all sitch as don't go on their knees to prayer."

"By that rule, then, you would call those who belong to the persuasion of my father, the sitting-order," observed Elizabeth.

"I'm sure I've never heer'n 'em spoken of by any other name than Quakers, so-called," returned Remarkable, betraying a slight uneasiness: "I should be the last one to call them otherwise, for I never in my life used a disparaging tarm of the Judge, or any of his family. I've always set store by the Quakers, they are sitch pretty-spoken, clever people; and it's a wonderment to me, how your daddy come to marry into a church family, for they are as contrary in religion as can be. One sits still, and for the most part, says nothing, while the church folks practyse all kinds of ways, so that I sometimes think it quite moosical to see them; for I went to a church-meeting once before, down country."

"You have found an excellence in the church liturgy, that has hitherto escaped me," said Miss Temple. "I will thank you to inquire whether the fire in my room burns: I feel fatigued with my day's journey, and will retire."

Remarkable felt a wonderful inclination to tell the young mistress of the mansion, that by opening a door she might see for herself; but prudence got the better of her resentment, and after pausing some little time, as a salvo to her dignity, she did as desired. The report was favourable, and the young lady, wishing Benjamin, who was filling the stove with wood, and the housekeeper, each a good night, withdrew.

The instant that the door closed on Miss Temple, Remarkable commenced a sort of mysterious, ambiguous discourse, that was neither abusive nor commendatory of the qualities of the absent personage; but which seemed to be drawing nigh, by regular degrees, to a most dissatisfied description. The Major-domo made no reply, but continued his occupation with great industry, which being happily completed, he took a look at the thermometer, and then, opening a drawer of the sideboard, he produced a supply of stimulants, that would have served to keep the warmth in his system, without the aid of the enormous fire he had been building. A small stand was drawn up near the stove, and the bottles and the glasses necessary for convenience, were quietly arranged. Two chairs were placed by the side of this comfortable situation, when Benjamin, for the first time, appeared to observe his companion.

"Come," he cried, "come, Mistress Remarkable, bring yourself to an anchor in this here chair.—It's a peeler without, I can tell you, good woman; but what cares I, blow high or blow low, d'ye see, it's all the same thing to Ben. The niggers are snug stowed below, before a fire that would roast an ox whole. The thermometer stands now at fifty-five, but if there's any vartue in good maple wood, I'll weather upon it, before one glass, as much as ten points more, so that the Squire, when he comes home from Betty Hollister's warm room, will feel as hot as a hand that has given the rigging a lick with bad tar. Come, Mistress, bring up in this here chair, and tell me how it is you like our new heiress."

"Why to my notion, Mr. Penguillum——"

"Pump—Pump," interrupted Benjamin; "it's Christmas-eve, Mistress Remarkable, and so d'ye see, you had better call me Pump. It's a shorter name, and as I mean to pump this here decanter till it sucks, why you may as well call me Pump."

"Did you ever!" cried Remarkable, with a laugh that seemed to unhinge every joint in her body; "You're a moosical creater, Benjamin, when the notion takes you. But as I was saying, I rather guess that times will be altered now in this house."

"Altered!" exclaimed the Major-domo, eyeing the bottle,

that was assuming the clear aspect of cut glass with astonishing rapidity; "it don't matter much, Mistress Remarkable, so long as I keep the keys of the lockers in my pocket."

"I can't say," continued the housekeeper, "but there's good eatables and drinkables enough in the house for a body's content—a little more sugar, Benjamin, in the glass—for Squire Jones is an excellent provider. But new lords, new laws; and I shouldn't wonder if you and I had an time on't in footer."

"Life is as unsartain as the wind that blows," said Benjamin, with a most imposingly moralizing air;—"and nothing is more vari'ble than the wind, Mistress Remarkable, unless you happen to fall in with the trades, d'ye see, and then you may run for the matter of a month at a time, with studding-sails on both sides alow and aloft, and with the cabin-boy at the wheel."

"I know that life is disp'ut unsartain," said Remarkable, compressing her features to the humour of her companion; "but I expect there will be great changes made in the house to rights; and that you will find a young man put over your head, as well as there is one that wants to be over mine; and after having been settled as long as you have, Benjamin, I should judge that to be hard."

"Promotion should go according to the length of sarvice," said the Major-domo; "and if-so-be that they ship a hand for my berth, or place a new steward aft, I shall throw up my commission in less time than you can put a pilot-boat in stays. Thof Squire Dickens," this was a common misnomer with Benjamin, "is a nice gentleman, and as good a man to sail with as heart could wish, yet I shall tell the Squire, d'ye see, in plain English, and that's my native tongue, that if-so-be he is thinking of putting any Johnny raw over my head, why I shall resign. I began forward, Mistress Pretty-bones, and worked my way aft, like a man. I was six months aboard a Garnsey lugger, hauling in the slack of the lee-sheet, and coiling up rigging. From that I went a few trips in a fore-and-after, in the same trade, which after all, was but a blind kind of sailing in the dark, where a man larns but little, excepting how to steer by the stars.—Well! then, d'ye see, I larnt how a topmast should be slushed, and how a top-gallant-sail was to be becketted; and then I did small jobs in the cabin, such as mixing the skipper's grog. 'Twas there I got my taste, which you must have often seen, is excellent.—Well, here's better acquaintance to us."

Remarkable nodded a return to the compliment, and took a sip of the beverage before her; for, provided it was well sweetened, she had no objection to a small potation now and then. After this observance of courtesy between the worthy couple, the dialogue proceeded as follows:

"You have had great experunces in your life, Benjamin; for, as the scripter says, 'they that go down to the sea in ships see the works of the Lord.' "

"Ay! for that matter, they in brigs and schooners too; and it mought say the works of the devil. The sea, Mistress Remarkable, is a great advantage to a man, in the way of knowledge, for he sees the fashions of nations, and the shape of a country. Now, I suppose, for myself here, who is but an unlarned man to some that follows the seas, I suppose that, taking the coast from cape Ler-Hogue as low down as Cape Finish-there, there isn't so much as a head-land, or an island, that I don't know either the name of it, or something more or less about it.—Take enough, woman, to colour the water. Here's sugar. It's a sweet tooth, that fellow that you hold on upon yet, Mistress Pretty-bones. But as I was saying, take the whole coast along, I know it as well as the way from here to the Bold Dragoon; and a devil of an acquaintance is that Bay of Biscay. Whew! I wish you could but hear the wind blow there. It sometimes takes two to hold one man's hair on his head. Scudding through the Bay is pretty much the same thing as travelling the roads in this country, up one side of a mountain, and down the other."

"*Do* tell!" exclaimed Remarkable; "and does the sea run as high as mountains, Benjamin?"

"Well, I will tell; but first let's taste the grog.—Hem! its the right kind of stuff, I must say, that you keeps in this country; but then you're so close aboard the West-Indies, you make but a small run of it. By the lord Harry, woman, if Garnsey only lay some where between Cape Hatteras and the Bite of Logann, but you'd see rum cheap! As to the seas, they runs more in lippers in the Bay of Biscay, unless it may be in sow-wester, when they tumble about quite handsomely; thof its not in the narrow seas that you are to look for a swell; just go off the Western Islands, in a westerly blow, keeping the land on your larboard hand, with the ship's head to the south'ard, and bring too, under a close-reef'd topsail; or mayhap a reef'd foresail, with a fore-top-mast-staysail; and mizzen-staysail, to keep her up to the sea, if she will bear it; and lay there for the matter of two watches, if you want to see mountains. Why, good woman, I've been off there in the Boadishey frigate when you could see nothing but some such matter as a piece of sky, mayhap, as big as the mainsail; and they again, there was a hole under your lee-quarter, big enough to hold the whole British navy."

"Oh! for massy's sake! and wan't you afeard, Benjamin? and how did you get off?"

"Afeard! who the devil do you think was to be frightened at a little salt water tumbling about his head? As for getting off, when we had enough of it, and had washed our decks down pretty well, we called all hands, for d'ye see, the watch below was in their hammocks, all the same as if they were in one of your best bed-rooms; and so we watched for a smooth time; clapt her helm hard a-weather, let fall the foresail, and got the tack aboard; and so, when we got her afore it, I ask you, Mistress Pretty-bones, if she didn't walk? didn't she! I'm no liar, good woman, when I say that I saw that ship jump from the top of one sea to another, just like one of these squirrels, that can fly, jumps from tree to tree."

"What, clean out of the water!" exclaimed Remarkable, lifting her two lank arms, with their bony hands spread in astonishment.

"It was no such easy matter to get out of the water, good woman, for the spray flew so that you couldn't tell which was sea and which was cloud. So there we kept her afore it, for the matter of two glasses. The First Lieutenant he cun'd the ship himself, and there was four quarter-masters at the wheel, besides the master, with six forecastle men in the gun-room, at the relieving tackles. But then she behaved herself so well! Oh! she was a sweet ship, mistress! That one frigate was well worth more, to live in, than the best house in the island. If I was king of England, I'd have her hauled up above Lon'on bridge, and fit her up for a palace; because why? If anybody can afford to live comfortably, his majesty can."

"Well! but Benjamin," cried this listener, who was in an ecstasy of astonishment, at this relation of the steward's dangers, "what *did* you do?"

"Do! why we did our duty, like good hearty fellows. Now if the countrymen of Mounsheer Ler Quaw had been aboard of her, they would have just struck her ashore on some of them small islands; but we run along the land until we found her dead to leeward off the mountains of Pico, and dam'me if I know to this day how we got there, whether we jumped over the island, or hauled round it; but there we was, and there we lay, under easy sail, fore-reaching, first upon one tack and then upon t'other, so as to poke her nose out now and then, and take a look to wind'ard, till the gale blow'd its pipe out."

"I wonder now," exclaimed Remarkable, to whom most of the terms used by Benjamin were perfectly unintelligible, but who got a confused idea of a raging tempest, "it must be an awful life, that going to sea! and I don't feel astonishment that you're so affronted with the thoughts of being forced to quit a comfortable home like this. Not that a body cares much for't, as there's more houses than one to live in. Why, when the Judge agreed with me to come and live with him, I'd no more notion of stopping any time, than any thing. I happened in, just to see how the family did, about a week after Miss Temple died, thinking to be back home agin night; but the family was in sitch a distressed way, that I couldn't but stop a while, and help 'em on. I thought the sitooation a good one, seeing that I was an unmarried body, and they were so much in want of help; so I tarried."

"And a long time have you left your anchors down in the same place, mistress; I think you must find that the ship rides easy?"

"How you talk, Benjamin! there's no believing a word you say. I must say that the Judge and Squire Jones have both acted quite clever, so long; but I see that now we shall have a specimen to the contrary. I heer'n say that the Judge was gone a great 'broad, and that he meant to bring his darter hum, but I didn't calcoolate on sitch carrins on. To my notion, Benjamin, she's likely to turn out a desput ugly gall."

"Ugly!" echoed the Major-domo, opening his eyes, that were beginning to close in a very suspicious sleepiness, in wide amazement; "by the Lord Harry, woman, I should as soon think of calling the Boadishey a clumsy frigate. What the devil would you have? arn't her eyes as bright as the morning and evening stars! and isn't her hair as black and glistening as rigging that has just had a lick of tar! doesn't she move as stately as a first-rate in smooth water, on a bow-line! Why, woman, the figure-head of the Boadishey was a fool to her, and that, as I've often heard the captain say, was an image of a great Queen; and arn't Queens always comely, woman? for who do you think would be a king, and not choose a handsome bedfellow."

"Talk decent, Benjamin," said the housekeeper, "or I won't keep your company. I don't gainsay her being comely to look on, but I will maintain that she's likely to show but poor conduct. She seems to think herself too good to talk to a poor body. From what Squire Jones had tell'd me, I some expected to be quite captivated by her company. Now, to my reckoning, Lowizy Grant is much more pritty behaved than Betsy Temple. She wouldn't so much as hold discourse with me, when I wanted to ask her how she felt on coming home and missing her mammy."

"Perhaps she didn't understand you, woman; you are none of the best linguister; and then Miss Lizzy has been exercising the King's English under a great Lon'on lady, and, for that matter, can talk the language almost as well as myself, or any native born British subject. You've forgot your schooling, and the young mistress is a great scollard."

"Mistress?" cried Remarkable; "don't make one out to be a nigger, Benjamin. She's no mistress of mine, and never will be. And as to speech, I hold myself as second to nobody out of New England. I was born and raised in Essex county; and I've always heer'n say, that the Bay State was provarbal for pronounsation."

"I've often heard of that Bay of State," said Benjamin, "but can' say that I've ever been in it, nor do I know exactly where away it is that it lays; but I suppose that there is good anchorage in it, and that it's no bad place for the taking of ling; but for size, it can't be so much as a yawl to a sloop of war; compared with the Bay of Biscay, or mayhap, Tor-bay. And as for language, if you want to hear the dictionary over-hauled, like a long-line in a blow, you must go to Wapping, and listen to the Lon'oners, as they deal out their lingo. How-somever, I see no such mighty matter that Miss Lizzy has been doing to you, good woman, so take another drop of your brew, and forgive and forget, like an honest soul."

"No, indeed! and I shan't do sitch a thing, Benjamin. This treatment is a newity to me, and what I won't put up with. I have a hundred and fifty dollars at use, besides a bed and twenty sheep, to good; and I don't crave to live in a house where a body mus'nt call a young woman by her given name to her face. I *will* call her Betsy as much as I please; its a free country, and no one can stop me. I did intend to stop while summer, but I shall quit to-morrow morning; and I will talk just as I please."

"For that matter, Mistress Remarkable," said Benjamin, "there's none here who will contradict you, for I'm of opinion that it would be as easy to stop a hurricane with a Barcelony hankerchy, as to bring up your tongue, when the stopper is off. I say, good woman, do they grow many monkeys along the shores of that Bay of State?"

"You're a monkey yourself, Mr. Penguillum," cried the en-raged housekeeper, "or a bear! a black, beastly bear! and an't fit for a decent woman to stay with. I'll never keep your com-pany agin, sir, if I should live thirty years with the Judge. Sitch talk is more befitting the kitchen than the keeping-room of a house of one who is well to do in the world."

"Look you, Mistress Pitty—Patty—Pretty-bones, mayhap I'm some such matter as a bear d'ye see, as they will find who come to grapple with me; but dam'me if I'm a monkey—a thing that chatters without knowing a word of what it says—a parrot; that will hold a dialogue, for what an honest man knows, in a dozen languages; mayhap in the Bay of State lingo; mayhap in Greek or High Dutch. But dost it know what it means itself? canst answer me that, good woman? Your Midshipman can sing out, and pass the word, when the Captain gives the order, but just set him adrift by himself, and let him work the ship of his own head, and, stop my grog, if you don't find all the Johny-raws laughing at him."

"Stop your grog indeed!" said Remarkable, rising with great indignation, and seizing a candle; "you're groggy now, Benjamin, and I'll quit the room before I hear any of your misbecoming word from you."

The housekeeper retired, with a manner but little less dignified, as she thought, than the air of the stately heiress, muttering as she drew the door after her, with a noise like the report of a musket, the opprobrious terms of "drunkard," "sot," and "beast."

"Who's that you say is drunk?" cried Benjamin, fiercely, rising and making a movement towards Remarkable. "You talk of mustering yourself with a lady! you're just fit to grumble and find fault. Where the devil should you larn behaviour and dictionary? in your damned Bay of State, ha?"

Benjamin here fell back in his chair, and soon gave vent to certain ominous sounds, which resembled, not a little, the growling of his favourite animal, the bear itself. Before, however, he was quite locked, to use the language that would suit the Della-cruscan humour of certain refined critics of the present day, "in the arms of Morpheus," he spoke aloud, observing due pauses between his epithets, the impressive terms of "monkey," "parrot," "pic-nic," "tar-pot," and "linguisters."

We will not attempt to explain his meaning, nor connect his sentences, and our readers must be satisfied with our informing them, that they were expressed with all that coolness of contempt that a man might well be supposed to feel for a monkey.

Nearly two hours passed in this sleep, before the Major-domo was awakened by the noisy entrance of Richard, Major Hartmann, and the master of the mansion: Benjamin so far rallied his confused faculties, as to shape the course of the two former to their respective apartments, when he disappeared himself, leaving the task of securing the house to him who was most interested in its safety. Locks and bars were but little attended to in the early day of that settlement; and so soon as Marmaduke had given an eye to the enormous fires of his dwelling, he retired. And with this act of prudence closes the first night of our tale.

· *Chapter XVI* ·

Watch. (*aside*) Some treason, masters—
Yet stand close.

MUCH ADO ABOUT NOTHING

It was fortunate for more than one of the bacchanalians, who left the "Bold Dragoon" late in the evening, that the severe cold of the season was becoming, rapidly, less dangerous, as they threaded the different mazes, through the snow-banks, that led to their respective dwellings. Thin, driving clouds began, towards morning, to flit across the heavens, and the moon sat behind a volume of vapour, that was impelled furiously towards the north, carrying with it the softer atmosphere from the distant ocean. The rising sun was obscured by denser and increasing columns of clouds, while the southerly wind that rushed up the valley, brought the never-failing symptoms of a thaw.

It was quite late in the morning, before Elizabeth, observing the faint glow which appeared on the eastern mountain, long after the light of the sun had struck the opposite hills, ventured from the house, with a view to gratify her curiosity with a glance by daylight at the surrounding objects, before the tardy revellers of the Christmas-eve should make their appearance at the breakfast-table. While she was drawing the folds of her pelisse more closely around her form, to guard against a cold that was yet great, though rapidly yielding, in the small enclosure that opened in the rear of the house on a little thicket of low pines, that were springing up where trees of a mightier growth had lately stood, she was surprised at the voice of Mr. Jones, crying aloud—

"Merry Christmas, merry Christmas to you, cousin Bess. Ah, ha! an early riser, I see; but I knew I should steal a march on you. I never was in a house yet, where I didn't get the first

Christmas greeting on every soul in it, man, woman, and child; great and small; black, white, and yellow. But stop a minute, till I can just slip on my coat; you are about to look at the improvements, I see, which no one can explain as well as I, who planned them all. It will be an hour before 'duke and the Major can sleep off Mrs. Hollister's confounded distillations, and so I'll come down and go with you."

Elizabeth turned, and observed her cousin in his night-cap, with his head out of his bed-room window, where his zeal for pre-eminence, in defiance of the weather, had impelled him to thrust it. She laughed, and promising to wait for his company, she re-entered the house, making her appearance again, holding in her hand a packet that was secured by several large and important seals, just in time to meet the gentleman.

"Come, Bessy, come," he cried, drawing one of her arms through his own; "the snow begins to give, but it will bear us yet. Don't you snuff old Pennsylvania in the very air? This is a vile climate, girl; now at sunset last evening it was cold enough to freeze a man's zeal, and that, I can tell you, takes a thermometer near zero for me; then about nine or ten it began to moderate; at twelve it was quite mild, and here all the rest of the night I have been so hot as not to bear a blanket on the bed.—Holla! Aggy,—merry Christmas, Aggy—I say, do you hear me, you black dog! there's a dollar for you; and if the gentleman get up before I come back, do you come out and let me know. I would'nt have 'duke get the start of me for the worth of your head."

The black caught the money from the snow, and promising a due degree of watchfulness, he gave the dollar a whirl in the air of twenty feet, and catching it as it fell, in the palm of his hand, he withdrew to the kitchen, to exhibit his present, with a heart as light as his face was happy in its expression.

"Oh, rest easy, my dear coz," said the young lady; "I took a look in at my father, who is likely to sleep an hour; and by using due vigilance you will secure all the honours of the season."

"Why, 'duke is your father, Elizabeth, but 'duke is a man who likes to be foremost, even in trifles. Now, as for myself, I care for no such things, except in the way of competition; for a thing which is of no moment in itself, may be made of importance in the way of competition. So it is with your father, he loves to be first; but I only struggle with him as a competitor, like."

"Oh! it's all very clear, sir," said Elizabeth; "you would not care a fig for distinction, if there were no one in the world but yourself; but as there happens to be a great many others, why you must struggle with them all—in the way of competition."

"Exactly so; I see you are a clever girl, Bess, and one who does credit to her masters. It was my plan to send you to that school; for when your father first mentioned the thing, I wrote a private letter for advice to a judicious friend in the city, who recommended the very school you went to. 'Duke was a little obstinate at first, as usual, but when he heard the truth, he was obliged to send you."

"Well, a truce to 'duke's foibles, sir; he is my father; and if you knew what he has been doing for you while we were in Albany, you would deal more tenderly with his character."

"For me!" cried Richard, pausing a moment in his walk to reflect. "Oh! he got the plans of the new Dutch meeting-house for me, I suppose; but I care very little about it, for a man, of a certain kind of talent, is seldom aided by any such foreign suggestions: his own brain is the best architect."

"No such thing," said Elizabeth, looking provokingly knowing.

"No! let me see—perhaps he had my name put in the bill for the new turnpike, as a director?"

"He might possibly; but it is not to such an appointment that I allude."

"Such an appointment!" repeated Mr. Jones, who began to fidget with curiosity; "then it is an appointment. If it is in the militia, I won't take it."

"No, no, it is not in the militia," cried Elizabeth, showing the packet in her hand, and then drawing it back, with a coquettish air; "it is an office of both honour and emolument."

"Honour and emolument!" echoed Richard, in painful suspense; "show me the paper, girl. Say, is it an office where there is any thing to *do?*"

"You have hit it, cousin Dickon; it is the executive office of the county; at least so said my father, when he gave me this packet to offer you as a Christmas-box—'Surely, if any thing will please Dickon,' he said, 'it will be to fill the executive chair of the county.'"

"Executive chair! what nonsense!" cried the impatient gentleman, snatching the packet from her hand; "there is no such office in the country. Eh! what! it is, I declare, a commission, appointing Richard Jones, Esquire, Sheriff of the county. Well, this is kind in 'duke, positively. I must say 'duke has a warm heart, and never forgets his friends. Sheriff! High Sheriff of——! It sounds well, Bess, but it shall execute better. 'Duke is a judicious man, after all, and knows human nature thoroughly. I'm much obliged to him," continued Richard, using the skirt of his coat, unconsciously, to wipe his eyes; "though I would do as much for him any day, as he shall see, if I have an opportunity to perform any of the duties of my office on him. It shall be done, cousin Bess—it shall be done, I say—How this cursed south wind makes my eyes water."

"Now, Richard," said the laughing maiden, "now I think you will find something to do. I have often heard you complain of old, that there was nothing to do in this new country, while to my eyes, it seemed as if every thing remained to be done."

"Do!" echoed Richard, who blew his nose, raised his little form to its greatest elevation, and looked prodigiously serious. "Every thing depends on system, my girl. I shall sit down this afternoon, and systematize the county. I must have deputies, you know. I will divide the county into districts, over which I will place my deputies; and I will have one for the village, which I will call my home department. Let me see—oh! Benjamin! yes, Benjamin will make a good deputy; he has been naturalized, and would answer admirably, if he could only ride on horseback."

"Yes, Mr. Sheriff," said his companion, "and as he understands ropes so well, he would be very expert, should occasion happen for his services, in the way of Jack Ketch."

"No," interrupted the other, "I flatter myself that no one could hang a man better than——that is—ha—oh! yes, Benjamin would do extremely well, in such an unfortunate dilemma, if he could be persuaded to attempt it. But I should despair of the thing. I never could induce him to hang, or teach him to ride on horseback. I must seek another deputy."

"Well, sir, as you have abundant leisure for all these important affairs, I beg that you will forget that you are High Sheriff, and devote some little of your time to gallantry. Where are the beauties and improvements which you were to show me?"

"Where! why every where. Here I have laid out some new streets; and when they are opened, and the trees felled, and they are all built up, will they not make a fine town? Well, 'duke is a liberal-hearted fellow, with all his stubbornness—Yes, yes, I must have at least four deputies, besides a jailer."

"I see no streets in the direction of our walk," said Elizabeth, "unless you call the short avenues through these pine bushes by that name.—Surely you do not contemplate building houses, very soon, in that forest before us, and in those swamps."

"We must run our streets by the compass, coz, and disregard trees, hills, ponds, stumps, or, in fact, any thing but posterity. Such is the will of your father, and your father, you know——"

"Had you made Sheriff, Mr. Jones," interrupted the lady, with a tone which said very plainly to the gentleman, that he was touching a forbidden subject.

"I know it, I know it," cried Richard; "and if it were in my power, I'd make 'duke a king. He is a noble-hearted fellow, and would make an excellent king; that is, if he had a good prime minister.—But who have we here? voices in the bushes;—a combination about mischief, I'll wager my commission. Let us draw near, and examine a little into the matter."

During this dialogue, as the parties had kept in motion, Richard and his cousin advanced some distance from the house, into the open space in the rear of the village, where, as may be gathered from the conversation, streets were planned, and future dwellings contemplated; but where, in truth, the only mark of improvement that was to be seen, was a neglected clearing along the skirt of a dark forest of mighty pines, over which the bushes or sprouts of the same tree had sprung up to a height that interspersed the fields of snow with little thickets of evergreen. The rushing of the wind, as it whistled through the tops of these mimic trees, prevented the footsteps of the pair from being heard, while their branches concealed their persons. Thus aided, the listeners drew nigh to a spot where the young hunter, Leather-stocking, and the Indian chief, were collected in an earnest consultation. The former was urgent in his manner, and seemed to think the subject of deep importance, while Natty appeared to listen with more than his usual attention, to what the other was saying. Mohegan stood a little on one side, with his head sunken on his chest, his hair falling forward, so as to conceal most of his features, and his whole attitude expressive of deep dejection, if not of shame.

"Let us withdraw," whispered Elizabeth; "we are intruders, and can have no right to listen to the secrets of these men."

"No right!" returned Richard, a little impatiently, in the same tone, and drawing her arm so forcibly through his own as to prevent her retreat; "you forget, cousin, that it is my duty to preserve the peace of the county, and see the laws executed. These wanderers frequently commit depredations; though I do not think John would do any thing secretly. Poor fellow! he was quite boozy last night, and hardly seems to be over it yet. Let us draw nigher, and hear what they say."

Notwithstanding the lady's reluctance, Richard, stimulated doubtless by his nice sense of duty, prevailed; and they were soon so near as distinctly to hear sounds.

"The bird must be had," said Natty, "by fair means or foul. Heigho! I've known the time, lad, when the wild turkeys wasn't over scarce in the country; though you must go into the Virginy gaps, if you want them for the feathers. To be sure, there is a different taste to a partridge, and a well-fattened turkey; though, to my eating, a beaver's tail and bear's hams makes the best of food. But then every one has his own appetite. I gave the last farthing, all to that shilling, to the French trader, this very morning, as I came through the town, for powder; so, as you have nothing, we can have but one shot for it. I know that Billy Kirby is out, and means to have a pull of the trigger at that very turkey. John has a true eye for a single fire, and somehow, my hand shakes so, whenever I have to do any thing extrawnary, that I often lose my aim. Now when I killed the she-bear this fall, with her cubs, though they were so mighty ravenous, I knocked them over one at a shot, and loaded while I dodged the trees in the bargain; but this is a very different thing, Mr. Oliver."

"This," cried the young man, with an accent that sounded as if he took a bitter pleasure in his poverty, while he held a shilling up before his eyes—"this is all the treasure that I possess—this and my rifle! Now, indeed, I have become a man of the woods, and must place my sole dependence on the chase. Come, Natty, let us stake the last penny for the bird; with your aim, it cannot fail to be successful."

"I would rather it should be John, lad; my heart jumps into my mouth, because you set your mind so much on't; and I'm sartain that I shall miss the bird. Them Indians can shoot one time as well as another; nothing ever troubles them. I say, John, here's a shilling; take my rifle, and get a shot at the big turkey they've put up at the stump. Mr. Oliver is over anxious for the creater, and I'm sure to do nothing when I have over anxiety about it."

The Indian turned his head gloomily, and after looking keenly for a moment, in profound silence, at his companions, he replied—

"When John was young, eyesight was not straighter than his bullet. The Mingo squaws cried out at the sound of his rifle. The Mingo warriors were made squaws. When did he ever shoot twice! The eagle went above the clouds, when he passed the wigwam of Chingachgook; his feathers were plenty with the women.—But see," he said, raising his voice from the low, mournful tones in which he had spoken, to a pitch of keen excitement, and stretching forth both hands—"they shake like a deer at the wolf's howl. Is John old? When was a Mohican a squaw, with seventy winters! No! the white man brings old age with him—rum is his tomahawk!"

"Why then do you use it, old man?" exclaimed the young hunter; "why will one so noble by nature, aid the devices of the devil, by making himself a beast?"

"Beast! is John a beast?" replied the Indian, slowly; "yes, you say no lie, child of the Fire-eater! John is a beast. The smokes were once few in these hills. The deer would lick the hand of a white man, and the birds rest on his head. They were strangers to him. My fathers came from the shores of the salt lake. They fled before rum. They came to their grandfather, and they lived in peace; or when they did raise the hatchet, it was to strike it into the brain of a Mingo. They gathered around the council-fire, and what they said was done. Then John was a man. But warriors and traders with light eyes followed them. One brought the long knife, and one brought rum. They were more than the pines on the mountains; and they broke up the councils, and took the lands. The evil spirit was in their jugs, and they let him loose.—Yes, yes—you say no lie, Young Eagle, John is a beast."

"Forgive me, old warrior," cried the youth, grasping his hand; "I should be the last to reproach you. The curses of Heaven light on the cupidity, that has destroyed such a race. Remember, John, that I am of your family, and it is now my greatest pride."

The muscles of Mohegan relaxed a little, and he said more mildly—

"You are a Delaware, my son; your words are not heard.—John cannot shoot."

"I thought that lad had Indian blood in him," whispered Richard, "by the awkward way he handled my horses last night. You see, coz, they never use harness. But the poor fellow shall have two shots at the turkey, if he wants it, for I'll give him another shilling myself; though, perhaps, I had better offer to shoot for him. They have got up their Christmas sports, I find, in the bushes yonder, where you hear the laughter;—though it is a queer taste this chap has for turkey; not but what it is good eating too."

"Hold, cousin Richard," exclaimed Elizabeth, clinging to his arm, "would it be delicate to offer a shilling to that gentleman?"

"Gentleman again! do you think a half breed, like him, will refuse money? no, no, girl; he will take the shilling; ay! and even rum too, notwithstanding he moralizes so much about it.

—But I'll give the lad a chance for his turkey, for that Billy Kirby is one of the best marksmen in the country; that is, if we except the—gentleman."

"Then," said Elizabeth, who found her strength unequal to her will; "then, sir, I will speak."—She advanced, with an air of proud determination, in front of her cousin, and entered the little circle of bushes that surrounded the trio of hunters. Her appearance startled the youth, who at first made an unequivocal motion towards retiring, but recollecting himself, bowed, by lifting his cap, and resumed his attitude of leaning on his rifle. Neither Natty nor Mohegan betrayed any emotion, though the appearance of Elizabeth was so entirely unexpected.

"I find," she said, "that the old Christmas sport of shooting the turkey is yet in use among you. I feel inclined to try my chance for a bird. Which of you will take this money, and after paying my fee, give me the aid of his rifle?"

"Is this a sport for a lady!" exclaimed the young hunter, with an emphasis that could not well be mistaken, and with a rapidity that showed he spoke without consulting any thing but feeling.

"Why not, sir?" returned the maiden. "If it be inhuman, the sin is not confined to one sex only. But I have my humour as well as others. I ask not your assistance, sir; but"—turning to Natty, and dropping a dollar in his hand—"this old veteran of the forest will not be so ungallant, as to refuse one fire for a lady."

Leather-stocking dropped the money into his pouch, and throwing up the end of his rifle, he freshened his priming; and first laughing in his usual manner, he threw the piece over his shoulder, and said—

"If Billy Kirby don't get the bird before me, and the Frenchman's powder don't hang fire this damp morning, you'll see as fine a turkey dead, in a few minutes, as ever was eaten in the Judge's shanty. I have know'd the Dutch women on the Mohawk and Scoharie count greatly on coming to them merry-makings; and so, lad, you shouldn't be short with the lady. Come, let us go forward, for if we wait, the finest bird will be gone."

"But I have a right before you, Natty, and shall try my own luck first. You will excuse me, Miss Temple; I have much reason to wish that bird, and may seem ungallant, but I must claim my privileges."

"Claim any thing that is justly your own, sir," returned the lady; "we are both adventurers, and this is my knight. I trust my fortune to his hand and eye. Lead on, Sir Leather-stocking, and we will follow."

Natty, who seemed pleased with the frank address of the young and beauteous maiden, who had so singularly intrusted him with such a commission, returned the bright smile with which she had addressed him, by his own peculiar mark of mirth, and moved across the snow, towards the spot whence the sounds of boisterous mirth proceeded with the long strides of a hunter. His companions followed in silence, the youth casting frequent and uneasy glances towards Elizabeth, who was detained by a motion from Richard.

"I should think, Miss Temple," he said, so soon as the others were out of hearing, "that if you really wished a turkey, you would not have taken a stranger for the office, and such a one as Leather-stocking. But I can hardly believe that you are serious, for I have fifty at this moment shut up in the coops, in every stage of fat, so that you might choose any quality you pleased. There are six that I am trying an experiment on, by giving them brick-bats with——"

"Enough, cousin Dickon," interrupted the lady; "I do wish the bird, and it is because I so wish, that I commissioned this Mr. Leather-stocking."

"Did you ever hear of the great shot that I made at the wolf, cousin Elizabeth, who was carrying off your father's sheep?" said Richard, drawing himself up into an air of displeasure.— "He had the sheep on his back; and had the head of the wolf been on the other side, I should have killed him dead; as it was——"

"You killed the sheep," again interrupted the young lady— "I know it all, my dear coz. But would it have been decorous, for the High Sheriff of——to mingle in such sports as these?"

"Surely you did not think I intended actually to fire with my own hands?" said Mr. Jones.—"But let us follow, and see the shooting. There is no fear of any thing unpleasant occurring to any female in this new country, especially to your father's daughter, and in my presence."

"My father's daughter fears nothing, sir," returned Elizabeth; "more especially when escorted by the highest executive officer in the county."

She took his arm, and he led her through the mazes of the bushes, to the spot where most of the young men of the village were collected for the sports of shooting a Christmas match, and whither Natty and his companions had already preceded him.

· *Chapter XVII* ·

I guess, by all this quaint array,
The burghers hold their sports to-day
SCOTT

The ancient amusement of shooting the Christmas turkey, is one of the few sports that the settlers of a new country seldom or never neglect to observe. It was connected with the daily practices of a people who often laid aside the axe or the scythe to seize the rifle, as the deer glided through the forests they were felling, or the bear entered their rough meadows to scent the air of a clearing, and to scan, with a look of sagacity, the progress of the invader.

On the present occasion, the usual amusement of the day had been a little hastened, in order to allow a fair opportunity to Mr. Grant, whose exhibition was not less a treat to the young sportsmen, than the one which engaged their present attention. The owner of the birds was a free black, who had been preparing for the occasion a collection of game, that was admirably qualified to inflame the appetite of an epicure, and was well adapted to the means and skill of the different competitors, who were of all ages. He had offered to the younger and more humble marksmen divers birds of an inferior quality, and some shooting had already taken place, much to the pecuniary advantage of the sable owner of the game. The order of the sports was extremely simple, and well understood. The bird was fastened by a string of tow, to the base of the stump of a large pine, the side of which, towards the point where the marksmen were placed, had been flattened with an axe, in order that it might serve the purpose of a target, by which the merit of each individual might be ascertained. The distance between the stump and this point was one hundred measured yards; a foot more or a foot less being thought an invasion of the right of one of the parties. The negro affixed his own price to every bird, and the terms of the chance: but when these were once established, he was obliged, by the strict principles of public justice that prevailed in the country to admit any adventurer who might offer.

The throng consisted of some twenty or thirty young men, most of whom had rifles, and a collection of all the boys in the village. The little urchins, clad in coarse but warm garments, stood gathered around the more distinguished marksmen, with their hands stuck under their waistbands, listening eagerly to the boastful stories of the skill that had been exhibited on former occasions, and were already emulating in their hearts these wonderful deeds in gunnery.

The chief speaker was the man who had been mentioned by Natty, as Billy Kirby. This fellow, whose occupation, when he did labour, was that of clearing lands, or chopping jobs, was of great stature, and carried, in his very air, the index of his character. He was a noisy, boisterous, reckless lad, whose good-natured eye contradicted the bluntness and bullying tenor of his speech. For weeks he would lounge around the taverns of the country, in a state of perfect idleness, or doing small jobs for his liquor and his meals, and cavilling with applicants about the prices of his labour: frequently preferring idleness to an abatement of a tittle of his independence, or a cent in his wages. But when these embarrassing points were once satisfactorily arranged, he would shoulder his axe and his rifle, slip his arms through the straps of his pack, and enter the woods with the tread of a Hercules. His first object was to learn his limits, round which he would pace, occasionally freshening with a blow of his axe, the marks on the boundary trees; and then he would proceed, with an air of great deliberation, to the centre of his premises, and throwing aside his superfluous garments, he would measure, with a knowing eye, one or two of the nearest trees, that were towering apparently into the very clouds, as he gazed upwards. Commonly selecting one of the most noble, for the first trial of his power, he would approach it with a listless air, whistling a low tune; and wielding his axe, with a certain flourish not unlike the salutes of a fencing-master, he would strike a light blow into the bark, and measure his distance. The pause that followed was ominous of the fall of the forest, that had flourished there for centuries. The heavy and brisk blows that he struck, were soon succeeded by the thundering report of the tree, as it came, first cracking and threatening, with the separation of its own last ligaments, then thrashing and tearing with its branches the tops of its surrounding brethren, and finally meeting the ground with a shock but little inferior to an earthquake. From that moment the sounds of the axe would be ceaseless, while the falling of the trees was like a distant cannonading; and the daylight broke into the depths of the woods, with almost the suddenness of a winter morning.

For days, weeks, nay months, Billy Kirby would toil, with an ardour that evinced his native spirit, and with an effect that seemed magical, until, his chopping being ended, his stentorian lungs could be heard emitting sounds, as he called to his patient oxen, the assistants in his labour, which rung through the hills like the cries of an alarm. He had been often heard, on a mild summer's evening, a long mile across the vale of Templeton; when the echoes from the mountains would take up his cries, until they died away in the feeble sounds from the distant rocks that overhung the lake. His piles, or, to use the language of the country, his logging, ended, with a despatch that could only accompany his dexterity and Herculean strength, the jobber would collect together his implements of labour, light the heaps of timber, and march away, under the blaze of the prostrate forest, like the conqueror of some city, who, having first prevailed over his adversary, places the final torch of destruction, as the finishing blow to his conquest. For a long time Billy Kirby would then be seen, sauntering around the taverns, the rider of scrub-races, the bully of cock-fights, and not unfrequently the hero of such sports as the one in hand.

Between him and the Leather-stocking there had long existed a jealous rivalry, on the point of their respective skill in shooting. Notwithstanding the long practice of Natty, it was commonly supposed that the steady nerves and quick eye of the wood-chopper rendered him his equal. Their competition had, however, been confined hitherto to boastings, and comparisons made from their successes in their various hunting excursions; but this was the first time they had ever come in upon collision. A good deal of higgling about the price of the choicest bird, had taken place between Billy Kirby and its owner, before Natty and his companions rejoined the sportsmen. It had, however, been settled at one shilling a shot, which was the highest sum ever exacted, the black taking care to protect himself from losses as much as possible, by the conditions of the sport. The turkey was already fastened at the "mark," but its body was entirely hid by the surrounding snow, nothing being visible but its red swelling head, and long, proud neck. If the bird was injured by any bullet that struck below the snow, it was still to continue the property of its present owner, but if a feather was touched in a visible part, the animal became the prize of the successful adventurer.

These terms were loudly proclaimed from the mouth of the negro, who was seated in the snow, in a somewhat hazardous vicinity to his favourite bird, as Elizabeth and her cousin, the newly appointed executive chief of the county, approached the noisy sportsmen. The sounds of mirth and contention sensibly lowered at this unexpected visit, but after a moment's pause, the curious interest exhibited in the face of the young lady, together with her smiling air, restored the freedom of the morning; though it was somewhat chastened both in language and vehemence, by the presence of such a spectator to their proceedings.

"Stand out of the way, boys!" cried the wood-chopper, who was placing himself at the shooting point—"stand out of the way, you little rascals, or I will shoot through you. Now, Brom, you may say good-by to that turkey."

"Stop!" cried the young hunter; "I am a candidate for a chance too. Here is my shilling, Brom; I wish a shot too."

"You may wish it in welcome," cried Kirby, "but if I ruffle the gobbler's feathers, how are you to get it? is money so plenty in your deer-skin pocket, that you pay for a chance that you may never have?"

"How know you, sir, how plenty money is in my pocket?" said the youth, fiercely. "Here is my shilling, Brom, and I claim a right to shoot."

"Don't be crabbed, my boy," said the other, who was very coolly fixing his flint. "They say you have a hole in your left shoulder, yourself: so I think Brom may give you a fire for half price. It will take a keen one to hit that bird, I can tell you, my lad, even if I give you a chance, which is a thing I have no mind to do."

"Don't be boasting, Billy Kirby," said Natty, throwing the breech of his rifle into the snow, and leaning on its barrel; "you'll get but one shot at the creater, for if the lad misses his aim, which wouldn't be a wonder if he did, with his arm so stiff and sore, you'll find a good piece and an old eye coming a'ter you. Maybe it's true that I can't shoot as I used to could, but a hundred yards is but a short distance for a long rifle."

"What, old Leather-stocking, are you out this morning," cried his reckless opponent. "Well, fair play's a jewel. But I've the lead of you, old fellow; so here goes, for a dry throat or a good dinner."

The countenance of the negro evinced not only all the interest which his pecuniary adventure might occasion, but also the keen excitement that the sport produced in the others, though with a very different wish as to the result. While the wood-chopper was slowly and steadily raising his rifle, he exclaimed—

"Fair play, Billy Kirby—stand back—make 'em stand back, boys,—gib a nigger fair play—poss-up, gobbler; shake a head, fool; don't a see 'em poking gun at 'em?"

These cries, which were intended as much to distract the attention of the marksman, as for any thing else, were, however, fruitless. The nerves of the wood-chopper were not so easily shaken, and he took his aim with the utmost deliberation. The dead stillness of expectation prevailed for a moment, and he fired. The head of the turkey was seen to dash on one side, and its wings were spread in momentary fluttering; but it settled itself down, calmly, into its bed of snow, and glanced its eyes uneasily around. For a time long enough to draw a deep breath, not a sound was heard. The silence was then broken, by the noise of the negro, who laughed, and shook his body, with all kinds of antics, rolling over in the snow with the excess of his delight.

"Well done a gobbler," he cried, jumping up, and affecting to embrace his bird; "I tell 'em to poss-up, and you see 'em dodge. Gib anoder shillin, Billy, and hab anoder shot."

"No—the shot is mine," said the young hunter; "you have my money already. Leave the mark, and let me try my luck."

"Ah! it's but money thrown away, lad," said Leather-stocking. "A turkey's head and neck is but a small mark for a new hand and a lame shoulder. You'd best let me take the fire, and maybe we can make some sittlement with the lady about the bird."

"The chance is mine," said the young hunter. "Clear the ground, that I may take it."

The discussions and disputes concerning the last shot were now abating, it having been determined, that if the turkey's head had been any where but just where it was at the moment, the bird must certainly have been killed. There was not much excitement produced by the preparations of the youth, who proceeded in a hurried manner to take his aim, and was in the act of pulling the trigger, when he was stopped by Natty.

"Your hand shakes, lad," he said, "and you seem over eager. Bullet wounds are apt to weaken the flesh, and, to my judgment, you'll not shoot so well as in common. If you will fire, you should shoot quick, before there is time to shake off the aim."

"Fair play," again shouted the negro; "fair play—gib a nigger fair play. What right a Nat-Bumppo tell a young man? Let 'em shoot—clear a ground."

The youth fired with great rapidity; but no motion was made by the turkey; and when the examiners for the ball returned from the "mark," they declared that he had missed the stump.

Elizabeth observed the change in his countenance, and could not help feeling surprise, that one so evidently superior to his companions, should feel a trifling loss so sensibly. But her own champion was now preparing to enter the lists.

The mirth of Brom, which had been again excited, though in a much smaller degree than before, by the failure of the second adventurer, vanished, the instant that Natty took his stand. His skin became mottled with large brown spots, that sullied the lustre of his native ebony most fearfully, while his enormous lips gradually compressed around the two rows of ivory, that had hitherto been shining in his visage, like pearls set in jet. His nostrils, at all times the most conspicuous features of his face, dilated, until they covered the greater part of the diameter of his countenance; while his brown and bony hands unconsciously grasped the snow-crust near him, the excitement of the moment completely overcoming his native dread of cold.

While these indications of apprehension were exhibited in the sable owner of the turkey, the man who gave rise to this extraordinary emotion was as calm and collected, as if there was not to be a single spectator of his skill.

"I was down in the Dutch settlements on the Scoharie," said Natty, carefully removing the leather guard from the lock of his rifle, "jist before the breaking out of the last war, and there was a shooting-match among the boys; so I took a hand in it myself. I think I opened a good many Dutch eyes that very day, for I won the powder-horn, three bars of lead, and a pound of as good powder as ever flashed in the pan of a gun. Lord! how they did swear in Garman! They did tell of one drunken Dutchman, who said he'd have the life of me, before I got back to the lake ag'in. But if he had put his rifle to his shoulder, with evil intent, God would have punished him for it; and even if the Lord didn't, and he had missed his aim, I know one that would have given him as good as he sent, and better too, if good shooting could come into the 'count."

By this time the old hunter was ready for his business, and throwing his right leg far behind him, and stretching his left arm along the barrel of his piece, he raised towards the bird. Every eye glanced rapidly from the marksman to the mark; but at the moment when each ear was expecting the report of the rifle, they were disappointed by the ticking sound of the flint only.

"A snap—a snap," shouted the negro, springing from his crouching posture, like a madman, before his bird. "A snap as good as a fire—Natty Bumppo gun he snap—Natty Bumppo miss a turkey."

"Natty Bumppo hit a nigger," said the indignant old hunter, "if you don't get out of the way, Brom. It's contrary to the reason of the thing, boy, that a snap should count for a fire, when one is nothing more than a fire-stone striking a steel pan, and the other is good lead, ay! and with a good aim; so get out of my way, boy, and let me show Billy Kirby how to shoot a Christmas turkey."

"Gib a nigger fair play!" cried the black, who continued resolutely to maintain his post. "Ebbery body know dat snap as good as fire. Leab it to Massa Jone—leab it to lady."

"Sartain," said the wood-chopper; "it's the law of the game in this part of the country, Leather-stocking. If you fire ag'in, you must pay up the other shilling. I b'lieve I'll try luck once more myself; so, Brom, here's my money, and I take the next fire."

"It's likely you know the laws of the woods better than I do, Billy Kirby!" returned Natty. "You come in with the settlers, with an ox goad in your hand, and I come in with moccasins on my feet, and with a good rifle on my shoulder, so long back as afore the old war; which is likely to know the best? I say, no man need tell me that snapping is as good as firing, when I pull the trigger."

"Leab it to Massa Jone," said the alarmed negro; "he know ebbery ting."

This appeal to the knowledge of Richard was too flattering to be unheeded. He therefore advanced a little from the spot whither the delicacy of Elizabeth had induced her to withdraw, and gave the following opinion, with all the gravity that the subject and his own rank demanded:—

"There seems to be a difference in opinion," he said, "on the subject of Nathaniel Bumppo's right to shoot at Abraham Freeborn's turkey, without the said Nathaniel paying one shilling for the privilege." This fact was too self-evident to be denied, and after pausing a moment, that the audience might digest his premises, Richard proceeded:—"It seems proper that I should decide this question, as I am bound to preserve the peace of the county; and men with deadly weapons in their hands, should not be heedlessly left to contention, and their own malignant passions. It appears that there was agreement, either in writing or in words, on the disputed point; therefore we must reason from analogy, which is, as it were, comparing one thing with another. Now, in duels, where both parties shoot, it is generally the rule that a snap is a fire; and if such is the rule, where the party has a right to fire back again, it seems to me unreasonable, to say that a man may stand snapping at that turkey all day. I therefore am of opinion, that Nathaniel Bumppo has lost his chance, and must pay another shilling before he renews his right."

As this opinion came from such a high quarter, and was delivered with so much effect, it silenced all murmurs, for the whole of the spectators had begun to take sides with great warmth, except from the Leather-stocking himself.

"I think Miss Elizabeth's thoughts should be taken," said Natty. "I've known the squaws give very good counsel, when the Indians have been dumb foundered in their notions. If she says that I ought to lose, I agree to give it up."

"Then I adjudge you to be a loser, for this time," said Miss Temple; "but pay your money, and renew your chance; unless Brom will sell me the bird for a dollar. I will give him the money, and save the life of the poor victim."

This proposition was evidently but little relished by any of the listeners, even the negro feeling unwilling to lose the sport, though he lost his turkey. In the mean while, as Billy Kirby was preparing himself for another shot, Natty left the goal, with an extremely dissatisfied manner, muttering to himself, and speaking aloud—

"There hasn't been such a thing as a good flint sold at the foot of the lake, since the time when the Indian traders used to come into the country;—and if a body should go into the flats along the streams in the hills, to hunt for such a thing, it's ten to one but they will be all covered up with the plough. Heigho! it seems to me, that just as the game grows scarce, and a body wants the best of ammunition, to get a livelihood, every thing that's bad falls on him, like a judgment. But

I'll change the stone, for Billy Kirby hasn't the eye for such a mark, I know."

The wood-chopper seemed now entirely sensible that his reputation in a great measure depended on his care; nor did he neglect any means to ensure his success. He drew up his rifle, and renewed his aim, again and again, still appearing reluctant to fire. No sound was heard from even Brom, during these portentous movements, until Kirby discharged his piece, with the same want of success as before. Then, indeed, the shouts of the negro rung through the bushes, and sounded among the trees of the neighbouring forest, like the outcries of a tribe of Indians. He laughed, rolling his head, first on one side, then on the other, until nature seemed exhausted with mirth. He danced, until his legs were wearied with motion, in the snow; and, in short, he exhibited all that violence of joy that characterizes the mirth of a thoughtless negro.

The wood-chopper had exerted all his art, and felt a proportionate degree of disappointment at his failure. He first examined the bird with the utmost attention, and more than once suggested that he had touched its feathers; but the voice of the multitude was against him, for it felt disposed to listen to the often-repeated cries of the black, to "gib a nigger fair play."

Finding it impossible to make out a title to the bird, Kirby turned fiercely to the black, and said—

"Shut your oven, you crow! where is the man that can hit a turkey's head at a hundred yards? I was a fool for trying. You needn't make an uproar, like a falling pine-tree, about it. Show me the man who can do it."

"Look this a-way, Billy Kirby," said Leather-stocking, "and let them clear the mark, and I'll show you a man who's made better shots afore now, and that when he's been hard pressed by the savages and wild beasts."

"Perhaps there is one whose rights come before ours, Leather-stocking," said Miss Temple; "if so, we will waive our privilege."

"If it be me that you have reference to, madam," said the young hunter, "I shall decline another chance. My shoulder is yet weak, I find."

Elizabeth regarded his proud, but forced manner, and even thought that she could discern a tinge on his cheek, that spoke the shame of conscious poverty. She said no more, but suffered her own champion to make a trial.

Although Natty Bumppo had certainly made hundreds of more momentous shots, at his enemies or his game, yet he never exerted himself more to excel. He raised his piece three several times; once to get his range; once to calculate his distance; and once because the bird, alarmed by the deathlike stillness that prevailed, turned its head quickly, to examine its foes. But the fourth time he fired. The smoke, the report, and the momentary shock, prevented most of the spectators from instantly knowing the result; but Elizabeth, when she saw her champion drop the end of his rifle in the snow, and open his mouth in one of its silent laughs, and then proceed, very coolly, to recharge his piece, knew that he had been successful. The boys rushed to the mark, and lifted the turkey on high, lifeless, and with nothing but the remnant of a head.

"Bring in the creater," said Leather-stocking, "and put it at the feet of the lady. I was her deputy in the matter, and the bird is her property."

"And a good deputy you have proved yourself," returned Elizabeth—"so good, cousin Richard, that I would advise you to remember his qualities." She paused, and the gayety that beamed on her face gave place to a more serious earnestness. She even blushed a little, as she turned to the young hunter, and, with the insinuating charm of a woman's best manner, added—"But it was only to see an exhibition of the far-famed skill of Leather-stocking, that I tried my fortunes. Will you, sir, accept the bird, as a small peace-offering, for the hurt that prevented your own success?"

The expression with which the youth received this present was indescribable. He appeared to yield to the exquisite blandishment of her air, in opposition to a strong inward impulse to the contrary. He bowed, and raised the victim silently from her feet, but continued silent.

Elizabeth handed the black a piece of silver as a remuneration for his loss, which had some effect in again unbending his muscles, and then expressed to her companion her readiness to return homeward.

"Wait a minute, cousin Bess," cried Richard; there is an uncertainty about the rules of this sport, that it is proper I should remove. If you will appoint a committee, gentlemen, to wait on me this morning, I will draw up, in writing, a set of regulations——" He stopped, with some indignation, to see who it was that so familiarly laid his hand on the shoulder of the High Sheriff of——.

"A merry Christmas to you, cousin Dickon," said Judge Temple, who had approached the party unperceived: I must have a vigilant eye to my daughter, sir, if you are to be seized daily with these gallant fits. I admire the taste, which would introduce a lady to such scenes!"

"It is her own perversity, 'duke," cried the disappointed Sheriff, who felt the loss of the first salutation as grievously as many a man would a much greater misfortune; and I must say that she comes honestly by it. I led her out to show her the improvements, but away she scampered, through the snow, at the first sound of the fire-arms, the same as if she had been brought up in a camp, instead of a first-rate boarding-school. I do think, Judge Temple, that such dangerous amusements should be suppressed by law; nay, I doubt whether they are not already indictable at common law."

"Well, sir, as you are Sheriff of the county, it becomes your duty to examine into the matter," returned the smiling Marmaduke. "I perceive that Bess has executed her commission, and I hope it met with a favourable reception."

Richard glanced his eye at the packet, which he held in his hand, and the slight anger produced by his disappointment vanished instantly.

"Ah! 'duke, my dear cousin," he said, "step a little on one side; I have something I would say to you." Marmaduke complied, and the sheriff led him to a little distance in the bushes, and continued—"First, 'duke, let me thank you for your friendly interest with the Council and the Governor, without which, I am confident, that the greatest merit would avail but little. But we are sisters' children—we are sisters' children; and you may use me like one of your horses; ride me or drive me, 'duke, I am wholly yours. But in my humble opinion, this young companion of Leather-stocking requires looking after. He has a very dangerous propensity for turkey."

"Leave him to my management, Dickon," said the Judge, gravely, "and I will cure his appetite by indulgence. It is with him that I would speak. Let us rejoin the sportsmen."

· *Chapter XVIII* ·

Poor wretch! the mother that him bare,
If she had been in presence there,
In his wan face, and sun-burnt hair,
    She had not known her child.
                                    SCOTT

It diminished, in no degree, the effect produced by the conversation which passed between Judge Temple and the young
hunter, that the former took the arm of his daughter, and drew
it through his own, when he advanced from the spot whither
Richard had led him, to where the youth was standing, in a
musing attitude leaning on his rifle, and apparently contemplating the dead bird that lay at his feet. The presence of Marmaduke did not interrupt the sports, which were resumed, by
loud and clamorous disputes concerning the conditions of a
chance, that involved the life of a bird of much inferior quality
to the last. Leather-stocking and Mohegan had alone drawn
aside to the place where stood their youthful companion; and,
although in the immediate vicinity of such a throng, the following conversation was heard only by those who were interested in it.

"I have greatly injured you, Mr. Edwards," said the
Judge; but the sudden and inexplicable start with which the
person spoke to received this unexpected address, caused him
to pause a moment in manifest surprise, also. As no answer
was given, and the strong emotion exhibited in the countenance of the youth gradually passed away, he continued—
"But fortunately, it is in some measure in my power to compensate you for what I have done. My kinsman, Richard
Jones, has received an appointment that will, in future, de-
prive me of his assistance, and leaves me, just now, destitute

of one who might greatly aid me with his pen. Your manner, notwithstanding appearances, is a sufficient proof of your education, nor will thy shoulder suffer thee to labour, for some time to come. My doors are open to thee, my young friend, for in this infant country we harbour no suspicions: little offering to tempt the cupidity of the evil disposed. Become my assistant, for at least a season, and receive such compensation as thy services will deserve."

There was nothing in the manner of the offer of the Judge to justify the reluctance, amounting nearly to loathing, with which the youth listened to his speech: but after a powerful effort, as if for self-command, he replied—

"I would serve you, sir, or any other man, for an honest support, for I do not affect to conceal that my necessities are very great, even beyond what appearances would indicate; but I am fearful that such new duties would interfere too much with more important business: so that I must decline your offer, and depend on my rifle, as before, for my subsistence."

Richard here took occasion to whisper to the young lady, who had shrunk a little from the foreground of the picture—

"This, you see, cousin Bess, is the natural reluctance of a half-breed to leave the savage state. Their attachment to a wandering life is, I verily believe, unconquerable."

"It is a precarious life," observed Marmaduke, without hearing the sheriff's observation, "and one that brings more evils with it than present suffering. Trust me, my young friend, my experience is greater than thine, when I tell thee, that the unsettled life of these hunters is of vast disadvantage for temporal purposes, and it totally removes one from within the influence of more sacred things."

"No, no, Judge," interrupted the Leather-stocking, who was hitherto unseen, or disregarded; "take him into your shanty in welcome, but tell him the raal thing. I have lived in the woods for forty long years, and have spent five years at a time without seeing the light of a clearing bigger than a wind-row in the trees; and I should like to know where you'll find a man, in his sixty-eighth year, who can get an easier living, for all your betterments, and your deer-laws: and, as for honesty, or

doing what's right between man and man, I'll not turn my
back to the longest winded deacon on your patent."

"Thou art an exception, Leather-stocking," returned the
Judge, nodding good-naturedly at the hunter; "for thou hast
a temperance unusual in thy class, and a hardihood exceeding
thy years. But this youth is made of materials too precious to
be wasted in the forest. I entreat thee to join my family, if it
be but till thy arm be healed. My daughter here, who is mistress of my dwelling, will tell thee that thou art welcome."

"Certainly," said Elizabeth, whose earnestness was strongly
checked by the assumption of a woman's dignity. "The unfortunate would be welcome at any time, but doubly so, when
we feel that we have occasioned the evil ourselves."

"Yes," said Richard, "and if you relish turkey, young
man, there are plenty in the coops, and those of the best kind,
I can assure you."

Finding himself thus ably seconded, Marmaduke pushed
his advantage to the utmost. He entered into a detail of the
duties that would attend the situation, and circumstantially
mentioned the reward, and all those points which are deemed
of importance among men of business. The youth listened in
extreme agitation. There was an evident contest in his feelings; at times he appeared to wish eagerly for the change, and
then again the incomprehensible expression of disgust would
cross his handsome features, like a dark cloud obscuring a
noonday sun.

The Indian, in whose manner the depression of self-abase-
ment was most powerfully exhibited, listened to the offers of
the Judge, with an interest that increased with each syllable.
Gradually he drew nigher to the group; and when, with his
keen glance, he detected the most marked evidence of yielding
in the countenance of his young companion, he changed at
once from his attitude and look of shame to the fearless and
proud front of an Indian warrior, and moving, with great dignity, closer to the parties, he spoke in his turn.

"Listen to your Father," he said, "for his words are old. Let
the Young Eagle and the Great Land Chief eat together; let
them sleep, without fear, near to each other. The children of
Miquon love not blood; they are just, and will do right. The

sun must rise and set often, before men can make one family; it is not the work of a day, but of many winters. The Mingoes and the Delawares are born enemies; their blood can never mix in the wigwam: it never will run in the same stream in the battle. What makes the brother of Miquon and Young Eagle foes? they are of the same tribe: their fathers and mothers are one. Learn to wait, my son: you have Delaware blood, and an Indian warrior knows how to be patient."

This figurative address seemed to have great weight with the young man, who gradually yielded to the representations of Marmaduke, and eventually consented to his proposal. It was, however, to be an experiment only; and if either of the parties thought fit to rescind the engagement, it was left at his option so to do. The remarkable and ill-concealed reluctance of the youth, to accept of an offer, which most men in his station would consider as an unhoped-for elevation, occasioned no little surprise in those of the spectators to whom he was a stranger; and it left a slight impression to his disadvantage. When the parties separated, they very naturally made the subject the topic of a conversation, which we shall relate; first commencing with the Judge, his daughter, and Richard, who were slowly pursuing the way back to the Mansion-house.

"I have surely endeavoured to remember the holy mandates of our Redeemer, when he bids us to 'love them who despitefully use you,' in my intercourse with this incomprehensible boy," said Marmaduke. "I know not what there is in my dwelling, to frighten a lad of his years, unless it may be thy presence and visage, Bess."

"No, no," said Richard, with great simplicity in his manner; "it is not cousin Bess. But when did you ever know a half-breed, 'duke, who could bear civilization? for that matter, they are worse than the savages themselves. Did you notice how knock-kneed he stood, Elizabeth, and what a wild look he had in his eyes?"

"I heeded not his eyes, sir," returned the maiden, "nor his knees, which would be all the better for a little humbling. Really, my dear sir, I think you did exercise the Christian virtue of patience to the utmost. I was disgusted with his airs, long before he consented to make one in our family. Truly, we are much honoured by the association! In what apartment is he to be placed, sir; and at what table is he to receive his nectar and ambrosia?"

"With Benjamin and Remarkable," interrupted Mr. Jones; "you surely would not make the youth eat with the blacks! He is part Indian, it is true, but the natives hold the negroes in great contempt. No, no—he would starve before he would break a crust with the negroes."

"I am but too happy, Dickon, to tempt him to eat with our-selves," said Marmaduke, "to think of offering even the in-dignity you propose."

"Then, sir," said Elizabeth, with an air that was slightly affected, as if submitting to her father's orders in opposition to her own will, "it is your pleasure that he be a gentleman."

"Certainly; he is to fill the station of one; let him receive the treatment that is due to his place, until we find him un-worthy of it."

"Well, well, 'duke," cried the Sheriff, "you will find it no easy matter to make a gentleman of him. The old proverb says, 'that it takes three generations to make a gentleman.' There was my father whom every body knew; my grandfather was an M.D., and his father a D.D.; and his father came from England. I never could come at the truth of his origin, but he was either a great merchant, in London, or a great country lawyer."

"Here is a true American genealogy for you," said Marma-duke, laughing. "It does very well, 'till you get across the water, where, as every thing is obscure, it is certain to deal in the superlative. You are sure that your English progenitor was great, Dickon, whatever his profession might be?"

"To be sure I am," returned the other; "I have heard my old aunt talk of him by the month. We are of good family, Judge Temple, and have never filled any but honourable sta-tions in life."

"I marvel that you should be satisfied with so scanty a pro-vision of gentility, in the olden time, Dickon. Most of the American genealogists commence their traditions, like the stories for children, with three brothers, taking special care that one of the triumvirate shall be the progenitor of any of the same name who may happen to be better furnished with worldly gear than themselves. But, here, all are equal who know how to conduct themselves with propriety; and Oliver Edwards comes into my family, on a footing with both the High Sheriff and the Judge."

"Well, 'duke, I call this democracy, not republicanism; but I say nothing; only let him keep within the law, or I shall show him, that the freedom of even this country is under wholesome restraint."

"Surely, Dickon, you will not execute till I condemn!" said Marmaduke. "But what says Bess to the new inmate? We must pay a deference to the ladies, in this matter, after all."

"Oh! sir," returned Elizabeth, "I believe I am much like a certain Judge Temple, in this particular; not easily to be turned from my opinion. But, to be serious, although I must think the introduction of a demisavage into the family a somewhat startling event, whomsoever you think proper to countenance, may be sure of my respect."

The Judge drew her arm more closely in his own, and smiled, while Richard led the way through the gate of the little court-yard in the rear of the dwelling, dealing out his ambiguous warnings, with his accustomed loquacity.

On the other hand, the foresters, for the three hunters, notwithstanding their great difference in character, well deserved this common name, pursued their course along the skirts of the village in silence. It was not until they had reached the lake, and were moving over its frozen surface, towards the foot of the mountain, where their hut stood, that the youth exclaimed—

"Who could have foreseen this, a month since! I have consented to serve Marmaduke Temple! to be an inmate in the dwelling of the greatest enemy of my race! yet what better could I do? The servitude cannot be long, and when the motive for submitting to it ceases to exist, I will shake it off, like the dust from my feet."

"Is he a Mingo, that you will call him enemy?" said Mohegan. "The Delaware warrior sits still, and waits the time of the Great Spirit. He is no woman, to cry out like a child."

"Well, I'm mistrustful, John," said Leather-stocking, in

whose air there had been, during the whole business, a strong expression of doubt and uncertainty. "They saw that there's new laws in the land, and I am sartain that there's new ways in the mountains. One hardly knows the lakes and streams, they've altered the country so much. I must say I'm mistrustful of such smooth speakers; for I've known the whites talk fair, when they wanted the Indian lands most. This I will say, though I'm white myself, and was born nigh York, and of honest parents, too."

"I will submit," said the youth; "I will forget who I am. Cease to remember, old Mohegan, that I am the descendant of a Delaware chief, who once was master of these noble hills, these beautiful vales, and of this water, over which we tread. Yes, yes—I will become his bondsman—his slave! Is it not an honourable servitude, old man?"

"Old man!" repeated the Indian, solemnly, and pausing in his walk, as usual when much excited—"yes; John is old. Son of my brother! if Mohegan was young, when would his rifle be still? where would the deer hide, and he not find him? But John is old; his hand is the hand of a squaw; his tomahawk is a hatchet; brooms and baskets are his enemies—he strikes no other.—Hunger and old age come together. See, Hawk-eye! when young, he would go days and eat nothing; but should he not put the brush on the fire now, the blaze would go out. Take the son of Miquon by the hand, and he will help you."

"I'm not the man I was, I'll own, Chingachgook," returned the Leather-stocking; "but I can go without a meal now, on occasion. When we tracked the Iroquois through the 'Beech-woods,' they druv the game afore them, for I hadn't a morsel to eat from Monday morning, come Wednesday sundown; and then I shot as fat a buck, on the Pennsylvanny line, as you ever laid eyes on. It would have done your heart raal good to have seen the Delawares eat,—for I was out scouting and scrimmaging with their tribe, at the very time. Lord! the Indians, lad, lay still, and just waited till Providence should send them their game; but I foraged about, and put a deer up, and put him down too, 'fore he had made a dozen jumps. I was too weak, and too ravenous to stop for his flesh; so I took a good drink of his blood, and the Indians eat of his meat raw.

John was there, and John knows. But then starvation would be apt to be too much for me now, I will own, though I'm no great eater at any time."

"Enough is said, my friends," cried the youth. "I feel that every where the sacrifice is required at my hands, and it shall be made; but say no more, I entreat you; I cannot bear this subject now."

His companions were silent, and they soon reached the hut, which they entered, after removing certain complicated and ingenious fastenings, that were put there, apparently, to guard a property of but very little value. Immense piles of snow lay against the log wall of this secluded habitation, on one side, while fragments of small trees, and branches of oak and chestnut, that had been torn from their parent stems by the winds, were thrown into a pile, on the other. A small column of smoke rose through a chimney of sticks, cemented with clay, along the side of the rock; and had marked the snow above with its dark tinges, in a wavy line, from the point of emission to another where the hill receded from the brow of a precipice, and held a soil that nourished trees of a gigantic growth, that overhung the little bottom beneath.

The remainder of the day passed off as such days are commonly spent in a new country.—The settlers thronged to the academy again, to witness the second effort of Mr. Grant; and Mohegan was one of his hearers. But, notwithstanding the Divine fixed his eyes intently on the Indian, when he invited his congregation to advance to the table, the shame of last night's abasement was yet too keen in the old chief to suffer him to move.

When the people were dispersing, the clouds that had been gathering all the morning, were dense and dirty; and before half of the curious congregation had reached their different cabins, that were placed in every glen and hollow of the mountains, or perched on the summits of the hills themselves, the rain was falling in torrents. The dark edges of the stumps began to exhibit themselves as the snow settled rapidly; the fences of logs and brush, which before had been only traced by the long lines of white mounds, that ran across the valley and up the mountains, peeped out, in spots, from their light covering; and the black stubs were momentarily becoming more distinct, as large masses of snow and ice fell from their sides, under the influence of the thaw.

Sheltered in the warm hall of her father's comfortable mansion, Elizabeth accompanied by Louisa Grant, looked abroad with admiration at the ever-varying face of things without. Even the village, which had just before been glittering with the colour of the frozen element, reluctantly dropped its mask, and the houses exposed their dark roofs and smoked chimneys. The pines shook off their covering of snow, and every thing seemed to be assuming its proper hue, with a rapidity of transition that bordered on the supernatural.

· *Chapter XIX* ·

And yet, poor Edwin was no vulgar boy.
BEATTIE

The close of Christmas day, A.D. 1793, was tempestuous, but comparatively warm. When darkness had again hid the objects in the village from the gaze of Elizabeth, she turned from the window, where she had remained while the least vestige of light lingered over the tops of the dark pines, with a curiosity that was rather excited than appeased by the passing glimpses of woodland scenery that she had caught during the day.

With her arm locked in that of Miss Grant, the young mistress of the mansion walked slowly up and down the hall, musing on the scenes that were rapidly recurring in her memory, and possibly dwelling, at times, in the sanctuary of her thoughts, on the strange occurrences that had led to the introduction to her father's family, of one, whose manners so singularly contradicted the inferences to be drawn from his situation. The expiring heat of the apartment, for its great size required a day to reduce its temperature, had given to her cheeks a richness of bloom that exceeded their natural colour, while the mild and melancholy features of Louisa were brightened with a faint tinge, that, like the hectic glow of disease, gave a painful interest to her beauty.

The eyes of the gentlemen who were yet seated around the rich wines of Judge Temple, frequently wandered from the table, that was placed at one end of the hall, to the lovely forms that were silently moving over its length. Much mirth, and that, at times, of a boisterous kind, proceeded from the mouth of Richard; but Major Hartmann was not yet excited to his pitch of merriment, and Marmaduke respected the presence of his clerical guest too much, to indulge in even the innocent humour that formed no small ingredient in his character.

Such were, and such continued to be, the pursuits of the party, for half an hour after the shutters were closed, and candles were placed in various parts of the hall, as substitutes for the departing daylight. The appearance of Benjamin staggering under the burthen of an armful of wood, was the first interruption to the scene.

"How now, Master Pump!" roared the newly appointed Sheriff; "is there not warmth enough in 'duke's best Madeira, to keep up the animal heat through this thaw? Remember, old boy, that the Judge is particular with his beech and maple, beginning to dread, already, a scarcity of the precious articles. Ha! ha! ha! 'duke, you are a good, warm-hearted relation, I will own, as in duty bound, but you have some queer notions about you, after all. 'Come, let us be jolly, and cast away folly!'"

The notes gradually sunk into a hum, while the Major-domo threw down his load, and turning to his interrogator with an air of great earnestness, he replied—

"Why, look you, Squire Dickens, mayhap there's a warm latitude round about the table there, thof it's not the stuff to raise the heat in my body, neither; the raal Jamaiky being the only thing to do that, beside good wood, or some such matter as Newcastle coal. But if I know any thing of weather, d'ye see, it's time to be getting all snug, and for putting the ports in, and stirring the fires a bit. Mayhap I've not followed the seas twenty-seven years, and lived another seven in these here woods for nothing, gemmen."

"Why, does it bid fair for a change in the weather, Benjamin?" inquired the master of the house.

"There's a shift of wind, your honour," returned the steward; "and when there's a shift of wind, you may look for a change, in this here climate. I was aboard of one of Rodney's fleet, d'ye see, about the time we licked De Grasse, Mounsheer Lew Quaw's countryman, there; and the wind was here at the south'ard and east'ard; and I was below, mixing a toothful of hot-stuff for the Captain of marines, who dined, d'ye see, in the cabin, that there very same day; and I suppose he wanted to put out the Captain's fire with a gun-room ingyne; and so, just as I got it to my own liking, after tasting pretty often, for the soldier was difficult to please, slap come the foresail ag'in the mast, whiz went the ship round on her heel, like a whirligig. And a lucky thing was it that our helm was down; for as she gathered starnway she payed off, which was more than every ship in the fleet did, or could do. But she strained herself in the trough of the sea, and she shipped a deal of water over her quarter. I never swallowed so much clear water at a time, in my life, as I did then, for I was looking up the after-hatch at the instant."

"I wonder, Benjamin, that you did not die with a dropsy!" said Marmaduke.

"I mought, Judge," said the old tar, with a broad grin; "but there was no need of the med'cine chest for a cure; for, as I thought the brew was spoilt for the marine's taste, and there was no telling when another sea might come and spoil it for mine, I finished the mug on the spot. So then all hands was called to the pumps, and there we began to ply the pumps——"

"Well, but the weather?" interrupted Marmaduke; "what of the weather without doors?"

"Why, here the wind has been all day at the south and now there's a lull, as if the last blast was out of bellows; and there's a streak along the mountain, to the north'ard, that, just now, wasn't wider than the bigness of your hand; and then the clouds drive afore it as you'd brail a mainsail, and the stars are heaving in sight, like so many lights and beacons, put there to warn us to pile on the wood; and, if-so-be that I'm a judge of weather, it's getting to be time to build on a fire; or you'll have half of them there porter-bottles, and them dimmy-johns of wine, in the locker here, breaking with the frost, afore the morning watch is called."

"Thou art a prudent sentinel," said the Judge. "Act thy pleasure with the forests, for this night at least."

Benjamin did as he was ordered; nor had two hours elapsed, before the prudence of his precautions became very visible. The south wind had, indeed, blown itself out, and it was succeeded by the calmness that usually gave warning of a serious change in the weather. Long before the family retired to rest, the cold had become cuttingly severe; and when Monsieur Le Quoi sallied forth, under a bright moon, to seek his own abode, he was compelled to beg a blanket in which he might envelop his form, in addition to the numerous garments that his sagacity had provided for the occasion. The divine and his daughter remained, as inmates of the Mansion-house, during the night, and the excess of last night's merriment induced the gentlemen to make an early retreat to their several apartments. Long before midnight, the whole family were invisible.

Elizabeth and her friend had not yet lost their senses in sleep, when the howlings of the northwest wind were heard around the buildings, and brought with them that exquisite sense of comfort, that is ever excited under such circumstances, in an apartment where the fire has not yet ceased to glimmer; and curtains, and shutters, and feathers, unite to preserve the desired temperature in the air. Once, just as her eyes had opened, apparently in the last stage of drowsiness, the roaring winds brought with them a long and plaintive howl, that seemed too wild for a dog, and yet strongly resembled the cries of that faithful animal, when night awakens his vigilance, and gives sweetness and solemnity to his alarms. The form of Louisa Grant instinctively pressed nearer to that of the young heiress, who, finding her companion was yet awake, said, in a low tone, as if afraid to break a charm with her voice—

"Those distant cries are plaintive, and even beautiful. Can they be the hounds from the hut of Leather-stocking?"

"They are wolves, who have ventured from the mountain, on the lake," whispered Louisa, "and who are only kept from the village by the lights. One night, since we have been here, hunger drove them to our very doors. Oh! what a dreadful night it was! But the riches of Judge Temple have given him too many safeguards, to leave room for fear in this house."

"The enterprise of Judge Temple is taming the very forests!" exclaimed Elizabeth, proudly, throwing off the covering, and partly rising in the bed. "How rapidly is civilization treading on the footsteps of nature!" she continued, as her eye glanced over, not only the comforts, but the luxuries of her apartment, and her ear again listened to the distant, but often repeated howls from the lake. Finding, however, that the timidity of her companion rendered the sounds painful to her, Elizabeth resumed her place by her side, and soon forgot the changes in the country, with those in her own condition, in a deep sleep.

The following morning, the noise of the female servant, who entered the apartment to light their fire, awoke the young maidens who form such conspicuous subjects in our tale. They arose, and finished the slight preparations of their toilettes in a clear, cold atmosphere, that penetrated through all the defences of even Miss Temple's warm room. When Elizabeth was attired, she approached a window and drew its curtain, and, throwing open its shutters, she endeavoured to look abroad on the village and the lake. But a thick covering of frost, on the panes of glass, while it admitted the light, hid the view. She raised the sash, and then, indeed, a most glorious scene met her delighted eye.

The lake had exchanged its covering of unspotted snow, for a face of dark ice, that reflected the rays of the rising sun, like a polished mirror. The houses were clothed in a dress of the same description, but which, owing to its position, shone like bright steel; while the enormous icicles that were pendent from every roof, caught the brilliant light, apparently throwing it from one to the other, as each glittered, on the side next to the luminary, with a golden lustre, that melted away, on its opposite, into the dusky shades of a background. But it was the appearance of the boundless forests, that covered the hills, as they rose, in the distance, one over the other, that most attracted the gaze of Miss Temple. The huge branches of the pines and hemlocks, on the western mountains, bent with the weight of the ice they supported, while their summits rose above the swelling tops of the oaks, beeches, and maples, like spires of burnished silver issuing from domes of the same material. The limits of the view, in this direction, were marked by an undulating outline of bright light, as if, reversing the order of nature, numberless suns might momentarily be expected to heave above the western horizon. In the foreground of the picture, along shores of the lake, and near to the village, each tree seemed studded with diamonds, that emitted their dancing rays, as the branches waved gently under the impulse of the air. Even the sides of the mountains where the rays of the sun could not yet fall, were decorated with a glassy coat, that presented every gradation of brilliancy, from the first touch of the luminary to the dark foliage of the hemlock, glistening through its coat of crystal. In short, the whole view was one scene of quivering radiancy, as lake, mountains, village, and woods, each emitted a portion of light, tinged with its peculiar hue, and varied by its position and its magnitude.

"See!" cried Elizabeth—"see, Louisa; hasten to the window, and observe the miraculous change."

Miss Grant complied; and, after bending for a moment in silence from the opening, she observed, in a low tone, as if afraid to trust the sound of her voice—

"The change is indeed wonderful! I am surprised that he should be able to effect it so soon."

Elizabeth turned in amazement, to hear such a skeptical sentiment from one educated like her companion; but was surprised to find that, instead of looking at the view, the mild, blue eyes of Miss Grant were dwelling on the form of a well-dressed young man, who was standing before the door of the building, in earnest conversation with her father. A second look was necessary, before she was able to recognise the person of the young hunter, in a plain, but assuredly, the ordinary garb of a gentleman.

"Every thing in this magical country seems to border on the marvellous," said Elizabeth; "and among all the changes, this is certainly not the least wonderful. I am not surprised, that your eye caught this transformation, without noticing the changes in the view. The actors are as unique as the scenery."

Miss Grant coloured highly, and drew in her head, as she answered—

"I am a simple girl, Miss Temple, and I am afraid you will find me but a poor companion. I—I am not sure that I understand all that you say. But I really thought that you wished me to notice the alteration in Mr. Edwards. Is it not more wonderful, when we recollect his origin? They say he is part Indian."

"He is certainly a genteel savage," returned the smiling Elizabeth. "But let us go down, and give the Sachem his tea;

—for I suppose he is a descendant of King Philip, if not a grandson of Pocahontas."

The ladies were met in the hall by Judge Temple, who took his daughter aside, to apprise her of that alteration in the appearance of their new inmate with which she was already acquainted.

"He appears reluctant to converse on his former situation," continued Marmaduke; "but I gather from his discourse, as is apparent from his manner, that he has seen better days; and I really am inclining to the opinion of Richard, as to his origin; for it was no unusual thing for the Indian Agents to rear their children in a laudable manner, and——"

"Very well, my dear sir," interrupted his daughter, laughing and averting her eyes; "it is all well enough, I dare say; but as I do not understand a word of the Mohawk language, he must be content to speak English; and as for his behavior, I trust to your discernment to control it."

"Ay! but, Bess," said the Judge, detaining her gently with his hand, "nothing must be said to him of his past life. This he has begged particularly of me, as a favour. He is, perhaps, a little soured, just now, with his wounded arm; but the injury seems very light, and another time he may be more communicative."

"Oh! I am not much troubled, sir, with that laudable thirst after knowledge, that is called curiosity. I shall believe him to be the child of Corn-stalk, or Corn-planter, or some other renowned chieftain; possibly of the Big Snake himself; and shall treat him as such, until he sees fit to shave his good-looking head, borrow some half-dozen pair of my best earrings, shoulder his rifle again, and disappear as suddenly as he made his entrance. So come, my dear sir, and let us not forget the rites of hospitality, for the short time he is to remain with us."

Judge Temple smiled at the graceful playfulness of his child, and taking her arm, they entered the breakfast parlour, where the young hunter was seated, with an air that showed his determination to domesticate himself in the family, with as little parade as possible.

Such were the incidents that led to this extraordinary increase in the family of Judge Temple, where, having once established the youth, the subject of our tale requires us to leave him, for a time, to pursue with diligence and intelligence, the employments that were assigned him by Marmaduke.

Major Hartmann made his customary visit, and took his leave of the party, for the next three months. Mr. Grant was compelled to be absent much of his time, in remote parts of the country, and his daughter became almost a constant visiter at the Mansion-house. Richard entered, with his constitutional eagerness, on the duties of his new office; and, as Marmaduke was much employed, with the constant applications of adventurers for farms, the winter passed swiftly away. The lake was a principal scene for the amusements of the young people; where the ladies, in their one-horse cutter, driven by Richard, and attended, when the snow would admit of it, by young Edwards, on his skates, spent many hours, taking the benefit of exercise in the clear air of the hills. The reserve of the youth gradually gave way to time and his situation, though it was still evident, to a close observer, that he had frequent moments of bitter and intense feeling.

Elizabeth saw many large openings appear in the sides of the mountains, during the three succeeding months, where different settlers had, in the language of the country, "made their pitch;" while the numberless sleighs that passed through the village, loaded with wheat and barrels of pot-ashes, afforded a clear demonstration that all these labours were not undertaken in vain. In short, the whole country was exhibiting the bustle of a thriving settlement, where the highways were thronged with sleighs, bearing piles of rough household furniture; studded, here and there, with the smiling faces of women and children, happy in the excitement of novelty; or with loads of produce, hastening to the common market at Albany, as served as so many snares, to induce the emigrants to enter into those wild mountains in search of competence and happiness.

The village was alive with business; the artisans increasing in wealth with the prosperity of the country, and each day witnessing some nearer approach to the manners and usages of an old-settled town. The man who carried the mail, or "the post," as he was called, talked much of running a stage, and once or twice, during the winter, he was seen taking a single passenger in his cutter, through the snow-banks towards the Mohawk, along which a regular vehicle glided, semi-weekly, with the velocity of lightning, and under the direction of a knowing whip from the "down countries." Towards spring, divers families, who had been into the "old states," to see their relatives, returned, in time to save the snow, frequently bringing with them whole neighborhoods, who were tempted by their representations to leave the farms of Connecticut and Massachusetts, and make a trial in the woods for fortune.

During all this time, Oliver Edwards, whose sudden elevation excited no surprise in that changeful country, was earnestly engaged in the service of Marmaduke, during the days; but his nights were often spent in the hut of Leather-stocking. The intercourse between the three hunters was maintained with a certain air of mystery, it is true, but with much zeal and apparent interest to all the parties. Even Mohegan seldom came to the Mansion-house, and Natty, never; but Edwards sought every leisure moment to visit his former abode, from which he would often return in the gloomy hours of night, through the snow, or, if detained beyond the time at which the family retired to rest, with the morning sun. These visits certainly excited much speculation in those to whom they were known, but no comments were made, excepting occasionally, in whispers from Richard, who would say—

"It is not at all remarkable;—a half-breed can never be weaned from the savage ways, any more than a full-blooded Indian."

· *Chapter XX* ·

Away! nor let me loiter in my song,
For we have many a mountain path to tread.
BYRON

As the spring gradually approached, the immense piles of snow, that by alternate thaws and frosts, and repeated storms, had obtained a firmness that threatened a tiresome durability, began to yield to the influence of milder breezes and a warmer sun. The gates of Heaven at times seemed to open, and a bland air diffused itself over the earth, when animate and inanimate nature would awaken, and, for a few hours, the gayety of spring shone in every eye, and smiled on every field. But the shivering blasts from the north would carry their chill influence over the scene again, and the dark and gloomy clouds that intercepted the rays of the sun, were not more cold and dreary, than the reaction which crossed the creation. These struggles between the seasons became, daily, more frequent, while the earth, like a victim to contention, slowly lost the animated brilliancy of winter, without obtaining the decided aspect of spring.

Several weeks were consumed in this cheerless manner, during which the inhabitants of the country gradually changed their pursuits from the social and bustling movements of the time of snow, to the laborious and domestic engagements of the coming season. The village was no longer thronged with visiters; the trade, that had enlivened the shops for several months, began to disappear; the highways lost their shining coats of beaten snow in impassable sloughs, and were deserted by the gay and noisy travellers who, in sleighs, had, during the winter, glided along their windings; and, in short, everything seemed indicative of a mighty change, not only in the earth itself, but in those also, who derived their sources of comfort and happiness from her bosom.

The younger members of the family in the Mansion-house, of which Louisa Grant was now habitually one, were by no means indifferent observers of these fluctuating and tardy changes. While the snow rendered the roads passable, they had partaken largely in the amusements of the winter, which included not only daily rides over the mountains, and through every valley within twenty miles of them, but divers ingenious and varied sources of pleasure, on the bosom of their frozen lake. There had been rides in the equipage of Richard, when, with his four horses, he had outstripped the winds with its speed, as it flew over the glassy ice which invariably succeeded a thaw. Then the exciting and dangerous "whirligig" would be suffered to possess its moment of notice. Cutters, drawn by a single horse, and hand-sleds, impelled by the gentlemen, on skates, would each in their turn be used; and, in short, every source of relief against the tediousness of a winter in the mountains was resorted to by the family. Elizabeth was compelled to acknowledge to her father, that the season, with the aid of his library, was much less irksome than she had anticipated.

As exercise in the open air, was in some degree necessary to the habits of the family, when the constant recurrence of frosts and thaws rendered the roads, which were dangerous, at the most favourable times, utterly impassable for wheels, saddle horses were used as substitutes for their other conveyances. Mounted on small and sure-footed beasts, the ladies would again attempt the passages of the mountains, and penetrate into every retired glen, where the enterprise of a settler had induced him to establish himself. In these excursions they were attended by some one or all of the gentlemen of the family, as their different pursuits admitted. Young Edwards was hourly becoming more familiarized to his situation, and not unfrequently mingled in their parties, with an unconcern and gayety, that for a short time, would, apparently, expel all unpleasant recollections from his mind. Habit, and the buoyancy of youth, seemed to be getting the ascendency over the secret causes of his uneasiness; though there were moments, when the same remarkable expression of disgust would cross his intercourse with Marmaduke, that had distinguished their conversations in the first days of their acquaintance.

It was at the close of the month of March, that the Sheriff succeeded in persuading his cousin and her young friend to accompany him in a ride to a hill, that was said to overhang the lake in a manner peculiar to itself.

"Besides, cousin Bess," continued the indefatigable Richard, "we will stop and see the 'sugar bush' of Billy Kirby; he is on the east end of the Ransom lot, making sugar for Jared Ransom. There is not a better hand over a kettle in the county, than that same Kirby. You remember, 'duke, that I had him his first season, in our own camp; and it is not a wonder that he knows something of his trade."

"He's a good chopper, is Billy," observed Benjamin, who held the bridle of the horse while the Sheriff mounted; "and he handles an axe, much the same as a forecastle-man does his marling spike, or a tailor his goose. They say he'll lift a potash kettle off the arch with his own hands, thof I can't say that I've ever seen him do it with my own eyes; but that is the say. And I've seen sugar of his making, which, maybe, wasn't as white as an old top-gallantsail, but which my friend Mistress Pretty-bones, within there, said, had the true molasses smack to it; and you are not the one, Squire Dickens, to be told that Mistress Remarkable has a remarkable tooth for sweet things in her nut grinder."

The loud laugh that succeeded the wit of Benjamin, and in which he participated, with no very harmonious sounds, himself, very fully illustrated the congenial temper which existed between the pair. Most of its point was, however, lost on the rest of the party, who were either mounting their horses, or assisting the ladies to do so, at the moment. When all were safely in their saddles, the whole moved through the village in great order. They paused for a moment, before the door of Monsieur Le Quoi, until he could bestride his steed, and then issuing from the little cluster of houses, they took one of the principal highways, that centred in the village.

As each night brought with it a severe frost, which the heat of the succeeding day served to dissipate, the equestrians were compelled to proceed singly, along the margin of the road, where the turf, and firmness of the ground, gave their horses a secure footing. Very trifling indications of approaching vegetation were to be seen, the surface of the earth presenting a cold, wet, and cheerless aspect that almost chilled the blood of the spectator. The snow yet lay scattered over most of those distant clearings that were visible in different parts of the mountains; though here and there an opening might be seen, where, as the white covering yielded to the season, the bright and lively green of the wheat served to enkindle the hopes of the husbandman. Nothing could be more marked, than the contrast between the earth and the heavens; for, while the former presented the dreary view that we have described, a warm and invigorating sun was dispensing his heats, from a sky that contained but a solitary cloud, that lingered near the mountain, and through an atmosphere that softened the colours of the sensible horizon until it shone like a sea of virgin blue.

Richard led the way, on this, as on all other occasions, that did not require the exercise of unusual abilities; and as he moved along, he essayed to enliven the party with the sounds of his experienced voice.

"This is your true sugar weather, 'duke," he cried; "a frosty night and a sunshiny day. I warrant me that the sap runs like a mill-tail up the maples this warm morning. It is a pity, Judge, that you do not introduce a little more science into the manufactory of sugar among your tenants. It might be done, sir, without knowing as much as Doctor Franklin—it might be done, Judge Temple."

"The first object of my solicitude, friend Jones," returned Marmaduke, "is to protect the sources of this great mine of comfort and wealth from the extravagance of the people themselves. When this important point shall be achieved, it will be in season to turn our attention to an improvement in the manufacture of the article. But thou knowest, Richard, that I have already subjected our sugar to the process of the refiner, and that the result has produced loaves as white as the snow on yon fields, and possessing the saccharine quality in its utmost purity."

"Saccharine, or turpentine, or any other 'ine, Judge Temple, you have never made a loaf larger than a good sized sugar-plum," returned the Sheriff. "Now, sir, I assert that no experiment is fairly tried, until it be reduced to practical purposes. If, sir, I owned a hundred, or, for that matter, two hundred thousand acres of land, as you do, I would build a sugar-house in the village; I would invite learned men to an investigation of the subject,—and such are easily to be found, sir; yes, sir, they are not difficult to find,—men who unite theory with practice; and I would select a wood of young and thrifty trees; and instead of making loaves of the size of a lump of candy, dam'me, 'duke, but I'd have them as big as a hay-cock."

"And purchase the cargo of one of those ships that, they say, are going to China," cried Elizabeth; "turn your potash-kettles into teacups, the scows on the lakes into saucers; bake your cake in yonder lime-kiln, and invite the county to a tea-party. How wonderful are the projects of genius! Really, sir, the world is of the opinion that Judge Temple has tried the experiment fairly, though he did not cause his loaves to be cast in moulds of the magnitude that would suit your magnificent conceptions."

"You may laugh, cousin Elizabeth—you may laugh, madam," retorted Richard, turning himself so much in his saddle as to face the party, and making extremely dignified gestures with his whip; "but I appeal to common sense, good sense, or what is of more importance than either, to the sense of taste, which is one of the five natural senses, whether a big loaf of sugar is not likely to contain a better illustration of a proposition than such a lump as one of your Dutch women puts under her tongue when she drinks her tea. There are two ways of doing every thing; the right way, and the wrong way. You make sugar now, I will admit, and you may, possibly, make loaf-sugar; but I take the question to be, whether you make the best possible sugar, and into the best possible loaves."

"Thou art very right, Richard," observed Marmaduke, with a gravity in his air, that proved how much he was interested in the subject. "It is very true that we manufacture sugar, but the inquiry is quite useful to make, how much? and in what

manner? I hope to live to see the day, when farms and plantations shall be devoted to this branch of business. Little is
known concerning the properties of the tree itself, the source
of all this wealth; how much it may be improved by cultivation, by the use of the hoe and plough."

"Hoe and plough," roared the Sheriff;—"would you set a
man hoeing round the root of a maple like this,"—pointing to
one of those noble trees, that occur so frequently in that part
of the country.—"Hoeing trees! are you mad, 'duke? This is
next to hunting for coal! Poh! poh! my dear cousin, hear reason, and leave the management of the sugarbush to me. Here
is Mr. Le Quoi, he has been in the West-Indies, and seen sugar
made often. Let him give an account of how it is made there,
and you will hear the philosophy of the thing.—Well, Monsieur, how is it that you make sugar in the West-Indies; any
thing in Judge Temple's fashion?"

The gentleman to whom this query was put, was mounted on
a small horse, of no very fiery temperament, and was riding
with his stirrups so short, as to bring his knees, while the animal rose a small ascent in the wood-path they were now travelling, into a somewhat hazardous vicinity to his chin. There
was no room for gesticulation or grace in the delivery of his
reply, for the mountain was steep and slippery; and although
the Gaul had an eye of uncommon magnitude on either side
of his face, they did not seem to be half competent to forewarn
him of the impediments of bushes, twigs and fallen trees, that
were momentarily crossing his path. With one hand employed
in averting these dangers, and the other grasping his bridle,
to check an untoward speed that his horse was assuming, the
native of France responded as follows—

"Sucre! dey do make eet in Martinique: mais—mais eet
is not from von tree; eet is from—ah—ah—vat you call—Je
voudrois que ces chemins fussent au diable—vat you call—
von steeck pour le promenade."

"Cane," said Elizabeth, smiling at the imprecation which
the wary Frenchman supposed was understood only by himself.

"Oui, Mam'selle, cane."

"Yes, yes," cried Richard, "cane is the vulgar name for it,

but the real term is saccharum officinarum; and what we call the sugar, or hard maple, is acer saccharinum. These are the learned names, Monsieur, and are such as, doubtless, you well understand."

"Is this Greek or Latin, Mr. Edwards?" whispered the heiress to the youth, who was opening a passage for herself and her companions through the bushes—"or perhaps it is a still more learned language, for an interpretation of which we must look to you."

The dark eye of the young man glanced towards the maiden, with a keenness bordering on ferocity; but its expression changed, in a moment, to the smiling playfulness of her own face, as he answered—

"I shall remember your doubts, Miss Temple, when next I visit my old friend Mohegan, and either his skill, or that of Leather-stocking shall solve them."

"And are you then, really ignorant of their language?" asked Elizabeth, with an impetuosity that spoke a lively interest in the reply.

"Not absolutely; but the deep learning of Mr. Jones is more familiar to me, or even the polite masquerade of Monsieur Le Quoi."

"Do you speak French?" said the lady, with a quickness that equalled her former interest.

"It is a common language with the Iroquois, and through the Canadas," he answered with an equivocal smile.

"Ah! but they are Mingoes, and your enemies."

"It will be well for me, if I have no worse," said the youth, dashing ahead with his horse, and thus putting an end to the evasive dialogue.

The discourse, however, was maintained with great vigour by Richard, until they reached an open wood on the summit of the mountain, where the hemlocks and pines totally disappeared, and a grove of the very trees that formed the subject of debate, covered the earth with their tall, straight trunks and spreading branches, in stately pride. The underwood had been entirely removed from this grove, or bush, as in conjunction with the simple arrangements for boiling, it was called, and a wide space of many acres was cleared, which might be likened to the dome of a mighty temple, to which the maples, with their stems formed the columns, their tops composing the capitals, and the heavens the arch. A deep and careless incision had been made into each tree, near its root, into which little spouts, formed of the bark of the alder, or of the sumach, were fastened; and a trough, roughly dug out of the linden, or basswood, was lying at the root of each tree, to catch the sap that flowed from this extremely wasteful and inartificial arrangement.

The party paused a moment, on gaining the flat, to breathe their horses, and, as the scene was entirely new to several of their number, to view the manner of collecting the fluid. A fine powerful voice aroused them from their momentary silence, as it rung under the branches of the trees, singing the following words of that inimitable doggerel, whose verses, if extended, would reach from the waters of the Connecticut to the shores of Ontario. The tune was, of course, that familiar air, which, although it is said to have been first applied to his nation in derision, circumstances have since rendered so glorious, that no American ever hears its jingling cadence, without feeling a thrill at his heart.

> "The Eastern States be full of men,
> The Western full of woods, Sir!
> The hills be like a cattle pen,
> The roads be full of goods sir!
> Then flow away, my sweety sap,
> And I will make you boily;
> Nor catch a woodman's hasty nap,
> For fear you should get roily.

> "The maple tree's a precious one,
> 'Tis fuel, food, and timber;
> And when your stiff day's work is done.
> Its juice will make you limber.
> Then flow away, &c.

> "And what's a man without his glass,
> His wife without her tea, sir?
> But neither cup nor mug will pass,
> Without this honey-bee, sir!
> Then flow away," &c.

During the execution of this sonorous ditty, Richard kept time with his whip on the mane of his charger, accompanying the gestures with a corresponding movement of his head and body. Towards the close of the song, he was overheard humming the chorus, and at its last repetition, to strike in as "sweety sap," and carry a second through, with a prodigious addition to the "effect" of the noise, if not to that of the harmony.

"Well done us!" roared the Sheriff, on the same key with the tune; "a very good song, Billy Kirby, and very well sung. Where got you the words, lad? is there more of it, and can you furnish me with a copy?"

The sugar-boiler, who was busy in his "camp," at a short distance from the equestrians, turned his head with great indifference, and surveyed the party, as they approached, with admirable coolness. To each individual, as he or she rode close by him, he gave a nod that was extremely good-natured and affable, but which partook largely of the virtue of equality, for not even to the ladies did he in the least vary his mode of salutation, by touching the apology for a hat that he wore, or by any other motion than the one we have mentioned.

"How goes it, how goes it, Sheriff?" said the woodchopper; "what's the good word to-day?"

"Why, much as usual, Billy," returned Richard. "But how is this! where are your four kettles, and your troughs, and your iron coolers? Do you make sugar in this slovenly way! I thought you were one of the best sugar-boilers in the county."

"I'm all that, Squire Jones," said Kirby, who continued in his occupation; "I'll turn my back to no man in the Otsego hills for chopping and logging; for boiling down the maple sap; for tending brick-kiln; splitting out rails; making potash, and parling too; or hoeing corn. Though I keep myself, pretty much, to the first business, seeing that the axe comes most nateral to me."

"You be von Jack All-trade, Mister Beel," said Monsieur Le Quoi.

"How?" said Kirby, looking up, with a simplicity which coupled with his gigantic frame and manly face, was a little ridiculous—"if you be for trade, Mounsher, here is some as good sugar as you'll find the season through. It's as clear from dirt as the Garman Flats is from stumps, and it has the raal maple flavour. Such stuff would sell in York for candy."

The Frenchman approached the place where Kirby had deposited his cakes of sugar, under the cover of a bark roof, and commenced the examination of the article, with the eye of one who well understood its value. Marmaduke had dismounted, and was viewing the works and the trees very closely, and not without frequent expressions of dissatisfaction, at the careless manner in which the manufacture was conducted.

"You have much experience in these things, Kirby," he said; "what is the course you pursue in making your sugar? I see that you have but two kettles."

"Two is as good as two thousand, Judge; I'm none of your polite sugar-makers, that boils for the great folks; but if the raal sweet maple is wanted, I can answer your turn. First, I choose, and then I tap my trees; say along about the last of February, or in these mountains, maybe not afore the middle of March; but any way, just as the sap begins to cleverly run——"

"Well, in this choice," interrupted Marmaduke, "are you governed by any outward signs that prove the quality of the tree?"

"Why, there's judgment in all things," said Kirby, stirring the liquor in his kettles briskly. "There's something in knowing when and how much to stir the pot. It's a thing that must be larnt. Rome wasn't built in a day, nor, for that matter, Templetown 'ither, though it may be said to be a quick-growing place. I never put my axe into a stunty tree, or one that hasn't a good, fresh-looking bark; for trees have disorders just like creaters: and where's the policy of taking a tree that's sickly, any more than you'd choose a foundered horse to ride post, or an overheated ox to do your logging——"

"All this is true: But what are your signs of illness? how do you distinguish a tree that is well from one that is diseased?"

"How does the doctor tell who has fever, and who colds?" interrupted Richard—"by examining the skin, and feeling the pulse, to be sure."

"Sartain," continued Billy, "the Squire an't far out of the

way. It's by the look of the thing, sure enough.—Well, when the sap begins to get a free run, I hang over the kettles, and set up the bush. My first boiling I push pretty smart, till I get the vartoo of the sap; but when it begins to grow of a molasses nater, like this in the kettle, one musn't drive the fires too hard, or you'll burn the sugar: and burny sugar is always bad to the taste, let it be never so sweet. So you ladle out from one kettle into the other, till it gets so, when you put the stirring stick into it, that it will draw into a thread: when it takes a kerful hand to manage it. There is a way to drain it off, after it has grained, by putting clay into the pans: but it isn't always practysed: some doos, and some doosn't.—Well, Mounsher, be we likely to make a trade?"

"I vill give you, Mister Beel, for von pound—dix sous."

"No, I expect cash for't: I never dicker away my sugar. But, seeing that it's you, Mounsher," said Billy, with a coaxing smile, "I'll agree to take a gallon of rum, and cloth enough for two shirts, if you will take the molasses in the bargain. It's raal good: I wouldn't deceive you or any man: and to my drinking it's about the best molasses I ever seed come out of a sugar-bush."

"Mr. Le Quoi has offered you ten pence," said young Edwards.

The manufacturer stared at the speaker, with an air of great freedom, but made no reply.

"Oui," said the Frenchman, "ten penny. Je vous remercie, Monsieur: ah! mon Anglois! je l'oublie toujours."

The wood-chopper looked from one to the other, with some displeasure: and evidently imbibed the opinion that they were amusing themselves at his expense. He seized the enormous ladle, which was lying in one of his kettles, and began to stir the boiling liquid with great diligence. After a moment, passed in dipping the ladle full, and then raising it on high, as the thick rich fluid fell back into the kettle, he suddenly gave it a whirl, as if to cool what yet remained, and offered the bowl to Mr. Le Quoi, saying—

"Taste that, Mounsher, and I guess you will say it is worth more than you offer. The molasses itself would fetch twice the money."

The complaisant Frenchman, after several timid efforts to trust his lips in contact with the bowl of the ladle, got a good swallow of the scalding liquid. He clapped his hand on his breast, and looked most piteously at the ladies, for a single instant, and then, to use the language of Billy, when he afterwards recounted the tale, "no drumsticks ever went faster on the skin of a sheep, than the Frenchman's legs, for a round or two: and then, such swearing and spitting, in French, you never seen. But it's a knowing one, from the old countries, that thinks to get his jokes smoothly over a Yankee wood-chopper."

The air of innocence with which Kirby resumed the occupation of stirring the contents of his kettle, would have completely deceived the spectators, as to his agency in the temporary suffering of Mr. Le Quoi, had not the reckless fellow thrust his tongue into his cheek, and cast his eyes over the party, with a simplicity of expression that was too exquisite to be true to nature. Mr. Le Quoi soon recovered his presence of mind, and his decorum; he briefly apologized to the ladies for one or two very intemperate expressions, that had escaped him in a moment of extraordinary excitement, and remounting his horse, he continued in the back-ground during the remainder of their visit, the wit of Kirby putting a violent termination, at once, to all negotiations on the subject of trade. During all this time, Marmaduke had been wandering about the grove, making his observations on his favourite trees, and the wasteful manner in which the wood-chopper conducted his manufacture.

"It grieves me to witness the extravagance that pervades this country," said the Judge, "where the settlers trifle with the blessings they might enjoy, with the prodigality of successful adventurers. You are not exempt from the censure yourself, Kirby, for you make dreadful wounds in these trees, where a small incision would effect the same object. I earnestly beg you will remember, that they are the growth of centuries, and when once gone, none living will see their loss remedied."

"Why, I don't know, Judge," returned the man he addressed: "It seems to me, if there's a plenty of any thing in this mountaynious country, it's the trees. If there's any sin in chopping them, I've a pretty heavy account to settle; for I've chopped over the best half of a thousand acres, with my own hands, counting both Varmount and York states; and I hope to live to finish the whull, before I lay up my axe. Chopping comes quite nateral to me, and I wish no other empl'yment; but Jared Ransom said that he thought the sugar was likely to be scarce this season, seeing that so many folks was coming into the settlement, and so I concluded to take the 'bush' on sheares for this one spring. What's the best news, Judge, consarning ashes? do pots hold so that a man can live by them still? I s'pose that they will if they keep on fighting."

"Thou reasonest with judgement, William," returned Marmaduke. "So long as the old world is to be convulsed with wars, so long will the harvest in America continue."

"Well it's an ill wind, Judge, that blows nobody any good. I'm sure the country is in a thriving way; and, though I know you calkilate greatly on the trees, setting as much store by them as some men would by their children, yet, to my eyes they are a sore sight at any time, unless I'm privileged to work my will on them; in which case, I can't say but that they are more to my liking. I have heern the settlers from the old countries say, that their rich men keep great oaks and elms, that would make a barrel of pots to the tree, standing round their doors and humsteads, and scattered over their farms, just to look on. Now, I call no country much improved, that is pretty well covered with trees. Stumps are a different thing, for they don't shade the land; and besides, if you dig them, they will make a fence that will turn any thing bigger than a hog, being grand for breachy cattle."

"Our notions on such subjects vary much, in different countries," said Marmaduke; "but it is not as ornaments that I value the noble trees of this country, it is for their usefulness. We are stripping the forests, as if a single year would replace what we destroy. But the hour approaches, when the laws will take notice of not only the woods but the game they contain also."

With this consoling reflection, Marmaduke remounted, and the equestrians passed the sugar-camp, on their way to the promised landscape of Richard. The wood-chopper was left alone, in the bosom of the forest to pursue his labours. Elizabeth turned her head, when they reached the point where they were to descend the mountain, and thought that the slow fires, that were glimmering under his enormous kettles, his little brush shelter, covered with pieces of hemlock bark, his gigantic size, as he wielded his ladle with a steady and knowing air, aided by the background of stately trees, with their spouts and troughs, formed, altogether, no unreal picture of human life in its first stages of civilization. Perhaps whatever the scene possessed of a romantic character was not injured by the powerful tones of Kirby's voice, ringing through the woods, as he again awoke his strains to another tune, which was but little more scientific than the former. All that she understood of the words, were——

> "And when the proud forest is falling,
>   To my oxen cheerfully calling,
>   From morn until night I am bawling,
>   Woe, back there, and hoy and gee;
>   Till our labour is mutually ended,
>   By my strength and cattle befriended,
>   And against the musquitoes defended,
>   By the bark of the walnut-tree.——

>> "Away! then, you lads who would buy land,
>>   Choose the oak that grows on the high land,
>>   Or the silvery pine on the dry land,
>>   It matters but little to me."

· Chapter XXI ·

Speed! Malise, speed! such cause of haste
Thine active sinews never brac'd.

SCOTT

The roads of Otsego, if we except the principal highways, were, at the early day of our tale, but little better than wood-paths of unusual width. The high trees that were growing on the very verge of the wheel-tracks, excluded the sun's rays, unless at meridian, and the slowness of the evaporation, united with the rich mould of vegetable decomposition, that covered the whole county, to the depth of several inches, occasioned but an indifferent foundation for the footing of travellers. Added to these, there were the inequalities of a natural surface, and the constant recurrence of enormous and slippery roots, that were laid bare by the removal of the light soil, together with stumps of trees, to make a passage not only difficult but dangerous. Yet the riders, among these numerous obstructions, which were such as would terrify an unpractised eye, gave no demonstrations of uneasiness, as their horses toiled through the sloughs, or trotted with uncertain paces along their dark route. In many places, the marks on the trees were the only indications of a road, with, perhaps, an occasional remnant of a pine, that, by being cut close to the earth, so as to leave nothing visible but its base of roots, spreading for twenty feet in every direction, was apparently placed there as a beacon, to warn the traveller that it was the centre of the highway.

Into one of these roads the active Sheriff led the way, first striking out of the footpath, by which they had descended from the sugar-bush, across a little bridge, formed of round logs laid loosely on sleepers of pine, in which large openings were frequent, and in one instance, of a formidable width. The nag of Richard, when it reached this barrier, laid its nose along the logs, and stepped across the difficult passage with the sagacity of a man; but the blooded filly which Miss Temple rode disdained so humble a movement. She made a step or two with an unusual caution, and then, on reaching the broadest opening, obedient to the curb and whip of her fearless mistress, she bounded across the dangerous pass, with the activity of a squirrel.

"Gently, gently, my child," said Marmaduke, who was following in the manner of Richard—"this is not a country for equestrian feats. Much prudence is requisite, to journey through our rough paths with safety. Thou mayst practise thy skill in horsemanship on the plains of New Jersey, with safety, but in the hills of Otsego, they must be suspended for a time."

"I may as well, then, relinquish my saddle at once, dear sir," returned his daughter; "for if it is to be laid aside until this wild country be improved, old age will overtake me, and put an end to what you term my equestrian feats."

"Say not so, my child," returned her father; "but if thou venturest again, as in crossing this bridge, old age will never overtake thee, but I shall be left to mourn thee, cut off in thy pride, my Elizabeth. If thou hadst seen this district of country, as I did, when it lay in the sleep of nature, and witnessed its rapid changes, as it awoke to supply the wants of man, thou wouldst curb thy impatience for a little time, though thou shouldst not check thy steed."

"I have a remembrance of hearing you speak, sir, of your first visit to these woods, but the recollection of it is faint, and blended with the confused images of childhood. Wild and unsettled as it may yet seem, it must have been a thousand times more dreary then. Will you repeat, dear sir, what you then thought of your enterprise, and what you felt?"

During this speech of Elizabeth, which was uttered with the interested fervour of affection, young Edwards rode more closely to the side of the Judge, and bent his dark eyes on his countenance with an expression that seemed to read his thoughts.

"Thou wast then young, my child, but must remember when I left thee and thy mother, to take my first survey of these uninhabited mountains," said Marmaduke. "But thou dost not feel all the secret motives that can urge a man to endure privations in order to accumulate wealth. In my case they have not been trifling, and God has been pleased to smile on my efforts. If I have encountered pain, famine, and disease, in accomplishing the settlement of this rough territory, I have not the misery of failure to add to the grievances."

"Famine!" echoed Elizabeth; "I thought this was the land of abundance! had you famine to contend with?"

"Even so, my child," said her father. "Those who look around them now, and see the loads of produce that issue out of every wild path in these mountains, during the season of travelling, will hardly credit that no more than five years have elapsed, since the tenants of these woods were compelled to eat the scanty fruits of the forest to sustain life, and with their unpractised skill, to hunt the beasts as food for their starving families."

"Ay!" cried Richard, who happened to overhear the last of this speech, between the notes of the wood-chopper's song, which he was endeavouring to breathe aloud; "that was the starving-time, cousin Bess. I grew as lank as a weasel that fall, and my face was as pale as one of your fever-and-ague visages. Monsieur Le Quoi, there, fell away like a pumpkin in drying; nor do I think you have got fairly over it yet, Monsieur. Benjamin, I thought, bore it with a worse grace than any of the family, for he swore it was harder to endure than a short allowance in the calm latitudes. Benjamin is a sad fellow to swear, if you starve him ever so little. I had half a mind to quit you then, 'duke, and go into Pennsylvania to fatten; but, damn it, thinks I, we are sisters' children, and I will live or die with him, after all."

"I do not forget thy kindness," said Marmaduke, "nor that we are of one blood."

"But my dear father," cried the wondering Elizabeth, "was there actual suffering? where were the beautiful and fertile vales of the Mohawk? could they not furnish food for your wants?"

"It was a season of scarcity; the necessities of life commanded a high price in Europe, and were greedily sought after by the speculators. The emigrants, from the east to the west, invariably passed along the valley of the Mohawk, and swept away the means of subsistence, like a swarm of locusts. Nor were the people on the Flats in a much better condition. They were in want themselves, but they spared the little excess of provisions, that nature did not absolutely require, with the justice of the German character. There was no grinding of the poor. The word speculator was then unknown to them. I have seen many a stout man, bending under the load of the bag of meal, which he was carrying from the mills of the Mohawk, through the rugged passes of these mountains, to feed his half-famished children, with a heart so light, as he approached his hut, that the thirty miles he had passed seemed nothing. Remember, my child, it was in our very infancy, we had neither mills nor grain, nor roads, nor often clearings;—we had nothing of increase, but the mouths that were to be fed; for, even at that inauspicious moment, the restless spirit of emigration was not idle, nay, the general scarcity, which extended to the east, tended to increase the number of adventurers."

"And how, dearest father, didst thou encounter this dreadful evil?" said Elizabeth, unconsciously adopting the dialect of her parent in the warmth of her sympathy. "Upon thee must have fallen all the responsibility, if not the suffering."

"It did, Elizabeth," returned the Judge, pausing for a single moment, as if musing on his former feelings. "I had hundreds, at that dreadful time, daily looking up to me for bread. The sufferings of their families, and the gloomy prospect before them, had paralysed the enterprise and efforts of my settlers; hunger drove them to the woods for food, but despair sent them, at night, enfeebled and wan, to a sleepless pillow. It was not a moment for inaction. I purchased cargoes of wheat from the granaries of Pennsylvania; they were landed at Albany, and brought up the Mohawk in boats; from thence it was transported on pack-horses into the wilderness, and distributed among my people. Seines were made, and the lakes and rivers were dragged for fish. Something like a miracle was wrought in our favour, for enormous shoals of herring were discovered to have wandered five hundred miles, through the windings of the impetuous Susquehanna, and the lake was alive with their numbers. They were at length caught, and dealt out to the people, with proper portions of salt; and from that moment, we again began to prosper."

"Yes," cried Richard, "and I was the man who served out both the fish and the salt. When the poor devils came to receive their rations, Benjamin, who was my deputy, was obliged to keep them off by stretching ropes around me, for they smelt so of garlic, from eating nothing but the wild onion, that the fumes put me out, often, in my measurement. You were a child then, Bess, and knew nothing of the matter, for great care was observed to keep both you and your mother from suffering. That year put me back, dreadfully, both in the breed of my hogs, and of my turkeys."

"No, Bess," cried the Judge, in a more cheerful tone, utterly disregarding the interruption of his cousin, "he who hears of the settlement of a country, knows but little of the actual toil and suffering by which it is accomplished. Unimproved and wild as this district now seems to your eyes, what was it when I first entered the hills! I left my party, the morning of my arrival, back near the farms of the Cherry Valley, and following a deer-path, rode to the summit of the mountain, that I have since called Mount Vision; for the sight that there met my eyes seemed to me as the deceptions of a dream. The fire had run over the pinnacle, and in a great measure, laid open the view. The leaves were fallen, and I mounted a tree, and sat for an hour looking on the silent wilderness. Not an opening was to be seen in the boundless forest, except where the lake lay, like a mirror of glass. The water was covered by myriads of the wild-fowl that migrate with the changes in the season; and while in my situation on the branch of the beech, I saw a bear, with her cubs, descend to the shore to drink. I had met many deer, gliding through the woods, in my journey; but not the vestige of a man could I trace, during my progress, nor from my elevated observatory. No clearing, no hut, none of the winding roads that are now to be seen, were there, nothing but mountains rising behind mountains, and the valley, with its surface of branches, enlivened here and there with the faded foliage of some tree, that parted from its leaves with more than ordinary reluctance. Even the little Susquehanna was then hid, by the height and density of the forest."

"And were you there alone?" asked Elizabeth; "passed you the night in that solitary state?"

"Not so my child," returned her father. "After musing on the scene for an hour, with a mingled feeling of pleasure and desolation, I left my perch and descended the mountain. My horse was left to browse on the twigs that grew within his reach, while I explored the shores of the lake, and the spot where Templeton stands. A pine of more than ordinary growth stood where my dwelling is now placed! A wind-row had been opened through the trees from thence to the lake, and my view was but little impeded. Under the branches of that tree I made my solitary dinner; I had just finished my repast as I saw a smoke curling from under the mountain, near the eastern bank of the lake. It was the only indication of the vicinity of man that I had then seen. After much toil I made my way to the spot, and found a rough cabin of logs, built against the foot of a rock, and bearing the marks of a tenant, though I found no one within it.—"

"It was the hut of Leather-stocking," said Edwards quickly.

"It was; though I, at first, supposed it to be a habitation of the Indians. But while I was lingering around the spot, Natty made his appearance, staggering under the load of the carcass of a buck that he had slain. Our acquaintance commenced at that time; before, I had never heard that such a being tenanted the woods. He launched his bark canoe, and set me across the foot of the lake, to the place where I had fastened my horse, and pointed out a spot where he might get a scanty browsing until the morning; when I returned and passed the night in the cabin of the hunter."

Miss Temple was so much struck by the deep attention of young Edwards, during this speech, that she forgot to resume her interrogatories; but the youth himself continued the discourse, by asking, with a smile lurking around his features—

"And how did the Leather-stocking discharge the duties of a host, sir?"

"Why, simply but kindly, until late in the evening, when he discovered my name and object, and the cordiality of his manner very sensibly diminished, or, I might better say, disappeared. He considered the introduction of the settlers as an innovation on his rights, I believe; for he expressed much dissatisfaction at the measure, though it was in his confused and ambiguous manner. I hardly understood his objections myself, but suppose they referred chiefly to an interruption of the hunting."

"Had you then purchased the estate, or were you examining it with an intent to buy?" asked Edwards, a little abruptly.

"It had been mine for several years. It was with a view to people the land that I visited the lake. Natty treated me hospitably, but coldly, I thought, after he learnt the nature of my journey. I slept on his own bear-skin, however, and in the morning joined my surveyors again."

"Said he nothing of the Indian rights, sir?" continued Edwards. "The Leather-stocking is much given to impeach the justice of the tenure by which the whites hold the country."

"I remember that he spoke of them, but I did not clearly comprehend him, and may have forgotten what he then said; for the Indian title was extinguished so far back as the close of the old war; and if it had not been at all, I hold under the patents of the Royal Governors, confirmed by an act of our own State Legislature, and no court in our country can affect my title."

"Doubtless, sir, your title is both legal and equitable," returned the youth, coldly, reining his horse back, and remaining silent until the subject was changed.

It was seldom that Mr. Jones suffered any conversation to continue, for a great length of time, without his participation. It seems that he was of the party that Judge Temple had designated as his surveyors; and he embraced the opportunity of the pause that succeeded the retreat of young Edwards, to take up the discourse, and with it a narration of their further proceedings, after his own manner. As it wanted, however, the interest that had accompanied the description of the Judge, we must decline the task of committing his sentences to paper.

They soon reached the point where the promised view was to be seen. It was one of those picturesque and peculiar scenes that belong to the Otsego, but which required the absence of the ice, and the softness of a summer's landscape, to be enjoyed in all its beauty. Marmaduke had early forewarned his daughter of the season and of its effect on the prospect, and after casting a cursory glance at its capabilities, the party returned homeward, perfectly satisfied that its beauties would repay them for the toil of a second ride, at a more propitious season.

"The spring is the gloomy time of the American year," said the Judge; "and it is more peculiarly the case in these mountains. The winter seems to retreat to the fastnesses of the hills, as to the citadel of its dominion, and is only expelled, after a tedious seige, in which either party, at times, would seem to be gaining the victory."

"A very just and apposite figure, Judge Temple," observed the Sheriff; "and the garrison under the command of Jack Frost make formidable sorties—you understand what I mean by sorties, Monsieur; sallies, in English—and sometimes drive General Spring and his troops back again into the low countries."

"Yes, sair," returned the Frenchman, whose prominent eyes were watching the precarious footsteps of the beast he rode, as it picked its dangerous way among the roots of trees, holes, log-bridges, and sloughs that formed the aggregate of the highway. "Je vous entend; de low countrie, it ees freeze up for half de year."

The error of Mr. Le Quoi was not noticed by the Sheriff; and the rest of the party were yielding to the influence of the changeful season, that was already teaching the equestrians that a continuance of its mildness was not to be expected for any length of time. Silence and thoughtfulness succeeded the gayety and conversation that had prevailed during the commencement of their ride, as clouds began to gather about the heavens, apparently collecting from every quarter, in quick motion, without the agency of a breath of air.

While riding over one of the cleared eminences that occurred in their route, the watchful eye of Judge Temple pointed out to his daughter the approach of a tempest. Flurries of snow already obscured the mountain that formed the northern boundary of the lake, and the genial sensation which had quickened the blood through their veins was already succeeded by the deadening influence of an approaching *north-wester*.

All of the party were now busily engaged in making the best of their way to the village, though the badness of the roads frequently compelled them to check the impatience of their animals, which often carried them over places that would not admit of any gait faster than a walk.

Richard continued in advance, and was followed by Mr. Le Quoi; next to whom rode Elizabeth, who seemed to have imbibed the distance which pervaded the manner of young Edwards, since the termination of the discourse between the latter and her father. Marmaduke followed his daughter, giving her frequent and tender warnings as to her safety and the management of her horse. It was, possibly, the evident dependence that Louisa Grant placed on his assistance, which induced the youth to continue by her side, as they pursued their way through a dreary and dark wood, where the rays of the sun could but rarely penetrate, and where even the daylight was obscured and rendered gloomy by the deep forests that surrounded them. No wind had yet reached the spot where the equestrians were in motion, but that dead stillness that often precedes a storm, contributed to render their situation more irksome than if they were already subjected to the fury of the tempest. Suddenly the voice of young Edwards was heard shouting, in those appalling tones that carry alarm to the very soul, and which curdle the blood of those that hear them—

"A tree! a tree! whip—spur for your lives! a tree! a tree!"

"A tree! a tree!" echoed Richard, giving his horse a blow that caused the alarmed beast to jump nearly a rod, throwing the mud and water into the air, like a hurricane.

"Von tree! von tree!" shouted the Frenchman, bending his body on the neck of his charger, shutting his eyes, and playing on the ribs of his beast with his heels, at a rate that caused him to be conveyed on the crupper of the Sheriff, with a marvellous speed.

Elizabeth checked her filly, and looked up, with an unconscious but alarmed air, at the very cause of their danger, while she listened to the crackling sounds that awoke the stillness of the forest; but, the next instant, her bridle was seized by her father, who cried—

"God protect my child!" and she felt herself hurried onward, impelled by the vigour of his nervous arm.

Each one of the party bowed to their saddle-bows, as the tearing of branches was succeeded by a sound like the rushing of the winds, which was followed by a thundering report, and a shock that caused the very earth to tremble, as one of the noblest ruins in the forest fell directly across their path.

One glance was enough to assure Judge Temple that his daughter and those in front of him were safe, and he turned his eyes, in dreadful anxiety, to learn the fate of the others. Young Edwards was on the opposite side of the tree, with his form thrown back in his saddle to its utmost distance, his left hand drawing up his bridle with its greatest force, while the right grasped that of Miss Grant, so as to draw the head of her horse under its body. Both the animals stood shaking in every joint with terror, and snorting fearfully. The maiden herself had relinquished her reins, and with her hands pressed on her face sat bending forward in her saddle, in an attitude of despair mingled strongly with resignation.

"Are you safe?" cried the Judge, first breaking the awful silence of the moment.

"By God's blessing," returned the youth; "but if there had been branches to the tree we must have been lost——"

He was interrupted by the figure of Louisa, slowly yielding in her saddle; and but for his arm, she would have sunken to the earth. Terror, however, was the only injury that the clergyman's daughter had sustained, and, with the aid of Elizabeth, she was soon restored to her senses. After some little time was lost in recovering her strength, the young lady was replaced in her saddle, and supported on either side by Judge Temple and Mr. Edwards, she was enabled to follow the party in their slow progress.

"The sudden falling of the trees," said Marmaduke, "are the most dangerous of our accidents in the forest, for they are not to be foreseen, being impelled by no winds, nor any extraneous or visible cause, against which we can guard."

"The reason of their falling, Judge Temple, is very obvious," said the Sheriff. "The tree is old and decayed, and it is gradually weakened by the frosts, until a line drawn from the centre of gravity falls without its base, and then the tree comes of a certainty; and I should like to know, what greater compulsion there can be for any thing, than a mathematical certainty. I studied mathe——"

"Very true, Richard," interrupted Marmaduke; "thy reasoning is true, and if my memory be not over treacherous, was furnished by myself on a former occasion. But how is one to guard against the danger? canst thou go through the forests, measuring the bases, and calculating the centres of the oaks? answer me that, friend Jones, and I will say thou wilt do the country a service."

"Answer thee that, friend Temple!" returned Richard; "a well-educated man can answer thee any thing, sir. Do any trees fall in this manner, but such as are decayed? Take care not to approach the roots of any rotten tree, and you will be safe enough."

"That would be excluding us entirely from the forests," said Marmaduke. "But, happily, the winds usually force down most of these dangerous ruins, as their currents are admitted into the woods by the surrounding clearings, and such a fall as this has been is very rare."

Louisa, by this time, had recovered so much of her strength, as to allow the party to proceed at a quicker pace; but long before they were safely housed, they were overtaken by the storm; and when they dismounted at the door of the Mansion-house, the black plumes in Miss Temple's hat were drooping with the weight of a load of damp snow, and the coats of the gentlemen were powdered with the same material.

While Edwards was assisting Louisa from her horse, the warm-hearted girl caught his hand with fervour, and whispered—

"Now, Mr. Edwards, both father and daughter owe their lives to you."

A driving, northwesterly storm succeeded; and before the sun was set, every vestige of spring had vanished; the lake, the mountains, the village, and the fields, being again hid under one dazzling coat of snow.

· *Chapter XXII* ·

Men, boys, and girls,
Desert th' unpeopled village; and wild crowds
Spread o'er the plain, by the sweet frenzy driven.
                                        SOMERVILLE

From this time to the close of April, the weather continued to be a succession of great and rapid changes. One day, the soft airs of spring would seem to be stealing along the valley, and, in unison with an invigorating sun, attempting, covertly, to rouse the dormant powers of the vegetable world; while on the next, the surly blasts from the north would sweep across the lake, and erase every impression left by their gentle adversaries. The snow, however, finally disappeared, and the green wheat fields were seen in every direction, spotted with the dark and charred stumps that had, the preceding season, supported some of the proudest trees of the forest. Ploughs were in motion, wherever those useful implements could be used, and the smokes of the sugar-camps were no longer seen issuing from the summits of the woods of maple. The lake had lost all the characteristic beauty of a field of ice, but still a dark and gloomy covering concealed its waters, for the absence of currents left them yet hid under a porous crust, which, saturated with the fluid, barely retained enough of its strength to preserve the contiguity of its parts. Large flocks of wild geese were seen passing over the country, which hovered, for a time, around the hidden sheet of water, apparently searching for an opening, where they might find a resting-place; and then, on finding themselves excluded by the chill covering, would soar away to the north, filling the air with their discordant screams, as if venting their complaints at the tardy operations of nature.

For a week, the dark covering of the Otsego was left to the undisturbed possession of two eagles, who alighted on the cen-

tre of its field, and sat proudly eyeing the extent of their undisputed territory. During the presence of these monarchs of the
air, the flocks of migrating birds avoided crossing the plain of
ice, by turning into the hills, apparently seeking the protection
of the forests, while the white and bald heads of the tenants of
the lake were turned upward, with a look of majestic contempt,
as if penetrating to the very heavens with the acuteness of
their vision. But the time had come, when even these kings of
birds were to be dispossessed. An opening had been gradually
increasing, at the lower extremity of the lake, and around the
dark spot where the current of the river had prevented the
formation of ice, during even the coldest weather; and the
fresh southerly winds, that now breathed freely up the valley,
obtained an impression on the waters. Mimic waves began to
curl over the margin of the frozen field, which exhibited an
outline of crystallizations, that slowly receded towards the
north. At each step the power of the winds and the waves increased, until, after a struggle of a few hours, the turbulent little billows succeeded in setting the whole field in an undulating
motion, when it was driven beyond the reach of the eye, with a
rapidity that was as magical as the change produced in the
scene by this expulsion of the lingering remnant of winter.
Just as the last sheet of agitated ice was disappearing in the
distance, the eagles rose over the border of crystals, and
soared with a wide sweep far above the clouds, while the waves
tossed their little caps of snow into the air, as if rioting in their
release from a thraldom of five months' duration.

The following morning Elizabeth was awakened by the exhilarating sounds of the martins, who were quarreling and
chattering around the little boxes that were suspended above
her windows, and the cries of Richard, who was calling, in
tones as animating as the signs of the season itself—

"Awake! awake! my lady fair! the gulls are hovering over
the lake already, and the heavens are alive with the pigeons.
You may look an hour before you can find a hole, through
which to get a peep at the sun. Awake! awake! lazy ones!
Benjamin is overhauling the ammunition, and we only wait
for our breakfasts, and away for the mountains and pigeon
shooting."

There was no resisting this animated appeal, and in a few minutes Miss Temple and her friend descended to the parlour. The doors of the hall were thrown open, and the mild, balmy air of a clear spring morning was ventilating the apartment, where the vigilance of the ex-steward had been so long maintaining an artificial heat with such unremitted diligence. The gentlemen were impatiently waiting for their morning's repast, each being equipt in the garb of a sportsman. Mr. Jones made many visits to the southern door, and would cry—

"See, cousin Bess! see, 'duke, the pigeon-roosts of the south have broken up! They are growing more thick every instant. Here is a flock that the eye cannot see the end of. There is food enough in it to keep the army of Xerxes for a month, and feathers enough to make beds for the whole county. Xerxes, Mr. Edwards, was a Grecian king, who—no, he was a Turk, or a Persian, who wanted to conquer Greece, just the same as these rascals will overrun our wheat-fields, when they come back in the fall. Away! away! Bess, I long to pepper them from the mountain."

In this wish both Marmaduke and young Edwards seemed equally to participate, for the sight was most exhilarating to a sportsman; and the ladies soon dismissed the party, after a hasty breakfast.

If the heavens were alive with pigeons, the whole village seemed equally in motion, with men, women, and children. Every species of fire-arms, from the French ducking-gun, with its barrel of near six feet in length, to the common horseman's pistol, was to be seen in the hands of the men and boys; while bows and arrows, some made of the simple stick of a walnut sapling, and others in a rude imitation of the ancient cross-bows, were carried by many of the latter.

The houses and the signs of life apparent in the village, drove the alarmed birds from the direct line of their flight, towards the mountains, along the sides and near the bases of which they were glancing in dense masses, that were equally wonderful by the rapidity of their motion, as by their incredible numbers.

We have already said, that across the inclined plane which fell from the steep ascent of the mountain to the banks of the

Susquehanna, ran the highway, on either side of which a clearing of many acres had been made at a very early day. Over those clearings, and up the eastern mountain, and along the dangerous path that was cut into its side, the different individuals posted themselves, as suited their inclinations; and in a few moments the attack commenced.

Among the sportsmen was to be seen the tall, gaunt form of Leather-stocking, who was walking over the field, with his rifle hanging on his arm, his dogs following close at his heels, now scenting the dead or wounded birds, that were beginning to tumble from the flocks, and then crouching under the legs of their master, as if they participated in his feelings at this wasteful and unsportsmenlike execution.

The reports of the fire-arms became rapid, whole volleys rising from the plain, as flocks of more than ordinary numbers darted over the opening, covering the field with darkness, like an interposing cloud; and then the light smoke of a single piece would issue from among the leafless bushes on the mountain, as death was hurled on the retreat of the affrighted birds, who were rising from a volley, for many feet into the air, in a vain effort to escape the attacks of man. Arrows, and missiles of every kind, were seen in the midst of the flocks; and so numerous were the birds, and so low did they take their flight, that even long poles, in the hands of those on the sides of the mountain, were used to strike them to earth.

During all this time, Mr. Jones, who disdained the humble and ordinary means of destruction used by his companions, was busily occupied, aided by Benjamin, in making arrangements for an assault of a more than ordinarily fatal character. Among the relics of the old military excursions, that occasionally are discovered throughout the different districts of New-York, there had been found in Templeton, at its settlement, a small swivel, which would carry a ball of a pound weight. It was thought to have been deserted by a war party of the whites, in one of their inroads into the Indian settlements, when, perhaps their convenience or the necessities induced them to leave such an encumbrance behind them in the woods. This miniature cannon had been released from the rust, and being mounted on little wheels, was now in a state for actual

service. For several years, it was the sole organ for extraordinary rejoicings that was used in those mountains. On the mornings of the Fourths of July, it would be heard, with its echoes
ringing among the hills, and telling forth its sounds, for thirteen times, with all the dignity of a two-and-thirty pounder;
and even Captain Hollister, who was the highest authority in
that part of the country on all such occasions, affirmed that
considering its dimensions, it was no despicable gun for a salute. It was somewhat the worse for the service it had performed, it is true, there being but a trifling difference in size
between the touch-hole and the muzzle. Still, the grand conceptions of Richard had suggested the importance of such an
instrument, in hurling death at his nimble enemies. The swivel
was dragged by a horse into a part of the open space, that the
Sheriff thought most eligible for planting a battery of the kind,
and Mr. Pump proceeded to load it. Several handfuls of duck-
shot were placed on top of the powder, and the Major-domo
soon announced that his piece was ready for service.

The sight of such an implement collected all the idle spectators to the spot, who, being mostly boys, filled the air with
their cries of exultation and delight. The gun was pointed on
high, and Richard, holding a coal of fire in a pair of tongs, patiently took his seat on a stump, awaiting the appearance of
a flock that was worthy of his notice.

So prodigious was the number of the birds, that the scattering fire of the guns, with the hurling of missiles, and the cries
of the boys, had no other effect than to break off small flocks
from the immense masses that continued to dart along the valley, as if the whole creation of the feathered tribe were pouring
through that one pass. None pretended to collect the game,
which lay scattered over the fields in such profusion as to
cover the very ground with the fluttering victims.

Leather-stocking was a silent, but uneasy spectator of all
these proceedings, but was able to keep his sentiments to himself until he saw the introduction of the swivel into the sports.

"This comes of settling a country!" he said—"here have I
known the pigeons to fly for forty long years, and, till you
made your clearings, there was nobody to skear or to hurt
them. I loved to see them come into the woods, for they were

company to a body; hurting nothing; being, as it was, as harmless as a garter-snake. But now it gives me sore thoughts when I hear the frighty things whizzing through the air, for I know its only a motion to bring out all the brats in the village at them. Well! the Lord won't see the waste of his creaters for nothing, and right will be done to the pigeons, as well as others, by-and-by. There's Mr. Oliver, as bad as the rest of them, firing into the flocks as if he was shooting down nothing but the Mingo warriors."

Among the sportsmen was Billy Kirby, who, armed with an old musket, was leading, and without even looking into the air, was firing and shouting as his victims fell even on his own person. He heard the speech of Natty, and took upon himself to reply—

"What's that, old Leather-stocking!" he cried, "grumbling at the loss of a few pigeons! If you had to sow your wheat twice, and three times, as I have done, you wouldn't be so massyfully feeling'd to'ards the divils.—Hurrah, boys! scatter the feathers. This is better than shooting at a turkey's head and neck, old fellow."

"It's better for you, maybe, Billy Kirby," replied the indignant old hunter, "and all them as don't know how to put a ball down a rifle barrel, or how to bring it up ag'n with a true aim; but it's wicked to be shooting into flocks in this wasty manner; and none do it, who know how to knock over a single bird. If a body has a craving for pigeon's flesh, why! it's made the same as all other creater's, for man's eating, but not to kill twenty and eat one. When I want such a thing I go into the woods till I find one to my liking, and then I shoot him off the branches without touching a feather of another, though there might be a hundred on the same tree. But you couldn't do such a thing, Billy Kirby—you couldn't do it if you tried."

"What's that you say, you old dried cornstalk! you sapless stub!" cried the wood-chopper. "You've grown mighty boasting, sin' you killed the turkey; but if you're for a single shot, here goes at that bird which comes on by himself."

The fire from the distant part of the field had driven a single pigeon below the flock to which it had belonged, and frightened with the constant reports of the muskets, it was approaching the spot where the disputants stood, darting first from one side, and then to the other, cutting the air with the swiftness of lightning, and making a noise with its wings, not unlike the rushing of a bullet. Unfortunately for the wood-chopper, notwithstanding his vaunt, he did not see his bird until it was too late for him to fire as it approached, and he pulled his trigger at the unlucky moment when it was darting immediately over his head. The bird continued its course with incredible velocity.

Natty lowered the rifle from his arm, when the challenge was made, and, waiting a moment, until the terrified victim had got in a line with his eyes, and had dropped near the bank of the lake, he raised it again with uncommon rapidity, and fired. It might have been chance, or it might have been skill, that produced the result; it was probably a union of both; but the pigeon whirled over in the air, and fell into the lake with a broken wing. At the sound of his rifle, both his dogs started from his feet, and in a few minutes the "slut" brought out the bird, still alive.

The wonderful exploit of Leather-stocking was noised through the field with great rapidity, and the sportsmen gathered in to learn the truth of the report.

"What," said young Edwards, "have you really killed a pigeon on the wing, Natty, with a single ball?"

"Haven't I killed loons before now, lad, that dive at the flash?" returned the hunter. "It's much better to kill only such as you want, without wasting your powder and lead, than to be firing into God's creaters in such a wicked manner. But I come out for a bird, and you know the reason why I like small game, Mr. Oliver, and now I have got one I will go home, for I don't relish to see these wasty ways that you are all practysing, as if the least thing wasn't made for use, and not to destroy."

"Thou sayest well, Leather-stocking," cried Marmaduke, "and I begin to think it time to put an end to this work of destruction."

"Put an ind, Judge, to your clearings. An't the woods His work as well as the pigeons? Use, but don't waste. Wasn't the woods made for the beasts and birds to harbour in? and when man wanted their flesh, their skins, or their feathers, there's the place to seek them. But I'll go to the hut with my own game, for I wouldn't touch one of the harmless things that kiver the ground here, looking up with their eyes on me, as if they only wanted tongues to say their thoughts."

With this sentiment in his mouth, Leather-stocking threw his rifle over his arm, and followed by his dogs, stepping across the clearing with great caution, taking care not to tread on one of the wounded birds that lay in his path, he soon entered the bushes on the margin and was hid from view.

Whatever impression the morality of Natty made on the Judge, it was utterly lost on Richard. He availed himself of the gathering of the sportsmen, to lay a plan for one "fell swoop" of destruction. The musket-men were drawn up in battle array, in a line extending on each side of his artillery, with orders to await the signal of firing from himself.

"Stand by, my lads," said Benjamin, who acted as an aid-de-camp on this momentous occasion, "stand by, my hearties, and when Squire Dickens heaves out the signal for to begin firing, d'ye see, you may open upon them in a broadside. Take care and fire low, boys, and you'll be sure to hull the flock."

"Fire low!" shouted Kirby—"hear the old fool! If we fire low we may hit the stumps, but not ruffle a pigeon."

"How should you know, you lubber?" cried Benjamin, with a very unbecoming heat for an officer on the eve of battle— "how should you know, you grampus? Haven't I sailed aboard of the Boadishy for five years? and wasn't it a standing order to fire low, and to hull your enemy? Keep silence at your guns, boys, and mind the order that is passed."

The loud laughs of the musket-men were silenced by the authoritative voice of Richard, who called to them for attention and obedience to his signals.

Some millions of pigeons were supposed to have already passed, that morning over the valley of Templeton; but nothing like the flock that was now approaching had been seen before. It extended from mountain to mountain in one solid blue mass, and the eye looked in vain over the southern hills to find its termination. The front of this living column was distinctly marked by a line, but very slightly indented, so regular and even was the flight. Even Marmaduke forgot the morality of Leather-stocking as it approached, and, in common with the rest, brought his musket to his shoulder.

"Fire!" cried the Sheriff, clapping his coal to the priming of the cannon. As half of Benjamin's charge escaped through the touch-hole, the whole volley of the musketry preceded the report of the swivel. On receiving this united discharge of small arms, the front of the flock darted upward, while, at the same instant, myriads of those in their rear rushed with amazing rapidity into their places, so that when the column of white smoke gushed from the mouth of the little cannon, an accumulated mass of objects was gliding over its point of direction.— The roar of the gun echoed along the mountains, and died away to the north, like distant thunder, while the whole flock of alarmed birds seemed, for a moment, thrown into one disorderly and agitated mass. The air was filled with their irregular flights, layer rising over layer, far above the tops of the highest pines, none daring to advance beyond the dangerous pass; when, suddenly, some of the leaders of the feathered tribe shot across the valley, taking their flight directly over the village, and the hundreds of thousands in their rear followed their example, deserting the eastern side of the plain to their persecutors and their fallen.

"Victory!" shouted Richard, "victory! we have driven the enemy from the field."

"Not so, Dickon," said Marmaduke, "the field is covered with them; and like the Leather-stocking, I see nothing but eyes, in every direction, as the innocent sufferers turn their heads in terror to examine my movements. Full one half of those that have fallen are yet alive: and I think it is time to end the sport; if sport it be."

"Sport!" cried the Sheriff; "it is princely sport! There are some thousands of the blue-coated boys on the ground, so that every old woman in the village may have a pot-pie for the asking."

"Well, we happily frightened the birds from this side of the valley," said Marmaduke, "and our carnage must of necessity end, for the present. Boys, I will give you sixpence a hundred for the pigeons' heads only; so go to work, and bring them into the village, where I will pay you."

This expedient produced the desired effect, for every urchin on the ground went industriously to work to wring the necks of the wounded birds. Judge Temple retired towards his dwelling with that kind of feeling, that many a man has experienced before him, who discovers, after the excitement of the moment has passed, that he has purchased pleasure at the price of misery to others. Horses were loaded with the dead; and, after the first burst of sporting, the shooting of pigeons became a business, for the remainder of the season, more in proportion to the people. Richard, however, boasted for many a year, of his shot with the "cricket;" and Benjamin gravely asserted, that he thought they killed nearly as many pigeons on that day, as there were Frenchmen destroyed on the memorable occasion of Rodney's victory.

· *Chapter XXIII* ·

Help, masters, help; here's a fish hangs in the net, like
a poor man's right in the law.

PERICLES OF TYRE

The advance of the season now became as rapid as its first
approach had been tedious and lingering. The days were uniformly mild, and genial to vegetation, while the nights, though
cool, were no longer chilled by frosts. The whip-poor-will was
heard whistling his melancholy notes along the margin of the
lake, and the ponds and meadows were sending forth the music of their thousand tenants. The leaf of the native poplar
was seen quivering in the woods; the sides of the mountains
began to lose their hue of brown, as the lively green of the different members of the forest blended their shades with the
permanent colours of the pine and hemlock; and even the buds
of the tardy oak were swelling with the promise of the coming
summer. The gay and fluttering bluebird, the social robin, and
the industrious little wren, were all to be seen enlivening the
fields with their presence and their songs; while the soaring
fish-hawk was already hovering over the waters of the Otsego,
watching, with his native voracity, for the appearance of his
prey.

The tenants of the lake were far-famed for both their quantities and their quality, and the ice had hardly disappeared,
before numberless little boats were launched from the shores,
and the lines of the fishermen were dropped into the inmost
recesses of its deepest caverns, tempting the unwary animals
with every variety of bait that the ingenuity or the art of man
had invented. But the slow, though certain adventures with a
hook and line were ill-suited to the profusion and impatience of
the settlers.—More destructive means were resorted to; and,
as the season had now arrived when the bass-fisheries were al-

lowed by the provisions of the law that Judge Temple had procured, the Sheriff declared his intention of availing himself of the first dark night, to enjoy the sport in person—

"And you shall be present, cousin Bess," he added, when he announced his intention, "and Miss Grant, and Mr. Edwards; and I will show you what I call fishing—not nibble, nibble, nibble, as 'duke does when he goes after the salmon-trout. There he will sit for hours, in a broiling sun, or perhaps, over a hole in the ice, in the coldest days in winter, under the lee of a few bushes, and not a fish will he catch, after all this mortification of the flesh. No, no—give me a good seine that's fifty or sixty fathoms in length, with a jolly parcel of boatmen to crack their jokes the while, and with Benjamin to steer, and let us haul them in by the thousands, and I shall call that fishing."

"Ah! Dickon," cried Marmaduke, "thou knowest but little of the pleasure there is in playing with the hook and line, or thou wouldst be more saving of the game. I have known thee to leave fragments enough behind thee, when thou hast headed a night-party on the lake, to feed a half-dozen famishing families."

"I shall not dispute the matter with you, Judge Temple," said the Sheriff with much dignity; "this night will I go; and I invite the company to attend, and then let them decide between us."

Richard was busy during most of the afternoon, making his preparations for the important occasion. Just as the light of the setting sun had disappeared, and a new moon had begun to cause faint shadows to be seen on the earth, the fishermen took their departure in a boat, for a point that was situated on the western shore of the lake, at the distance of rather more than half a mile from the village. The ground had become settled, and the walking was good and dry. Marmaduke, with his daughter, her friend, and young Edwards, continued on the high grassy banks at the outlet of the placid sheet of water, watching the dark object that was moving with great rapidity across the lake, until it entered the shade of the western hills, and was lost to the eye. The distance round by land to the point of their destination, was a mile, and he observed—

"It is time for us to be moving; the moon will be down ere we reach the point, and then the miraculous hauls of Dickon will commence."

The evening was warm, and after the long and dreary winter from which they had just escaped, delightfully invigorating, both to the mind and body. Inspirited by the scene and their anticipated amusement the youthful companions of the Judge followed his steps, as he led them along the shores of the Otsego, and through the skirts of the little village.

"See!" said young Edwards, "they are building their fire already; it glimmers for a moment, and then dies again like the light of a fire-fly."

"Now it blazes like a bonfire," cried Elizabeth, "you can see the figures moving around the light. Oh! I would bet my jewels against the gold beads of Remarkable, that my impatient cousin Dickon had an agency in raising that bright flame; —and see; it begins to fade again, like most of his brilliant schemes."

"Thou hast guessed the truth, Bess," said her father; "he has thrown an armful of brush on the pile, which has burnt out as soon as lighted. But it has enabled them to find a better fuel, for their fire begins to burn with a more steady flame. It is the true fisherman's beacon now; observe how beautifully it throws its little circle of light on the water!"

The appearance of the fire urged the pedestrians on, for even the ladies had become eager to witness the draught of the seine. By the time they reached the bank, which rose above the low point where the fisherman had landed, the moon had sunk behind the tops of the western pines, and as most of the stars were obscured by the clouds, there was but little other light, by which to view the scene, than that which proceeded from the large piles of brush, branches, and roots, that had been collected under the superintendence of Richard. At the suggestion of Marmaduke, his companions paused to listen to the conversation of those below them, and examine the party, for a moment, before they descended to the shore.

The whole group was seated around the fire, on the ground, with the exception of Richard and Benjamin; the former of whom occupied the root of a decayed stump, that had been drawn to the spot as part of their fuel, and the latter was standing, with his arms a-kimbo, so near to the flame, that the smoke occasionally obscured his solemn visage, as it waved around the pile, in obedience to the light night-airs, that swept gently over the surface of the water.

"Why, look you, Squire," said the Major-domo, "you may call a lake-fish that will weigh twenty or thirty pounds, a serious matter; but to a man who has hauled in a shovel-nosed shirk, d'ye see, it's but a poor kind of fishing, after all."

"I don't know, Benjamin," returned the Sheriff; "a haul of one thousand Otsego bass, without counting pike, pickerel, perch, bull-pouts, salmon-trouts, and suckers, is no bad fishing, let me tell you. There may be sport in sticking a shark, but what is he good for after you have got him? Now any one of the fish that I have named is fit to set before a king."

"Well, Squire," returned Benjamin, "just listen to the philosophy of the thing. Would it stand to reason that such fish should live and be catched in this here little pond of water, where it's hardly deep enough to drown a man, as you'll find in the wide ocean, where, as every body knows, that is, every body that has followed the seas, whales and grampuses are to be seen, that are as long as one of them pine trees on yonder mountain?"

"Softly, softly, Benjamin," said the Sheriff, using a soothing manner, as if he wished to save the credit of his favourite; "why some of the pines will measure full two hundred feet, and even more."

"Two hundred or two thousand, it's all the same thing," cried Benjamin, with an air which manifested that he was not easily to be bullied out of his opinion, on a subject like the present—"Haven't I been there, and haven't I seen? I have said that you fall in with whales as long as one of them there pines; and I'll stand to what I have once said."

During this dialogue, which was evidently but the close of a much longer discussion, the huge frame of Billy Kirby was seen extended on one side of the fire, where he was picking his teeth with the splinters of the chips that were near him, and occasionally shaking his head, with the distrust that was engendered by the marvellous qualities of Benjamin's assertions. It seems that he now thought it time to advance his sentiments on the subject.

"I've a notion," said the wood-chopper, "that there's water in this lake to swim the biggest whale that ever was invented; and, as to the pines, I think I ought to know so'thing consarning them; and I have chopped many a one that was sixty times the length of my helve, without counting the eyes; and I b'lieve, Benny, that if the old pine that stands in the hollow of the Vision Mountain, just over the village, and you may see the tree itself by looking up, for the moon is on its top yet;—well, now I b'lieve, that if that same tree was planted out in the deepest part of the lake, there would be water enough for the biggest ship that ever was built to float over it, without touching its upper branches, I do."

"Did'ee ever see a ship, Master Kirby?" roared the steward—"did'ee ever see a ship, man? or any craft bigger than a lime-scow, or a wood-boat, on this here small bit of fresh water?"

"Yes, I have," said the wood-chopper, stoutly; "I can say that I have, and tell no lie."

"Did'ee ever see a British ship, Master Kirby? an English line-of-battle ship, boy? Where away did'ee ever fall in with a regular built vessel, with starn-post and cut-water, garboard streak and plank-shear, gangways and hatchways, and water-ways, quarterdeck and forecastle, ay, and flush-deck?—tell me that, man, if you can; where away did'ee ever fall in with such a hooker; a full-rigged, regular-built, decked vessel?"

The whole company were a good deal astounded with this overwhelming question, and even Richard afterward remarked, that it "was a thousand pities that Benjamin could not read, or he must have made a valuable officer to the British marine. It was no wonder that they overcome the French so easily on the water, when even the lowest sailor so well understood the different parts of a vessel." But Billy Kirby was a fearless wight, and had great jealousy of foreign dictation; he had arisen on his feet, and turned his back to the fire, during the voluble delivery of this interrogatory; and when the steward ended, contrary to all expectation, he gave the following spirited reply:—

"Where! why on the North River, and maybe on Champlain. There's sloops on the river, boy, that would give a hard time on't the stoutest vessel King George owns. They carry masts of ninety feet in the clear, of good, solid pine, for I've been at the chopping of many a one in Varmount state. I wish I was captain of one of them, and you was in that Board-dish that you tell so much about; and we'd soon see what good Yankee stuff is made on, and whether a Varmounter's hide an't as thick as an Englishman's."

The echoes from the opposite hills, which were more than half a mile from the fishing point, sent back the discordant laugh that Benjamin gave forth at this challenge; and the woods that covered their sides, seemed, by the noise that issued from their shades to be full of mocking demons.

"Let us descend to the shore," whispered Marmaduke, "or there will soon be ill blood between them. Benjamin is a fearless boaster, and Kirby, though good-natured, is a careless son of the forest, who thinks one American more than a match for six Englishmen. I marvel that Dickon is silent, where there is such a trial of skill in the superlative!"

The appearance of Judge Temple and the ladies produced, if not a pacification, at least a cessation of hostilities. Obedient to the directions of Mr. Jones, the fishermen prepared to launch their boat, which had been seen in the back-ground of the view, with the net carefully disposed on a little platform in its stern, ready for instant service. Richard gave vent to his reproaches at the tardiness of the pedestrians, when all the turbulent passions of the party were succeeded by a calm, as mild and as placid as that which prevailed over the beautiful sheet of water, that they were about to rifle of its best treasures.

The night had now become so dark as to render objects, without the reach of the light from their fire, not only indistinct, but in most cases, invisible. For a little distance the water was discernible, glistening, as the glare from the fire danced over its surface, touching it, here and there, with red, quivering streaks; but at a hundred feet from the shore, a boundary of impenetrable gloom opposed itself to the vision.

One or two stars were shining through the openings of the clouds, and the lights were seen in the village, glimmering faintly, as if at an immeasurable distance. At times, as their fire lowered, or as the horizon cleared, the outline of the mountain, on the other side of the lake, might be traced, by its undulations; but its shadow was cast, wide and dense, on the bosom of the waters, rendering the darkness, in that direction, trebly deep.

Benjamin Pump was invariably the cockswain and net-caster of Richard's boat, unless the Sheriff saw fit to preside in person; and, on the present occasion, Billy Kirby, and a youth of about half his strength, were assigned to the duty at the oars. The remainder of the assistants were stationed at the ropes, for the laborious service of hauling the net to land. The arrangements were speedily made, and Richard gave the signal to "shove-off."

Elizabeth watched the motion of the batteau, as it pulled from the shore, letting loose its rope as it went, but it soon disappeared in the darkness, when her ear was her only guide to its evolutions. There was a great affectation of stillness, during all these manœuvres, in order, as Richard assured them, "not to frighten the bass, who were running into the shoal waters, and who would approach the light, if not disturbed by the sounds from the fishermen."

The hoarse voice of Benjamin was alone heard, issuing out of the gloom, as he uttered, in authoritative tones, "pull larboard oar," "pull starboard," "give way together, boys," and such other dictative mandates as were necessary for the right disposition of his seine. A long time was passed in this necessary part of the process, for Benjamin prided himself greatly on his skill in throwing the net, and, in fact, most of the success of the sport depended on its being done with judgment. At length, a loud splash in the water, as he threw away the "staff," or "stretcher," with a hoarse call from the steward, of "clear," announced that the boat was returning to the shore; when Richard seized a brand from the fire, and ran to a point, as far above the centre of the fishing ground, as the one from which the batteau had started was below it.

"Stick her in dead for the Squire, boys," said the steward, "and we'll have a look at what there is that grows in this here pond."

In place of the falling net, were now to be heard the quick strokes of the oars, and the noise of the rope running out of the boat. Presently the batteau shot into the circle of light, and in an instant she was pulled to shore. Several eager hands were extended, to receive the "hauling line," and, both ropes being equally well manned, the fishermen commenced hauling in, with slow and steady drags, Richard standing in the centre, giving orders, first to one party and then to the other, to increase or slacken their efforts, as the occasion required. The visiters were posted near him, and enjoyed a fair view of the whole operation, which was slowly advancing to an end.

Opinions, as to the result of their adventure, were now freely hazarded by all the men, some declaring that the net came in as light as a feather, and others affirming that it seemed to be full of logs. As the ropes were many hundred feet in length, these opposing sentiments were thought to be of little moment by the Sheriff, who would go first to one line and then to the other, giving each a small pull, in order to enable him to form an opinion for himself.

"Why, Benjamin," he cried, as he made his first effort in this way, "you did not throw your net clear. I can move it with my little finger. The rope slackens in my hand."

"Did you ever see a whale, Squire?" responded the steward: "I say that if that there net is foul, the devil is in the lake in the shape of a fish, for I cast it as fair as ever rigging was rove over the quarter-deck of a flag-ship."

But Richard discovered his mistake, when he saw Billy Kirby before him, standing with his feet to the water, at an angle of forty-five degrees, inclining shorewards, and expending his gigantic strength in sustaining himself in that posture. He ceased his remonstrances, and proceeded to the party at the other line.

"I see the 'staffs,'" shouted Mr. Jones;—"gather in, boys, and away with it; to shore with her—to shore with her."

At this cheerful sound, Elizabeth strained her eyes and saw the ends of the two sticks on the seine, emerging from the darkness, while the men closed, near to each other, and formed a deep bag of their net. The exertions of the fishermen sensibly increased, and the voice of Richard was heard, encouraging them to make their greatest efforts, at the present moment.

"Now's the time, my lads," he cried; "let us get the ends to land, and all we have will be our own—away with her!"

"Away with her it is," echoed Benjamin—"hurrah! ho-a-hoy, hoy-a-hoy, ho-a!"

"In with her," shouted Kirby, exerting himself in a manner that left nothing for those in his rear to do, but to gather up the slack of the rope which he passed through his hands.

"Staff, ho!" shouted the steward.

"Staff, ho!" echoed Kirby, from the other rope.

The men rushed to the water's edge, some seizing the upper rope, and some the lower, or lead-rope, and began to haul with great activity and zeal. A deep semicircular sweep, of the little balls that supported the seine in its perpendicular position, was plainly visible to the spectators, and as it rapidly lessened in size, the bag of the net appeared, while an occasional flutter on the water announced the uneasiness of the prisoners it contained.

"Haul in, my lads," shouted Richard—"I can see the dogs kicking to get free. Haul in, and here's a cast that will pay you for the labour."

Fishes of various sorts now were to be seen, entangled in the meshes of the net, as it was passed through the hands of the labourers; and the water, at a little distance from the shore, was alive with the agitated movements of the alarmed victims. Hundreds of white sides were glancing up to the surface of the water, and glistening in the firelight, when frightened at the uproar and the change, the fish would again dart to the bottom, in fruitless efforts for freedom.

"Hurrah!" shouted Richard again; "one or two more heavy drags, boys, and we are safe."

"Cheerily, boys, cheerily!" cried Benjamin; "I see a salmon-trout that is big enough for a chowder."

"Away with you, you varmint!" said Billy Kirby, plucking a bull-pout from the meshes and casting the animal back into the lake with great contempt. "Pull, boys, pull; here's all kinds, and the Lord condemn me for a liar, if there an't a thousand bass!"

Inflamed beyond the bounds of discretion at the sight, and forgetful of the season, the wood-chopper rushed to his middle in the water, and began to drive the reluctant animals before him from their native element.

"Pull heartily, boys," cried Marmaduke, yielding to the excitement of the moment, and laying his hands to the net, with no trifling addition to the force. Edwards had preceded him, for the sight of the immense piles of fish, that were slowly rolling over on the gravelly beach, had impelled him also to leave the ladies, and join the fishermen.

Great care was observed in bringing the net to land, and, after much toil, the whole shoal of victims were safely deposited in a hollow of the bank, where they were left to flutter away their brief existence, in their new and fatal element.

Even Elizabeth and Louisa were greatly excited and highly gratified, by seeing two thousand captives thus drawn from the bosom of the lake, and laid prisoners at their feet. But when the feelings of the moment were passing away, Marmaduke took in his hands a bass, that might have weighed two pounds, and after viewing it a moment, in melancholy musing, he turned to his daughter, and observed—

"This is a fearful expenditure of the choicest gifts of providence. These fish, Bess, which thou seest lying in such piles before thee, and which, by tomorrow evening will be rejected food on the meanest table in Templeton, are of a quality and flavour that, in other countries, would make them esteemed a luxury on the tables of princes or epicures. The world has no better fish than the bass of Otsego; it unites the richness of the shad to the firmness of the salmon."

"But surely, dear sir," cried Elizabeth, "they must prove a great blessing to the country, and a powerful friend to the poor."

"The poor are always prodigal, my child, where there is plenty, and seldom think of a provision against the morrow. But if there can be any excuse for destroying animals in this manner, it is in taking the bass. During the winter, you know, they are entirely protected from our assaults by the ice, for they ever refuse the hook; and during the hot months they are not seen. It is supposed they retreat to the deep and cool waters of the lake, at that season, and it is only in the spring and autumn, that for a few days, they are to be found around the points where they are within the reach of a seine. But, like all the other treasures of the wilderness, they already begin to disappear, before the wasteful extravagance of man."

"Disappear, 'duke! disappear!" exclaimed the Sheriff; "if you don't call this appearing, I know not what you will. Here are a good thousand of the shiners, some hundreds of suckers, and a powerful quantity of other fry. But this is always the way with you, Marmaduke; first it's the trees, then it's the deer, after that it's the maple sugar, and so on to the end of the chapter. One day you talk of canals, through a country where there's a river or a lake every half-mile, just because the water won't run the way you wish it to go; and the next, you say something about mines of coal, though any man who has good eyes like myself—I say with good eyes—can see more wood than would keep the city of London in fuel for fifty years; wouldn't it, Benjamin?"

"Why, for that, Squire," said the steward, "Lon'on is no small place. If it was stretched an end, all the same as a town on one side of a river, it would cover some such matter as this here lake. Thof I dar'st to say, that the wood in sight might sarve them a good turn, seeing that the Lon'oners mainly burn coal."

"Now we are on the subject of coal, Judge Temple," interrupted the Sheriff, "I have a thing of much importance to communicate to you; but I will defer it until to-morrow. I know that you intend riding into the eastern part of the patent, and I will accompany you, and conduct you to a spot, where some of your projects may be realized. We will say no more now, sir, for there are listeners; but a secret has this evening been revealed to me, 'duke, that is of more consequence to your welfare, than all your estates united."

Marmaduke laughed at the important inelligence, to which in a variety of shapes he was accustomed, and the Sheriff, with

an air of great dignity, as if pitying his want of faith, proceeded in the business more immediately before them. As the
labour of drawing the net had been very great, he directed one
party of his men to commence throwing the fish into piles,
preparatory to the usual division, while another, under the
superintendence of Benjamin, prepared the seine for a second
haul.

· Chapter XXIV ·

While from its margin, terrible to tell!
Three sailors with their gallant boatswain fell.

FALCONER

While the fishermen were employed in making the preparations for an equitable division of their spoils, Elizabeth and her friend strolled to a short distance from the group, along the shores of the lake. The shades of evening had been gradually gathering around the scene, during the draught of the net, and, while the objects in the vicinity of the fire were still distinct, and even vivid, the surrounding darkness became deeper, both by the contrast, and the advancing dominion of the night. After reaching a point, to which even the brightest of the occasional gleams of light from the fire did not extend, the ladies turned, and paused a moment, in contemplation of the busy and lively party they had left, and of the obscurity, which, like the gloom of oblivion, seemed to envelope the rest of the creation.

"This is indeed a subject for the pencil!" exclaimed Elizabeth. "Observe the countenance of that wood-chopper, while he exults in presenting a larger fish than common to my cousin Sheriff; and see, Louisa, how handsome and considerate my dear father looks, by the light of that fire, where he stands viewing the havoc of the game. He seems really melancholy, as if he actually thought that a day of retribution was to follow this hour of abundance and prodigality! Would they not make a fine picture, Louisa?"

"You know that I am ignorant of all such accomplishments, Miss Temple."

"Call me by my Christian name," interrupted Elizabeth; "this is not a place, neither is this a scene, for the observance of forms."

"Well, then, if I may venture an opinion," said Louisa, timidly, "I should think it might indeed make a picture. The selfish earnestness of that Kirby over his fish, would contrast finely with the—the—expression of Mr. Edwards's face. I hardly know what to call it; but it is—a—is—you know what I would say, dear Elizabeth."

"You do me too much credit, Miss Grant," said the heiress; "I am no diviner of thoughts, or interpreter of expressions."

There was certainly nothing harsh, or even cold, in the manner of the speaker, but still it repressed the conversation for a moment, and the maidens continued to stroll still further from their party, retaining each other's arm, but observing a profound silence. Elizabeth, perhaps, conscious of the improper phraseology of her last speech, or perhaps excited by the new object that met her wandering gaze, was the first to break the present awkward cessation in the discourse, by exclaiming, in all the richness of her animated and animating voice—

"Look, Louisa! we are not alone; there are fishermen lighting a fire on the other side of the lake, immediately opposite to us; it must be in front of the cabin of the Leatherstocking!"

For some cause or other, Miss Grant had kept her eyes bent in the direction of the pebbles, over which she was walking; probably because, being less adventurous than her companion, she was disposed to view what could be faintly discerned, without attempting the gloom, in a vain effort to pierce its mysteries; or probably for some better reason, that we leave our readers to imagine; but thus awakened, she looked up, in the direction pointed out by her friend, and saw, at once, the cause of her sudden exclamation.

Through the obscurity, which prevailed most immediately under the eastern mountain, a small and uncertain light was plainly to be seen, though as it was occasionally lost to the eye, it seemed struggling for its existence. They observed it to move, and sensibly to lower, as if carried down the descent of the bank to the shore. Here, in a very short time, its flame gradually expanded, and grew brighter, until it became of the size of a man's head, when it continued to shine, a steady and glaring ball of fire.

Such an object, lighted as it were by magic, under the brow of the mountain, and in that retired and unfrequented spot, gave double interest to the beauty and singularity of its appearance. It did not at all resemble the large and unsteady light of their own fire, being much more clear and bright, and retaining its size and shape with perfect uniformity.

There are moments when the best regulated minds are, more or less, subjected to the injurious impressions which few have escaped in infancy, and Elizabeth smiled at her own weakness, while she remembered the idle tales which were circulated through the village, at the expense of the Leatherstocking. The same ideas seized her companion, and at the same instant, for Louisa pressed nearer to her friend, as she said, in a low voice, stealing a timid glance towards the bushes and trees that overhung the bank near them—

"Did you ever hear the singular ways of this Natty spoken of, Miss Temple? They say that, in his youth, he was an Indian warrior, or, what is the same thing, a white man leagued with the savages; and it is thought he has been concerned in many of their inroads, in the old wars."

"The thing is not at all improbable," returned Elizabeth, "but he is not alone in that particular."

"No, surely; but is it not strange that he is so cautious with his hut? he never leaves it, without fastening it in a remarkable manner; and, in several instances, when the children, or even the men of the village, have wished to seek a shelter there from the storms, he has been known to drive them from his door, with rudeness and threats. That surely is singular in this country!"

"It is certainly not being very hospitable; but we must remember his aversion to the customs of civilized life. You heard my father say, a few days since, how kindly he was treated by him on his first visit to this place." Elizabeth paused, and smiled, with an expression of peculiar archness, though the darkness hid its meaning from her companion, as she continued: —"Besides, he certainly admits the visits of Mr. Edwards, whom we both know to be far from a savage."

To this speech Louisa made no reply, but continued gazing on the object which had elicited her remarks. In addition to the bright and circular flame was now to be seen a fainter though a vivid light, of an equal diameter to the other at the upper end, but which, after extending downward for many feet, gradually tapered to a point at its lower extremity. A dark space was plainly visible between the two, and the new illumination was placed beneath the other, the whole forming an appearance not unlike an inverted note of admiration. It was soon evident that the latter was nothing but the reflection, from the water, of the former, and that the object, whatever it might be, was advancing across, or rather over the lake, for it seemed to be several feet above its surface, in a direct line with themselves. Its motion was amazingly rapid, the ladies having hardly discovered that it was moving at all, before the waving light of a flame was discerned, losing its regular shape, while it increased in size, as it approached them.

"It appears to be supernatural!" whispered Louisa, beginning to retrace her steps towards the party.

"It is beautiful!" exclaimed Elizabeth.

A brilliant, though wavering flame was now plainly visible, gracefully gliding over the lake, and throwing its light on the water in such a manner as to tinge it slightly; though, in the air, so strong was the contrast, the darkness seemed to have the distinctness of material substances, as if the fire were imbedded in a setting of ebony. This appearance, however, gradually wore off and the rays from the torch struck out, and enlightened the atmosphere in front of it, leaving the background in a darkness that was more inpenetrable than ever.

"Ho! Natty, is that you?" shouted the Sheriff—"paddle in, old boy, and I'll give you a mess of fish that is fit to place before the Governor."

The light suddenly changed its direction, and a long and slightly-built boat hove up out of the gloom, while the red glare fell on the weather-beaten features of the Leatherstocking, whose tall person was seen erect in the frail vessel, wielding, with all the grace of an experienced boatman, a

long fishing spear, which he held by its centre, first dropping one end then the other into the water, to aid in propelling
the little canoe of bark, we will not say through, but over the
water. At the farther end of the vessel, a form was faintly
seen, guiding its motions, and using a paddle with the ease of
one who felt there was no necessity for extraordinary exertions. The Leather-stocking struck his spear lightly against
the short staff which upheld, on a rude grating framed of old
hoops of iron, the knots of pine that composed the fuel, and
the light, which glared high, for an instant fell on the swarthy
features, and dark, glancing eyes of Mohegan.

The boat glided along the shore until it arrived opposite to
the fishing-ground, when it again changed its direction, and
moved on to the land, with a motion so graceful, and yet so
rapid, that it seemed to possess the power of regulating its
progress by its own volition. The water in front of the canoe
was hardly ruffled by its passage and no sound betrayed the
collision, when the light fabric shot on the gravelly beach, for
nearly half its length, Natty receding a step or two from its
bow, in order to facilitate the landing.

"Approach, Mohegan," said Marmaduke: "approach,
Leather-stocking, and load your canoe with bass. It would be
a shame to assail the animals with the spear, when such mul-
titudes of victims lie here, that will be lost as food for the
want of mouths to consume them."

"No, no, Judge," returned Natty, his tall figure stalking
over the narrow beach and ascending to the little grassy bottom where the fish were laid in piles; "I eat of no man's nasty
ways. I strike my spear into the eels, or the trout, when I crave
the creaters, but I wouldn't be helping to such a sinful kind
of fishing, for the best rifle that was ever brought out from
the old countries. If they had fur like a beaver, or you could
tan their hides, like a buck, something might be said in favour
of taking them by the thousands with your nets; but as God
made them for man's food, and for no other disarnable reason, I call it sinful and wasty to catch more than can be eat."

"Your reasoning is mine," cried Marmaduke; "for once, old
hunter, we agree in our opinions; and I heartily wish we could

make a convert of the Sheriff. A net of half the size of this would supply the whole village with fish, for a week, at one haul."

The Leather-stocking did not relish this alliance in sentiment, and he shook his head doubtingly, as he answered—

"No, no; we are not much of one mind, Judge, or you'd never turn good hunting grounds into stumpy pastures. And you fish and hunt out of rule; but to me, the flesh is sweeter, where the creater has some chance for its life; for that reason, I always use a single ball, even if it be at a bird or a squirrel; besides, it saves lead, for when a body knows how to shoot, one piece of lead is enough for all, except hard-lived animals."

The Sheriff heard these opinions with great indignation, and when he completed the last arrangement for the division, by carrying, with his own hands, a trout of a large size, and placing it on four different piles in succession, as his changeful ideas of justice required, he gave vent to his spleen by exclaiming—

"A very pretty confederacy, indeed! Judge Temple, the landlord and owner of a township, with Nathaniel Bumppo, a lawless squatter, and professed deer-killer, in order to preserve the game in the county! But, 'duke, when I fish, I fish, and don't play;—so, away, boys, for another haul, and we'll send our wagons and carts, in the morning, to bring in our prizes!"

Marmaduke appeared to understand that all opposition to the will of the Sheriff would be useless, and he strolled from the fire, to the place where the canoe of the hunters lay, whither the ladies and Oliver Edwards had already preceded him.

Curiosity induced the females to approach this spot, but it surely was a different motive that led the youth thither. Elizabeth examined the light ash timbers and thin bark covering of the canoe, in admiration of its neat but simple execution, and with wonder that any human being could be so daring as to trust his life in so frail a vessel. But the youth explained to her the buoyant properties of the boat, and its perfect safety, when under proper management, adding, in such glowing terms, a description of the manner in which the fish were struck with the spear, that she changed suddenly, from an apprehension of the danger of the excursion, to a desire to participate in its pleasures. She even ventured a proposition to that effect to her father, laughing at the same time, at her own wish, and accusing herself of acting under a woman's caprice.

"Say not so, Bess," returned the Judge; "I would have you above the idle fears of a silly girl. These canoes are the safest kind of boats, to those who have skill and steady nerves. I have crossed the broadest part of the Oneida in one much smaller than this."

"And I the Ontary," interrupted the Leather-stocking; "and that with squaws in the canoe, too. But the Delaware women be used to the paddle, and are down good hands in a boat of this nater. If the young woman would like to see an old man strike a trout for his breakfast, she is welcome to a seat and a sight. John will say the same, seeing that he built the canoe, which was only launched yesterday; for I'm not over curious at such small work as brooms, and basket-making, and other like Indian trades."

Natty gave the heiress one of his significant laughs, with a kind nod of his head, when he concluded this invitation; but Mohegan, with the native grace of an Indian, approached, and taking her soft white hand into his own swarthy and wrinkled palm, said—

"Come, grand-daughter of Miquon, and John will be glad. Trust the Indian; his head is old, though his hand is not steady. The young Eagle will go, and see that no harm hurts his sister."

"Well, Mr. Edwards," cried Elizabeth, blushing slightly, "your friend, Mohegan, you see, has given a promise for you. Do you redeem the pledge?"

"With my life, if necessary, Miss Temple," cried the youth, with fervour. "The sight is worth some little apprehension, for of real danger there is none. I will go with you and Miss Grant, however, to save appearances."

"With me!" exclaimed Louisa; "no, not with me, Mr. Edwards, nor surely do you mean to trust yourself in that slight canoe."

"But I shall, for I have no apprehensions any longer," said Elizabeth, stepping into the boat, and taking a seat where the Indian directed. "Mr. Edwards, you may remain, as three do seem to be enough for such an egg-shell."

"It shall hold a fourth," cried the young man, springing to her side, with a violence that nearly shook the weak fabric of the vessel asunder;—"pardon me, Miss Temple, that I do not permit these venerable Charons to take you to the shades unattended by your genius."

"Is it a good or evil spirit?" asked Elizabeth.

"Good to you."

"And mine," added the maiden, with an air that strangely blended pique with satisfaction. But the motion of the canoe gave rise to new ideas, and fortunately afforded a good excuse to the young man to change the discourse.

It appeared to Elizabeth that they glided over the water by magic, so easy and graceful was the manner in which Mohegan guided his little bark. A slight gesture with his spear, indicated the way in which the Leather-stocking wished to go, and a profound silence was observed by the whole party, as a precaution necessary to the success of their fishery. The shore, at that point of the lake, ran gradually off, and the water shoaled regularly, differing, in this particular, altogether, from those parts where the mountains rose, nearly in perpendicular precipices, from the beach. There, the largest vessels could have lain, with their yards locked in the branches of the pines; while here, a scanty growth of rushes lifted their tops above the lake, gently curling the waters, as their bending heads slowly waved with the passing breath of the night air. It was at the shallow points, only, that the bass could be found, or the net cast with success.

Elizabeth saw thousands of these fish, swimming in shoals along the shallow and warm waters of the shore; for the flaring light of their torch exposed all the mysteries of the lake, laying them open to the eye, with a slight variation in colour, as plainly as if the limpid sheet of the Otsego was but another atmosphere. Every instant she expected to see the impending spear of Leather-stocking darting into the thronging hosts that were rushing beneath her, where it would seem that a blow could not go amiss; and where, as her father had already said, the prize that would be obtained was worthy of the notice of any epicure. But Natty had his peculiar habits, and, it would seem, his peculiar tastes also. His tall stature, and his erect posture, enabled him to see much further than those who, from motives of safety, were seated in the bottom of the canoe; and he turned his head warily, in every direction, frequently bending his body forward, and straining his vision, as if desirous of penetrating the darkness in the water, that surrounded their boundary of light. At length his anxious scrutiny was rewarded with success, and, waving his spear from the shore, he said in a cautious tone—

"Send her outside the bass, John; I see a laker there that has run out of the school. It's sildom one finds such a creater in the shallow waters, where a spear can touch it."

Mohegan gave a wave of assent with his hand, and in the next instant the canoe was without the "run of the bass," and in water of nearly twenty feet in depth. A few additional knots were laid on the grating, and the light from the fire made to reach the bottom. Elizabeth then saw a fish of unusual size, floating above the small pieces of logs and sticks that were lying on the bottom. The animal was only distinguishable, at that distance, by a slight but almost imperceptible motion of its fins and tail. The curiosity excited by this unusual exposure of the secrets of the lake, seemed to be mutual between the heiress of the land and the lord of these waters, for the "salmon-trout" soon announced his interest by raising his head and body, for a few degrees above a horizontal line, and then dropping them again into the position of nature.

"Whist! whist!" said Natty, in a low voice, on hearing a slight sound made by Elizabeth, in bending over the side of the canoe, in eager curiosity;—

" 'tis a skeary animal, and it's a far stroke for a spear. My handle is but fourteen foot, and the creatur lies at a good eighteen from the top of the water; but I'll try him, for he's a ten-pounder."

While speaking, the Leather-stocking was poising and directing his weapon. Elizabeth saw the bright, polished tines, as they slowly and silently entered the water, where the refraction pointed them many degrees from the true direction to the fish; and she thought that the intended victim saw them also, as he seemed to increase the play of his tail and fins, though without moving his station. At the next instant, the tall body of Natty bent to the water's edge, and the handle of his spear disappeared in the lake. The long, dark streak of the gliding weapon, and the little bubbling vortex, which followed its rapid flight, were easily to be seen; but it was not until the handle shot again high into the air, by its own reaction, and its master, catching it in his hand, threw its tines uppermost, that Elizabeth was acquainted with the success of the blow. A fish of great size was transfixed by the barbed steel, and was very soon shaken from its impaled situation into the bottom of the canoe.

"That will do, John," said Natty, raising his prize by one of his fingers, and exhibiting it before the torch; "enough is as good as a feast; I shall not strike another blow to-night."

The Indian again waved his hand, and replied with the simple and energetic monosyllable of—

"Good."

Elizabeth was awakened from the trance, created by this scene, and by gazing in that unusual manner at the bottom of the lake, by the hoarse sounds of Benjamin's voice, and the dashing of oars, as the heavier boat of the seine-drawers approached the spot where the canoe lay, dragging after its toilsome way, the folds of the net, which was already spreading on the water.

"Haul off, haul off, Master Bumppo," cried Benjamin; "your top-light frightens the fish, who see the net and sheer off soundings. A fish knows as much as a horse, or, for that matter, more, seeing that its brought up on the water. Haul off, Master Bumppo, haul off, I say, and give a wide berth to the seine."

Mohegan guided their little canoe to a point where the movements of the fishermen could be observed, without interruption to the business, and then suffered it to lie quietly on the water, looking like an imaginary vessel floating in the air. There appeared to be much ill-humour among the party in the batteau, for the directions of Benjamin were not only frequent, but issued in a voice that partook largely of the tones of dissatisfaction.

"Pull larboard oar, will ye, Master Kirby," cried the old seaman; "Pull larboard best. It would puzzle the oldest admiral in the British fleet to cast this here net fair, with a wake like a corkscrew. Pull starboard oar, boy, starboard oar, with a will."

"Harkee, Mister Pump," said Kirby, ceasing to row, and speaking with some spirit; "I'm a man that likes civil language and decent treatment; such as is right 'twixt man and man. If you want us to go hoy, say so, and hoy I'll go, for the benefit of the company; but I'm not used to being ordered about like dumb cattle."

"Who's dumb cattle?" echoed Benjamin, fiercely, turning his forbidding face to the glare of the light from the canoe, and exhibiting every feature teeming with the expression of his disgust. "If you want to come aft and cun the boat round, come and be damned, and a pretty steerage you'll make of it too. There's but another heave of the net in the stern-sheets, and we're clear of the thing. Give way, will ye? and shoot her ahead for a fathom or two, and if you catch me afloat again with such a horsemarine as yourself, why rate me a ship's jackass, that's all."

Probably encouraged by the prospect of a speedy termination to his labour, the wood-chopper resumed his oar, and, under the strong excitement of his feelings, gave a stroke with it, that not only cleared the boat of the net, but of the steward, at the same instant, also. Benjamin had stood on the little platform that held the seine, in the stern of the boat, and the violent whirl occasioned by the wood-chopper's arm, completely destroyed his balance. The position of the lights rendered objects in the batteau distinguishable, both from the canoe and the shore; and the heavy fall on the water drew all eyes to the steward, as he lay struggling, for a moment, in sight.

A loud burst of merriment, to which the lungs of Kirby contributed no small part, broke out like a chorus of laughter, and rung along the eastern mountain, in echoes, until it died away in distant, mocking mirth, among the rocks and woods.

The body of the steward was seen slowly to disappear, as was expected; but when the light waves, which had been raised by his fall, began to sink in calmness, and the water finally closed over his head, unbroken and still, a very different feeling pervaded the spectators.

"How fare you, Benjamin?" shouted Richard from the shore.

"The dumb devil can't swim a stroke!" exclaimed Kirby, rising, and beginning to throw aside his clothes.

"Paddle up, Mohegan," cried young Edwards, "where the light will show us how he lies, and let me dive for the body."

"Oh! save him! for God's sake, save him!" exclaimed Elizabeth, bowing her head on the side of the canoe in horror.

A powerful and dexterous sweep of Mohegan's paddle sent the canoe directly over the spot where the steward had fallen, and a loud shout from the Leather-stocking announced that he saw the body.

"Then steady the boat while I dive," again cried Edwards.

"Gently, lad, gently," said Natty; "I'll spear the creater up in half the time, and no risk to any body."

The form of Benjamin was lying, about half way to the bottom, grasping with either hand the bottoms of some broken rushes, by whose strength it was maintained in that position. The blood of Elizabeth curdled to her heart, as she saw the figure of a fellow-creature thus extended under an immense sheet of water, apparently in motion, by the undulations of the dying waves, with its face and hands, viewed by that light, and through the medium of the fluid, already coloured with livid hues like death.

At the same instant, she saw the shining tines of Natty's spear approaching the motionless head of the sufferer, and entwining themselves, rapidly and dexterously in the hairs of his queue and the cape of his coat. The body was now raised slowly, looking ghastly and grim, as its features turned upward to the light, and approached the surface. The arrival of the nostrils of Benjamin into their own atmosphere, was announced by a breathing that would have done credit to a full-grown porpoise. For a moment, Natty held the steward suspended, with his head just above the water, while his eyes slowly opened, and stared about him, as if he thought that he had reached a new and unexplored country.

As all the parties acted and spoke together, much less time was consumed in the occurrence of these events, than in their narration. To bring the batteau to the end of the spear, and to raise the form of Benjamin from its liquid element into the boat, and for the whole party to gain the shore, and land, required but a minute. Kirby, aided by Richard, whose anxiety induced him to run into the water to meet his favourite assistant, carried the motionless steward up the bank, and seated him before the fire, where he was supported, while the Sheriff proceeded to order the most approved measures then in use, for the resuscitation of the drowned.

"Run, Billy," he cried, "to the village, and bring up the rum-hogshead that lies before the door, in which I am making vinegar in cold weather, and be quick, boy, don't stay to empty the vinegar; and stop at Mr. Le Quoi's, and buy a paper of tobacco and half-a-dozen pipes; and ask Remarkable for some salt, and one of her flannel petticoats; and ask Dr. Todd to send his lancet, and to come himself; and——ha! 'duke, what are you about? would you strangle a man who is full of water, by giving him rum! Help me to open this hand, that I may pat it."

All this time Benjamin sat with his muscles fixed, his mouth shut, and his hands clenching the rushes, which he had seized in the confusion of the moment, and which, as he held fast, like a true seaman, had been the means of preventing his body from rising again to the surface. His eyes, however, were open, and stared wildly on the group about the fire, while his lungs were playing like a blacksmith's bellows, as if to compensate themselves for the minute of inaction to which they had been subjected. As he kept his lips compressed, with a most inveterate determination, the air was compelled to pass through his nostrils, and he rather snorted than breathed, and in such a manner that nothing, but the excessive agitation of the Sheriff, could at all justify his precipitous orders.

The bottle, applied to the steward's lips by Marmaduke, acted like a charm. His mouth opened instinctively; his hands dropped the rushes, and seized the black glass; his éyes raised from their horizontal stare to the heavens; and the whole man was lost, for a moment, in a new sensation. Unhappily for the propensity of the steward, breath was as necessary after one of these draughts, as after his submersion, and the time at length arrived when he was compelled to let go of the bottle.

"Why, Benjamin!" roared the Sheriff; "you amaze me! for a man of your experience in drownings to act so foolishly! just now you were half full of water, and now you are"——

"Full of grog," interrupted the steward, his features settling down, with amazing flexibility, into their natural economy. "But, d'ye see, Squire, I kept my hatches close, and it is but little water that ever gets into my scuttle-butt. Harkee, Master Kirby! I've followed the salt water for the better part of a man's life, and have seen some navigation on the fresh; but this here matter I will say in your favour, and that is, that you're the awk'ardest green'un that ever straddled a boat's thwart. Them that likes you for a shipmate, may sail with you, and no thanks; but dam'me if I even walk on the lake shore in your company. For why? you'd as lief drown a man as one of them there fish; not to throw a Christian creature so much as a rope's end, when he was adrift, and no life-buoy in sight! —Natty Bumppo, give us your fist. There's them that says you're an Indian, and a scalper, but you've sarved me a good turn, and you may set me down for a friend; thof it would have been more ship-shape to lower the bight of a rope, or running bow line, below me, than to seize an old seaman by his head-lanyard; but I suppose you are used to taking men by the hair, and seeing you did me good instead of harm thereby, why, it's the same thing, d'ye see."

Marmaduke prevented any reply, and assuming the direction of matters, with a dignity and discretion that at once silenced all opposition from his cousin, Benjamin was dispatched to the village by land, and the net was hauled to shore, in such a manner that the fish, for once, escaped its meshes with impunity.

The division of the spoils was made in the ordinary manner, by placing one of the party with his back to the game, who declared the owner of each pile. Billy Kirby stretched his large frame on the grass, by the side of the fire, as a sentinel until morning, over the net and the fish; and the remainder of the party embarked in the batteau, to return to the village.

The wood-chopper was seen broiling his supper on the coals, as they lost sight of the fire; and when the boat approached the shore, the torch of Mohegan's canoe was shining again under the gloom of the eastern mountain. Its motion ceased suddenly; a scattering of brands was exhibited in the air, and then all remained dark as the conjunction of night, forests, and mountains, could render the scene.

The thoughts of the heiress wandered from the youth, who was holding a canopy of shawls over herself and Louisa, to the hunter and the Indian warrior; and she felt an awakening curiosity to visit a hut, where men of such different habits and temperament were drawn together, as if by one common impulse.

· *Chapter XXV* ·

Cease all this parlance about hills and dales;
None listen to thy scenes of boyish frolic,
Fond dotard! with such tickled ears as thou dost;
Come! to thy tale.

DUO

Mr. Jones arose, on the following morning, with the sun, and ordering his own and Marmaduke's steeds to be saddled, he proceeded, with a countenance that was big with some business of unusual moment, to the apartment of the Judge. The door was unfastened, and Richard entered, with the freedom that characterized, not only the intercourse between the cousins, but the ordinary manners of the Sheriff.

"Well, 'duke, to horse," he cried, "and I will explain to you my meaning in the allusions I made last night. David says, in the Pslams—no, it was Solomon, but it was all in the family —Solomon said, there was a time for all things; and in my humble opinion, a fishing party is not the moment for discussing important subjects—Ha! why, what the devil ails you, Marmaduke? an't you well? let me feel your pulse; my grandfather you know"—

"Quite well in the body, Richard," interrupted the Judge, repulsing his cousin, who was about to assume the functions that properly belonged to Dr. Todd; "but ill at heart. I received letters by the post of last night, after we returned from the point, and this among the number."

The Sheriff took the letter, but without turning his eyes on the writing, for he was examining the appearance of the other with astonishment. From the face of his cousin, the gaze of Richard wandered to the table, which was covered with letters, packets, and newspapers; then to the apartment, and all that it contained. On the bed there was the impression that had been made by a human form, but the coverings were unmoved, and every thing indicated that the occupant of the room had passed a sleepless night. The candles had burned to the sockets, and had evidently extinguished themselves in their own fragments. Marmaduke had drawn his curtains, and opened both the shutters and sashes, to admit the balmy air of a spring morning; but his pale cheek, his quivering lip, and his sunken eye, presented, altogether, so very different an appearance from the usual calm, manly, and cheerful aspect of the Judge, that the Sheriff grew each moment more and more bewildered with his astonishment. At length Richard found time to cast his eyes on the direction of the letter, which he still held unopened, crumbling it in his hand.

"What! a ship-letter!" he exclaimed: "and from England! ha! 'duke, here must be news of importance indeed!"

"Read it," said Marmaduke, waving his hand for silence, and pacing the floor in excessive agitation.

Richard, who commonly thought aloud, was unable to read a letter, without suffering part of its contents to escape him in audible sound. So much of the epistle as was divulged in that manner, we shall lay before the reader, accompanied by the passing remarks of the Sheriff:—

" 'London, February 12th, 1793.' What a devil of a passage she had! but the wind has been northwest for six weeks, until within the last fortnight. 'Sir, your favours of August 10th, September 23rd, and of December 1st, were received in due season, and the fist answered by return of packet. Since the receipt of the last, I'—Here a long passage was rendered indistinct, by a most significant kind of humming noise made by the Sheriff. 'I grieve to say that'—hum, hum, bad enough to be sure—'but trust that a merciful Providence has seen fit'—hum, hum, hum; seems to be a good, pious sort of man, 'duke; belongs to the established church, I dare say; hum, hum—'vessel sailed from Falmouth on or about the 1st September of last year, and'—hum, hum, hum. 'If any thing should transpire on this afflicting subject, shall not fail'— hum, hum; really a good-hearted man, for a lawyer—'but can communicate nothing further at present'—Hum, hum. 'The

national convention'—hum, hum—'unfortunate Louis'—
hum, hum—'example of your Washington'—a very sensible
man, I declare, and none of your crazy democrats. Hum, hum
—'our gallant navy'—hum, hum—'under our most excellent
monarch'—ay, a good man enough, that King George, but
bad advisers; hum, hum—'I beg to conclude with assurances
of my perfect respect,'—hum, hum—'ANDREW HOLT.'
Andrew Holt—a very sensible, feeling man, this Mr. Andrew
Holt—but the writer of evil tidings. What will you do next,
cousin Marmaduke?"

"What can I do, Richard, but trust to time and the will of
Heaven? Here is another letter, from Connecticut, but it only
repeats the substance of the last. There is but one consoling
reflection to be gathered from the English news, which is, that
my last letter was received by him before the ship sailed."

"This is bad enough indeed! 'duke, bad enough indeed!
and away go all my plans of putting wings to the house, to the
devil. I had made my arrangements for a ride, to introduce
you to somethng of a very important nature. You know how
much you think of mines"—

"Talk not of mines," interrupted the Judge; "there is a
sacred duty to be performed, and that without delay. I must
devote this day to writing; and thou must be my assistant,
Richard; it will not do to employ Oliver in a matter of such
secrecy and interest."

"No, no, 'duke," cried the Sheriff, squeezing his hand; "I
am your man, just now; we are sisters' children, and blood,
after all, is the best cement to make friendship stick together.
Well, well, there is no hurry about the silver mine, just now;
another time will do as well. We shall want Dirky Van, I suppose?"

Marmaduke assented to this indirect question, and the
Sheriff relinquished all his intentions on the subject of his
ride, and repairing to the breakfast parlour, he dispatched a
messenger to require the immediate presence of Dirck Van
der School.

The village of Templeton, at that time, supported but two
lawyers, one of whom was introduced to our readers in the
bar-room of the "Bold Dragoon," and the other was the gen-

tleman of whom Richard spoke, by the friendly yet familiar appellation of Dirck, or Dirky Van. Great good-nature, a very tolerable share of skill in his profession, and considering the circumstances, no contemptible degree of honesty, were the principal ingredients to be found in the character of this man; who was known to the settlers as Squire Van der School, and sometimes by the flattering, though anomalous title of the "Dutch," or "honest lawyer." We would not wish to mislead our readers in their conceptions of any of our characters, and we therefore feel it necessary to add, that the adjective, in the preceding agnomen of Mr. Van der School, was used in direct reference to its substantive. Our orthodox friends need not be told, that all merit in this world is comparative; and, once for all, we desire to say, that where any thing which involves qualities or character is asserted, we must be understood to mean, "under the circumstances."

During the remainder of the day, the Judge was closeted with his cousin and his lawyer; and no one else was admitted to his apartment, excepting his daughter. The deep distress, that so evidently afflicted Marmaduke, was, in some measure, communicated to Elizabeth, also; for a look of dejection shaded her intelligent features, and the buoyancy of her animated spirits was sensibly softened. Once on that day, young Edwards, who was a wondering and observant spectator of the sudden alteration produced in the heads of the family, detected a tear stealing over the cheek of the heiress, and suffusing her bright eyes with a softness that did not always belong to their proud and laughing expression.

"Have any evil tidings been received, Miss Temple?" he inquired, with an interest and voice that caused Louisa Grant to raise her head from her needlework, with a quickness at which she instantly blushed herself. "I would offer my services to your father, if, as I suspect, he needs an agent in some distant place, and I thought it would give you relief."

"We have certainly heard bad news," returned Elizabeth, "and it may be necessary that my father should leave his home for a short period; unless I can persuade him to trust my cousin Richard with the business, whose absence from the county, just at this time, too, might be inexpedient."

The youth paused a moment, and the blood gathered slowly to his temples, as he continued—

"If it be of a nature that I could execute"——

"It is such that can only be confided to one we know—one of ourselves."

"Surely, you know me, Miss Temple!" he added, with a warmth that he seldom exhibited, but which did sometimes escape him, in the moments of their frank communications— "Have I lived five months under your roof, and yet a stranger?"

Elizabeth was engaged with her needle also, and she bent her head to one side, affecting to arrange her muslin; but her hand shook, her colour heightened, and her eyes lost their moisture in an expression of ungovernable interest, as she said—

"How much do we know of you, Mr. Edwards?"

"How much!" echoed the youth, gazing from the speaker to the mild countenance of Louisa, that was also illuminated with awakened curiosity; "how much! have I been so long an inmate with you, and not known?"

The head of Elizabeth turned slowly from its affected position, and the look of confusion that had blended so strongly with an expression of interest, changed to a smile of archness, as she answered—

"We know you, sir, indeed: you are called Mr. Oliver Edwards. I understand that you have informed my friend, Miss Grant, that you are a native"——

"Elizabeth!" exclaimed Louisa, blushing to her eyes, and trembling like an aspen; "you misunderstood me, dear Miss Temple; I—I—it was only conjecture. Besides, if Mr. Edwards is related to the natives, why should we reproach him? In what are we better? at least I, who am the child of a poor and unsettled clergyman?"

Elizabeth shook her head, doubtingly, and even laughed, but made no reply, until, observing the melancholy which pervaded the countenance of her companion, who was thinking of the poverty and labours of her father, she continued—

"Nay, Louisa, your humility carries you too far. The daughter of a minister of the church can have no superiors. Neither

I nor Mr. Edwards is quite your equal, unless," she added, again smiling, "he is in secret a king."

"A faithful servant of the King of kings, Miss Temple, is inferior to none on earth," said Louisa; "but his honours are his own; I am only the child of a poor and friendless man, and can claim no other distinction. Why, then, should I feel myself elevated above Mr. Edwards, because—because—perhaps he is only very, very distantly related to John Mohegan?"

Glances of a very comprehensive meaning were exchanged between the heiress and the young man, as Louisa betrayed, while vindicating his lineage, the reluctance with which she admitted his alliance to the old warrior; but not even a smile at the simplicity of their companion was indulged by either.

"On reflection, I must acknowledge that my situation here is somewhat equivocal," said Edwards, "though I may be said to have purchased it with my blood."

"The blood, too, of one of the native lords of the soil!" cried Elizabeth, whose melancholy had vanished in the excitement of their dialogue.

"Do I bear the marks of my lineage so very plainly impressed on my appearance?" asked the youth, with a little pique in his manner. "I am dark, but not very red—not more so than common?"

"Rather more so, just now," said the heiress.

"I am sure, Miss Temple," cried Louisa, "you cannot have taken much notice of Mr. Edwards. His eyes are not so black as Mohegan's, or even your own, nor is his hair!"

"Very possibly, then, I can lay claim to the same descent. It would be a great relief to my mind to think so, for I own that I grieve when I see old Mohegan walking about these lands, like the ghost of one of their ancient possessors, and feel how small is my right to possess them."

"Do you?" cried the youth, with a vehemence that startled the ladies.

"I do, indeed," returned Elizabeth, after suffering a moment to pass in her surprise; "but what can I do? what can my father do? Should we offer the old man a home and a maintenance, his habits would compel him to refuse us.

Neither, were we so silly as to wish such a thing, could we convert these clearings and farms, again, into hunting-grounds, as the Leather-stocking would wish to see them."

"You speak the truth, Miss Temple," said Edwards. "What can you do, indeed! But there is one thing that I am certain you can and will do, when you become the mistress of these beautiful valleys—use your wealth with indulgence to the poor and charity to the needy;—indeed, you can do no more."

"And that will be doing a good deal," said Louisa, smiling in her turn. "But there will, doubtless, be one to take the direction of such things from her hands."

"I am not about to disclaim matrimony," cried the heiress, "like a silly girl, who dreams of nothing else from morning till night; but I am a nun, here, without the vow of celibacy. Where should I find a husband in these forests?"

"There is none, Miss Temple," said Edwards, quickly, "there is none who has a right to aspire to you, and I know that you will assert the dignity of your sex, and wait to be sought by your equal; or die, as you live, loved, respected, and admired, by all who know you."

The young man seemed to think that he had said all that was required by gallantry, for he arose, and taking his hat, hurried from the apartment. Perhaps Louisa thought that he had said more than was necessary, for she sighed, with an aspiration so low that it was scarcely audible to herself, and bent her head over her work again. And it is possible that Miss Temple wished to hear more, for her eyes continued fixed for a minute, on the door through which the youth had passed, then glanced quickly towards her companion, when the long silence that succeeded manifested how much zest may be given to the conversation of two maidens under eighteen, by the presence of a youth of three and twenty.

The first person encountered by Mr. Edwards, as he rather rushed than walked from the house, was the little, square-built lawyer, with a large bundle of papers under his arm, a pair of green spectacles on his nose, with glasses at the sides, as if to multiply his power of detecting frauds, by additional organs of vision.

Mr. Van der School was a well-educated man, but of a slow comprehension, who had imbibed a wariness in his speeches and actions, from having suffered by his collisions with his more mercurial and apt brethren who had laid the foundations of their practice in the eastern courts, and who had sucked in shrewdness with their mothers' milk. The caution of this gentleman was exhibited in his actions, by the utmost method and punctuality, tinctured with a good deal of timidity; and in his speeches by a parenthetical style, that frequently left to his auditors a most delightful search after his meaning.

"A good morning to you, Mr. Van der School," said Edwards; "it seems to be a busy day with us at the Mansion-house."

"Good morning, Mr. Edwards, (if that is your name, (for, being a stranger, we have no other evidence of the fact than your own testimony,) as I understand you have given it to Judge Temple,) good morning, sir. It is, apparently, a busy day, (but a man of your discretion need not be told, (having, doubtless, discovered it of your own accord,) that appearances are often deceitful,) up at the Mansion-house."

"Have you papers of consequence, that will require copying? can I be of assistance to you in any way?"

"There are papers, (as doubtless, you see, (for your eyes are young,) by the outsides) that require copying."

"Well, then I will accompany you to your office, and receive such as are most needed, and by night I shall have them done, if there be much haste."

"I shall be always glad to see you, sir, at my office, (as in duty bound, (not that it is obligatory to receive any man within your dwelling, (unless, so inclined,) which is a castle,) according to the forms of politeness,) or at any other place; but the papers are most strictly confidential, (and as such, cannot be read by any one,) unless so directed,) by Judge Temple's solemn injunctions) and are invisible to all eyes) excepting those whose duties (I mean assumed duties) require it of them."

"Well, sir, as I perceive that I can be of no service, I wish you another good morning; but beg you will remember that

I am quite idle, just now, and I wish you would intimate as
much to Judge Temple, and make him a tender of my services, in any part of the world; unless—unless—it be far from
Templeton."

"I will make the communication, sir, in your name, (with
your own qualifications,) as your agent. Good morning, sir.
— But stay proceedings, Mr. Edwards, (so called,) for a moment. Do you wish me to state the offer of travelling, as a
final contract, (for which consideration has been received,
at former dates, (by sums advanced,) which would be binding,) or as a tender of services for which compensation is to
be paid (according to future agreement between the parties)
on performance of the conditions?"

"Any way—any way," said Edwards,—"he seems in distress, and I would assist him."

"The motive is good, sir, (according to appearances,
(which are often deceitful,) on first impressions,) and does
you honour. I will mention your wish, young gentleman, (as
you now seem) and will not fail to communicate the answer,
by five o'clock, P.M. of this present day, (God willing,) if
you give me an opportunity so to do."

The ambiguous nature of the situation and character of
Mr. Edwards, had rendered him an object of peculiar suspicion to the lawyer, and the youth was consequently too
much accustomed to similar equivocal and guarded speeches,
to feel any unusual disgust at the present dialogue. He saw,
at once, that it was the intention of the practitioner to conceal the nature of his business, even from the private secretary of Judge Temple; and he knew too well, the difficulty
of comprehending the meaning of Mr. Van der School, when
the gentleman most wished to be luminous in his discourse,
not to abandon all thoughts of a discovery, when he perceived that the attorney was endeavouring to avoid any
thing like an approach to a cross examination. They parted
at the gate, the lawyer walking, with an important and hurried air, towards his office, keeping his right hand firmly
clenched on the bundle of papers that his left arm pressed
to his side with a kind of convulsive motion.

It must have been obvious to all our readers, that the

youth entertained an unusual and deeply seated prejudice against the character of the Judge; but, owing to some counteracting cause, his sensations were now those of powerful interest in the state of his patron's present feelings, and in the cause of his secret uneasiness.

He remained gazing after the lawyer, until the door closed on both the bearer and the mysterious packet, when he returned slowly to the dwelling, and endeavoured to forget his curiosity, in the usual avocations of his office.

When the Judge made his reappearance in the circles of his family, his cheerfulness was tempered by a shade of melancholy, that lingered for many days around his manly brow; but the magical progression of the season aroused him from his temporary apathy, and his smiles returned with the animated looks of summer.

The heats of the days, and the frequent occurrence of balmy showers, had completed, in an incredibly short period, the growth of plants, which the lingering spring had so long retarded in the germ; and the woods presented every shade of green that the American forests know. The stumps in the cleared fields were already hid beneath the tops of the stalks of rich wheat that were waving with every breath of the summer air, shining and changing their hues, like velvet.

During the continuance of his cousin's dejection, Mr. Jones forbore, with much consideration, to press on his attention a business that each hour was drawing nearer to the heart of the Sheriff, and which, if any opinion could be formed by his frequent private conferences with the man who was introduced in these pages, by the name of Jotham, at the bar-room of the Bold Dragoon, was becoming also of great importance.

At length the Sheriff ventured to allude again to the subject, and one evening, in the beginning of July, Marmaduke made him a promise of devoting the following day to the desired excursion.

· *Chapter XXVI* ·

Speak on, my dearest father!
Thy words are like the breezes of the west.

MILMAN

It was a mild and soft morning, when Marmaduke and Richard mounted their horses, to proceed on the expedition that had so long been uppermost in the thoughts of the latter; and Elizabeth and Louisa appeared at the same instant in the hall, attired for an excursion on foot.

The head of Miss Grant was covered by a neat little hat of green silk, and her modest eyes peered from under its shade, with the soft languor that characterized her whole appearance; but Miss Temple trod her father's wide apartments with the step of their mistress, holding in her hand, dangling by one of its ribands, the gipsy that was to conceal the glossy locks that curled around her polished forehead, in rich profusion.

"What, are you for a walk, Bess!" cried the Judge, suspending his movements for a moment, to smile, with a father's fondness, at the display of womanly grace and beauty that his child presented.

"Remember the heats of July, my daughter, nor venture further than thou canst retrace before the meridian. Where is thy parasol, girl? thou wilt lose the polish of thy brow, under this sun and southern breeze, unless thou guard it with unusual care."

"I shall then do more honour to my connexions," returned the smiling daughter. "Cousin Richard has a bloom that any lady might envy. At present, the resemblance between us is so trifling that no stranger would know us to be 'sisters' children.'"

"Grand-children, you mean, cousin Bess," said the Sheriff. "But on, Judge Temple; time and tide wait for no man; and if you take my counsel, sir, in twelve months from this day, you may make an umbrella for your daughter of her camel's-hair shawl, and have its frame of solid silver. I ask nothing for myself, 'duke, you have been a good friend to me already; besides, all that I have will go to Bess, there, one of these melancholy days, so it's as long as it's short, whether I or you leave it. But we have a day's ride before us, sir; so move forward, or dismount, and say you won't go, at once."

"Patience, patience, Dickon," returned the Judge, checking his horse, and turning again to his daughter. "If thou art for the mountains, love, stray not too deep into the forest, I entreat thee; for, though it is done often with impunity, there is sometimes danger."

"Not at this season, I believe, sir," said Elizabeth; "for, I will confess, it is the intention of Louisa and myself to stroll among the hills."

"Less at this season than in the winter, dear; but still there may be danger in venturing too far. But though thou art resolute, Elizabeth, thou art too much like thy mother not to be prudent."

The eyes of the parent turned reluctantly from the brilliant beauty of his child, and the Judge and Sheriff rode slowly through the gateway and disappeared among the buildings of the village.

During this short dialogue, young Edwards had stood, an attentive listener, holding in his hand a fishing-rod, the day and the season having tempted him also to desert the house, for the pleasure of exercise in the air. As the equestrians turned through the gate, he approached the young maidens, who were already moving on to the gravelled walk that led to the street, and was about to address them, as Louisa paused, and said quickly—

Here is Mr. Edwards, would speak to us, Elizabeth."

The other stopped also, and turned to the youth, politely, but with a slight coldness in her air, that sensibly checked the freedom with which the gentleman had approached them.

"Your father is not pleased that you should walk unattended in the hills, Miss Temple. If I might offer myself as a
protector"—

"Does my father select Mr. Oliver Edwards as the organ of
his displeasure?" interrupted the lady.

"Good Heaven! you misunderstood my meaning," cried the
youth; "I should have said uneasy, for not pleased. I am his
servant, madam, and in consequence yours. I repeat that,
with your consent, I will change my rod for a fowling piece,
and keep nigh you on the mountain."

"I thank you, Mr. Edwards," returned Elizabeth, suffering one of her fascinating smiles to chase the trifling frown
from her features; "but where there is no danger, no protection is required. We are not yet, sir, reduced to wandering
among these free hills accompanied by a bodyguard. If such
an one is necessary, there he is, however.—Here, Brave,—
Brave,—my noble Brave!"

The huge mastiff that has been already mentioned, appeared from his kennel, gaping and stretching himself, with
a pampered laziness; but as his mistress again called—
"Come, dear Brave; once have you served your Master well;
let us see how you can do your duty by his daughter"—the
dog wagged his tail, as if he understood her language,
walked with a stately gait to her side, where he seated himself, and looked up at her face, with an intelligence but little
inferior to that which beamed in her own lovely countenance.

She resumed her walk, but again paused, after a few steps,
and added, in tones of conciliation—

"You can be serving us equally, and, I presume, more
agreeably to yourself, Mr. Edwards, by bringing us a string
of your favourite perch, for the dinner table."

When they again began to walk, Miss Temple did not look
back, to see how the youth bore this repulse; but the head of
Louisa was turned several times, before they reached the gate,
on that considerate errand.

"I am afraid, Elizabeth," she said, "that we have morti-
fied Oliver. He is still standing where we left him, leaning on
his rod. Perhaps he thinks us proud."

"He thinks justly," exclaimed Miss Temple, as if awaking from a deep musing; "he thinks justly, then. We are too proud to admit of such particular attentions from a young man in an equivocal situation. What! make him the companion of our most private walks! It is pride, Louisa, but it is the pride of a woman."

It was several minutes before Oliver aroused himself from the abstracted position in which he was standing when Louisa last saw him; but when he did, he muttered something, rapidly and incoherently, and throwing his rod over his shoulder, he strode down the walk, through the gate and along one of the streets of the village, until he reached the lakeshore, with the air of an emperor. At this spot boats were kept, for the use of Judge Temple and his family. The young man threw himself into a light skiff, and seizing the oars, he sent it across the lake towards the hut of Leather-stocking, with a pair of vigorous arms. By the time he had rowed a quarter of a mile, his reflections were less bitter; and when he saw the bushes that lined the shore in front of Natty's habitation gliding by him, as if they possessed the motion which proceeded from his own efforts, he was quite cooled in mind, though somewhat heated in body. It is quite possible, that the very same reason which guided the conduct of Miss Temple, suggested itself to a man of the breeding and education of the youth; and it is very certain, that if such were the case, Elizabeth rose instead of falling in the estimation of Mr. Edwards.

The oars were now raised from the water, and the boat shot close in to the land, where it lay gently agitated by waves of its own creating, while the young man, first casting a cautious and searching glance around him in every direction, put a small whistle to his mouth, and blew a long, shrill note, that rung far among the echoing rocks behind the hut. At this alarm, the hounds of Natty rushed out of their bark kennel, and commenced their long, piteous howls, leaping about as if half frantic, though restrained by the leashes of buckskin, by which they were fastened.

"Quiet, Hector, quiet," said Oliver, again applying his whistle to his mouth, and drawing out notes still more shrill than before. No reply was made, the dogs having returned to their kennel at the sounds of his voice.

Edwards pulled the bows of the boat on to the shore, and landing, ascended the beach and approached the door of the cabin. The fastenings were soon undone, and he entered, closing the door after him, when all was as silent, in that retired spot, as if the foot of man had never trod the wilderness. The sounds of the hammers, that were in incessant motion in the village, were faintly heard across the water; but the dogs had crouched into their lairs, well satisfied that none but the privileged had approached the forbidden ground.

A quarter of an hour elapsed before the youth reappeared, when he fastened the door again and spoke kindly to the hounds. The dogs came out at the well-known tones, and the slut jumped upon his person, whining and barking, as if entreating Oliver to release her from her prison. But Old Hector raised his nose to the light current of air, and opened a long howl, that might have been heard for a mile.

"Ha! what do you scent, my old veteran of the woods?" cried Edwards. "If a beast, it is a bold one, and if a man, an impudent."

He sprung through the top of a pine, that had fallen near the side of the hut, and ascended a small hillock, that sheltered the cabin to the south, where he caught a glimpse of the formal figure of Hiram Doolittle, as it vanished with an unusual rapidity for the architect, amid the trees and bushes.

"What can that fellow be wanting here?" muttered Oliver. "He has no business in this quarter, unless it be his curiosity, which is an endemic in these woods. But against that I will effectually guard, though the dogs should take a liking to his ugly visage, and let him pass." The youth returned to the door, while giving vent to this soliloquy, and completed the fastenings, by placing a small chain through a staple, and securing it there by a padlock. "He is a pettifogger, and surely must know that there is such a thing as feloniously breaking into a man's house."

Apparently well satisfied with this arrangement, the youth again spoke to the hounds; and, descending to the shore, he launched his boat, and taking up his oars, pulled off into the lake.

There were several places in the Otsego that were celebrated as fishing-ground for the perch. One was nearly opposite to the cabin, and another, still more famous, was near a point, at the distance of a mile and a half above it, under the brow of the mountain, and on the same side of the lake with the hut. Oliver Edwards pulled his little skiff over the first, and sat, for a minute, undecided whether to continue there, with his eyes on the door of the cabin, or to change his ground, with a view to get superior game. While gazing about him, he saw the light-coloured bark canoe of his old companions, riding on the water, at the point we have mentioned, and containing two figures, that he at once knew to be Mohegan and the Leather-stocking. This decided the matter, and the youth pulled his little boat, in a very few minutes, to the place where his friends were fishing, and fastened it to the light vessel of the Indian.

The old men received Oliver with welcoming nods of their heads, but neither drew his line from the water, nor, in the least, varied his occupation. When Edwards had secured his own boat, he baited his hook and threw it into the lake, without speaking.

"Did you stop at the wigwam, lad, as you rowed by?" asked Natty.

"Yes, and I found all safe; but that carpenter and justice of the peace, Mr. or, as they call him, Squire Doolittle, was prowling through the woods, nigh by. But I made sure of the door, before I left the hut, and I think he is too great a coward to approach the hounds."

"There's little to be said in favour of that man," said Natty, while he drew in a perch and baited his hook. "He craves dreadfully to come into the cabin, and has as good as asked me as much to my face; but I put him off with unsartin answers, so that he is no wiser than Solomon. This comes of having so many laws that such a man may be called on to intarpret them."

"I fear he is more knave than fool," cried Edwards; "I see that he makes a tool of that simple man, the Sheriff, and I dread that his impertinent curiosity may yet give us much trouble."

"If he harbours too much about the cabin, lad, I'll shoot the creater," said the Leather-stocking, quite cooly.

"No, no, Natty, you must remember the law," said Edwards, "or we shall have you in trouble; and that, odd man, would be an evil day, and sore tidings to us all."

"Would it, boy!" exclaimed the hunter, raising his eyes with a look of friendly interest towards the youth. "You have the true blood in your veins, Mr. Oliver, and I'll support it, to the face of Judge Temple, or in any court in the country. How is it, John? do I speak the true word? is the lad staunch, and of the right blood?"

"He is a Delaware," said Mohegan, "and my brother. The Young Eagle is brave, and he will be a chief. No harm can come."

"Well, well," cried the youth impatiently; "say no more about it, my good friends; if I am not all that your partiality would make me, I am yours through life—in prosperity as in poverty. But now we will talk of other matters."

The old hunters yielded to his wish, which seemed to be their law. For a short time, a profound silence prevailed, during which each man was very busy with his hook and line; but Edwards, probably feeling that it remained with him to renew the discourse, soon observed, with the air of one who knew not what he said—

"How beautifully tranquil and glassy the lake is. Saw you it ever more calm and even than at this moment, Natty?"

"I have known the Otsego water for five-and-forty years," said Leather-stocking, "and I will say that for it, which is, that a cleaner spring or a better fishing is not to be found in the land. Yes, yes—I had the place to myself once; and a cheerful time I had of it. The game was as plenty as heart could wish, and there was none to meddle with the ground, unless there might have been a hunting party of the Delawares crossing the hills, or, maybe, a rifling scout of them thieves, the Iroquois. There was one or two Frenchmen that squatted in the flats, further west, and married squaws; and some of the Scotch-Irishers, from the Cherry Valley, would come on to the lake, and borrow my canoe, to take a mess of parch, or drop a line for a salmon-trout; but, in the main, it was a cheerful place, and I had but little to disturb me in it. John would come, and John knows."

Mohegan turned his dark face, at this appeal, and, moving his hand forward with a graceful motion of assent, he spoke, using the Delaware language—

"The land was owned by my people; we gave it to my brother, in council—to the Fire-Eater; and what the Delawares give, lasts as long as the waters run. Hawk-eye smoked at that council, for we loved him."

"No, no, John," said Natty, "I was no chief, seeing that I know'd nothing of scholarship, and had a white skin. But it was a comfortable hunting-ground then, lad, and would have been so to this day, but for the money of Marmaduke Temple, and, maybe, the twisty ways, of the law."

"It must have been a sight of melancholy pleasure, indeed," said Edwards, while his eye roved along the shores and over the hills, where the clearings, groaning with the golden corn, were cheering the forests with the signs of life, "to have roamed over these mountains, and along this sheet of beautiful water, without a living soul to speak to, or to thwart your humour."

"Haven't I said it was a cheerful!" said Leather-stocking. "Yes, yes—when the trees begun to be kivered with the leaves, and the ice was out of the lake, it was a second paradise. I have travelled the woods for fifty-three years, and have made them my home for more than forty, and I can say that I have met but one place that was more to my liking; and that was only to eyesight, and not for hunting or fishing."

"And where was that?" asked Edwards.

"Where! why up on the Cattskills. I used often to go up into the mountains after wolves' skins, and bears; once they bought me to get them a stuffed painter; and so I often went. There's a place in them hills that I used to climb to when I wanted to see the carryings on of the world, that would well pay any man for a barked shin or a torn moccasin. You know the Cattskills, lad, for you must have seen them on your left, as you followed the river up from York, looking as blue as a piece of clear sky, and holding the clouds on their tops, as the smoke curls over the head of an Indian chief at a council fire. Well, there's the High-peak and the Round-top, which lay back, like a father and mother among their children, seeing they are far above all the other hills. But the place I mean is next to the river, where one of the ridges juts out a little from the rest, and where the rocks fall for the best part of a thousand feet, so much up and down, that a man standing on their edges is fool enough to think he can jump from top to bottom."

"What see you when you get there?" asked Edwards.

"Creation!" said Natty, dropping the end of his rod into the water, and sweeping one hand around him in a circle— "all creation, lad. I was on that hill when Vaughan burnt 'Sopus, in the last war, and I seen the vessels come out of the highlands as plain as I can see that lime-scow rowing into the Susquehanna, though one was twenty times further from me than the other. The river was in sight for seventy miles, under my feet, looking like a curled shaving, though it was eight long miles to its banks. I saw the hills in the Hampshire grants, the high lands of the river, and all that God had done or man could do, as far as eye could reach— you know that the Indians named me for my sight, lad— and from the flat on the top of that mountain, I have often found the place where Albany stands; and as for 'Sopus! the day the royal troops burnt the town, the smoke seemed so nigh, that I thought I could hear the screeches of the women."

"It must have been worth the toil, to meet with such a glorious view!"

"If being the best part of a mile in the air, and having men's farms and housen at your feet, with rivers looking like rib-ands, and mountains bigger than the 'Vision,' seeming to be haystacks of green grass under you, gives any satisfaction to a man, I can recommend the spot. When I first come into the woods to live, I used to have weak spells, and I felt lonesome; and then I would go into the Cattskills and spend a few days on that hill, to look at the ways of man; but it's now many a year since I felt any such longings, and I'm getting too old for them rugged rocks. But there's a place, a

short two miles back of that very hill, that in late times I relished better than the mountain; for it was more kivered with
the trees, and more nateral."

"And where was that?" inquired Edwards, whose curiosity
was strongly excited by the simple description of the hunter.

"Why, there's a fall in the hills, where the water of two
little ponds that lie near each other breaks out of their
bounds, and runs over the rocks into the valley. The stream
is, maybe, such a one as would turn a mill, if so useless a
thing was wanted in the wilderness. But the hand that made
that 'Leap' never made a mill! There the water comes crook-
ing and winding among the rocks, first so slow that a trout
could swim in it, and then starting and running just like any
creater that wanted to make a far spring, till it gets to where
the mountain divides, like the cleft hoof of a deer, leaving a
deep hollow for the brook to tumble into. The first pitch is
nigh two hundred feet, and the water looks like flakes of
driven snow, afore it touches the bottom; and there the
stream gathers itself together again for a new start, and maybe
flutters over fifty feet of flat-rock, before it falls for another
hundred, when it jumps about from shelf to shelf, first turning this-away and then turning that-away, striving to get
out of the hollow, till it finally comes to the plain."

"I have never heard of this spot before!" exclaimed
Edwards; "it is not mentioned in the books."

"I never read a book in my life," said Leather-stocking;
"and how should a man who has lived in towns and schools
know any thing about the wonders of the woods! No, no,
lad; there has that little stream of water been playing
among them hills, since He made the world, and not a dozen
white men have ever laid eyes on it. The rock sweeps like
masonwork, in a half-round, on both sides of the fall and
shelves over the bottom for fifty feet; so that when I've been
sitting at the foot of the first pitch, and my hounds have run
into the caverns behind the sheet of water, they've looked no
bigger than so many rabbits. To my judgment, lad, it's the
best piece of work that I've met with in the woods; and
none know how often the hand of God is seen in a wilderness,
but them that rove it for a man's life."

"What becomes of the water? in which direction does it run? Is it a tributary of the Delaware?"

"Anan!" said Natty.

"Does the water run into the Delaware?"

"No, no, it's a drop for the old Hudson; and a merry time it has till it gets down off the mountain. I've sat on the shelving rock many a long hour, boy, and watched the bubbles as they shot by me, and thought how long it would be before that very water, which seemed made for the wilderness, would be under the bottom of a vessel, and tossing in the salt sea. It is a spot to make a man solemnize. You can see right down into the valley that lies to the east of the High-Peak, where, in the fall of the year, thousands of acres of woods are before your eyes, in the deep hollow, and along the side of the mountain, painted like ten thousand rainbows, by no hand of man, though without the ordering of God's providence."

"Why, you are eloquent, Leather-stocking," exclaimed the youth.

"Anan!" repeated Natty.

"The recollection of the sight has warmed your blood, old man. How many years is it since you saw the place?"

The hunter made no reply; but bending his ear near to the water, he sat for a minute, holding his breath, and listening attentively, as if to some distant sound. At length, he raised his head, and said—

"If I hadn't fastened the hounds with my own hands, with a fresh leash of green buck-skin, I'd take a Bible oath that I heard old Hector ringing his cry on the mountain."

"It is impossible," said Edwards, "It is not an hour since I saw him in his kennel."

By this time the attention of Mohegan was attracted to the sounds; but, notwithstanding the youth was both silent and attentive, he could hear nothing but the lowing of some cattle from the western hills. He looked at the old men, Natty sitting with his hand to his ear, like a trumpet, and Mohegan bending forward, with his arm raised to a level with his face, holding the fore-finger elevated as a signal for attention, and laughed aloud at what he deemed to be their imaginary sounds.

"Laugh if you will, boy," said Leather-stocking, "the hounds be out, and are hunting a deer. No man can deceive me in such a matter. I wouldn't have had the thing happen for a beaver's skin. Not that I care for the law! but the venison is lean now, and the dumb things run the flesh off their bones for no good. Now do you hear the hounds?"

Edwards started, as a full cry broke on his ear, changing from the distant sounds that were caused by some intervening hill, to the confused echoes that rung among the rocks that the dogs were passing, and then directly to a deep and hollow baying that pealed under the forest on the lake shore. These variations in the tones of the hounds passed with amazing rapidity, and while his eyes were glancing along the margin of the water, a tearing of the branches of the alder and dog-wood caught his attention, at a spot near them, and, at the next moment a noble buck sprung on the shore, and buried himself in the lake. A full-mouthed cry, directly from the lungs of the hounds, followed, when Hector and the slut shot through the opening in the bushes, and darted into the lake also, bearing their breasts most gallantly to the water.

Chapter XXVII

Oft in the full descending flood he tries
To lose the scent, and lave his burning sides.
THOMSON

"I KNOWED it—I know'd it!" cried Natty, when both deer
and hounds were in full view;—"the buck has gone by them
with the wind, and it has been too much for the poor rogues;
but I must break them of these tricks, or they'll give me a
deal of trouble. He-ere, he-ere—shore with you, rascals—
shore with you—will ye?—Oh! off with you, old Hector, or
I'll hatchel your hide with my ramrod when I get ye."

The dogs knew their master's voice, and after swimming in
a circle, as if reluctant to give over the chase, and yet afraid
to persevere, they finally obeyed, and returned to the land,
where they filled the air with their howlings and cries.

In the mean time the deer, urged by his fears, had swam
over half the distance between the shore and the boats, before his terror permitted him to see the new danger. But at
the sounds of Natty's voice, he turned short in his course,
and for a few moments seemed about to rush back again, and
brave the dogs. His retreat in this direction was, however, effectually cut off, and turning a second time, he urged his
course obliquely for the centre of the lake, with an intention
of landing on the western shore. As the buck swam by the
fishermen, raising his nose high into the air, curling the
water before his slim neck like the beak of a galley, throwing his legs forward, and gliding along with incredible velocity, the Leather-stocking began to sit very uneasy in his
canoe.

"'Tis a noble creater!" he exclaimed; "what a pair of
horns! a man might hang up all his garments on the
branches. Let me see—July is the last month, and the flesh

must be getting good." While he was talking, Natty had instinctively employed himself in fastening the inner end of
the bark rope, that served him for a cable, to a paddle, and,
rising suddenly on his legs, he cast this buoy away from him,
and cried—"Strike out, John! Let her go. The creater's a fool
to tempt a man in this way."

Mohegan threw the fastening of the youth's boat off the
canoe, and with one stroke of his paddle sent the light bark
over the water like a meteor.

"Hold!" exclaimed Edwards. "Remember the law, my old
friends. You are in plain sight of the village, and I know that
Judge Temple is determined to prosecute all, indiscriminately,
who kill the deer out of season."

But the remonstrance came too late: the canoe was already far from the skiff, and the two hunters too much engaged in their pursuit to listen to his voice.

The buck was now within fifty yards of his pursuers, cutting the water most gallantly, and snorting at each breath
with his terror and his exertions, while the canoe seemed to
dance over the waves as it rose and fell with the undulations
made by its own motion. Leather-stocking raised his rifle and
freshened the priming, but stood in suspense whether to slay
his victim or not.

"Shall I, John, or no?" he said. "It seems but a poor advantage to take of the dumb thing too. I won't; it has taken
to the water on its own nater, which is the reason that God has
given to a deer, and I'll give it the lake play; so, John, lay
out your arm, and mind the turn of the buck; it's easy to
catch them, but they'll turn like a snake."

The Indian laughed at the conceit of his friend, but continued to send the canoe forward with a velocity that proceeded much more from his skill than his strength. Both of
the old men now used the language of the Delawares when
they spoke.

"Hooh!" exclaimed Mohegan; "the deer turns his head.
Hawk-eye, lift your spear."

Natty never moved abroad without taking with him every
implement that might, by possibility, be of service in his pursuits. From his rifle he never parted; and, although intend-

ing to fish with the line, the canoe was invariably furnished with all of its utensils, even to its grate. This precaution grew out of the habits of the hunter, who was often led, by his necessities or his sports, far beyond the limits of his original destination. A few years earlier than the date of our tale, the Leather-stocking had left his hut on the shores of the Otsego, with his rifle and his hounds, for a few days' hunting in the hills; but before he returned he had seen the waters of the Ontario. One, two, or even three hundred miles had once been nothing to his sinews, which were now a little stiffened by age. The hunter did as Mohegan advised, and prepared to strike a blow with the barbed weapon into the neck of the buck.

"Lay her more to the left, John," he cried, "lay her more to the left; another stroke of the paddle, and I have him."

While speaking, he raised the spear, and darted it from him like an arrow. At that instant the buck turned, the long pole glanced by him, the iron striking against his horn, and buried itself, harmlessly, in the lake.

"Back water," cried Natty, as the canoe glided over the place where the spear had fallen, "hold water, John."

The pole soon reappeared, shooting upward from the lake, and as the hunter seized it in his hand, the Indian whirled the light canoe round, where it lay, and renewed the chase. But this evolution gave the buck a great advantage; and it also allowed time for Edwards to approach the scene of action.

"Hold your hand, Natty," cried the youth, "hold your hand; remember it is out of season."

This remonstrance was made as the batteau arrived close to where the deer was struggling with the water, his back now rising to the surface, now sinking beneath it, as the waves curled from his neck, the animal sustaining itself nobly against the odds.

"Hurrah!" shouted Edwards, inflamed beyond prudence at the sight; "mind him as he doubles—mind him as he doubles; sheer more to the right, Mohegan, more to the right, and I'll have him by the horns; I'll throw the rope over his antlers."

The dark eye of the old warrior was dancing in his head,

with a wild animation, as bright and natural as the rays that shot from the glancing eyes of the terrified deer himself, and the sluggish repose in which his aged frame had been resting in the canoe, was now changed to all the rapid inflections of practised agility. The canoe whirled with each cunning evolution of the chase, like a bubble floating in a whirlpool; and when the direction of the pursuit admitted, for a short distance, of a straight course, the little bark skimmed the lake with a velocity that urged the deer to seek its safety in some new and unexpected turn. It was the frequency of these circuitous movements, that, by confining the action to so small a compass, enabled the youth to keep near his companions. More than twenty times both the pursued and the pursuers glided by him, just without the reach of his oars, until he thought the best way to view the sport was to remain stationary, and by watching a favourable opportunity, assist as much as he could in taking their intended victim.

He was not required to wait long, for no sooner had he adopted this resolution, and risen in the boat, than he saw the deer coming bravely towards him, with an apparent intention of pushing for a point of land at some distance from the hounds, who were still barking and howling on the shore. Edwards caught the painter of his skiff, and, making a noose, cast it from him with all his force, and luckily succeeded in drawing its knot close around one of the antlers of the buck.

For one instant, the skiff was drawn through the water, but in the next, the canoe glided before it, and Natty, bending low, passed his knife across the throat of the animal, whose blood followed the wound, dying the waters for many feet. The short time that was passed in the last struggles of the animal, was spent by the hunters in bringing their boats together, and securing them in that position, when Leatherstocking drew the deer from the water, and laid its lifeless form in the bottom of the canoe. He placed his hands on the ribs, and on different parts of the body of his prize, and then, raising his head, he laughed in his peculiar manner, saying—

"So much for Marmaduke Temple's law! This warms a body's blood, old John; I haven't killed a buck in the lake afore this, 'sin this many a year. I call that good venison, lad;

and I know them that will relish the creater's steaks, for all the betterments in the land."

The Indian had long been drooping with his years, and perhaps under the calamities of his race, but this invigorating and exciting sport had caused a gleam of sunshine to cross his swarthy face that had long been absent from his features. It was evident that the old man enjoyed the chase more as a memorial of his youthful sports and deeds, than with any expectation of profiting by the success. He felt the deer, however, lightly, his hand already trembling with the reaction of his unusual exertions, and smiled with a nod of approbation, as he said, in the emphatic and sententious manner of his people—

"Good."

"I am afraid, Natty," said Edwards, when the heat of the moment had passed, and his blood began to cool, "that we have all been equally transgressors of the law. But keep your own counsel, and there are none here to betray us. Yet, how came those dogs at large? I left them securely fastened, I know, for I felt the thongs, and examined the knots, when I was at the hut."

"It has been too much for the poor things," said Natty, "to have such buck take the wind of them. See, lad, the pieces of the buck-skin are hanging from their necks yet. Let us paddle up, John, and I will call them in, and look a little into the matter."

When the old hunter landed, and examined the thongs that were yet fast to the hounds, his countenance sensibly changed, and he shook his head doubtingly.

"Here has been a knife at work," he said—"this skin was never torn, nor is this the mark of a hound's tooth. No, no— Hector is not in fault, as I feared."

"Has the leather been cut?" cried Edwards.

"No, no—I didn't say it had been cut, lad; but this is a mark that was never made by a jump or a bite."

"Could that rascally carpenter have dared!" exclaimed the impetuous youth.

"Ay! he durst to do any thing, where there is no danger," said Natty; "he is a curious body, and loves to be helping other people on with their consarns. But he had best not harbour so much near the wigwam!"

In the mean time, Mohegan had been examining, with an Indian's sagacity, the place where the leather thong had been separated. After scrutinizing it closely, he said, in Delaware—

"It was cut with a knife—a sharp blade and a long handle —and the man was afraid of the dogs."

"How is this, Mohegan?" exclaimed Edwards; "You saw it not! how can you know these facts?"

"Listen, son," said the warrior. "The knive was sharp, for the cut is smooth;—the handle was long, for a man's arm would not reach from this gash to that cut that did not go through the skin;—he was a coward, or he would have cut the thongs around the necks of the hounds."

"On my life," cried Natty, "John is on the scent! It was that carpenter; and he has got on the rock back of the kennel, and let the dogs loose by fastening his knife to a stick. It would be an easy matter to do it, when a man is so minded."

"And why should he do so?" asked Edwards; "who has done him wrong, that he should trouble two old men like you?"

"It's a hard matter lad, to know men's ways, I find, since the settlers have brought in their new fashions. But is there nothing to be found out in this place? and maybe he is troubled with his longings after other people's business, as he often is."

"Your suspicions are just," cried the youth, "Give me the canoe: I am young and strong, and will get down there yet, perhaps, in time to interrupt his plans. Heaven forbid, that we should be at the mercy of such a man!"

His proposal was instantly accepted, the deer being placed in the skiff in order to lighten the canoe, and in less than five minutes the little vessel of bark was gliding over the glassy lake, and was soon hid by the points of land, as it shot close along the shore.

Mohegan followed slowly with the skiff, while Natty called his hounds to him, bade them keep close, and, shouldering his rifle, he ascended the mountain, with an intention of going to the hut by land.

· *Chapter XXVIII* ·

Ask me not what the maiden feels,
Left in that dreadful hour alone;
Perchance, her reason stoops, or reels;
Perchance, a courage not her own,
Braces her mind to desperate tone.
                                        SCOTT

While the chase was occurring on the lake, Miss Temple and her companion pursued their walk with the activity of youth. Male attendants, on such excursions, were thought to be altogether unnecessary, for none were ever known, there, to offer an insult to a female who respected the dignity of her own sex. After the embarrassment that had been created by their parting discourse with Edwards, had dissipated itself, the girls maintained a conversation that was as innocent and cheerful as themselves.

The path they had taken led them but a short distance above the hut of Leather-stocking, and there was a point in the road which commanded a birds-eye view of the sequestered spot.

From a feeling, that might have been natural, but must have been powerful, neither of the maidens, in their frequent and confidential dialogues, had ever trusted herself to utter one syllable concerning the equivocal situation in which the young man, who was now so intimately associated with them, had been found. If Judge Temple had deemed it prudent to make any inquiries on the subject, he had also thought it proper to keep the answers to himself; though it was so common an occurrence to find the well-educated youth of the eastern states, in every stage of their career to wealth, that the simple circumstance of his intelligence, connected with his poverty, would not, at that day, and in that country, have excited any very powerful curiosity. With his breeding, it might have been different; but the youth himself had so effectually guarded against any surprise on this subject, by his cold, and even in some cases, rude deportment, that when his manners seemed to soften by time, the Judge, if he thought about it at all, would have been most likely to imagine that the improvement was the result of his late association. But women are always more alive to such subjects than men; and what the abstraction of the father had overlooked, the observation of the daughter had easily detected. In the thousand little courtesies of polished life, she had early discovered that Edwards was not wanting, though his gentleness was so often crossed by marks of what she conceived to be fierce and uncontrollable passions. It may, perhaps, be unnecessary to tell the reader that Louisa Grant never reasoned so much after the fashions of the world. The gentle girl, however, had her own thoughts on the subject, and, like others, she drew her own conclusions.

"I would give all my other secrets, Louisa," exclaimed Miss Temple, laughing, and shaking back her dark locks, with a look of childish simplicity that her intelligent face seldom expressed, "to be mistress of all that those rude logs have heard and witnessed."

They were both looking at the secluded hut, at the instant, and Miss Grant raised her mild eyes, and she answered—

"I am sure they would tell nothing to the disadvantage of Mr. Edwards."

"Perhaps not; but they might tell who he is."

"Why, dear Miss Temple, we know all that already," returned the other; "I have heard it all very rationally explained by your cousin"——

"The executive chief!" interrupted Elizabeth—"yes, yes, he can explain any thing. His ingenuity will one day discover the philosopher's stone. But what did he say?"

"Say!" echoed Louisa, with a look of surprise; "why every thing that seemed to me to be satisfactory; and I have believed it to be true. He said that Natty Bumppo had lived most of his life in the woods, and among the Indians, by which means he had formed an acquaintance with old John, the Delaware chief."

"Indeed! that was quite a matter of fact tale for cousin Dickon. What came next?"

"I believe he accounted for their close intimacy, by some story about the Leather-stocking saving the life of John in a battle."

"Nothing more likely," said Elizabeth, a little impatiently; "but what is all this to the purpose?"

"Nay, Elizabeth, you must bear with my ignorance, and I will repeat all that I remember to have overheard; for the dialogue was between my father and the Sheriff, so lately as the last time they met. He then added, that the kings of England used to keep gentlemen as agents among the different tribes of Indians, and sometimes officers in the army, who frequently passed half their lives on the edge of the wilderness."

"Told with a wonderful historical accuracy! And did he end there?"

"Oh! no—then he said that these agents seldom married; and—and—they must have been wicked men, Elizabeth! but than he said—that—that"——

"Never mind," said Miss Temple, blushing and smiling, though so slightly, that both were unheeded by her companion—"skip all that."

"Well, then he said that they often took great pride in the education of their children, whom they frequently sent to England, and even to the colleges; and this is the way that he accounts for the liberal manner in which Mr. Edwards has been taught; for he acknowledges that he knows almost as much as himself, or your father—or even mine."

"Quite a climax in learning!" cried the heiress—"commencing with the last, I suppose. And so he made Mohegan the grand uncle or grandfather of Oliver Edwards."

"You have heard him yourself, then?" said Louisa.

"Often; but not on this subject. Mr. Richard Jones, you know, dear, has a theory for every thing; but has he one which will explain the reason why that hut is the only habitation within fifty miles of us, whose door is not open to every person that may choose to lift its latch?"

"I have never heard him say any thing on this subject," returned the clergyman's daughter; "but I suppose that, as they are poor, they very naturally are anxious to keep the little that they honestly own. It is sometimes dangerous to be rich, Miss Temple; but you cannot know how hard it is to be very, very poor."

"Nor you neither, I trust, Louisa; at least I should hope, that in this land of abundance, no minister of the church could be left to absolute suffering."

"There cannot be actual misery," returned the other, in a low and humble tone, "where there is a dependence on our Maker; but there may be such suffering as will cause the heart to ache."

"But not you—not you," said the impetuous Elizabeth— "not you, dear girl; you have never known the misery that is connected with poverty."

"Ah! Miss Temple, you little understand the troubles of this life, I believe. My father has spent many years as a missionary, in the new countries, where his people were poor, and frequently we have been without bread; unable to buy, and ashamed to beg, because we would not disgrace his sacred calling. But how often have I seen him leave his home, where the sick and the hungry felt, when he left them, that they had lost their only earthly friends, to ride on a duty which could not be neglected for domestic evils. Oh! how hard it must be, to preach consolation to others, when your own heart is bursting with anguish!"

"But it is all over now!" exclaimed Elizabeth, "your father's income must now be equal to his wants—it must be—it shall be."

"It is," replied Louisa, dropping her head on her bosom to conceal the tears which flowed in spite of her gentle Christianity, "for there are none left to be supplied but me."

The turn the conversation had taken drove from the minds of the young maidens all other thoughts but those of holy charity, and Elizabeth folded her friend in her arms, who gave vent to her momentary grief in audible sobs. When this burst of emotion had subsided, Louisa raised her mild countenance, and they continued their walk in silence.

By this time they had gained the summit of the mountain, where they left the highway, and pursued their course, under the shade of the stately trees that crowned the eminence. The day was becoming warm, and the girls plunged more deeply into the forest, as they found its invigorating coolness agreeably contrasted to the excessive heat they had experienced in their ascent. The conversation, as if by mutual consent, was entirely changed to the little incidents and scenes of their walk, and every tall pine, and every shrub or flower, called forth some simple expression of admiration.

In this manner they proceeded along the margin of the precipice, catching occasional glimpses of the placid Otsego, or pausing to listen to the rattling of wheels and the sounds of hammers, that rose from the valley, to mingle the signs of men with the scenes of nature, when Elizabeth suddenly started, and exclaimed—

"Listen! there are the cries of a child on this mountain! is there a clearing near us? or can some little one have strayed from its parents?"

"Such things frequently happen," returned Louisa. "Let us follow the sounds; it may be a wanderer starving on the hill."

Urged by this consideration, the females pursued the low, mournful sounds, that proceeded from the forest, with quick and impatient steps. More than once, the ardent Elizabeth was on the point of announcing that she saw the sufferer, when Louisa caught her by the arm, and pointing behind them, cried—

"Look at the dog!"

Brave had been their companion, from the time the voice of his young mistress lured him from his kennel, to the present moment. His advanced age had long before deprived him of his activity; and when his companions stopped to view the scenery, or to add to their bouquets, the mastiff would lay his huge frame on the ground, and await their movements, with his eyes closed, and a listlessness in his air that ill accorded with the character of a protector. But when, aroused by this cry from Louisa, Miss Temple turned, she saw the dog with his eyes keenly set on some distant object, his head bent near the ground, and his hair actually rising on his body, either through fright or anger. It was most probably the latter, for he was growling in a low key, and occasionally showing his teeth, in a manner that would have terrified his mistress, had she not so well known his good qualities.

"Brave!" she said, "be quiet, Brave! what do you see, fellow?"

At the sounds of her voice, the rage of the mastiff, instead of being at all diminished, was very sensibly increased. He stalked in front of the ladies, and seated himself at the feet of his mistress, growling louder than before, and occasionally giving vent to his ire by a short, surly barking.

"What does he see?" said Elizabeth, "there must be some animal in sight."

Hearing no answer from her companion, Miss Temple turned her head, and beheld Louisa, standing with her face whitened to the colour of death, and her finger pointing upward, with a sort of flickering, convulsed motion. The quick eye of Elizabeth glanced in the direction indicated by her friend, where she saw the fierce front and glaring eyes of a female panther, fixed on them in horrid malignity, and threatening instant destruction.

"Let us fly!" exclaimed Elizabeth, grasping the arm of Louisa, whose form yielded like melting snow, and sunk lifeless to the earth.

There was not a single feeling in the temperament of Elizabeth Temple, that could prompt her to desert a companion in such an extremity; and she fell on her knees, by the side of the inanimate Louisa, tearing from the person of her friend, with an instinctive readiness, such parts of her dress as might obstruct her respiration, and encouraging their only safeguard, the dog, at the same time, by the sounds of her voice.

"Courage, Brave!" she cried, her own tones beginning to tremble, "courage, courage, good Brave."

A quarter-grown cub, that had hitherto been unseen, now appeared, dropping from the branches of a sapling that grew under the shade of the beech which held its dam. This ignorant, but vicious creature, approached the dog, imitating the actions and sounds of its parent, but exhibiting a strange mixture of the playfulness of a kitten with the ferocity of its race. standing on its hind legs, it would rend the bark of a tree with its fore paws, and play all the antics of a cat, for a moment; and then, by lashing itself with its tail, growling and scratching the earth, it would attempt the manifestations of anger that rendered its parent so terrific.

All this time Brave stood firm and undaunted, his short tail erect, his body drawn backward on its haunches, and his eyes following the movements of both dam and cub. At every gambol played by the latter, it approached nigher to the dog, the growling of the three becoming more horrid at each moment, until the younger beast overleaping its intended bound, fell directly before the mastiff. There was a moment of fearful cries and struggles, but they ended almost as soon as commenced, by the cub appearing in the air, hurled from the jaws of Brave, with a violence that sent it against a tree so forcibly, as to render it completely senseless.

Elizabeth witnessed the short struggle, and her blood was warming with the triumph of the dog, when she saw the form of the old panther in the air, springing twenty feet from the branch of the beech to the back of the mastiff. No words of ours can describe the fury of the conflict that followed. It was a confused struggle on the dried leaves, accompanied by loud and terrific cries. Miss Temple continued on her knees, bending over the form of Louisa, her eyes fixed on the animals with an interest so horrid, and yet so intense, that she almost forgot her own stake in the result. So rapid and vigorous were the bounds of the inhabitant of the forest, that its active frame seemed constantly in the air, while the dog nobly faced his foe, at each successive leap. When the panther lighted on the shoulders of the mastiff, which was its constant aim, old Brave, though torn with her talons, and stained with his own blood, that already flowed from a dozen wounds, would shake off his furious foe, like a feather, and rearing on his hind legs, rush to the fray again, with his jaws distended, and a dauntless eye. But age, and his pampered life, greatly disqualified the noble mastiff for such a struggle. In every thing but courage, he was only the vestige of what he had once been. A higher bound than ever, raised the wary and furious beast far beyond the reach of the dog, who was making a desperate but fruitless dash at her, from which she alighted in a favourable position, on the back of her aged foe.—For a single moment, only, could the panther remain there, the great strength of the dog returning with a convulsive effort. But Elizabeth saw, as Brave fastened his teeth in the side of his enemy, that the collar of brass around his neck, which had been glittering throughout the fray, was of the colour of blood, and directly, that his frame was sinking to the earth, where it soon lay prostrate and helpless. Several mighty efforts of the wild-cat to extricate herself from the jaws of the dog, followed, but they were fruitless, until the mastiff turned on his back, his lips collapsed, and his teeth loosened; when the short convulsions and stillness that succeeded, announced the death of poor Brave.

Elizabeth now lay wholly at the mercy of the beast. There is said to be something in the front of the image of the Maker, that daunts the hearts of the inferior beings of his creation; and it would seem that some such power, in the present instance, suspended the threatened blow. The eyes of the monster and the kneeling maiden met, for an instant, when the former stooped to examine her fallen foe; next to scent her luckless cub. From the latter examination, it turned, however, with its eyes apparently emitting flashes of fire, its tail lashing its sides furiously, and its claws projecting for inches from its broad feet.

Miss Temple did not, or could not move. Her hands were clasped in the attitude of prayer, but her eyes were still drawn to her terrible enemy; her cheeks were blanched to the whiteness of marble, and her lips were slightly separated with horror. The moment seemed now to have arrived for the fatal termination, and the beautiful figure of Elizabeth was bowing meekly to the stroke, when a rustling of leaves from behind seemed rather to mock the organs, than to meet her ears.

"Hist! hist!" said a low voice—"stoop lower, gal, your bunnet hides the creater's head."

It was rather the yielding of nature than a compliance with this unexpected order, that caused the head of our heroine to sink on her bosom; when she heard the report of the rifle, the whizzing of the bullet, and the enraged cries of the beast, who was rolling over on the earth, biting its own flesh, and tearing the twigs and branches within its reach. At the next instant the form of the Leather-stocking rushed by her, and he called aloud—

"Come in, Hector, come in, you old fool; 'tis a hard-lived animal, and may jump ag'in."

Natty maintained his position in front of the maidens, most fearlessly, notwithstanding the violent bounds and threatening aspect of the wounded panther, which gave several indications of returning strength and ferocity, until his rifle was again loaded, when he stepped up to the enraged animal, and placing the muzzle close to its head, every spark of life was extinguished by the discharge.

The death of her terrible enemy appeared to Elizabeth like a resurrection from her own grave. There was an elasticity in the mind of our heroine, that rose to meet the pressure of instant danger, and the more direct to the senses her apprehensions came, the more her nature had struggled to overcome them. But still she was woman. Had she been left to herself in her late extremity, she would probably have used her faculties to the utmost, and with discretion, in protecting her person, but encumbered with her inanimate friend, retreat was a thing not to be attempted.—Notwithstanding the fearful aspect of her foe, the eye of Elizabeth had never shrunk from its gaze, and long after the event, her thoughts would recur to her passing sensations, and the sweetness of her midnight sleep would be disturbed, as her active fancy conjured in dreams, the most trifling movements of savage fury, that the beast had exhibited in its moment of power.

We shall leave the reader to imagine the restoration of Louisa's senses, and the expressions of gratitude which fell from the young women. The former was effected by a little water, that was brought from one of the thousand springs of those mountains, in the cap of the Leather-stocking; and the latter were uttered with all the warmth that might be expected from the character of Elizabeth. Natty received her vehement protestations of gratitude, with a simple expression of good-will, and with indulgence for her present excitement, but with a carelessness that showed how little he thought of the service he had rendered.

"Well, well," he said, "be it so, gal; let it be so, if you wish it—we'll talk the thing over another time; but I'm sore afeared you'll find Mr. Oliver a better companion than an old hunter, like me. Come, come—let us get into the road, for you've had tirror enough to make you wish yourself in your father's house ag'in."

This was uttered as they were proceeding, at a pace that was adapted to the weakness of Louisa, towards the highway: on reaching which the ladies separated from their guide, declaring themselves equal to the remainder of their walk without his assistance, and feeling encouraged by the sight of the village, which lay beneath their feet like a picture, with its limpid lake in front, the winding stream along its margin, and its hundred chimneys of whitened bricks.

The reader need not be told the nature of the emotions which two youthful, ingenuous, and well-educated girls would experience at their escape from a death so horrid as the one which had impended over them, while they pursued their way in silence along the track on the side of the mountain; nor how deep were their mental thanks to that Power which had given them their existence, and which had not deserted them in their extremity; neither how often they pressed each other's arms, as the assurance of their present safety came, like a healing balm, athwart their troubled spirits, when their thoughts were recurring to the recent moments of horror.

Leather-stocking remained on the hill, gazing after their retiring figures, until they were hid by a bend in the road, when he whistled in his dogs, and shouldering his rifle, he returned into the forest.

"Well, it was a skeary thing to the young creaters," said Natty, while he retrod the path towards the slain. "It might frighten an older woman, to see a she painter so near her, with a dead cub by its side. I wonder if I had aimed at the varmint's eye, if I shouldn't have touched the life sooner than in the forehead? but they are hard-lived animals and it was a good shot consid'ring that I could see nothing but the head and the peak of its tail. Hah! who goes there?"

"How goes it, Natty?" said Mr. Doolittle, stepping out of the bushes, with a motion that was a good deal accelerated by the sight of the rifle, that was already lowered in his direction. "What! shooting this warm day! mind, old man, the law don't get hold on you."

"The law, Squire! I have shook hands with the law these forty years," returned Natty; "for what has a man who lives in the wilderness to do with the ways of the law?"

"Not much, maybe," said Hiram; "but you sometimes trade in ven'son. I s'pose you know, Leather-stocking, that there is an act passed to lay a fine of five pounds currency, or twelve dollars and fifty cents, by decimals, on every man who kills a deer betwixt January and August. The Judge had a great hand in getting the law through."

"I can believe it," returned the old hunter; "I can believe that or any thing, of a man who carries on as he does in the country."

"Yes, the law is quite positive, and the Judge is bent on putting it in force—five pounds penalty. I thought I heerd your hounds out on the scent of so'thing this morning: I didn't know but they might get you in difficulty."

"They know their manners too well," said Natty, carelessly. "And how much goes to the state's evidence, Squire?"

"How much!" repeated Hiram, quailing under the honest but sharp look of the hunter—"the informer gets half, I—I b'lieve;—yes, I guess it's half. But there's blood on your sleeve, man—you haven't been shooting any thing this morning?"

"I have, though," said the hunter, nodding his head significantly to the other, "and a good shot I made of it."

"H-e-m!" ejaculated the magistrate; "and where is the game? I s'pose it's of a good nater, for your dogs won't hunt at any thing that isn't choish."

"They'll hunt any thing I tell them to, Squire," cried Natty, favouring the other with his laugh: "They'll hunt you, if I say so. He-e-e-re, he-e-e-re, Hector—he-e-e-re, slut—come this a-way, pups—come this a-way—come hither."

"Oh! I've always heern a good character of the dogs," returned Mr. Doolittle, quickening his pace by raising each leg in rapid succession, as the hounds scented around his person. "And where is the game, Leather-stocking?"

During this dialogue, the speakers had been walking at a very fast gait, and Natty swung the end of his rifle round, pointing through the bushes, and replied—

"There lays one. How do you like such meat?"

"This!" exclaimed Hiram, "why this is Judge Temple's dog Brave. Take kear, Leather-stocking, and don't make an inimy of the Judge. I hope you haven't harmed the animal?"

"Look for yourself, Mr. Doolittle," said Natty, drawing his knife from his girdle, and wiping it, in a knowing manner, once or twice across his garment of buck-skin; "does his throat look as if I had cut it with this knife?"

"It is dreadfully tore! it's an awful wownd—no knife never did this deed. Who could have done it?"

"That painter behind you, Squire—look, there's two of them."

"Painters!" echoed Hiram, whirling on his heel, with an agility that would have done credit to a dancing master; "where's a painter?"

"Be easy, man," said Natty; "there's two of the vinimous things; but the dog finished one, and I have fastened the other's jaws for her; so you needn't look so skeared, Squire; they won't hurt you."

"And where's the deer?" cried Hiram, staring about him with a bewildered air.

"Anan! deer!" repeated Natty.

"Sartain, an't there ven'son here, or didn't you kill a buck?"

"What! when the law forbids the thing, Squire!" said the old hunter. "I hope there's no law ag'in killing the painters."

"No; there's a bounty on the scalps—but—will your dogs hunt painters, Natty?"

"Any thing; didn't I tell you they'd hunt a man? He-e-re, he-e-re, pups"——

"Oh! yes, yes, I remember. Well, they are strange dogs, I must say—I am quite in a wonderment."

Natty had seated himself on the ground, and having laid the grim head of his late ferocious enemy in his lap, was drawing his knife with a practised hand, around the ears, which he tore from the head of the beast in such a manner as to preserve their connexion, when he answered—

"What at, Squire? did you never see a painter's scalp afore? Come, you be a magistrate, I wish you'd make me out an order for the bounty."

"The bounty!" repeated Hiram, holding the ears on the end of his finger, for a moment, as if uncertain how to proceed. "Well, let us go down to your hut, where you can take the oath, and I will write out the order. I s'pose you have a bible? all the law wants is the four Evangelists and the Lord's prayer."

"I rather guess not," said Natty, a little coldly; "not such a bible as the law needs."

"Oh! there's but one sort of bible, at least that's good in law," returned the magistrate; "and yourn will do as well as another's. Come, the carcasses are worth nothing, man; let us go down and take the oath."

"Softly, softly, Squire," said the hunter, lifting his trophies very deliberately from the ground, and shouldering his rifle; "why do you want an oath at all, for a thing that your own eyes has seen? won't you believe yourself, that another man must swear to a fact that you know to be true? You seen me scalp the creaters, and if I must swear to it, it shall be before Judge Temple, who needs an oath."

"But we have no pen or paper, here, Leather-stocking; we must go to the hut for them, or how can I write the order?"

Natty turned his simple features on the cunning magistrate with another of his laughs, as he said—

"And what should I be doing with such scholars' tools? I want no pens or paper, not knowing the use of 'ither; and so I keep none. No, No, I'll bring the scalps into the village, Squire, and you can make out the order on one of your law-books, and it will be all the better for it. The deuce take this leather on the neck of the dog, it will strangle the old fool. Can you lend me a knife, Squire?"

Hiram, who seemed particularly anxious to be on good terms with his companion, unhesitatingly complied. Natty cut the thong from the neck of the hound, and, as he returned the knife to its owner, carelessly remarked—

" 'Tis a good bit of steel, and has cut such leather as this very same before now, I dare to say."

"Do you mean to charge me with letting your hounds loose?" exclaimed Hiram, with a consciousness that disarmed his caution.

"Loose!" repeated the hunter—"I let them loose myself. I always let them loose before I leave the hut."

The ungovernable amazement with which Mr. Doolittle listened to this falsehood, would have betrayed his agency in the liberation of the dogs, had Natty wanted any further confirmation; and the coolness and management of the old man now disappeared in open indignation.

"Look you here, Mr. Doolittle," he said, striking the breech of his rifle violently on the ground; "what there is in the wigwam of a poor man like me, that one like you can crave, I don't know; but this I tell you to your face, that you never shall put a foot under the roof of my cabin with my consent, and that if you harbour round the spot as you have done lately, you may meet with treatment that you won't over and above relish."

"And let me tell you, Mr. Bumppo," said Hiram, retreating, however, with a quick step, "that I know you've broke the law, and that I'm a magistrate, and will make you feel it too, before you are a day older."

"That for you and your law too," cried Natty, snapping his fingers at the justice of the peace—"away with you, you varmint, before the divil tempts me to give you your just desarts. Take kear, if I ever catch your prowling face in the woods ag'in, that I don't shoot it for an owl."

There is something at all times commanding in honest indignation, and Hiram did not stay to provoke the wrath of the old hunter to extremities. When the intruder was out of sight,

Natty proceeded to the hut, where he found all quiet as the grave. He fastened his dogs, and tapping at the door, which was opened by Edwards, asked—

"Is all safe, lad?"

"Every thing," returned the youth. "Some one attempted the lock, but it was too strong for him."

"I know the creater," said Natty, "but he'll not trust himself within reach of my rifle ag'in very soon, for I'll——What more was uttered by the Leather-stocking, in his vexation, was rendered inaudible by the closing of the door of the cabin.

· *Chapter XXIX* ·

It is noised he hath a mass of treasure.
TIMON OF ATHENS

When Marmaduke Temple and his cousin rode through the gate of the former, the heart of the father had been too recently touched with the best feeling of our nature, to leave inclination for immediate discourse. There was an importance in the air of Richard, which would not have admitted of the ordinary informal conversation of the Sheriff, without violating all the rules of consistency; and the equestrians pursued their way with great diligence, for more than a mile, in profound silence. At length the soft expression of parental care, blended with affection, was slowly chased from the handsome features of the Judge, and was gradually supplanted by the cast of humour and benevolence that was usually seated on his brow.

"Well, Dickon," he said, "since I have yielded myself, so far, implicitly to your guidance, I think the moment has arrived, when I am entitled to further confidence. Why and wherefore are we journeying together in this solemn gait?"

The Sheriff gave a loud hem, that rung far in the forest, which they had now entered, and keeping his eyes fixed on objects before him, like a man who is looking deep into futurity, he replied as follows:—

"There has always been one point of difference between us, Judge Temple, I may say, since our nativity; not that I would insinuate that you are at all answerable for the acts of nature; for a man is no more to be condemned for the misfortunes of his birth, than he is to be commended for the natural advantages he may possess; but on one point we may be said to have differed since our births, and they, you know, occurred within two days of each other."

"I really marvel, Richard, what this one point can be; for, to my eyes, we seem to differ so materially and so often"——

"Mere consequences, sir," interrupted the Sheriff, "all our minor differences proceed from one cause, and that is, our opinions of the universal attainments of genius."

"In what, Dickon!" exclaimed the Judge.

"I speak plain English, I believe, Judge Temple; at least I ought; for my father, who taught me, could speak"——

"Greek and Latin," interrupted Marmaduke—"I well know the qualifications of your family in tongues, Dickon. But proceed to the point; why are we travelling over this mountain to-day?"

"To do justice to any subject, sir, the narrator must be suffered to proceed in his own way," continued the Sheriff. "You are of opinion, Judge Temple, that a man is to be qualified by nature and education to do only one thing well, whereas I know that genius will supply the place of learning, and that a certain sort of man can do any thing and every thing."

"Like yourself, I suppose," said Marmaduke, smiling.

"I scorn personalities, sir," returned the Sheriff; "I say nothing of myself; but there are three men on your patent, of the kind that I should term talented by nature for her general purposes, though acting under the influence of different situations."

"We are better off then, than I had supposed," said Marmaduke. "Who are they?"

"Why, sir, one is Hiram Doolittle; he is a carpenter by trade, as you know, and I need only point to the village to exhibit his merits. Then he is a magistrate, and might shame many a man, in his distribution of justice, who has had better opportunities than himself."

"Well, he is one," said Marmaduke, with the air of a man that was determined not to dispute the point.

"Yes, sir, and Jotham Riddel is another."

"Who!" exclaimed the Judge.

"Jotham Riddel."

"What, that dissatisfied, shiftless, lazy, speculating fellow!

he who changes his county every three years, his farm every six months, and his occupation every season! an agriculturist yesterday, a shoemaker to-day, and a schoolmaster to-morrow! that epitome of all the unsteady and profitless propensities of the settlers without one of their good qualities to counterbalance the evil! Nay, Richard, this is too bad or even—but who is the third?"

"As the third is not used to hearing such comments on his character, Judge Temple, I shall not name him," said the indignant Sheriff.

"The amount of all this, then, Dickon, is, that the trio of which you are one, and the principal, have made some important discovery."

"I have not said that I am one, Judge Temple. As I told you before, I say nothing of myself. But a discovery has been made, and you are deeply interested in it."

"Proceed—I am all ears."

"No, no, 'duke, you are bad enough, I own, but not so bad as that either; your ears are not quite full grown."

The Sheriff laughed heartily at his wit, and put himself in good humour thereby, when he gratified his patient cousin with the following explanation:—

"You know, 'duke, that there is a man living on your estate that goes by the name of Natty Bumppo. Here has this man lived, by what I can learn, for more than forty years—by himself, until lately; and now with strange companions."

"Part very true, and all very probable," said the Judge.

"All true, sir, all true. Well, within these last few months have appeared as his companions, an old Indian chief, the last, or one of the last of his tribe that is to be found in this part of the country, and a young man, who is said to be the son of some Indian agent, by a squaw."

"Who says that?" cried Marmaduke, with an interest he had not manifested before.

"Who! why common sense—common report. But listen till you know all. This youth has very pretty talents—yes, what I call very pretty talents—and has been well educated, has seen very tolerable company, and knows how to behave himself, when he has a mind to. Now, Judge Temple, can you tell me what has brought three such men as Indian John, Natty Bumppo, and Oliver Edwards, together?"

Marmaduke turned his countenance, in evident surprise, to his cousin, and replied quickly—

"Thou hast unexpectedly hit on a subject, Richard, that has often occupied my mind. But knowest thou any thing of this mystery, or are they only the crude conjectures of"——

"Crude nothing, 'duke, crude nothing; but facts, stubborn facts. You know there are mines in these mountains; I have often heard you say that you believed in their existence"——

"Reasoning from analogy, Richard, but not with any certainty of the fact."

"You have heard them mentioned, and have seen specimens of the ore, sir; you will not deny that! and, reasoning from analogy, as you say, if there be mines in South America, ought there not to be mines in North America too?"

"Nay, nay, I deny nothing, my cousin. I certainly have heard many rumours of the existence of mines, in these hills; and I do believe that I have seen specimens of the precious metals that have been found here. It would occasion me no surprise to learn that tin and silver, or, what I consider of more consequence, good coal,"—

"Damn your coal, sir," cried the Sheriff; "who wants to find coal in these forests? No, no, silver, 'duke; silver is the one thing needful and silver is to be found. But listen: you are not to be told that the natives have long known the use of gold and silver; now who so likely to be acquainted where they are to be found, as the ancient inhabitants of a country? I have the best reasons for believing that both Mohegan and the Leather-stocking have been privy to the existence of a mine, in this very mountain, for many years."

The Sheriff had now touched his cousin in a sensitive spot; and Marmaduke lent a more attentive ear to the speaker, who, after waiting a moment, to see the effect of this extraordinary developement, proceeded——

"Yes, sir, I have my reasons, and at a proper time you shall know them."

"No time is so good as the present," exclaimed Marmaduke.

"Well, well, be attentive," continued Richard, looking cautiously about him, to make certain that no eavesdropper was
hid in the forest, though they were in constant motion. "I
have seen Mohegan and the Leather-stocking, with my own
eyes—and my eyes are as good as any body's eyes—I have
seen them, I say, both going up the mountain and coming
down it, with spades and picks; and others have seen them
carrying things into their hut, in a secret and mysterious
manner, after dark. Do you know what they could be?"

The Judge did not reply, but his brow had contracted, with
a thoughtfulness that he always wore when much interested,
and his eyes rested on his cousin in expectation of hearing
more. Richard continued—

"It was ore. Now, sir, I ask if you can tell me who this Mr.
Oliver Edwards is, that has made a part of your household
since last Christmas?"

Marmaduke again raised his eyes, but continued silent,
shaking his head in the negative.

"That he is a half-breed we know, for Mohegan does not
scruple to call him, openly, his kinsman; that he is well educated, we know. But as to his business here—do you remember that about a month before this young man made his
appearance among us, Natty was absent from home several
days? You do; for you inquired for him, as you wanted some
venison to take to your friends, when you went for Bess.
Well, he was not to be found. Old John was left in the hut
alone; and when Natty did appear, although he came on in
the night, he was seen drawing one of those jumpers that they
carry their grain to mill in, and to take out something, with
great care, that he had covered up under his bear—skins.
Now let me ask you, Judge Temple, what motive could induce a man like the Leather-stocking to make a sled, and
toil with a load over these mountains, if he had nothing but
his rifle or his ammunition to carry?"

"They frequently make these jumpers to convey their game
home, and you say he had been absent many days."

"How did he kill it? His rifle was in the village to be

mended. No, no—that he was gone to some unusual place is certain; that he brought back some secret utensils is also certain; and since then he has not allowed a soul to approach his hut."

"He was never fond of intruders"——

"I know it," interrupted Richard; "but did he drive them from his cabin morosely? Within a fortnight of his return, this Mr. Edwards appears. They spent whole days in the mountains, pretending to be shooting, but in reality exploring; the frosts prevented their digging at that time, and he availed himself of a lucky accident to get into good quarters. But even now, he is quite half of his time in that hut—many hours in each night. They are smelting, 'duke, they are smelting, and as they grow rich you grow poor."

"How much of this is thine own, Richard, and how much comes from others? I would sift the wheat from the chaff."

"Part is my own, for I saw the jumper, though it was broken up and burnt in a day or two. I have told you that I saw the old man with his spades and picks. Hiram met Natty, as he was crossing the mountain, the night of his arrival with the sled, and very good-naturedly offered—Hiram *is* good natured—to carry up part of his load, for the old man had a heavy pull up the back of the mountain, but he wouldn't listen to the thing, and repulsed the offer in such a manner that the Squire said he had half a mind to swear the peace against him. Since the snow has been off, more especially after the frosts got out of the ground, we have kept a watchful eye on the gentlemen, in which we have found Jotham to be very useful."

Marmaduke did not much like the associates of Richard in this business, still he knew them to be cunning and ready in expedients; and as there was certainly something mysterious, not only in the connexion between the old hunters and Edwards, but in what his cousin had just related, he began to revolve the subject in his own mind with care. On reflection, he remembered various circumstances that tended to corroborate these suspicions, and as the whole business favoured one of his infirmities, he yielded the more readily to their impression. The mind of Judge Temple, at all times comprehensive, had received from his peculiar occupations, a bias to look far into futurity, in speculations on the improvements that posterity were to make in his lands. To his eye, where others saw nothing but a wilderness, towns, manufactories, bridges, canals, mines, and all the other resources of an old country, were constantly presenting themselves, though his good sense suppressed, in some degree, the exhibition of these expectations.

As the Sheriff allowed his cousin full time to reflect on what he had heard, the probability of some pecuniary adventure being the connecting link in the chain that brought Oliver Edwards into the hut of Leather-stocking, appeared to him each moment to be stronger. But Marmaduke was too much in the habit of examining both sides of a subject, not to perceive the objections, and reasoned with himself aloud:—

"It cannot be so, or the youth would not be driven so near the verge of poverty."

"What so likely to make a man dig for money, as being poor?" cried the Sheriff.

"Besides, there is an elevation of character about Oliver, that proceeds from education, which would forbid so clandestine a proceeding."

"Could an ignorant fellow smelt?" continued Richard.

"Then Bess hints that he was reduced to his last shilling, when we took him into our dwelling."

"He has been buying tools. And would he spend his last sixpence for a shot at a Turkey, had he not known where to get more."

"Can I have possibly been so long a dupe! His manner has been rude to me at times; but I attributed it to his conceiving himself injured, and to his mistaking the forms of the world."

"Haven't you been a dupe all your life, 'duke? and an't what you call ignorance of forms deep cunning, to conceal his real character?"

"If he were bent on deception, he would have concealed his knowledge, and passed with us for an inferior man."

"He cannot. I could no more pass for a fool, myself, than I could fly. Knowledge is not to be concealed, like a candle under a bushel."

"Richard," said the Judge, turning to his cousin, "there are many reasons against the truth of thy conjectures; but thou hast awakened suspicions which must be satisfied. But why are we travelling here?"

"Jotham, who has been much in the mountain latterly, being kept there by me and Hiram, has made a discovery, which he will not explain, he says, for he is bound by an oath; but the amount is, that he knows where the ore lies, and he has this day begun to dig. I would not consent to the thing, 'duke, without your knowledge, for the land is yours; and now you know the reason of our ride. Don't you call this a countermine for their mine, ha!"

"And where is the desirable spot?" asked the Judge, with an air half comical, half serious.

"Close by; and when we have visited that, I will show you one of the places that we have found within a week, where our gentlemen hunters have been amusing themselves for six months past."

The gentlemen continued to discuss the matter, while their horses picked their way under the branches of trees, and over the uneven ground of the mountain. They soon arrived at the end of their journey, where, in truth, they found Jotham already buried to his neck in a hole that he had been digging.

Marmaduke questioned the miner very closely, as to his reasons for believing in the existence of the precious metals near that particular spot; but the fellow maintained an obstinate mystery in his answers. He asserted that he had the best of reasons for what he did, and inquired of the Judge what portion of the profits would fall to his own share, in the event of success, with an earnestness that proved his faith. After spending an hour near the place, examining the stones, and searching for the usual indications of the proximity of ore, the Judge remounted, and suffered his cousin to lead the way to the place where the mysterious trio had been making their excavation.

The spot chosen by Jotham was on the back of the mountain that overhung the hut of Leather-stocking, and the place selected by Natty and his companions was on the other side of the same hill, but above the road, and, of course, in an opposite direction to the route taken by the ladies in their walk.

"We shall be safe in approaching the place now," said Richard, while they dismounted and fastened their horses; "for I took a look with the glass, and saw John and Leather-stocking in their canoe fishing, before we left home, and Oliver is in the same pursuit; but these may be nothing but shams, to blind our eyes, so we will be expeditious, for it would not be pleasant to be caught here by them."

"Not on my own land!" said Marmaduke sternly. "If it be as you suspect, I will know their reasons for making this excavation."

"Mum," said Richard, laying his finger on his lip, and leading the way down a very difficult descent to a sort of a natural cavern, which was formed in the face of the rock, and not unlike a fire-place in shape. In front of this place lay a pile of earth, which had evidently been taken from the recess, and part of which was yet fresh. An examination of the exterior of the cavern, left the Judge in doubt whether it was one of nature's frolics that had thrown it into that shape, or whether it had been wrought by the hands of man, at some earlier period. But there could be no doubt that the whole of the interior was of recent formation, and the marks of the pick were still visible, where the soft, lead-coloured rock had opposed itself to the progress of the miners. The whole formed an excavation of about twenty feet in width, and nearly twice that distance in depth. The height was much greater than was required for the ordinary purposes of experiment; but this was evidently the effect of chance, as the roof of the cavern was a natural stratum of rock, that projected many feet beyond the base of the pile. Immediately in front of the recess, or cave, was a little terrace, partly formed by nature, and partly by the earth that had been carelessly thrown aside by the labourers. The mountain fell off precipitately in front of the terrace, and the approach by its sides under the ridge of the rocks, was difficult, and a little dangerous. The whole was wild, rude, and apparently incomplete: for, while looking among the bushes, the Sheriff found the very implements that had been used in the work.

When the Sheriff thought that his cousin had examined the spot sufficiently, he cried—

"Well, Judge Temple, are you satisfied?"

"Perfectly that there is something mysterious, and to me perplexing in this business. It is a secret spot, and cunningly devised, Richard; yet I see no symptoms of ore."

"Do you expect, sir, to find gold and silver lying like pebbles on the surface of the earth?—dollars and dimes ready coined to your hands! No, no—the treasure must be sought after to be won. But let them mine; I shall countermine."

The Judge took an accurate survey of the place, and noted in his memorandum-book such marks as were necessary to find it again, in the event of Richard's absence; when the cousins returned to their horses.

On reaching the highway they separated, the Sheriff to summon twenty-four "good men and true," to attend as the inquest of the county, on the succeeding Monday, when Marmaduke held his stated court of "common pleas and general sessions of the peace," and the Judge to return, musing deeply on what he had seen and heard in the course of the morning.

When the horse of the latter reached the spot where the highway fell towards the valley, the eye of Marmaduke rested, it is true, on the same scene that had, ten minutes before, been so soothing to the feelings of his daughter and her friend, as they emerged from the forest; but it rested in vacancy. He threw the reins to his sure-footed beast, and suffered the animal to travel at its own gait, while he soliloquized as follows:—

"There may be more in this than I at first supposed. I have suffered my feelings to blind my reason, in admitting an unknown youth in this manner to my dwelling;—yet this is not the land of suspicion. I will have the Leather-stocking before me, and, by a few direct questions, extract the truth from the simple old man."—

At that instant the Judge caught a glimpse of the figures of Elizabeth and Louisa, who were slowly descending the mountain, but a short distance before him. He put spurs to his horse, and riding up to them, dismounted, and drove his steed along the narrow path. While the agitated parent was listening to the vivid description that his daughter gave of her recent danger, and her unexpected escape, all thoughts of mines, vested rights, and examinations, were absorbed in his emotions; and when the image of Natty again crossed his recollection, it was not as a lawless and depredating squatter, but as the preserver of his child.

Chapter XXX

The court awards it, and the law doth give it.
MERCHANT OF VENICE

Remarkable Pettibone, who had forgotten the wound received by her pride, in the contemplation of the ease and comforts of her situation, and who still retained her station in the family of Judge Temple, was despatched to the humble dwelling which Richard styled "the Rectory," in attendance on Louisa, who was soon consigned to the arms of her father.

In the mean time, Marmaduke and his daughter were closeted for more than an hour, nor shall we invade the sanctuary of parental love, by relating the conversation for that period. At its expiration, when the curtain rises on the reader, the Judge is seen walking up and down the apartment, with a tender melancholy in his air, softening the manly expression of his features, and his child reclining on a settee, with a flushed cheek, and her dark eyes seeming to float in crystals.

"It was a timely rescue! it was, indeed, a timely rescue, my child!" cried the Judge. "Then thou didst not desert thy friend, my noble Bess?"

"I believe I may as well take the credit of fortitude," said Elizabeth, "though I much doubt if flight would have availed me any thing, had I even courage to execute such an intention. But I thought not of the expedient."

"Of what didst thou think, love? where did thy thoughts dwell most, at that fearful moment?"

"The beast! the beast!" cried Elizabeth, veiling her face with her fair hand; "Oh! I saw nothing, I thought of nothing, but the beast. I tried to think of better things, but the horror was too glaring, the danger too much before my eyes."

"Well, well, thou art safe, and we will converse no more on the unpleasant subject. I did not think such an animal yet remained in our forests; but they will stray far from their haunts when pressed by hunger, and"—

A loud knocking at the door of the apartment interrupted what he was about to utter, and he bid the applicant enter. The door was opened by Benjamin, who came in with a discontented air, as if he felt that he had a communication to make that would be out of season.

"Here is Squire Doolittle below, sir," commenced the Major-domo. "He has been standing off and on in the dooryard, maybe for the matter of a glass; and he has sum'mat on his mind that he wants to heave up, d'ye see; but I tells him, says I, man, would you be coming aboard with your complaints, said I, when the Judge has gotten his own child, as it were, out of the jaws of a lion? But damn the bit of manners has the fellow any more than if he was one of them Guineas, down in the kitchen there; and so as he was shearing alongside, every stretch he made towards the house, I could do no better than to let your honour know that the chap was in the offing."

"He must have business of importance," said Marmaduke; "something in relation to his office, most probably, as the court sits so shortly."

"Ay, ay, you have it, sir," cried Benjamin, "it's sum'mat about a complaint that he has to make of the old Leather-stocking, who, to my judgment, is the better man of the two. It's a very good sort of man is this Master Bumppo, and he has a way with a spear, all the same as if he was brought up at the bow oar of the captain's barge, or was born with a boat-hook in his hand."

"Against the Leather-stocking!" cried Elizabeth, rising from her reclining posture.

"Rest easy, my child," said the Judge, smiling, "it is some trifle, I pledge you; I believe I am already acquainted with its import. Trust me, Bess, your champion shall be safe in my care.—Show Mr. Doolittle in, Benjamin."

Miss Temple appeared satisfied with this assurance, but fastened her dark eyes on the person of the architect, who profited by the permission, and instantly made his appearance.

All the impatience of Hiram seemed to vanish the instant he entered the apartment. After saluting the Judge and his daughter, he took the chair to which Marmaduke pointed, and sat for a minute, composing his straight black hair, with a gravity in his demeanour that was intended to do honour to his official station. At length he said—

"It's likely from what I hear, that Miss Temple had a pretty narrow chance with painters on the mountain."

Marmaduke made a gentle inclination of his head, by way of assent, but continued silent.

"I s'pose the law gives a bounty on the scalps," continued Hiram, "in which case the Leather-stocking will make a good job on't."

"It shall be my care, sir, to see that he is rewarded," returned the Judge.

"Yes, yes, I rather guess that nobody hereabouts doubts the Judge's generosity. Does he know whether the Sheriff has fairly made up his mind to have a reading desk or a deacon's pew under the pulpit?"

"I have not heard my cousin speak on that subject lately," replied Marmaduke.

"I think it's likely that we will have a pretty dull court on't, from what I can gather. I hear that Jotham Riddel and the man who bought his betterments have agreen to leave their difference to men, and I don't think there'll be more than two civil cases in the calendar."

"I am glad of it," said the Judge, "nothing gives me more pain, than to see my settlers wasting their time and substance in the unprofitable struggles of the law, I hope it may prove true, sir."

"I rather guess 'twill be left out to men," added Hiram, with an air equally balanced between doubt and assurance, but which Judge Temple understood to mean certainly; "I some think that I am appointed a referee in the case myself; Jotham as much as told me that he should take me. The defendant, I guess, means to take Captain Hollister, and we two have partly agreen on Squire Jones for the third man."

"Are there any criminals to be tried?" asked Marmaduke.

"There's the counterfeiters," returned the magistrate; "as they were caught in the fact, I think it likely that they'll be indicted, in which case, it's probable they will be tried."

"Certainly, sir; I had forgotten these men. There are no more I hope."

"Why, there is a threaten to come forrard with an assault, that happened at the last independence day; but I'm not sartain that the law'll take hold on't. There was plaguey hard words passed, but whether they struck or not I haven't heern. There's some folks talk of a deer or two being killed out of season, over on the west side of the patent, by some of the squatters on the 'Fractions'."

"Let a complaint be made, by all means," cried the Judge; "I am determined to see the law executed to the letter on all such depredators."

"Why, yes, I thought the Judge was of that mind; I come partly, on such a business myself."

"You!" exclaimed Marmaduke, comprehending in an instant, how completely he had been caught by the other's cunning; "and what have you to say, Sir?"

"I some think that Natty Bumppo has the carcass of a deer in his hut at this moment, and a considerable part of my business was to get a sarch warrant to examine."

"You think, sir! do you know that the law exacts an oath, before I can issue such a precept. The habitation of a citizen is not to be idly invaded on light suspicion.

"I rather think I can swear to it myself," returned the immovable Hiram; "and Jotham is in the street, and as good as ready to come in and make oath to the same thing."

"Then issue the warrant thyself; thou art a magistrate, Mr. Doolittle; why trouble me with the matter?"

"Why, seeing it's the first complaint under the law, and knowing the Judge set his heart on the thing, I thought it best that the authority to sarch should come from himself. Besides, as I'm much in the woods, among the timber, I don't altogether like making an enemy of the Leather-stocking.

Now the Judge has a weight in the county that puts him above all fear." Miss Temple turned her beautiful face to the callous architect, with a scornful smile, as she said—

"And what has any honest person to dread from so kind a man as poor Bumppo?"

"Why, it's as easy, Miss, to pull a rifle-trigger on a magistrate as on a painter. But if the Judge don't conclude to issoo the warrant, I must go home and make it out myself."

"I have not refused your application, sir," said Marmaduke, perceiving at once, that his reputation for impartiality was at stake; "go into my office, Mr. Doolittle, where I will join you, and sign the warrant."

Judge Temple stopped the remonstrances which Elizabeth was about to utter, after Hiram had withdrawn, by laying his hand playfully on her mouth, and saying—

"It is more terrific in sound than frightful in reality, my child. I suppose the Leather-stocking has shot a deer, for the season is nearly over, and you say that he was hunting with his dogs, when he came so timely to your assistance. But it will be only to examine his cabin, and find the animal, when you can pay the penalty out of your own pocket, Bess. Nothing short of the twelve dollars and a half will satisfy this harpy, I perceive; and surely my reputation as a Judge is worth that trifle."

Elizabeth was a good deal pacified with this assurance, and suffered her father to leave her, to fulfill his promise to Hiram.

When Marmaduke left his office, after executing his disagreeable duty, he met Oliver Edwards, walking up the gravelled walk in front of the Mansion-house, with great strides, and with a face agitated by some powerful passion. On seeing Judge Temple, the youth turned aside, and with a warmth in his manner that was not often exhibited to Marmaduke, he cried—

"I congratulate you, sir; from the bottom of my soul I congratulate you, Judge Temple. Oh! it would have been too horrid to have recollected for a moment! I have just left the hut, where, after showing me his scalps, old Natty told me of the escape of the ladies, as a thing to be mentioned last. Indeed,

indeed, sir, no words of mine can express half of what I felt"
—the youth paused a moment, as if suddenly recollecting
that he was overstepping prescribed limits, and concluded
with a good deal of embarrassment—"what I have felt, at this
danger to Miss—Grant, and—and your daughter, sir."

But the heart of Marmaduke was too much softened by his
recent emotions, to admit of his cavilling with trifles, and
without regarding the confusion of the other, he replied—

"I thank thee, thank thee, Oliver; as thou sayest, it is almost too horrid to be remembered. But come, let us hasten to
Bess, for Louisa has already gone to the Rectory."

The young man sprung forward, and, throwing open a door,
barely permitted the Judge to precede him, when he was in
the presence of Elizabeth in a moment.

The cold distance that often crossed the demeanour of the
heiress, in her intercourse with Edwards, was now entirely
banished, and two hours were passed by the party, in the
free, unembarrassed, and confiding manner of old and esteemed friends. Judge Temple had forgotten the suspicions
engendered during his morning's ride, and the youth and
maiden conversed, laughed, and were sad by turns, as if
directed by a common impulse. At length Edwards, after repeating his intention to do so for the third time, left the Mansion-house to go to the Rectory on a similar errand of friendship.

During this short period, a scene was passing at the hut,
that completely frustrated the benevolent intentions of Judge
Temple in favour of the Leather-stocking, and at once destroyed the short-lived harmony between the youth and
Marmaduke.

When Hiram Doolittle had obtained his search warrant,
his first business was to procure a proper officer to see it executed. The Sheriff was absent, summoning, in person, the
grand inquest for the county; the deputy, who resided in the
village, was riding on the same errand, in a different part of
the settlement; and the regular constable of the township
had been selected for his station from motives of charity, being lame of one leg, and an invalid. Hiram intended to accompany the officer as a spectator, but felt no very strong

desire to bear the brunt of the battle. It was, however, Saturday, and the sun was already turning the shadows of the pines towards the east; on the morrow the conscientious magistrate could not engage in such an expedition at the peril of his soul; and long before Monday, the venison, and all vestiges of the death of the deer, might be secreted or destroyed. Happily, the lounging form of Billy Kirby met his eye, and Hiram, at all times fruitful in similar expedients, saw his way clear at once. Jotham, who was associated in the whole business, and who had left the mountain in consequence of a summons from his coadjutor, but who failed, equally with Hiram, in the unfortunate particular of nerve, was directed to summon the wood-chopper to the dwelling of the magistrate.

When Billy appeared, he was very kindly invited to take the chair in which he had already seated himself, and was treated, in all respects, as if he were an equal.

"Judge Temple has set his heart on putting the deer law in force," said Hiram, after the preliminary civilities were over, "and a complaint has been laid before him that a deer has been killed. He has issooed a sarch-warrant, and sent for me to get somebody to execute it."

Kirby, who had no idea of being excluded from the deliberative part of any affair in which he was engaged, drew up his bushy head in a reflecting attitude, and, after musing a moment, replied by asking a few questions.

"The Sheriff is gone out of the way?"

"Not to be found."

"And his deputy too?"

"Both gone on the skirts of the patent."

"But I seen the constable hobbling about town an hour ago."

"Yes, yes," said Hiram, with a coaxing smile and knowing nod, "but this business wants a man—not a cripple."

"Why," said Billy, laughing, "will the chap make fight?"

"He's a little quarrelsome at times, and thinks he's the best man in the county at rough-and-tumble."

"I heerd him brag once," said Jotham, "that there wasn't a

man 'twixt the Mohawk Flats and the Pennsylvany line that was his match at a close hug."

"Did you!" exclaimed Kirby, raising his huge frame in his seat, like a lion stretching in his lair, "I rather guess he never felt a Varmounter's to knuckles on his back-bone. But who is the chap?"

"Why," said Jotham, "it's"——

"It's ag'in law to tell," interrupted Hiram, "unless you'll qualify to sarve. You'd be the very man to take him, Bill; and I'll make out a spicial deputation in a minute, when you will get the fees."

"What's the fees?" said Kirby, laying his large hand on the leaves of a statute-book that Hiram had opened in order to give dignity to his office, which he turned over, in his rough manner, as if he were reflecting on a subject, about which he had, in truth, already decided; "will they pay a man for a broken head?"

"They'll be something handsome," said Hiram.

"Damn the fees," said Billy, again laughing—"doos the fellow think he's the best wrestler in the county, though? what's his inches?"

"He's taller than you be," said Jotham, "and one of the biggest!"——

Talkers, he was about to add, but the impatience of Kirby interrupted him. The wood-chopper had nothing fierce, or even brutal in his appearance; the character of his expression was that of good-natured vanity. It was evident he prided himself on the powers of the physical man, like all who have nothing better to boast of; and, stretching out his broad hand, with the palm downward, he said, keeping his eyes fastened on his own bones and sinews—

"Come, give us a touch of the book. I'll swear, and you'll see that I'm a man to keep my oath."

Hiram did not give the wood-chopper time to change his mind, but the oath was administered without any unnecessary delay. So soon as this preliminary was completed, the three worthies left the house, and proceeded by the nearest road towards the hut. They had reached the bank of the lake, and were diverging from the route of the highway, before Kirby recollected that he was now entitled to the privileges of the initiated, and repeated his question, as to the name of the offender.

"Which way, which way, Squire?" exclaimed the hardy wood-chopper; "I thought it was to sarch a house that you wanted me, not the woods. There is nobody lives on this side of the lake, for six miles, unless you count the Leather-stocking and old John for settlers. Come, tell me the chap's name, and I warrant me that I lead you to his clearing by a straighter path than this, for I know every sapling that grows within two miles of Templetown."

"This is the way," said Hiram, pointing forward, and quickening his step, as if apprehensive that Kirby would desert, "and Bumppo is the man."

Kirby stopped short, and looked from one of his companions to the other in astonishment. He then burst into a loud laugh, and cried—

"Who? Leather-stocking! he may brag of his aim and his rifle, for he has the best of both, as I will own myself, for 'sin he shot the pigeon I knock under to him; but for a wrestle! Why, I would take the divil between my finger and thumb, and tie him in a bow knot around my neck for a Barcelony. Why, Jotham, you could take him down yourself, as you'd take down a two years' pine with an axe. The man is seventy, and was never any thing particular for strength."

"He's a deceiving man," said Hiram, "like all the hunters; he is stronger than he seems;—besides, he has a rifle."

"That for his rifle!" cried Billy, "he'd no more hurt me with his rifle than he'd fly. He is a harmless creater, and I must say that I think he has as good right to kill deer as any man on the patent. It's his main support, and this is a free country, where a man is privileged to follow any calling he likes."

"According to that doctrine," said Jotham, "anybody may shoot a deer."

"This is the man's calling, I tell you," returned Kirby, "and the law was never made for such as him."

"The law was made for all," observed Hiram, who bagan to think the danger was likely to fall to his own share, notwithstanding his management; "and the law is particular in noticing parjury."

"See here, Squire Doolittle," said the reckless wood-chopper, "I don't kear the valie of a beetle-ring for you and your parjury too. But as I have come so far, I'll go down and have a talk with the old man, and maybe we'll fry a steak of the deer together."

"Well, if you can get in paceably, so much the better," said the magistrate. "To my notion, strife is very unpopular; I prefar, at all times, clever conduct to an ugly temper."

As the whole party moved at a great pace, they soon reached the hut, where Hiram thought it prudent to halt on the outside of the top of the fallen pine, which formed a chevaux-de-frieze, to defend the approach to the fortress, on the side next to the village. The delay was but little relished by Kirby, who clapped his hands to his mouth, and gave a loud halloo, that brought the dogs out of their kennel, and, almost at the same instant, the scantily covered head of Natty also from the door.

"Lie down, you old fool," cried the hunter; "do you think there's more painters about you."

"Ha! Leather-stocking, I've an arrand with you," cried Kirby; "here's the good people of the state have been writing you a small letter and they've hired me to ride post."

"What would you have with me, Billy Kirby?" said Natty, stepping across his threshold, and raising his hand over his eyes to screen them from the rays of the setting sun, while he took a survey of his visiter. "I've no land to clear; and heaven knows I would set out six trees afore I would cut down one. Down, Hector, I say, into your kennel with ye."

"Would you, old boy?" roared Billy, "then so much the better for me. But I must do my arrand. Here's a letter for you, Leather-stocking. If you can read it it's all well, and if you can't, here's Squire Doolittle at hand, to let you know what it means. It seems you mistook the twentieth of July for the first of August, that's all."

By this time Natty had discovered the lank person of Hiram, drawn up under the cover of a high stump; and all that was complacent in his manner instantly gave way to marked distrust and dissatisfaction. He placed his hand within the door of his hut, and said a few words in an undertone, when he again appeared, and continued—

"I've nothing for ye; so away, afore the evil one tempts me to do you harm. I owe you no spite, Billy Kirby, and what for should you trouble an old man who has done you no harm?"

Kirby advanced through the top of the pine, to within a few feet of the hunter, where he seated himself on the end of a log with great composure, and began to examine the nose of Hector, with whom he was familiar, from their frequently meeting in the woods, where he sometimes fed the dog from his own basket of provisions.

"You've outshot me, and I'm not ashamed to say it," said the wood-chopper, "but I don't owe you a grudge for that, Natty! though it seems, that you've shot once too often, for the story goes that you've killed a buck."

"I've fired but twice to-day, and both times at the painters," returned the Leather-stocking; "see! here's the scalps! I was just going in with them to the Judge's to ask the bounty."

While Natty was speaking, he tossed the ears to Kirby, who continued playing with them, with a careless air, holding them to the dogs and laughing at their movements when they scented the unusual game.

But Hiram, emboldened by the advance of the deputed constable, now ventured to approach also, and took up the discourse with the air of authority that became his commission. His first measure was to read the warrant aloud, taking care to give due emphasis to the most material parts, and concluding with the name of the Judge in very audible and distinct tones.

"Did Marmaduke Temple put his name to that bit of paper!" said Natty, shaking his head;—"well, well, that man loves the new ways, and his betterments, and his lands, afore his own flesh and blood. But I won't mistrust the gal; she has an eye like a full-grown buck! poor thing, she didn't choose her father and can't help it. I know but little of the law, Mr. Doolittle; what is to be done, now you have read your commission?"

"Oh! it's nothing but form, Natty," said Hiram, endeavouring to assume a friendly aspect. Let's go in and talk the thing over in reason. I dare to say that the money can be easily found, though I conclude, from what passed, that Judge Temple will pay it himself."

The old hunter had kept a keen eye on the movements of his three visiters, from the beginning, and had maintained his position, just without the threshold of his cabin, with a determined manner, that showed he was not to be easily driven from his post. When Hiram drew nigher, as if expecting that his proposition would be accepted, Natty lifted his hand and motioned for him to retreat.

"Haven't I told you, more than once, not to tempt me," he said. "I trouble no man; why can't the law leave me to myself? Go back—go back, and tell your Judge that he may keep his bounty; but I won't have his wasty ways brought into my hut."

This offer, however, instead of appeasing the curiosity of Hiram, seemed to inflame it the more; while Kirby cried—

"Well, that's fair, Squire; he forgives the county his demand, and the county should forgive him the fine; it's what I call an even trade, and should be concluded on the spot. I like quick dealings, and what's fair 'twixt man and man."

"I demand entrance into this house," said Hiram, summoning all the dignity he could muster to his assistance, "in the name of the people, and by vartoo of this warrant, and of my office, and with this peace officer."

"Stand back, stand back, Squire, and don't tempt me," said the Leather-stocking, motioning for him to retire, with great earnestness.

"Stop us at your peril," continued Hiram—"Billy! Jotham! close up—I want your testimony."

Hiram had mistaken the mild but determined air of Natty for submission, and had already put his foot on the threshold to enter, when he was seized unexpectedly by his shoulders, and hurled over the little bank towards the lake, to the distance of twenty feet. The suddenness of the movement, and the unexpected display of strength on the part of Natty, created a momentary astonishment in his invaders, that silenced all noises, but at the next instant Billy Kirby gave vent to his mirth in loud peals of laughter that he seemed to heave up from his very soul.

"Well done, old stub!" he shouted, "the Squire know'd you better than I did. Come, come, here's a green spot; take it out like men, while Jotham and I see fair play."

"William Kirby, I order you to do your duty," cried Hiram, from under the bank, "seize that man; I order you to seize him in the name of the people."

But the Leather-stocking now assumed a more threatening attitude; his rifle was in his hand, and its muzzle was directed towards the wood-chopper.

"Stand off, I bid ye," said Natty, "you know my aim, Billy Kirby; I don't crave your blood, but mine and yourn both shall turn this green grass red, afore you put your foot into the hut."

While the affair appeared trifling, the wood-chopper seemed disposed to take sides with the weaker party; but when the fire-arms were introduced, his manner very sensibly changed. He raised his large frame from the log, and facing the hunter with an open front, he replied—

"I didn't come here as your enemy, Leather-stocking; but I don't vallie the hollow piece of iron in your hand so much as a broken axe-helve;—so, Squire, say the word, and keep within the law, and we'll soon see who's the best man of the two."

But no magistrate was to be seen! The instant the rifle was produced Hiram and Jotham vanished; and when the wood-chopper bent his eyes about him in surprise at receiving no answer, he discovered their retreating figures, moving towards the village, at a rate that sufficiently indicated that they had not only calculated the velocity of a rifle-bullet, but also its probable range.

"You've skeared the creaters off," said Kirby, with great contempt expressed on his broad features; "but you are not a-going to skear me; so, Mr. Bumppo, down with your gun, or there'll soon be trouble 'twixt us."

Natty dropped his rifle, and replied—

"I wish you no harm, Billy Kirby; but I leave it to yourself, whether an old man's hut is to be run down by such varmint as them. I won't deny the buck to you, Billy, and you may take the skin in, if you please, and show it as a tisti-mony. The bounty will pay the fine, and that ought to satisfy any man."

" 'Twill, old boy, 'twill," cried Kirby, every shade of dis-pleasure vanishing from his open brow at the peace-offering; "throw out the hide, and that shall satisfy the law."

Natty entered his hut, and soon reappeared, bringing with him the desired testimonial, and the wood-chopper departed, as thoroughly reconciled to the hunter as if nothing had hap-pened. As he paced along the margin of the lake, he would burst into frequent fits of laughter, while he recollected the summerset of Hiram; and, on the whole, he thought the affair a very capital joke.

Long before Billy reached the village, however, the news of his danger, and of Natty's disrespect to the law, and of Hiram's discomfiture, were in circulation. A good deal was said about sending for the Sheriff; some hints were given about calling out the posse comitatus to avenge the insulted laws; and many of the citizens were collected, deliberating how to proceed. The arrival of Billy with the skin, by remov-ing all grounds for a search, changed the complexion of things materially. Nothing now remained but to collect the fine, and assert the dignity of the people; all of which, it was unani-mously agreed, could be done as well on the succeeding Mon-day as on a Saturday night, a time kept sacred by a large por-tion of the settlers. Accordingly, all further proceedings were suspended for six-and-thirty hours.

· *Chapter XXXI* ·

And dar'st thou, then,
To beard the lion in his den,
The Douglass in his hall?
MARMION

The commotion was just subsiding, and the inhabitants of the village had begun to disperse from the little groups they had formed, each retiring to his own home, and closing his door after him, with the grave air of a man who consulted public feeling in his exterior deportment, when Oliver Edwards, on his return from the dwelling of Mr. Grant, encountered the young lawyer who is known to the reader as Mr. Lippet. There was very little similarity in the manners or opinions of the two; but as they both belonged to the more intelligent class of a very small community, they were, of course, known to each other; and, as their meeting was at a point where silence would have been rudeness, the following conversation was the result of their interview;

"A fine evening, Mr. Edwards," commenced the lawyer, whose disinclination to the dialogue was, to say the least, very doubtful; "we want rain sadly;—that's the worst of this climate of ours, it's either a drought or a deluge. It's likely you've been used to a more equal temperatoore?"

"I am a native of this state," returned Edwards coldly.

"Well, I've often heerd that point disputed; but it's so easy to get a man naturalized, that it's of little consequence where he was born. I wonder what course the Judge means to take in this business of Natty Bumppo?"

"Of Natty Bumppo!" echoed Edwards; "to what do you allude, sir?"

"Haven't you heerd!" exclaimed the other, with a look of surprise, so naturally assumed as completely to deceive the

other; "why, it may turn out an ugly business. It seems that
the old man has been out in the hills, and has shot a buck, this
morning, and that, you know, is a criminal matter in the eyes
of Judge Temple."

"Oh! he has, has he!" said Edwards averting his face to
conceal the colour that collected in his sun-burnt cheek. "Well,
if that be all, he must even pay the fine."

"It's five pounds currency," said the lawyer; "could Natty
muster so much money at once?"

"Could he!" cried the youth. "I am not rich, Mr. Lippet;
far from it—I am poor, and I have been hoarding my salary
for a purpose that lies near my heart; but before that old man
should lie one hour in jail, I would spend the last cent to prevent it. Besides he has killed two panthers, and the bounty
will discharge the fine many times over."

"Yes, yes," said the lawyer, rubbing his hands together, with
an expression of pleasure that had no artifice about it; "we
shall make it out; I see plainly we shall make it out."

"Make what out, sir? I must beg an explanation."

"Why, killing the buck is but a small matter compared to
what took place this afternoon," continued Mr. Lippet, with
a confidential and friendly air, that insensibly won upon the
youth, as little as he liked the man. "It seems, that a complaint was made of the fact, and the suspicion that there was
venison in the hut was sworn to, all which is provided for in
the statoote, when Judge Temple granted a search-warrant"—

"A search-warrant!" echoed Edwards, in a voice of horror,
and with a face that should have been again averted, to conceal its paleness; "and how much did they discover? What
did they see?"

"They saw old Bumppo's rifle; and that is a sight which
will quiet most men's curiosity in the woods."

"Did they! did they!" shouted Edwards, bursting into a
convulsive laugh; so the old hero beat them back!—he beat
them back! did he?"

The lawyer fastened his eyes in astonishment on the youth;
but as his wonder gave way to the thoughts that were commonly uppermost in his mind, he replied—

"It's no laughing matter, let me tell you, sir; the forty dollars of bounty, and your six months of salary will be much reduced before you can get the matter fairly settled. Assaulting a magistrate in the execootion of his duty, and menacing a constable with fire-arms, at the same time, is a pretty serious affair, and is punishable with both fine and imprisonment."

"Imprisonment!" repeated Oliver; "imprison the Leather-stocking! no, no, sir; it would bring the old man to his grave. They shall never imprison the Leather-stocking."

"Well, Mr. Edwards," said Lippet, dropping all reserve from his manner, "you are called a curious man; but if you can tell me how a jury is to be prevented from finding a verdict of guilty, if this case comes fairly before them, and the proof is clear, I shall acknowledge that you know more law than I do, who have had a license in my pocket for three years."

By this time the reason of Edwards was getting the ascendancy of his feelings; and as he began to see the real difficulties in the case, he listened more readily to the conversation of the lawyer. The ungovernable emotion that escaped the youth, in the first moment of his surprise, entirely passed away, and although it was still evident that he continued to be much agitated by what he had heard, he succeeded in yielding a forced attention to the advice which the other uttered.

Notwithstanding the confused state of his mind, Oliver soon discovered that most of the expedients of the lawyer were grounded in cunning, and plans that required a time to execute them in, that neither suited his disposition nor his emergencies. After, however, giving Mr. Lippet to understand that he retained him in the event of a trial, an assurance that at once satisfied the lawyer, they parted, one taking his course, with a deliberate tread, in the direction of the little building that had a wooden sign over its door, with "Chester Lippet, Attorney at Law," painted on it; and the other, pacing over the ground, with enormous strides, towards the Mansion-house. We shall take leave of the attorney for the present, and direct the attention of the reader to his client.

When Edwards entered the hall, whose enormous doors

were opened to the passage of the air of a mild evening, he found Benjamin engaged in some of his domestic avocations, and in a hurried voice inquired where Judge Temple was to be found.

"Why, the Judge has just stept into his office, with that master carpenter, Mr. Doolittle; but Miss Lizzy is in that there parlour. I say, Master Oliver, we'd like to have had a bad job of that panther, or painter's work—some calls it one, and some calls it t'other—but I know little of the beast, seeing that it is not of British growth. I said as much as that it was in the hills, the last winter; for I heard it moaning on the lake shore one evening in the fall, when I was pulling down from the fishing point in the skiff. Had the animal come into the open water, where a man could see where and how to work his vessel, I would have engaged the thing myself; but looking aloft among the trees, is all the same to me as standing on the deck of one ship, and looking at another vessel's tops. I never can tell one rope from another"——

"Well, well," interrupted Edwards; "I must see Miss Temple."

"And you shall see her, sir," said the steward; "she's in this here room. Oh! Lord, Master Edwards, what a loss she'd have been to the Judge! Dam'me if I know where he would have gotten such another daughter; that is, full grown, d'ye see. I say, sir, this Master Bumppo is a worthy man, and seems to have a handy way with him, with fire-arms and boat-hooks. I'm his friend, Master Oliver, and he and you may both set me down as the same."

"We may want your friendship, my worthy fellow," cried Edwards, squeezing his hand convulsively—"We may want your friendship, in which case you shall know it."

Without waiting to hear the earnest reply that Benjamin meditated, the youth extricated himself from the vigorous grasp of the steward, and entered the parlour.

Elizabeth was alone, and still reclining on the sofa, where we last left her. A hand, which exceeded all that the ingenuity of art could model, in shape and colour, veiled her eyes; and the maiden was sitting in an abstracted posture, as if communing deeply with herself. Struck by the attitude and loveliness of the form that met his eye, the young man checked his impatience, and approached her with respect and caution.

"Miss Temple—Miss Temple," he said, "I hope I do not intrude; but I am anxious to see you, if it be only for a moment."

Elizabeth raised her face, and exhibited her dark eyes swimming in moisture; but a flush crossed her cheeks, that resembled the tints which the setting sun throws over the neighbouring clouds.

"Is it you, Edwards?" she said with a sweetness in her voice, and a softness in her air, that she often used to her father, but which, from its novelty to himself, thrilled on every nerve of the youth; "how left you our poor Louisa?"

"She is with her father, happy and grateful," said Oliver. "I never witnessed more feeling than she manifested when I ventured to express my pleasure at her escape. I know not how it was, Miss Temple, but when I first heard of your horrid situation, my feelings were too powerful for utterance; and I did not properly find my tongue, until the walk to Mr. Grant's had given me time to collect myself. I believe—I do believe, I acquitted myself better there, for Miss Grant even wept at my silly speeches."

For a moment Elizabeth did not reply, but again veiled her eyes with her hand. The feeling that caused the action, however, soon passed away, and, raising her face again to his gaze, she continued, with a smile—

"Your friend, the Leather-stocking, has now become my friend, Edwards; I have been thinking how I can best serve him; perhaps you, who know his habits and his wants so well, can tell me"——

"I can," cried the youth, with an impetuosity that startled the maiden—"I can, and may Heaven reward you for the wish. Natty has been so imprudent as to forget the law, and has this day killed a deer. Nay, I believe I must share in the crime and the penalty, for I was an accomplice throughout. A complaint has been made to your father, and he has granted a search"——

"I know it all," interrupted Elizabeth, beckoning with her

hand for silence; "I know it—I know it all. The forms of the law must be complied with, however; the search must be made, the deer found, and the penalty paid. But I must retort your own question. Have you lived so long in our family, not to know us? Look at me, Oliver Edwards. Do I appear like the girl who would permit the man who has just saved her life to linger in a jail, for so small a sum as this fine? No, no, sir; my father is a Judge, but he is a man and a Christian. It is all understood and no harm shall follow."

"What a load of apprehensions do your declarations remove!" exclaimed Edwards. "He shall not be disturbed again! your father will protect him! I have your assurance, Miss Temple, that he will, and I must believe it."

"You may have his own, Mr. Edwards," returned Elizabeth, "for here he comes to make it."

But the appearance of Marmaduke, who entered the apartment, contradicted the flattering anticipations of his daughter. His brow was contracted with a look of care, and his manner was disturbed. Neither Elizabeth nor the youth spoke; but the Judge was allowed to pace once or twice across the room without interruption, when he cried—

"Our plans are defeated, girl; the obstinacy of the Leatherstocking has brought down the indignation of the law on his devoted head, and it is out of my power to avert it."

"How? in what manner?" cried Elizabeth; "the fine is nothing; surely"——

"I did not—I could not anticipate that an old, a friendless man, like him would dare to oppose the officers of justice," interrupted the Judge; "I supposed that he would submit to the search, when the fine could have been paid, and the law would have been appeased; but now he will have to meet its rigour."

"And what must the punishment be, sir?" asked Edwards, in an agitated voice.

Marmaduke turned quickly to the spot where the youth had withdrawn, and exclaimed—

"You here! I did not observe you. I know not what it will be, sir; it is not usual for a Judge to decide, until he has heard the testimony, and the jury have convicted. Of one thing, however, you may be assured, Mr. Edwards; it shall be whatever the law demands, notwithstanding any momentary weakness I may have exhibited, because the luckless man has been of such eminent service to my daughter."

"No one, I believe, doubts the sense of justice which Judge Temple entertains!" returned Edwards, bitterly. "But let us converse calmly, sir. Will not the years, the habits, nay, the ignorance of my old friend, avail him any thing against such a charge?"

"Ought they? I may ask," returned Marmaduke. "They may extenuate, but can they acquit? Would any society be tolerable, young man, where the ministers of justice are to be opposed by men armed with rifles? Is it for this that I have tamed the wilderness?"

"Had you tamed the beasts that so lately threatened the life of Miss Temple, sir, your arguments would apply better."

"Edwards!" exclaimed Elizabeth——

"Peace, my child," interrupted her father;—"the youth is unjust; but I have not given him cause. I overlook thy remark, Oliver, for I know thee to be a friend of Natty, and thy zeal in his behalf has overcome thy discretion."

"Yes, he is my friend," cried Edwards, "and I glory in the title. He is simple, unlettered, even ignorant; prejudiced, perhaps, though I feel that his opinion of the world is too true; but he has a heart, Judge Temple, that would atone for a thousand faults; he knows his friends, and never deserts them, even if it be his dog."

"This is a good character, Mr. Edwards," returned Marmaduke, mildly; "but I have never been so fortunate as to secure his esteem, for to me he has been uniformly repulsive; yet I have endured it, as an old man's whim. However, when he appears before me, as his judge, he shall find that his former conduct shall not aggravate, any more than his recent services shall extenuate his crime."

"Crime!" echoed Edwards; "is it a crime to drive a prying miscreant from his door? Crime! Oh! no, sir; if there be a criminal involved in this affair, it is not he."

"And who may it be, sir?" asked Judge Temple, facing the

agitated youth, with his fine, manly features settled to their usual composure.

This appeal was more than the young man could bear. Hitherto he had been deeply agitated by his emotions; but now the volcano burst its boundaries.

"Who! and this to me!" he cried; "ask your own conscience, Judge Temple. Walk to that door, sir, and look out upon the valley, that placid lake, and those dusky mountains, and say to your own heart, if heart you have, whence came these riches, this vale, those hills, and why am I their owner? I should think, sir, that the appearance of Mohegan and the Leather-stocking, stalking through the country, impoverished and forlorn, would wither your sight."

Marmaduke heard this burst of passion, at first with deep amazement; but when the youth had ended, he beckoned to his impatient daughter for silence, and replied—

"Oliver Edwards, thou forgettest in whose presence thou standest. I have heard, young man, that thou claimest descent from the native owners of the soil; but surely thy education has been given thee to no effect, if it has not taught thee the validity of the claims that have transferred the title to the whites. These lands are mine by the very grants of thy ancestry, if thou art so descended; and I appeal to Heaven, for a testimony of the uses I have put them to. After this language, we must separate. I have too long sheltered thee in my dwelling; but the time has arrived when thou must quit it. Come to my office, and I will discharge the debt I owe thee. Neither shall thy present intemperate language mar thy future fortunes, if thou wilt hearken to the advice of one who is many years thy senior."

The ungovernable feeling that caused the violence of the youth had passed away, and he stood gazing after the retiring figure of Marmaduke, with a vacancy in his eye, that denoted the absence of his mind. At length he recollected himself, and, turning his head slowly around the apartment, he beheld Elizabeth, still seated on the sofa, but with her head dropped on her bosom, and her face again concealed by her hands.

"Miss Temple," he said—all violence had left his manner— "Miss Temple—I have forgotten myself—forgotten you. You have heard what your father has decreed, and this night I leave here. With you I would part in amity."

Elizabeth slowly raised her face, across which a momentary expression of sadness stole; but as she left her seat, her dark eyes lighted with their usual fire, her cheek flushed to burning, and her whole air seemed to belong to another nature.

"I forgive you, Edwards, and my father will forgive you," she said, when she reached the door. "You do not know us, but the time may come, when your opinions shall change"——

"Of you! never!" interrupted the youth: "I"——

"I would speak, sir, and not listen. There is something in this affair that I do not yet comprehend; but tell the Leatherstocking he has friends as well as judges in us. Do not let the old man experience unnecessary uneasiness at this rupture. It is impossible that you could increase his claims here; neither shall they be diminished by any thing you have said. Mr. Edwards, I wish you happiness, and warmer friends."

The youth would have spoken, but she vanished from the door so rapidly, that when he reached the hall her light form was nowhere to be seen. He paused a moment, in a stupor, and then, rushing from the house, instead of following Marmaduke to his "office," he took his way directly to the cabin of the hunters.

· *Chapter XXXII* ·

Who measured earth, described the starry spheres,
And traced the long records of lunar years.

Richard did not return from the exercise of his official duties,
until late in the evening of the following day. It had been one
portion of his business to superintend the arrest of part of a
gang of counterfeiters, that had, even at that early period,
buried themselves in the woods, to manufacture their base
coin, which they afterward circulated from one end of the
Union to the other. The expedition had been completely successful, and about midnight the Sheriff entered the village,
at the head of a posse of deputies and constables, in the centre
of whom rode, pinioned, four of the malefactors. At the gate
of the Mansion-house they separated, Mr. Jones directing his assistants to proceed with their charge to the county
jail, while he pursued his own way up the gravelled walk, with
that kind of self-satisfaction that a man of his organization
would feel, who had, really, for once, done a very clever thing.

"Holla! Aggy!" shouted the Sheriff, when he reached the
door; "where are you, you black dog? will you keep me here
in the dark all night?—Holla! Aggy! Brave! Brave! hoy, hoy
—where have you got to, Brave? Off his watch! Every body
is asleep but myself! poor I must keep my eyes open that others may sleep in safety. Brave! Brave! Well, I will say this for
the dog lazy as he's grown, that it is the first time I ever knew
him let any one come to the door after dark, without having
a smell to know whether it was an honest man or not. He could
tell by his nose, almost as well as I could myself by looking at
them. Holla! you Agamemnon! where are you? Oh! here
comes that dog at last."

By this time the Sheriff had dismounted, and observed a

form, which he supposed to be that of Brave, slowly creeping out of the kennel; when, to his astonishment, it reared itself on two legs instead of four, and he was able to distinguish by the star-light, the curly head and dark visage of the negro.

"Ha! what the devil are you doing there, you black rascal?" he cried; "is it not hot enough for your Guinea blood in the house, this warm night, but you must drive out the poor dog and sleep in his straw?"

By this time the boy was quite awake, and with a blubbering whine, he attempted to reply to his master.

"Oh! masser Richard! masser Richard! such a ting! such a ting! I nebber tink a could 'appen! nebber tink he die! Oh, Lor-a-gor! an't bury—keep 'em till masser Richard get back —got a grabe dug"——

Here the feelings of the negro completely got the mastery, and instead of making any intelligible explanation of the causes of his grief, he blubbered aloud.

"Eh! what! buried! grave! dead!" exclaimed Richard with a tremour in his voice; "nothing serious? nothing has happened to Benjamin, I hope? I know he has been bilious; but I gave him"——

"Oh! worser 'an a dat! worser 'an a dat? sobbed the negro. "Oh! de Lor! Miss 'Lizzy and a Miss Grant—walk—mountain —poor Bravy!—kill a lady—painter—Oh! Lor, Lor!—Natty Bumppo—tear he troat all open—come a see, masser Richard —such a booful copse—here he be—here he be."

As all this was perfectly inexplicable to the Sheriff, he was glad to wait patiently until the black brought a lantern from the kitchen, when he followed Aggy to the kennel, where he beheld poor Brave, indeed, lying in his blood, stiff and cold, but decently covered with the great-coat of the negro. He was on the point of demanding an explanation; but the grief of the black, who had fallen asleep on his voluntary watch, having burst out afresh on his waking, utterly disqualified the lad from giving one. Luckily, at this moment the principal door of the house opened, and the coarse features of Benjamin were thrust over the threshold, with a candle elevated above them, shedding its dim rays around in such a manner as to exhibit the lights and shadows of his countenance. Richard threw his bridle to the black, and bidding him look to the horse, he entered the hall.

"What is the meaning of the dead dog?" he cried. "Where is Miss Temple?"

Benjamin made one of his square gestures, with the thumb of his left hand pointing over his right shoulder, as he answered—

"Turned in."

"Judge Temple—where is he?"

"In his birth."

"But explain, why is Brave dead? and what is the cause of Aggy's grief?"

"Why, it's all down, Squire," said Benjamin, pointing to a slate that lay on the table, by the side of a mug of toddy, a short pipe in which the tobacco was yet burning, and a Prayer-book.

Among the other pursuits of Richard, it was a passion to keep a register of all passing events; and his diary, which was written in the manner of a journal, or log-book, embraced not only such circumstances as affected himself, but observations on the weather, and all the occurrences of the family, and frequently of the village. Since his appointment to the office of Sheriff, and his consequent absences from home, he had employed Benjamin to make memoranda, on a slate, of whatever might be thought worth remembering, which, on his return, were regularly transferred to the journal, with proper notations of the time, manner, and other little particulars. There was, to be sure, one material objection to the clerkship of Benjamin, which the ingenuity of no one but Richard could have overcome. The steward read nothing but his Prayer-book, and that only in particular parts, and by the aid of a good deal of spelling, and some misnomers; but he could not form a single letter with a pen. This would have been an insuperable bar to journalizing with most men; but Richard invented a kind of hieroglyphical character, which was intended to note all the ordinary occurrences of a day, such as how the wind blew, whether the sun shone, or whether it rained, the hours, &c.; and for the extraordinary, after giving certain elementary lectures on the subject, the Sheriff was obliged to trust to the ingenuity of the Major-domo. The reader will at once perceive, that it was to this chronicle that Benjamin pointed, instead of directly answering the Sheriff's interrogatory.

When Mr. Jones had drunk a glass of the toddy, he brought forth, from its secret place, his proper journal, and seating himself by the table, he prepared to transfer the contents of the slate to the paper, at the same time that he appeased his curiosity. Benjamin laid one hand on the back of the Sheriff's chair, in a familiar manner, while he kept the other at liberty, to make use of a fore-finger, that was bent like some of his own characters, as an index to point out his meaning.

The first thing referred to by the Sheriff was the diagram of a compass, that was cut in one corner of the slate for permanent use. The cardinal points were plainly marked on it, and all the usual divisions were indicated in such a manner, that no man who had ever steered a ship could mistake them.

"Oh!" said the Sheriff, settling himself down comfortably in his chair,—"you'd the wind southeast, I see, all last night; I thought it would have blown up rain."

"Devil the drop, sir," said Benjamin; "I believe that the scuttle-butt up aloft is emptied; for there hasn't so much water fell in the county, for the last three weeks, as would float Indian John's canoe, and that draws just one inch nothing, light."

"Well, but didn't the wind change here this morning? there was a change where I was."

"To be sure it did, Squire; and haven't I logged it as a shift of wind."

"I don't see where, Benjamin; I"——

"Don't see!" interrupted the steward, a little crustily; "ain't there a mark ag'in east-and-by-nothe-half-nothe, with sum'mat like a rising sun at the end of it, to show 'twas in the morning watch?"

"Yes, yes, that is very legible; but where is the change noted?"

"Where why doesn't it see this here tea-kettle, with a mark run from the spout straight, or mayhap a little crooked or so, into west-and-by-southe-half-southe? now I calls this a shift of wind, Squire. Well, do you see this here boar's head that you made for me alongside the compass"——

"Ay ay—Boreas—I see. Why you've drawn lines from its mouth, extending from one of your marks to the other."

"It's no fault of mine, Squire Dickens; 'tis your d—d climate. The wind has been at all them there marks this very day; and that's all round the compass, except a little matter of an Irishman's hurricane at meridium, which you'll find marked right up and down. Now, I've known a sow-wester blow for three weeks, in the Channel, with a clean drizzle, in which you might wash your face and hands, without the trouble of hauling in water from alongside."

"Very well, Benjamin," said the Sheriff, writing in his journal; "I believe I have caught the idea. Oh! Here's a cloud over the rising sun;—so you had it hazy in the morning?"

"Ay, ay, sir," said Benjamin.

"Ah! it's Sunday, and here are the marks for the length of the sermon—one, two, three, four— What! did Mr. Grant preach forty minutes!"

"Ay, sum'mat like it; it was a good half-hour by my own glass, and then there was the time lost in turning it, and some little allowance for leeway in not being over smart about it."

"But, Benjamin, this is as long as a Presbyterian sermon; you never could have been ten minutes in turning the glass!"

"Why, d'ye see, Squire, the parson was very solemn, and I just closed my eyes in order to think the better with myself, just the same as you'd put in the dead-lights to make all snug, and when I opened them ag'in I found the congregation were getting under weigh for home, so I calculated the ten minutes would cover the lee-way after the glass was out. It was only some such matter as a cat's nap."

"Oh, ho! Master Benjamin, you were asleep, were you! but I'll set down no such slander against an orthodox divine." Richard wrote twenty-nine minutes in his journal, and continued—"Why, what's this you've got opposite ten o'clock, A.M.? a full moon! had you a moon visible by day! I have heard of such portents before now, but—eh, what's this alongside of it? an hour-glass?"

"That!" said Benjamin, looking cooly over the Sheriff's shoulder, and rolling the tobacco about in his mouth with a jocular air; "why, that's a small matter of my own. It's no moon, Squire, but only Betty Hollister's face; for, d'ye see, sir, hearing all the same as if she had got up a new cargo of Jamaiky from the river, I called in as I was going to the church this morning—ten, A.M. was it? just the time—and tried a glass; and so I logged it, to put me in mind of calling to pay her like an honest man."

"That was it, was it?" said the Sheriff, with some displeasure at this innovation on his memoranda; "and could you not make a better glass than this? it looks like a death's head and an hour-glass."

"Why, as I liked the stuff, Squire," returned the steward, "I turned in, homeward bound, and took t'other glass, which I set down at the bottom of the first, and that gives the thing the shape it has. But as I was there ag'in to-night, and paid for the three at once, your honour may as well run the sponge over the whole business."

"I will buy you a slate for your own affairs, Benjamin," said the Sheriff; "for I don't like to have the journal marked over in this manner."

"You needn't—you needn't, Squire; for seeing that I was likely to trade often with the woman while this barrel lasted, I've opened a fair account with Betty, and she keeps her marks on the back of her bar door, and I keeps the tally on this here bit of a stick."

As Benjamin concluded he produced a piece of wood, on which five very honest large notches were apparent. The Sheriff cast his eyes on this new leger, for a moment, and continued—

"What have we here! Saturday, two P.M.—why here's a whole family piece! two wine-glasses upside-down!

"That's two women; the one this-away is Miss 'Lizzy and t'other is the parson's young'un."

"Cousin Bess and Miss Grant!" exclaimed the Sheriff, in amazement; "why, what have they to do with my journal?"

"They'd enough to do to get out of the jaws of that there

painter, or panther," said the immoveable steward. "This here thingum'y, Squire, that maybe looks sum'mat like a rat, is the beast, d'ye see; and this here t'other thing, keel uppermost, is poor old Brave, who died nobly, all the same as an admiral fighting for his king and country; and that there"——

"Scarecrow," interrupted Richard.

"Ay, mayhap it do look a little wild or so," continued the steward; "but to my judgment, Squire, it's the best imager I've made, seeing it's most like the man himself;— well, that's Natty Bumppo, who shot this here painter that killed that there dog, who would have eaten or done worse to them here young ladies."

"And what the devil does all this mean?" cried Richard, impatiently.

"Mean!" echoed Benjamin; "it's as true as the Boadishey's log-book"——

He was interrupted by the Sheriff, who put a few direct questions to him, that obtained more intelligible answers by which means he became possessed of a tolerably correct idea of the truth. When the wonder, and we must do Richard the justice to say, the feelings also, that were created by this narrative, had in some degree subsided, the Sheriff turned his eyes again on his journal, where more inexplicable hieroglyphics met his view.

"What have we here!" he cried; "two men boxing! has there been a breach of the peace? ah! that's the way, the moment my back is turned"——

"That's the Judge and young Master Edwards," interrupted the steward, very cavalierly.

"How! 'duke fighting with Oliver! what the devil has got into you all? more things have happened within the last thirty-six hours, than in the preceding six months."

"Yes, it's so indeed, Squire," returned the steward; "I've known a smart chase, and a fight at the tail of it, where less has been logged than I've got on that there slate. How-somenever, they didn't come to facers, only passed a little jaw fore and aft."

"Explain! explain!" cried Richard—"it was about the mines, ha!—ay, ay, I see it, I see it; here is a man, with a pick on his shoulder. So you heard it all, Benjamin?"

"Why, yes, it was about their minds, I believe, Squire," returned the steward; "and by what I can learn, they spoke them pretty plainly to one another. Indeed, I may say that I overheard a small matter of it myself, seeing that the windows was open, and I hard by. But this here is no pick, but an anchor on a man's shoulder; and here's the other fluke down his back, maybe a little too close, which signifies that the lad has got underway and left his moorings."

"Has Edwards left the house?" demanded Richard, peremptorily.

"He has," said the steward.

Richard pursued this advantage, and, after a long and close examination, he succeeded in getting out of Benjamin all that he knew, not only concerning the misunderstanding, but of the attempt to search the hut, and Hiram's discomfiture. The Sheriff was no sooner possessed of these facts, which Benjamin related with all possible tenderness to the Leather-stocking, then, snatching up his hat, and bidding the astonished steward to secure the doors and go to his bed, he left the house.

For at least five minutes after Richard disappeared, Benjamin stood with his arms a-kimbo, and his eyes fastened on the door; when, having collected his astonished faculties, he prepared to execute the orders he had received.

It has already been said, that the "court of common pleas and general sessions of the peace," or, as it is commonly called, the "county court," over which Judge Temple presided, held one of its stated sessions on the following morning. The attendants of Richard were officers who had come to the village as much to discharge their usual duties at this court, as to escort the prisoners; and the Sheriff knew their habits too well, not to feel confident he should find most, if not all of them, in the public room of the jail, discussing the qualities of the keeper's liquors. Accordingly he held his way, through the silent streets of the village, directly to the small and insecure building, that contained all the unfortunate debtors, and some of the criminals of the county, and where justice was administered to such unwary applicants as were so silly as to throw away two dollars, in order to obtain one from their neighbours. The arrival of four malefactors in the custody of a dozen officers, was an event, at that day, in Templeton; and when the Sheriff reached the jail, he found every indication that his subordinates intended to make a night of it.

The nod of the Sheriff brought two of his deputies to the door, who in their turn drew off six or seven of the constables. With this force Richard led the way through the village, towards the bank of the lake, undisturbed by any noise, except the barking of one or two curs, who were alarmed by the measured tread of the party, and by the low murmurs that ran through their own numbers, as a few cautious questions and answers were exchanged, relative to the object of their expedition. When they had crossed the little bridge of hewn logs that was thrown over the Susquehanna, they left the highway, and struck into that field which had been the scene of the victory over the pigeons. From this they followed their leader into the low bushes of pines and chestnuts which had sprung up along the shores of the lake, where the plough had not succeeded the fall of the trees, and soon entered the deep forest itself. Here Richard paused, and collected his troop around him.

"I have required your assistance, my friends," he said in a low voice, "in order to arrest Nathaniel Bumppo, commonly called the Leather-stocking. He has assaulted a magistrate, and resisted the execution of a search-warrant, by threatening the life of a constable with his rifle. In short, my friends, he has set an example of rebellion to the laws, and has become a kind of out-law. He is suspected of other misdemeanors and offences against private rights; and I have this night taken on myself, by the virtue of my office as Sheriff, to arrest the said Bumppo, and bring him to the county jail, that he may be present and forthcoming to answer to these heavy charges before the court to-morrow morning. In executing this duty, my friends and fellow-citizens, you are to use courage and discretion. Courage, that you may not be daunted by any lawless attempts that this man may make, with his rifle and his dogs, to oppose you; and discretion, which here means caution and prudence, that he may not escape from this sudden attack—and—for other good reasons that I need not mention. You will form yourselves in a complete circle around his hut, and at the word 'advance,' called aloud by me, you will rush forward, and without giving the criminal time for deliberation, enter his dwelling by force and make him your prisoner. Spread yourselves for this purpose, while I shall descend to the shore with a deputy, to take charge of that point; and all communications must be made directly to me, under the bank in front of the hut, where I shall station myself, and remain in order to receive them."

This speech, which Richard had been studying during his walk, had the effect that all similar performances produce, of bringing the dangers of the expedition immediately before the eyes of his forces. The men divided, some plunging deeper into the forest in order to gain their stations without giving an alarm, and others continuing to advance, at a gait that would allow the whole party to get in order; but all devising the best plans to repulse the attack of a dog, or escape a rifle-bullet. It was a moment of dread expectation and interest.

When the Sheriff thought time enough had elapsed for the different divisions of his force to arrive at their stations, he raised his voice in the silence of the forest, and shouted the watch-word. The sounds played among the arched branches of the trees in hollow cadences; but when the last sinking tone was lost on the ear, in place of the expected howls of the dogs, no other noises were returned but the crackling of torn branches and dried sticks, as they yielded before the advancing steps of the officers. Even this soon ceased, as if by a common consent, when, the curiosity and impatience of the Sheriff getting the complete ascendency over his discretion, he rushed up the bank, and in a moment stood on the little piece of cleared ground in front of the spot where Natty had so long lived. To his utter amazement, in place of the hut, he saw only smouldering ruins!

The party gradually drew together about the heap of ashes and ends of smoking logs, while a dim flame in the centre of the ruin, which still found fuel to feed its lingering life, threw its pale light, flickering with the passing currents of the air, around the circle, now showing a face with eyes fixed in astonishment, and then glancing to another countenance, leaving the former shaded in the obscurity of night. Not a voice was raised in inquiry, nor an exclamation made in astonishment. The transition from excitement to disappointment was too powerful in its effects for speech, and even Richard lost the use of an organ that was seldom known to fail him.

The whole groupe were yet in the fulness of their surprise, when a tall form stalked from the gloom into the circle, treading down the hot ashes and dying embers with callous feet, and standing over the light, lifted his cap, and exposed the bare head and weather-beaten features of the Leather-stocking. For a moment he gazed at the dusky figures who surrounded him, more in sorrow than in anger, before he spoke.

"What would ye have with an old and helpless man?" he said. "You've driven God's creaters from the wilderness, where his providence had put them for his own pleasure, and you've brought in the troubles and divilties of the law, where no man was ever known to disturb another. You have driven me, that have lived forty long years of my appointed time in this very spot, from my home and the shelter of my head, lest you should put your wicked feet and wasty ways into my cabin. You've driven me to burn these logs, under which I've eaten and drunk, the first of Heaven's gifts, and the other of the pure springs, for the half of a hundred years, and to mourn the ashes under my feet, as a man would weep and mourn for the children of his body. You've rankled the heart of an old man, that has never harmed you or your'n, with bitter feelings towards his kind, at a time when his thoughts should be on a better world; and you've driven him to wish that the beasts of the forest, who never feast on the blood of their own families, was his kindred and race; and now, when he has come to see the last brand of his hut, before it is melted into ashes, you follow him up, at midnight, like hungry hounds on the track of a worn-out and dying deer! What more would ye have? for I am here—one to many. I come to mourn, not to fight; and, if it is God's pleasure, work your will on me."

When the old man ended, he stood, with the light glimmering around his thinly-covered head, looking earnestly at the groupe, which receded from the pile, with an instinctive and involuntary movement, without the reach of the quivering rays, leaving a free passage for his retreat into the bushes, where pursuit, in the dark, would have been fruitless. Natty seemed not to regard the advantage, but stood facing each individual in the circle, in succession, as if to see who would be the first to arrest him. After a pause of a few moments, Richard began to rally his confused faculties, and advancing, apologized for his duty, and made him his prisoner. The party was now collected, and, preceded by the Sheriff, with Natty in their centre, they took their way towards the village.

During the walk, divers questions were put to the prisoner concerning his reasons for burning the hut, and whither Mohegan had retreated, but to all of them he observed a profound silence, until, fatigued with their previous duties, and the lateness of the hour, the Sheriff and his followers reached the village and dispersed to their several places of rest, after turning the key of a jail on the aged and apparently friendless Leather-stocking.

· Chapter XXXIII ·

Fetch here the stocks, ho!
You stubborn ancient knave, you reverend braggart,
We'll teach you.

LEAR

The long days and early sun of July allowed time for a gathering of the interested, before the little bell of the academy announced that the appointed hour had arrived for administering right to the wronged, and punishment to the guilty. Ever since the dawn of day, the highways and wood-paths that, issuing from the forests, and winding along the sides of the mountains, centered in Templeton, had been thronged with equestrians and footmen bound to the haven of justice. There was to be seen a well-clad yeoman, mounted on a sleek, switch-tailed steed, ambling along the highway, with his red face elevated in a manner that said, "I have paid for my land, and fear no man," while his bosom was swelling with the conscious pride of being one of the grand inquest for the county. At his side rode a companion, his equal in independence of feeling, perhaps, but his inferior in thrift, as in property and consideration. This was a professed dealer in lawsuits—a man whose name appeared in every calendar; whose substance, gained in the multifarious expedients of a settler's changeable habits, was wasted in feeding the harpies of the courts. He was endeavoring to impress the mind of the grand juror with the merits of a cause that was now at issue. Along with these two was a pedestrian, who, having thrown a rifle frock over his shirt, and placed his best wool hat above his sunburnt visage, had issued from his retreat in the woods by a footpath, and was striving to keep company with the others, at an unequal gait, on his way to hear and to decide the disputes of his neighbours as a petit juror.

By ten o'clock the streets of the village were filled with groupes of men with busy faces, some talking of their private concerns, some listening to a popular expounder of political creeds, and others gaping in at the open stores, admiring the finery, or examining sithes, axes, and such other manufactures as attracted their curiosity or excited their admiration. A few women were to be observed in the crowd, mostly carrying infants in their arms, and followed at a lounging, listless gait, by their rustic lords and masters. There was one young couple, in whom the warmth of connubial love was yet new, walking among the moving throng, both dressed in their back-wood finery, at a respectful distance from each other, while the swain directed the timid steps of his bride by the unbending motions of an extended arm, to which she was appended by grasping his thumb.

At the first stroke of the bell, Richard issued from the front door of the "Bold Dragoon," flourishing in his hand a sheathed sword, that he was fond of saying his ancestors had carried in one of Cromwell's victories, and crying, in an authoritative tone, to "clear the way for the court." The order was obeyed promptly, though not servilely; the members of the crowd nodding familiarly to the members of the procession, as it passed. A party of constables with their staves followed the Sheriff, preceding Marmaduke, and four plain, grave-looking yeomen, who were his associates on the bench. There was nothing to distinguish these subordinate judges from the better part of the spectators, except gravity, which they affected a little more than common, and that one of their number was attired in an old-fashioned military coat, with skirts that reached no lower than the middle of his thighs, and bearing two little silver epaulettes, not half so big as a modern pair of shoulder knots. This gentleman was a colonel of the militia, in attendance on a court-martial, who found leisure to steal a moment from his military to attend to his civil jurisdiction. But this incongruity was nothing; it excited neither notice nor comment. Three or four clean-shaved lawyers followed, as meekly as if they were lambs going to the slaughter, one or two of whom had contrived to obtain an air of scholastic gravity, by wearing spectacles. The rear was brought up by another posse of constables, and the mob followed the whole into the room where the court held its sittings.

The edifice was composed of a basement of squared logs, perforated here and there with small grated windows, through which a few wistful faces were gazing at the crowd without, among which were the guilty, downcast countenances of the counterfeiters, and the simple but honest features of the Leather-stocking. The dungeons were to be distinguished, externally, from the debtors' apartments, only by the size of the apertures, the thickness of the grates, and by the heads of spikes that were driven into the logs as a protection against the illegal use of edge-tools. The upper story was of frame-work, regularly covered with boards, and contained one room decently fitted up for the purposes of justice. A bench ran along one of its sides, and was raised on a narrow platform to the height of a man above the floor, and was protected in front by a light railing. In the centre was a seat, furnished with rude arms, that was always filled by the presiding judge. In front, on a level with the floor of the room, was a large table covered with green baize, and surrounded by benches; and at either of its ends were placed rows of seats rising one over the other, for jury boxes. Each of these several divisions were surrounded by a railing. The remainder of the room was an open space appropriated to the spectators.

When the judges were seated, the lawyers had taken possession of the table, and the noise of moving feet had ceased in the area, the proclamations were made in the usual form, the jurors were sworn, the charge was given, and the court proceeded to hear the business before them.

We shall not detain the reader with a description of the captious discussions that occupied the court for the first two hours. Judge Temple had impressed on the jury, in his charge, the necessity for despatch on their part, recommending to their notice, from motives of humanity, the prisoners in the jail as the first objects of their attention. Accordingly, after the period we have mentioned had elapsed, the cry of the officers to "clear the way for the grand jury," announced the entrance of that body. The usual forms were observed, when the foreman handed up to the bench two bills, on both of which the Judge observed, at the first glance of his eye, the name of Nathaniel Bumppo. It was a leisure moment with the court; some low whispering passed between the bench and the Sheriff, who gave a signal to his officers, and in a very few minutes the silence that prevailed there was interrupted by a general movement in the outer crowd; when presently the Leather-stocking made his appearance, ushered into the criminal's bar under the custody of two constables. The hum ceased, the people closed into the open space again and the silence soon became so deep that the hard breathing of the prisoner was audible.

Natty was dressed in his buck-skin garments, without his coat, in place of which he wore only a shirt of coarse linen-check, fastened at his throat by the sinew of a deer, leaving his red neck and weather-beaten face exposed and bare. It was the first time that he had ever crossed the threshold of a court of justice, and curiosity seemed to be strongly blended with his personal feelings. He raised his eyes to the bench, thence to the jury-boxes, the bar, and the crowd without, meeting every where looks that were fastened on himself. After surveying his own person, as if in search of the cause of this unusual attraction, he once more turned his face around the assemblage, and then opened his mouth in one of his silent and remarkable laughs.

"Prisoner, remove your cap," said Judge Temple.

The order was either unheard or unheeded.

"Nathaniel Bumppo, be uncovered," repeated the Judge.

Natty started at the sound of his name, and raising his face earnestly towards the bench, he said—

"Anan!"

Mr. Lippet arose from his seat at the table, and whispered in the ear of the prisoner, when Natty gave him a nod of assent, and took the deer-skin covering from his head.

"Mr. District Attorney," said the Judge, "the prisoner is ready; we wait for the indictment."

The duties of the public prosecutor were discharged by Dirck Van der School, who adjusted his spectacles, cast a cautious look around him at his brethren of the bar, which he ended by throwing his head aside so as to catch one glance over the glasses, when he proceeded to read the bill aloud. It was the usual charge for an assault and battery on the person of Hiram Doolittle, and was couched in the ancient language of such instruments, especial care having been taken by the scribe, not to omit the name of a single offensive weapon known to the law. When he had done, Mr. Van der School removed his spectacles, which he closed and placed in his pocket, seemingly, for the pleasure of again opening and replacing them on his nose. After this evolution was repeated once or twice, he handed the bill over to Mr. Lippet, with a cavalier air, that said as much as "pick a hole in that, if you can."

Natty listened to the charge against him with great attention, leaning forward towards the reader with an earnestness that denoted his interest; and when it was ended he raised his tall body to the utmost, and drew a long sigh. All eyes were turned to the prisoner, whose voice was vainly expected to break the stillness of the room.

"You have heard the presentment that the grand jury have made, Nathaniel Bumppo," said the Judge, "what do you plead to the charge?"

The old man dropped his head for a moment in a reflecting attitude, and then raising it, he laughed again, before he answered—

"That I handled the man a little rough or so, is not to be denied; but that there was occasion to make use of all them things that the gentleman has spoken of, is downright untrue. I am not much of a wrestler, seeing that I am getting old; but I was out among the Scotch-Irishers—lets me see —it must have been as long ago as the first year of the old war"——

"Mr. Lippet, if you are retained for the prisoner," interrupted Judge Temple, "instruct your client how to plead; if not, the court shall assign him counsel."

Aroused from studying the indictment by this appeal, the

attorney got up, and after a short dialogue with the hunter in a low voice, he informed the court that they were ready to proceed.

"Do you plead guilty or not guilty?" said the Judge.

"I may say not guilty with a clean conscience," returned Natty; "for there's no guilt in doing what's right; and I'd rather die on the spot, than had him put foot in the hut at that moment."

Richard started at this declaration, and bent his eyes significantly on Hiram, who returned the look with a slight movement of his eyebrows alone.

"Proceed to open the cause, Mr. District Attorney," continued the Judge. "Mr. Clerk, enter the plea of not guilty."

After a short opening address from Mr. Van der School, Hiram was summoned to the bar to give his testimony. It was delivered to the letter, perhaps, but with all the moral colouring which can be conveyed under such expressions as, "thinking no harm," "feeling it my bounden duty as a magistrate," and "seeing that the constable was back'ard in the business." When he had done, and the District Attorney declined putting any further interrogatories, Mr. Lippet arose, with an air of keen investigation, and asked the following questions:

"Are you a constable of this county, sir?"

"No sir," said Hiram, "I'm only a justice-peace."

"I ask you, Mr. Doolittle, in the face of this court, putting it to your conscience and your knowledge of the law, whether you had any right to enter that man's dwelling?"

"Hem!" said Hiram, undergoing a violent struggle between his desire for vengeance and his love for legal fame; "I do suppose—that in—that is—strict law—that supposing—maybe I hadn't a real—lawful right;—but as the case was—and Billy was so back'ard—I might come for'ard in the business."

"I ask you again, sir," continued the lawyer, following up his success, "whether this old, this friendless old man, did or did not repeatedly forbid your entrance?"

"Why, I must say," said Hiram, "that he was considerable cross-grained; not what I call clever, seeing that it was only one neighbour wanting to go into the house of another."

"Oh! then you own it was only meant for a neighbourly visit on your part, and without the sanction of the law. Remember, gentlemen, the words of the witness, 'one neighbour wanting to enter the house of another.' Now, sir, I ask you if Nathaniel Bumppo did not again and again order you not to enter?"

"There was some words passed between us," said Hiram, "but I read the warrant to him aloud."

"I repeat my question; did he tell you not to enter his habitation?"

"There was a good deal passed betwixt us—but I've the warrant in my pocket; maybe the court would wish to see it?"

"Witness," said Judge Temple, "answer the question directly; did or did not the prisoner forbid you entering his hut?"

"Why, I some shink"—

"Answer without equivocation," continued the Judge, sternly.

"He did."

"And then did you attempt to enter, after this order?"

"I did; but the warrant was in my hand."

"Proceed, Mr. Lippet, with your examination."

But the attorney saw that the impression was in favour of his client, and, waving his hand with a supercilious manner, as if unwilling to insult the understanding of the jury with any further defence, he replied—

"No, sir; I leave it for your honour to charge; I rest my case here."

"Mr. District Attorney," said the Judge, "have you any thing to say?"

Mr. Van der School removed his spectacles, folded them, and replacing them once more on his nose, eyed the other bill which he held in his hand, and then said, looking at the bar over the top of his glasses—

"I shall rest the prosecution here, if the court please."

Judge Temple arose and began the charge.

"Gentlemen of the Jury," he said, "you have heard the

testimony, and I shall detain you but a moment. If an officer meet with resistance in the execution of a process, he has an undoubted right to call any citizen to his assistance; and the acts of such assistance come within the protection of the law. I shall leave you to judge, gentlemen, from the testimony, how far the witness in this prosecution can be so considered, feeling less reluctance to submit the case thus informally to your decision, because there is yet another indictment to be tried, which involves heavier charges against the unfortunate prisoner."

The tone of Marmaduke was mild and insinuating, and as his sentiments were given with such apparent impartiality, they did not fail of carrying their due weight to the jury. The grave-looking yeomen, who composed this tribunal, laid their heads together for a few minutes without leaving their box, when the foreman arose, and after the forms of the court were duly observed, he pronounced the prisoner to be—

"Not guilty."

"You are acquitted of this charge, Nathaniel Bumppo," said the Judge.

"Anan," said Natty.

"You are found not guilty of striking and assaulting Mr. Doolittle."

"No, no, I'll not deny but that I took him a little roughly by the shoulders," said Natty, looking about him with great simplicity, "and that I"——

"You are acquitted," interrupted the Judge; "and there is nothing further to be said or done in the matter."

A look of joy lighted up the features of the old man, who now comprehended the case, and placing his cap eagerly on his head again, he threw up the bar of his little prison, and said feelingly—

"I must say this for you, Judge Temple, that the law has not been as hard on me as I dreaded. I hope God will bless you for the kind things you've done to me this day."

But the staff of the constable was opposed to his egress, and Mr. Lippet whispered a few words in his ear, when the aged hunter sunk back into his place, and removing his cap, stroked down the remnants of his gray and sandy locks, with an air of mortification mingled with submission.

"Mr. District Attorney," said Judge Temple, affecting to busy himself with his minutes, "proceed with the second indictment."

Mr. Van der School took great care that no part of the presentment, which he now read, should be lost on his auditors. It accused the prisoner of resisting the execution of a search-warrant by force of arms, and particularized in the vague language of the law, among a variety of other weapons, the use of the rifle. This was indeed a more serious charge than an ordinary assault and battery, and a corresponding degree of interest was manifested by the spectators in its result. The prisoner was duly arraigned, and his plea again demanded. Mr. Lippet had anticipated the answers of Natty, and in a whisper advised him how to plead. But the feelings of the old hunter were awakened by some of the expressions of the indictment, and forgetful of his caution, he exclaimed—

" 'Tis a wicked untruth; I crave no man's blood. Them thieves, the Iroquois, won't say it to my face, that I ever thirsted after man's blood. I have fought as a soldier that feared his Maker and his officer, but I never pulled a trigger on any but a warrior that was up and awake. No man can say that I ever struck even a Mingo in his blanket. I b'lieve there's some who thinks there's no God in a wilderness!"

"Attend to your plea, Bumppo," said the Judge; "you hear that you are accused of using your rifle against an officer of justice; are you guilty or not guilty?"

By this time the irritated feelings of Natty had found a vent; and he rested on the bar for a moment, in a musing posture, when he lifted his face, with his silent laugh, and pointing to where the wood-chopper stood, he said—

"Would Billy Kirby be standing there, d'ye think, if I had used the rifle?"

"Then you deny it," said Mr. Lippet, "you plead not guilty."

"Sartain," said Natty; "Billy knows that I never fired it

at all. Billy, do you remember the turkey last winter? ah! me! that was better than common firing; but I can't shoot as I used to could."

"Enter the plea of not guilty," said Judge Temple, strongly affected by the simplicity of the prisoner.

Hiram was again sworn, and his testimony given on the second charge. He had discovered his former error, and proceeded more cautiously than before.—He related very distinctly, and, for the man, with amazing terseness, the suspicion against the hunter, the complaint, the issuing of the warrant, and the swearing in of Kirby; all of which, he affirmed, were done in due form of law. He then added the manner in which the constable had been received; and stated distinctly that Natty had pointed the rifle at Kirby, and threatened his life, if he attempted to execute his duty. All this was confirmed by Jotham, who was observed to adhere closely to the story of the magistrate. Mr. Lippet conducted an artful cross examination of these two witnesses, but, after consuming much time, was compelled to relinquish the attempt to obtain any advantage in despair.

At length the District Attorney called the wood-chopper to the bar. Billy gave an extremely confused account of the affair, although he evidently aimed at the truth, until Mr. Van der School addressed him, by asking some direct questions:—

"It appears, from examining the papers; that you demanded admission into the hut legally; so you were put in bodily fear by his rifle and threats?"

"I didn't mind them that, man," said Billy, snapping his fingers; "I should be a poor stick, to mind such a one as old Leather-stocking."

"But I understood you to say, (referring to your previous words, (as delivered here in court,) in the commencement of your testimony,) that you thought he meant to shoot you?"

"To be sure, I did; and so would you too, Squire, if you had seen the chap dropping a muzzle that never misses, and cocking an eye that has a natural squint by long practice. I thought there would be a dust on't, and my back was up at once; but Leather-stocking gi'n up the skin, and so the matter ended."

"Ah! Billy," said Natty, shaking his head, " 'twas a lucky thought in me to throw out the hide, or there might have been blood spilt; and I'm sure, if it had been your'n, I should have mourn'd it sorely the little while I have to stay."

"Well, Leather-stocking," returned Billy, facing the prisoner, with a freedom and familiarity that utterly disregarded the presence of the court, "as you are on the subject, it may that you've no"—

"Go on with your examination, Mr. District Attorney."

That gentleman eyed the familiarity between his witness and the prisoner with manifest disgust, and indicated to the court that he was done.

"Then you didn't feel frightened, Mr. Kirby?" said the counsel for the prisoner.

"Me! no," said Billy, casting his eyes over his own huge frame with evident self-satisfaction; "I'm not to be skeared so easy."

"You look like a hardy man; where were you born, sir?"

"Varmount state; 'tis a mountaynious place, but there's a stiff soil, and it's pretty much wooded with beech and maple."

"I have always heerd so," said Mr. Lippet soothingly. "You have been used to the rifle yourself, in that country?"

"I pull the second best trigger in this county. I knock under to Natty Bumppo there, sin' he shot the pigeon."

Leather-stocking raised his head, and laughed again, when he thrust out a wrinkled hand, and said—

"You're young yet, Billy; and haven't seen the matches that I have; but here's my hand; I bear no malice to you, I don't."

Mr. Lippet allowed this conciliatory offering to be accepted, and judiciously paused, while the spirit of peace was exercising her influence over the two; but the Judge interposed his authority by saying—

"This is an improper place for such dialogues.—Proceed

with your examination of this witness, Mr. Lippet, or I shall order the next."

The attorney started, as if he were unconscious of any impropriety, and continued—

"So you settled the matter with Natty amicably on the spot, did you?"

"He gi'n me the skin, and I didn't want to quarrel with an old man; for my part, I see no such mighty matter in shooting a buck."

"And you parted friends? and you would never have thought of bringing the business up before a court, hadn't you been subpoenaed?"

"I don't think I should; he gi'n the skin, and I didn't feel a hard thought, though Squire Doolittle got some affronted."

"I have done, sir," said Mr. Lippet, probably relying on the charge of the Judge, as he again seated himself, with the air of a man who felt that his success was certain.

When Mr. Van der School arose to address the jury, he commenced by saying—

"Gentlemen of the jury, I should have interrupted the leading questions put by the prisoner's counsel, (by leading questions I mean telling him what to say,) did I not feel confident that the law of the land was superior to any advantages (I mean legal advantages) which he might obtain by his art. The counsel for the prisoner, gentlemen, has endeavoured to persuade you, in opposition to your good sense, to believe that pointing a rifle at a constable (elected or deputed) is a very innocent affair; and that society (I mean the commonwealth, gentlemen,) shall not be endangered thereby. But let me claim your attention, while we look over the particulars of this heinous offense." Here Mr. Van der School favoured the jury with an abridgment of the testimony, recounted in such a manner as utterly to confuse the faculties of his worthy listeners. After this exhibition he closed as follows—"and now, gentlemen, having thus made plain to your senses the crime of which this unfortunate man has been guilty (unfortunate both on account of his ignorance and his guilt,) I shall leave you to your own consciences; not in the least doubting that you will see the importance (notwithstanding the prisoner's counsel (doubtless relying on your former verdict) wishes to appear so confident of success) of punishing the offender, and assert the dignity of the laws."

It was now the duty of the Judge to deliver his charge. It consisted of a short, comprehensive summary of the testimony, laying bear the artifice of the prisoner's counsel, and placing the facts in so obvious a light that they could not well be misunderstood. "Living as we do, gentlemen," he concluded, "on the skirts of society, it becomes doubly necessary to protect the ministers of the law. If you believe the witnesses, in their construction of the acts of the prisoner, it is your duty to convict him; but if you believe that the old man, who this day appears before you, meant not to harm the constable, but was acting more under the influence of habit than by the instigations of malice, it will be your duty to judge him, but to do it with lenity."

As before, the jury did not leave their box, but, after a consultation of some little time, their foreman arose and pronounced the prisoner—

"Guilty."

There was but little surprise manifested in the court room at this verdict, as the testimony, the greater part of which we have omitted, was too clear and direct to be passed over. The judges seemed to have anticipated this sentiment, for a consultation was passing among them also, during the deliberation of the jury, and the preparatory movements of the "bench" announced the coming sentence.

"Nathaniel Bumppo," commenced the Judge, making the customary pause.

The old hunter, who had been musing again, with his head on the bar, raised himself and cried, with a prompt military tone—

"Here."

The Judge waved his hand for silence, and proceeded—

"In forming their sentence, the court have been governed as much by the consideration of your ignorance of the laws, as by a strict sense of the importance of punishing such outrages as this of which you have been found guilty. They have, therefore, passed over the obvious punishments of whipping on the bare back, in mercy to your years; but as the dignity of the law requires an open exhibition of the consequences of your crime, it is ordered, that you be conveyed from this room to the public stocks, where you are to be confined for one hour; that you pay a fine to the state of one hundred dollars; and that you be imprisoned in the jail of this county for one calendar month; and furthermore, that your imprisonment do not cease until the said fine shall be paid. I feel it my duty, Nathaniel Bumppo,"——

"And where should I get the money," interrupted the Leather-stocking, eagerly; "where should I get the money! you'll take away the bounty on the painters, because I cut the throat of a deer; and how is an old man to find so much gold or silver in the woods? No, no, Judge; think better of it, and don't talk of shutting me up in a jail for the little time I have to stay."

"If you have any thing to urge against the passing of the sentence, the court will yet hear you," said the Judge, mildly.

"I have enough to say ag'in it," cried Natty, grasping the bar, on which his fingers were working with a convulsed motion. "Where am I to get the money? Let me out into the woods and hills, where I've been used to breathe the clear air, and though I'm threescore and ten, if you've left game enough in the country, I'll travel night and day but I'll make you up the sum afore the season is over. Yes, yes— you see the reason of the thing, and the wickedness of shutting up an old man, that has spent his days, as one may say, where he could always look into the windows of heaven."

"I must be governed by the law"——

"Talk not to me of law, Marmaduke Temple," interrupted the hunter. "Did the beast of the forest mind your laws, when it was thirsty and hungry for the blood of your own child! She was kneeling to her God for a greater favour than I ask, and he heard her; and if you now say no to my prayers, do you think he will be deaf?"

"My private feelings must not enter into"——

"Hear me, Marmaduke Temple," interrupted the old man, with a melancholy tone of voice, "and hear reason. I've travelled these mountains when you was no judge, but an infant in your mother's arms; and I feel as if I had a right and privilege to travel them ag'in afore I die. Have you forgot the time you came on to the lake-shore, when there wasn't even a jail to lodge in; and didn't I give you my own bearskin to sleep on, and the fat of a noble buck to satisfy the cravings of your hunger? Yes, yes—you thought it no sin then to kill a deer! And this I did, though I had no reason to love you, for you had never done any thing but harm to them that loved and sheltered me. And now will you shut me up in your dungeons to pay me back fir my kindness? A hundred dollars! where should I get the money? No, no —there's them that says hard things of you, Marmaduke Temple, but you an't so bad as to wish to see an old man die in a prison, because he stood up for the right. Come, friend, let me pass; it's long sin' I've been used to such crowds, and I crave to be in the woods ag'in. Don't fear me, Judge—I bid you not to fear me; for if there's beaver enough left on the streams, or the buckskins will sell for a shilling a-piece, you shall have the last penny of the fine. Where are ye, pups! come away, dogs! come away! we have a grievous toil to do for our years, but it shall be done—yes, yes, I've promised it, and it shall be done!"

It is unnecessary to say that the movement of the Leather-stocking was again intercepted by the constable; but before he had time to speak, a bustling in the crowd, and a loud hem, drew all eyes to another part of the room.

Benjamin had succeeded in edging his way through the people, and was now seen balancing his short body, with one foot on a window and the other on the railing of the jury-box. To the amazement of the whole court, the steward was evidently preparing to speak. After a good deal of difficulty, he succeeded in drawing from his pocket a small bag, and then found utterance.

"If-so-be," he said, "that your honour is agreeable to trust the poor fellow out on another cruise among the beasts, here's a small matter that will help to bring down the risk, seeing that there's just thirty-five of your Spaniards in it; and I wish, from the bottom of my heart, that they were raal British guineas, for the sake of the old boy. But 'tis as it is; and if Squire Dickens will be just so good as to over-haul this small bit of an account, and take enough from the bag to settle the same, he's welcome to hold on to the rest, till such time as the Leather-stocking can grapple with them said beaver, or, for that matter, for ever, and no thanks asked."

As Benjamin concluded, he thrust out the wooden regis-ter of his arrears to the "Bold Dragoon" with one hand, while he offered his bag of dollars with the other. Astonish-ment at this singular interruption produced a profound still-ness in the room, which was only interrupted by the Sheriff, who struck his sword on the table, and cried—

"Silence!"

"There must be an end to this," said the Judge, strug-gling to overcome his feelings. "Constable, lead the prisoner to the stocks. Mr. Clerk, what stands next on the calendar?"

Natty seemed to yield to his destiny, for he sunk his head on his chest, and followed the officer from the court-room in silence. The crowd moved back for the passage of the pris-oner, and when his tall form was seen descending from the outer door, a rush of the people to the scene of his disgrace followed.

Ha! ha! look! he wears cruel garters!

LEAR

The punishments of the common law were still known at the time of our tale, to the people of New-York; and the whipping-post, with its companion, the stocks, were not yet supplanted by the more modern but doubtful expedients of the public prisons. Immediately in front of the jail, those relics of the elder times were situated, as a lesson of precautionary justice to the evil-doers of the settlement.

Natty followed the constables to this spot, bowing his head with submission to a power that he was unable to oppose, and surrounded by the crowd that formed a circle about his person, exhibiting in their countenances a strong curiosity. A constable raised the upper part of the stocks, and pointed with his finger to the holes where the old man was to place his feet. Without making the least objection to the punishment, the Leather-stocking quietly seated himself on the ground, and suffered his limbs to be laid in the openings, without even a murmur; though he cast one glance about him, as if in quest of that sympathy that human nature always seems to require under suffering. If he met no direct manifestations of pity, neither did he see any savage exultation expressed, nor hear a single reproachful epithet. The character of the mob, if it could be called by such a name, was that of attentive subordination.

The constable was in the act of lowering the upper plank, when Benjamin, who had pressed close to the side of the prisoner, said, in his hoarse tones, as if seeking for some cause to create a quarrel—

"Where away, master constable, is the use to be found of

clapping a man in them here bilboes? it neither stops his grog nor hurts his back; what for is it that you do the thing?"

" 'Tis the sentence of the court, Mr. Penguillum, and there's law for it, I s'pose."

"Ay, ay, I know that there's law for the thing; but where away do you find the use, I say? it does no harm, and it only keeps a man by the heels for the small matter of two glasses."

"Is it no harm, Benny Pump," said Natty, raising his eyes with a piteous look to the face of the steward—"is it no harm to show off a man in his seventy-first year, like a tame bear, for the settlers to look on! Is it no harm to put an old soldier, that has sarved through the war of 'fifty-six, and seen the inimy in the 'seventy-six business, into a place like this, where the boys can point at him and say, I have known the time when he was a spictacle for the country! is it no harm to bring down the pride of an honest man to be the equal of the beasts of the forest!"

Benjamin stared about him fiercely, and, could he have found a single face that expressed contumely, he would have been prompt to quarrel with its owner; but meeting every where with looks of sobriety, and occasionally of commiseration, he very deliberately seated himself by the side of the hunter, and placing his legs in the two vacant holes of the stocks, he said—

"Now lower away, master constable, lower away, I tell ye! If-so-be there's such a thing hereabouts as a man that wants to see a bear, let him look and be d—d, and he shall find two of them, and mayhap one of the same that can bite as well as growl."

"But I've no orders to put you in the stocks, Mr. Pump," cried the constable, "you must get up, and let me do my duty."

"You've my orders, and what do you need better, to meddle with my own feet? so lower away, will ye, and let me see the man that chooses to open his mouth with a grin on it."

"There can't be any harm in locking up a creater that will enter the pound," said the constable, laughing, and closing the stocks on them both.

It was fortunate that this act was executed with decision, for the whole of the spectators, when they saw Benjamin assume the position he took, felt an inclination for merriment, which few thought it worth their efforts to suppress. The steward struggled violently for his liberty again, with an evident intention of making battle on those who stood nearest to him; but the key was already turned, and all his efforts were made in vain.

"Hark ye, master constable," he cried, "just clear away your bilboes for the small matter of a log-glass, will ye, and let me show some of them there chaps who it is that they are so merry about."

"No, no, you would go in, and you can't come out," returned the officer, "until the time has expired that the Judge directed for the keeping of the prisoner."

Benjamin, finding that his threats and his struggles were useless, had good sense enough to learn patience from the resigned manner of his companion, and soon settled himself down by the side of Natty, with a contemptuousness expressed in his hard features, that showed that he had substituted disgust for rage. When the violence of the steward's feelings had in some measure subsided, he turned to his fellow-sufferer, and, with a motive that might have vindicated a worse effusion, he attempted the charitable office of consolation.

"Taking it by and large, Master Bump-ho, 'tis but a small matter, after all," he said. "Now I've known very good sort of men, aboard of the Boadishey, laid by the heels, for nothing, mayhap, but forgetting that they'd drunk their allowance already, when a glass of grog has come in their way. This is nothing more than riding with two anchors ahead, waiting for a turn in the tide, or a shift of wind, d'ye see, with a soft bottom and plenty of room for the sweep of your hawse. Now I've seen many a man, for over-shooting his reckoning, as I told ye, moored head and starn, where he couldn't so much as heave his broadside round, and mayhap a stopper clapt on his tongue too, in the shape of a pump-bolt lashed athwart-ship his jaws, all the same as an out-rigger along side of a taffrel-rail."

The hunter appeared to appreciate the kind intentions of the other, though he could not understand his eloquence; and raising his humbled countenance, he attempted a smile in vain, as he said—

"Anan!"

" 'Tis nothing, I say, but a small matter of a squall, that will soon blow over," continued Benjamin. "To you that has such a length of keel, it must be all the same as nothing; thof, seeing that I'm a little short in my lower timbers, they've triced my heels up aloft in such a way as to give me a bit of a slue. But what cares I, Master Bump-ho, if the ship strains a little at her anchor; it's only for a dog-watch, and dam'me but she'll sail with you then on that cruise after them said beaver. I'm not much used to small arms, seeing that I was stationed at the ammunition-boxes, being sum'mat too low-rigged to see over the hammock cloths; but I can carry the game, d'ye see, and mayhap make out to lend a hand with the traps; and if-so-be you're any way so handy with them as ye be with your boat-hook, 'twill be but a short cruise after all. I've squared the yards with Squire Dickens this morning, and I shall send him word that he needn't bear my name on the books again till such time as the cruise is over."

"You're used to dwell with me, Benny," said Leather-stocking, mournfully, "and the ways of the woods would be hard on you, if"——

"Not a bit—not a bit," cried the steward; "I'm none of your fair-weather chaps, Master Bump-ho, as sails only in smooth water. When I find a friend I sticks by him, d'ye see. Now there's no better man a-going than Squire Dickens, and I love him about the same as I loves Mistress Hollister's new keg of Jamaiky." The steward paused, and turning his uncouth visage on the hunter, he surveyed him with a roguish leer of his eye, and gradually suffered the muscles of his hard features to relax, until his face was illuminated by the display of white teeth, when he dropped his voice, and added—"I say, Mister Leather-stocking, 'tis fresher and livelier than any Hollands you'll get in Garnsey. But we'll send a hand over and ask the woman for a taste, for

I'm so jamb'd in these here bilboes, that I begin to want
sum'mat to lighten my upper works."

Natty sighed, and gazed about him on the crowd, that
already began to disperse, and which had now diminished
greatly, as its members scattered in their various pursuits.
He looked wistfully at Benjamin, but did not reply; a
deeply seated anxiety seeming to absorb every other sensation, and to throw a melancholy gloom over his wrinkled features, which were working with the movements of his mind.

The steward was about to act on the old principle that
silence gives consent, when Hiram Doolittle, attended by
Jotham, stalked out of the crowd, across the open space,
and approached the stocks. The magistrate passed by the
end where Benjamin was seated, and posted himself, at a
safe distance from the steward, in front of the Leather-
stocking. Hiram stood for a moment, cowering before the
keen looks that Natty fastened on him, and suffering under
an embarrassment that was quite new; when, having in
some degree recovered himself, he looked at the heavens,
and then at the smoky atmosphere, as if it were only an ordinary meeting with a friend, and said, in his formal, hesitating way—

"Quite a scurcity of rain lately; I some think we shall
have a long drought on't."

Benjamin was occupied in untying his bag of dollars and
did not observe the approach of the magistrate, while Natty
turned his face, in which every muscle was working, away
from him in disgust, without answering. Rather encouraged
than daunted by this exhibition of dislike, Hiram, after a
short pause, continued—

"The clouds look as if they'd no water in them, and the
earth is dreadfully parched. To my judgment, there'll be
short crops this season, if the rain doos'nt fall quite
speedily."

The air with which Mr. Doolittle delivered this propheti-
cal opinion was peculiar to his species. It was a jesuitical,
cold, unfeeling, and selfish manner, that seemed to say, "I
have kept within the law," to the man he had so cruelly injured. It quite overcame the restraint that the old hunter

had been labouring to impose on himself, and he burst out in a warm glow of indignation.

"Why should the rain fall from the clouds," he cried, "when you force the tears from the eyes of the old, the sick, and the poor! Away with ye—away with ye! you may be formed in the image of the Maker, but Satan dwells in your heart. Away with ye, I say! I am mournful and the sight of ye brings bitter thoughts."

Benjamin ceased thumbing his money, and raised his head, at the instant that Hiram, who was thrown off his guard by the invectives of the hunter, unluckily trusted his person within reach of the steward, who grasped one of his legs, with a hand that had the grip of a vice, and whirled the magistrate from his feet, before he had either time to collect his senses, or exercise the strength he really did possess. Benjamin wanted neither proportions nor manhood in his head, shoulders, and arms, though all the rest of his frame appeared to be originally intended for a very different sort of man. He exerted his physical powers, on the present occasion, with much discretion, and as their positions were a great disadvantage to his antagonist, without at all discomposing the steward, the struggle resulted, very soon in Benjamin getting the magistrate fixed in a posture somewhat similar to his own and manfully placed face to face.

"You're a ship's cousin, I tell ye, Master Doo-but-little," roared the steward,—"some such matter as a ship's cousin, sir. I know you, I do, with your fair-weather speeches to Squire Dickens, to his face, and then you go and sarve out your grumbling to all the old women in the town, do ye. An't it enough for any Christian, let him harbour never so much malice, to get an honest old fellow laid by the heels in this fashion, without carrying sail so hard on the poor dog, as if you would run him down as he lay at his anchors? but I've logged many a hard thing against your name, master, and now the time's come to foot up the day's work, d'ye see; so square yourself, you lubber, square yourself, and we'll soon know who's the better man."

"Jotham!" cried the frightened magistrate—"Jotham!

call in the constables. Mr. Penguillum, I command the peace—I order you to keep the peace."

"There's been more peace than love atwixt us, master," cried the steward, making some equivocal demonstrations towards hostility; "so mind yourself! square yourself, I say! do you smell this here bit of sledge-hammer?"

"Lay hands on me if you dare!" exclaimed Hiram, as well as he could under the grasp which the steward held on his throttle—"lay hands on me if you dare!"

"If you call this laying, master, you are welcome to the eggs," roared the steward.

It becomes our disagreeable duty to record here, that the acts of Benjamin now became perfectly unequivocal; for he darted his sledge-hammer violently on the anvil of Mr. Doolittle's countenance, and the place became, in an instant, a scene of tumult and confusion. The crowd rushed in a dense circle around the spot, while some ran to the court-room to give the alarm, and one or two of the more juvenile part of the multitude had a desperate trial of speed, to see who should be the happy man to communicate the critical situation of the magistrate to his wife.

Benjamin worked with great industry and a good deal of skill, at his occupation, using one hand to raise up his antagonist, while he knocked him over with the other; for he would have been disgraced in his own estimation, had he struck a blow on a fallen adversary. By this considerate arrangement, he found means, however, to hammer the visage of Hiram out of all shape, by the time Richard succeeded in forcing his way through the throng to the point of combat. The Sheriff afterward declared, independent of his mortifications, as a preserver of the peace of the county, at this interruption to its harmony, he was never so grieved in his life, as when he saw this breach of unity between his favourites. Hiram had in some degree become necessary to his vanity, and Benjamin, strange as it may appear, he really loved. This attachment was exhibited in the first words that he uttered.

"Squire Doolittle! Squire Doolittle! I am shamed to see a man of your character and office forget himself so much as to disturb the peace, insult the court, and beat poor Benjamin, in this manner!"

At the sound of Mr. Jones' voice, the steward ceased his employment, and Hiram had an opportunity of raising his discomfited visage towards the mediator. Emboldened by the sight of the Sheriff, Mr. Doolittle again had recourse to his lungs.

"I'll have the law on you for this," he cried desperately; "I'll have the law on you for this. I call on you, Mr. Sheriff, to seize this man, and I demand that you take his body into custody."

By this time Richard was master of the true state of the case, and, turning to the steward, he cried—

"Benjamin, how came you in the stocks? I always thought you were as mild and docile as a lamb. It was for your docility that I most esteemed you. Benjamin! Benjamin! you have not only disgraced yourself, but your friends, by this shameless conduct. Bless me! bless me! Mr. Doolittle, he seems to have knocked your face all on one side."

Hiram by this time had got on his feet again, and without the reach of the steward, when he broke forth in violent appeals for vengeance. The offense was too apparent to be passed over, and the Sheriff, mindful of the impartiality exhibited by his cousin in the recent trial of the Leatherstocking, came to the painful conclusion that it was necessary to commit his major-domo to prison. As the time of Natty's punishment was expired, and Benjamin found that they were to be confined, for that night at least, in the same apartment, he made no very strong objections to the measure, nor spoke of bail, though as the Sheriff preceded the party of constables that conducted them to the jail, he uttered the following remonstrance:—

"As to being birthed with Master Bump-ho for a night or so, it's but little I think of it, Squire Dickens, seeing that I calls him an honest man, and one as has a handy way with boat-hooks and rifles; but as for owning that a man desarves any thing worse than a double allowance, for knocking that carpenter's face a-one-side, as you call it, I'll maintain it's ag'in reason and Christianity. If there's a

blood-sucker in this 'ere country, it's that very chap. Ay! I
know him and if he hasn't got all the same as dead-wood in
his head-works, he knows sum'mat of me. Where's the
mighty harm, Squire, that you take it so much to heart? it's
all the same as any other battle, d'ye see, sir, being fair
broadside to broadside, only that it was fout at anchor,
which was what we did in Port Praya roads, when suff'ring
came in among us; and a suff'ring time he had of it, before
he got out again."

Richard thought it unworthy of him to make any reply
to this speech; but when his prisoners were safely lodged
in an outer dungeon, ordering the bolts to be drawn and the
key turned, he withdrew.

Benjamin held frequent and friendly dialogues with different people, through the iron gratings, during the afternoon; but his companion paced their narrow limits, in his
moccasins, with quick, impatient treads, his face hanging on
his breast in dejection, or when lifted, at moments, to the
idlers at the window, lighted, perhaps, for an instant, with
the childish aspect of aged forgetfulness, which would vanish directly in an expression of deep and obvious anxiety.

At the close of the day Edwards was seen at the window,
in close and earnest dialogue with his friend; and after he
departed it was thought that he had communicated words of
comfort to the hunter, who threw himself on his pallet, and
was soon in a deep sleep. The curious spectators had exhausted the conversation of the steward, who had drunk
good fellowship with half of his acquaintances, and as Natty
was no longer in motion, by eight o'clock, Billy Kirby, who
was the last lounger at the window, retired into the "Templetown Coffee-House," when Natty rose and hung a blanket
before the opening, and the prisoners apparently retired
for the night.

Chapter XXXV

And to avoid the foe's pursuit,
With spurring put their cattle to't;
And till all four were out of wind,
And danger too, ne'er look'd behind.

HUDIBRAS

As the shades of evening approached, the jurors, witnesses, and other attendants of the court, began to disperse, and before nine o'clock the village was quiet, and its streets nearly deserted. At that hour, Judge Temple and his daughter, followed at a short distance by Louisa Grant, walked slowly down the avenue, under the slight shadows of the young poplars, holding the following discourse:—

"You can best soothe his wounded spirit, my child," said Marmaduke; "but it will be dangerous to touch on the nature of his offence; the sanctity of the laws must be respected."

"Surely, sir," cried the impatient Elizabeth, "those laws that condemn a man like the Leather-stocking to so severe a punishment, for an offence that even I must think very venial, cannot be perfect in themselves."

"Thou talkest of what thou dost not understand, Elizabeth," returned her father. "Society cannot exist without wholesome restraints. Those restraints cannot be inflicted, without security and respect to the persons of those who administer them; and it would sound ill indeed, to report that a judge had extended favour to a convicted criminal, because he had saved the life of his child."

"I see—I see the difficulty of your situation, dear sir," cried the daughter; "but in appreciating the offence of poor Natty, I cannot separate the minister of the law from the man."

"There thou talkest as a woman, child; it is not for an assault on Hiram Doolittle, but for threatening the life of a constable, who was in the performance of"—

"It is immaterial whether it be one or the other," interrupted Miss Temple, with a logic that contained more feeling than reason; "I know Natty to be innocent, and thinking so, I must think all wrong who oppress him."

"His judge among the number! thy father, Elizabeth?"

"Nay, nay—nay, do not put such questions to me; give me my commission, father, and let me proceed to execute it."

The Judge paused a moment, smiling fondly on his child, and then dropped his hand affectionately on her shoulder, as he answered—

"Thou hast reason, Bess, and much of it too, but thy heart lies too near thy head. But listen: in this pocket-book are two hundred dollars. Go to the prison—there are none in this place to harm thee—give this note to the jailer, and when thou seest Bumppo, say what thou wilt to the poor old man; give scope to the feelings of thy warm heart; but try to remember, Elizabeth, that the laws alone remove us from the conditions of the savages; that he has been criminal, and that his judge was thy father."

Miss Temple made no reply, but she pressed the hand that held the pocket-book to her bosom, and taking her friend by the arm, they issued together from the enclosure into the principal street of the village.

As they pursued their walk in silence, under the row of houses, where the deeper blue of the evening effectually concealed their persons, no sound reached them, excepting the slow tread of a yoke of oxen, with the rattling of a cart, that were moving along the street in the same direction with themselves. The figure of the teamster was just discernible by the dim light, lounging by their side, with a listless air, as if equally fatigued with his beasts, by the toil of the day. At the corner, where the jail stood, the progress of the ladies was impeded for a moment, by the oxen, who were turned up to the side of the building, and given a lock of hay, which they had carried on their necks, as a reward for their patient labour. The whole of this was so natural, and so common, that Elizabeth saw nothing to induce a second glance at the team until she heard the teamster speaking to his cattle in a low voice—

"Mind yourself, Brindle; will you, sir! will you!"

The language itself was unusual to oxen, with which all who dwell in a new country are familiar; but there was something in the voice also, that startled Miss Temple. On turning the corner, she necessarily approached near to the man, and her searching look was enabled to detect the person of Oliver Edwards, concealed under the coarse garb of a teamster. Their eyes met at the same instant, and, notwithstanding the gloom, and the enveloping cloak of Elizabeth, the recognition was mutual.

"Miss Temple!" "Mr. Edwards!" were exclaimed simultaneously, though a feeling that seemed common to them both rendered their tones nearly inaudible.

"Is it possible," exclaimed Edwards, after the moment of doubt had passed; "do I see you so nigh the jail! but you are going to the Rectory, I beg pardon, Miss Grant, I believe; I did not recognize you at first."

The sigh which Louisa uttered, was so faint that it was only heard by Elizabeth, who replied quickly—

"We are going not only to the jail, Mr. Edwards, but into it. We wish to show the Leather-stocking that we do not forget his services, and that, at the same time we must be just, we are also grateful. I suppose you are on a similar errand; but let me beg that you will give us leave to precede you ten minutes. Good night, sir; I—I—am quite sorry, Mr. Edwards, to see you reduced to such labour; I am sure my father would"——

"I shall wait your pleasure, madam," interrupted the youth, coldly. "May I beg that you will not mention my being here?"

"Certainly, sir," said Elizabeth, returning his bow by a slight inclination of her head, and urging the tardy Louisa forward. As they entered the jailer's house, however, Miss Grant found leisure to whisper—

"Would it not be well to offer part of your money to Oliver? half of it will pay the fine of Bumppo; and he is so unused to hardships! I am sure my father will subscribe much of his little pittance, to place him in a station that is more worthy of him."

The involuntary smile that passed over the features of Elizabeth was transient as a gleam of flitting light, and was blended with an expression of deep and heartfelt pity. She did not reply, however, and the appearance of the jailer soon recalled the thoughts of both to the immediate object of their visit.

The rescue of the ladies, and their consequent interest in his prisoner, together with the informal manners that prevailed in the country, all united to prevent any surprise on the part of the jailer, at their request for admission to Bumppo. The note of Judge Temple, however, would have silenced all objections, if he had felt them, and he led the way without hesitation to the apartment that held the prisoners. The instant the key was put into the lock, the hoarse voice of Benjamin was heard, demanding—

"Yo! hoy! who comes there?"

"Some visitors that you'll be glad to see," returned the jailer. "What have you done to the lock, that it won't turn?"

"Handsomely, handsomely, master," cried the steward; "I've just drove a nail into a birth alongside of this here bolt, as a stopper, d'ye see, so that master Doo-but-little can't be running in and breezing up another fight atwixt us, for, to my account, there'll be but a banyan with me soon, seeing that they'll mulct me of my Spaniards, all the same as if I'd overflogged the lubber. Throw your ship into the wind, and lay by for a small matter, will ye? and I'll soon clear a passage."

The sounds of hammering gave an assurance that the steward was in earnest, and in a short time the lock yielded, when the door was opened.

Benjamin had evidently been anticipating the seizure of his money, for he had made frequent demands on the favourite cask at the "Bold Dragoon," during the afternoon and evening, and was now in that state which by marine imagery is called "half-seas-over." It was no easy thing to destroy the balance of the old tar by the effects of liquor, for, as he expressed it himself, "he was too low-rigged not to carry sail in all weathers;" but he was precisely in that condition which is so expressively termed "muddy." When he perceived who the visiters were, he retreated to the side of the room where his pallet lay, and regardless of the presence of his young mistress, seated himself on it with an air of great sobriety, placing his back firmly against the wall.

"If you undertake to spoil my locks in this manner, Mr. Pump," said the jailer, "I shall put a stopper, as you call it, on your legs, and tie you down to your bed."

"What for should ye, Master?" grumbled Benjamin; "I've rode out one squall today, anchored by the heels, and I wants no more of them. Where's the harm of doing all the same as yourself? Leave that there door free outboard, and you'll find no locking inboard, I'll promise ye."

"I must shut up for the night at nine," said the jailer, "and it's now forty-two minutes past eight." He placed the little candle he carried on a rough pine table, and withdrew.

"Leather-stocking!" said Elizabeth, when the key of the door was turned on them again, "my good friend Leatherstocking! I have come on a message of gratitude to you. Had you submitted to the search, worthy old man, the death of the deer would have been a trifle, and all would have been well"—

"Submit to the sarch!" interrupted Natty, raising his face from resting on his knees, without rising from the corner where he had seated himself; "d'ye think, gal, I would let such a varmint into my hut? No, no—I wouldn't have opened the door to your own sweet countenance then. But they are wilcome to sarch among the coals and ashes now they'll find only some such heap as is to be seen at every pot-ashery in the mountains."

The old man dropped his face again on one hand, and seemed to be lost in a melancholy musing.

"The hut can be rebuilt, and made better than before," returned Miss Temple; "and it shall be my office to see done, when your imprisonment is ended."

"Can ye raise the dead, child!" said Natty, in a sorrow

ful voice; "can ye go into the place where you've laid your fathers, and mothers, and children, and gather together their ashes, and make the same men, and women of them as afore! You do not know what 'tis to lay your head for more than forty years under the cover of the same logs, and to look on the same things for the better part of a man's life. You are young yet, child, but you are one of the most precious of God's creaters. I had a hope for ye that it might come to pass, but it's all over now; this put to that, will drive the thing quite out of his mind for ever."

Miss Temple must have understood the meaning of the old man better than the other listeners; for, while Louisa stood innocently by her side commiserating the griefs of the hunter, the heiress bent her head aside, so as to conceal her features, from the dim light, by her dark tresses. The action and the feeling that caused it lasted but a moment, when she faced the party, and continued—

"Other logs, and better, though, can be had, and shall be found for you, my old defender. Your confinement will soon be over, and before that time arrives I shall have a house prepared for you, where you may spend the close of your harmless life in ease and plenty."

"Ease and plenty! house!" repeated Natty, slowly. "You mean well, gal, you mean well, and I quite mourn that it cannot be; but he has seen me a sight and a laughing-stock for"——

"Damn your stocks," said Benjamin, flourishing his bottle with one hand, from which he had been taking hasty and repeated draughts, while he made gestures of disdain with the other; "who cares for his bilboes? there's a leg that's been stuck up an end like a gib-boom for an hour, d'ye see, and what's it the worse for't, ha! canst tell me, what's it the worser, ha?"

"I believe you forget, Mr. Pump, in whose presence you sit with so much composure," said Elizabeth.

"Forget you, Miss 'Lizzy," returned the steward; "if I do dam'me; you're not to be forgot, like Goody Pretty-bones, up at the big house there. I say, old sharp-shooter, she may have pretty bones, but I can't say so much for her flesh, d'ye see, for she looks sum'mat like an otomy with another man's jacket on. Now, for the skin of her face, it's all the same as a new top-sail with a taught bolt-rope, being snug at the leaches, but all in a bight about the inner cloth."

"Peace—I command you to be silent, sir," said Elizabeth.

"Ay, ay, ma'am," returned the steward. "You didn't say I shouldn't drink, though."

"We will not speak of what is to become of others," said Miss Temple, turning again to the hunter—"but of your own fortunes, Natty. It shall be my care to see that you pass the rest of your days in ease and plenty."

"Ease and plenty!" again repeated the Leather-stocking; "what ease can there be to an old man, who must walk a mile across the open fields, before he can find a shade to hide him from the scorching sun! or what plenty is there where you may hunt a day and not start a buck, or see any thing bigger than a mink, or maybe a stray fox! Ah! I shall have a hard time after them very beavers, for this fine. I must go low towards the Pennsylvany line in sarch of the creaters, maybe a hundred mile, for they are not to be got here-away. No, no—your betterments and clearings have druv the knowing things out of the country; and instead of beaver-dams, which is the nater of the animal, and according to Providence, you turn back the waters over the low grounds with your mill-dams, as if 'twas in man to stay the drops from going where He wills them to go. Benny, unless you stop your hand from going so often to your mouth, you won't be ready to start when the time comes."

"Hark'ee, Master Bump-ho," said the steward; "don't you fear for Ben. When the watch is called, set me on my legs, and give me the bearings and distance of where you want to steer, and I'll carry sail with the best of you, I will."

"The time has come now," said the hunter, listening; "I hear the horns of the oxen rubbing ag'in the side of the jail."

"Well, say the word, and then heave ahead, shipmate," said Benjamin.

"You won't betray us, gal?" said Natty, looking up simply into the face of Elizabeth—"you won't betray an old man, who craves to breathe the clear air of heaven? I mean no harm, and if the law says that I must pay the hundred dollars, I'll take the season through, but it shall be forthcoming; and this good man will help me."

"You catch them," said Benjamin, with a sweeping gesture of his arm, "and if they get away again, call me a slink, that's all."

"But what mean you!" cried the wondering Elizabeth. "Here you must stay for thirty days; but I have the money for your fine in this purse. Take it; pay it in the morning, and summon patience for your month. I will come often to see you, with my friend; we will make up your clothes with our own hands; indeed, indeed, you shall be comfortable."

"Would ye, children?" said Natty, advancing across the floor with an air of kindness, and taking the hand of Elizabeth; "would ye be so kearful of an old man, and just for shooting the beast which cost him nothing? Such things doesn't run in the blood, I believe, for you seem not to forget a favour. Your little fingers couldn't do much on a buckskin, nor be you used to such a thread as sinews. But if he hasn't got past hearing, he shall hear it and know it, that he may see, like me, there is some who know how to remember a kindness."

"Tell him nothing," cried Elizabeth, earnestly; "if you love me, if you regard my feelings, tell him nothing. It is of yourself only I would talk, and for yourself only I act. I grieve, Leather-stocking, that the law requires that you should be detained here so long; but, after all, it will be only a short month, and"——

"A month!" exclaimed Natty, opening his mouth with his usual laugh; "not a day, nor a night, nor an hour, gal. Judge Temple may sintence, but he can't keep, without a better dungeon than this. I was taken once by the French, and they put sixty-two of us in a block-house, nigh hand to old Frontinac; but 'twas easy to cut through a pine log to them that was used to timber." The hunter paused, and looked cautiously around the room, when, laughing again, he shoved the steward gently from his post, and removing the bed-clothes, discovered a hole recently cut in the logs with a mallet and chisel. "It's only a kick, and the outside piece is off, and then"—

"Off! ay, off!" cried Benjamin, rousing from his stupor; "well, here's off. Ay! ay! you catch 'em, and I'll hold on to them said beaver-hats."

"I fear this lad will trouble me much," said Natty; " 'twill be a hard pull for the mountain, should they take the scent soon, and he is not in a state of mind to run."

"Run!" echoed the steward; "no, sheer alongside, and let's have a fight of it."

"Peace!" ordered Elizabeth.

"Ay, ay, ma'am."

"You will not leave us surely, Leather-stocking," continued Miss Temple; "I beseech you, reflect that you will be driven to the woods entirely, and that you are fast getting old. Be patient for a little time, when you can go abroad openly, and with honour."

"Is there beaver to be catched here, gal?"

"If not, here is money to discharge the fine, and in a month you are free. See, here it is in gold."

"Gold!" said Natty, with a kind of childish curiosity; "it's long sin' I've seen a gold piece. We used to get the broad joes, in the old war, as plenty as the bears be now. I remember there was a man in Dieskau's army, that was killed, who had a dozen of the shining things sewed up in his shirt. I didn't handle them myself, but I seen them cut out, with my own eyes; they was bigger and brighter than them be."

"These are English guineas, and are yours," said Elizabeth; "an earnest of what shall be done for you."

"Me! why should you give me this treasure?" said Natty, looking earnestly at the maiden.

"Why! have you not saved my life? did you not rescue me from the jaws of the beast?" exclaimed Elizabeth, veiling her eyes, as if to hide some hideous object from her view.

The hunter took the money, and continued turning it in his hand for some time, piece by piece, talking aloud during the operation.

"There's a rifle, they say, out on the Cherry Valley, that will carry a hundred rods and kill. I've seen good guns in my day, but none quite equal to that. A hundred rods with any sartainty is great shooting! Well, well—I'm old, and the gun I have will answer my time. Here, child, take back your gold. But the hour has come; I hear him talking to the cattle, and I must be going. You won't tell of us, gal—you won't tell of us, will ye?"

"Tell of you!" echoed Elizabeth,—"but take the money, old man; take the money, even if you go into the mountains."

"No, no," said Natty, shaking his head kindly; "I wouldn't rob you so for twenty rifles. But there's one thing you can do for me, if ye will, that no other is at hand to do."

"Name it—name it."

"Why, it's only to buy a canister of powder;—'twill cost two silver dollars. Benny Pump has the money ready, but we daren't come into the town to get it. Nobody has it but the Frenchman. 'Tis of the best and just suits a rifle. Will you get it for me, gal?—say, will you get it for me?"

"Will I! I will bring it to you, Leather-stocking, though I toil a day in quest of you through the woods. But where shall I find you, and how?"

"Where!" said Natty, musing a moment—"to-morrow, on the Vision; on the very top of the Vision I'll meet you, child, just as the sun gets over our heads. See that it's the fine grain; you'll know it by the gloss, and the price."

"I will do it," said Elizabeth, firmly.

Natty now seated himself, and placing his feet in the hole, with a slight effort he opened a passage through into the street. The ladies heard the rustling of hay, and well understood the reason why Edwards was in the capacity of a teamster.

"Come, Benny," said the hunter; " 'twill be no darker to-night, for the moon will rise in an hour."

"Stay!" exclaimed Elizabeth; "it should not be said that you escaped in the presence of the daughter of Judge Temple. Return, Leather-stocking, and let us retire, before you execute your plan."

Natty was about to reply, when the approaching foot-steps of the jailer announced the necessity of his immediate return. He had barely time to regain his feet, and to conceal the hole with the bed-clothes, across which Benjamin very opportunely fell, before the key was turned, and the door of the apartment opened.

"Isn't Miss Temple ready to go?" said the civil jailer— "it's the usuooal hour for locking up."

"I follow you, sir," returned Elizabeth, "Good night, Leather-stocking."

"It's a fine grain, gal, and I think 'twill carry lead further than common. I am getting old, and can't follow up the game with the step that I used to could."

Miss Temple waved her hand for silence, and proceeded Louisa and the keeper from the apartment. The man turned the key once, and observed that he would return and secure his prisoners, when he had lighted the ladies to the street. Accordingly, they parted at the door of the building, when the jailer retired to his dungeons, and the ladies walked, with throbbing hearts, towards the corner.

"Now the Leather-stocking refuses the money," whispered Louisa, "it can all be given to Mr. Edwards, and that added to"——

"Listen!" said Elizabeth; "I hear the rustling of the hay; they are escaping at this moment. Oh! they will be de-tected instantly!"

By this time they were at the corner, where Edwards and Natty were in the act of drawing the almost helpless body of Benjamin through the aperture. The oxen had started back from their hay, and were standing with their heads down the street, leaving room for the party to act in.

"Throw the hay into the cart," said Edwards, "or they will suspect how it has been done. Quick, that they may not see it."

Natty had just returned from executing this order, when the light of the keeper's candle shone through the hole, and instantly his voice was heard in the jail, exclaiming for his prisoners.

"What is to be done, now?" said Edwards—"this drunken fellow will cause our detection, and we have not a moment to spare."

"Who's drunk, ye lubber!" muttered the steward.

"A break-jail! a break-jail!" shouted five or six voices from within.

"We must leave him," said Edwards.

" 'Twouldn't be kind, lad," returned Natty; "he took half the disgrace of the stocks on himself to-day, and the creater has feeling."

At this moment two or three men were heard issuing from the door of the "Bold Dragoon," and among them the voice of Billy Kirby.

"There's no moon yet," cried the wood-chopper; "but it's a clear, moonshiny night. Come, whose for home? Hark! what a rumpus they're kicking up in the jail—here's go and see what it's about."

"We shall be lost," said Edwards, "if we don't drop this man."

At that instant Elizabeth moved close to him, and said rapidly, in a low voice—

"Lay him in the cart, and start the oxen; no one will look there."

"By heaven, there's a woman's quickness in the thought," said the youth.

The proposition was no sooner made than executed. The steward was seated on the hay, and bid to hold his peace, and apply the goad that was placed in his hand while the oxen were urged on. So soon as this arrangement was completed, Edwards and the hunter stole along the houses for a short distance, when they disappeared through an opening that led into the rear of the buildings. The oxen were in brisk motion, and presently the cries of pursuit were heard in the street. The ladies quickened their pace, with a wish to escape the crowd of constables and idlers that were approaching, some execrating, and some laughing at the exploit of the prisoners. In the confusion, the voice of Kirby was plainly distinguishable above all the others, shouting and swearing that he would have the fugitives, threatening to bring back Natty in one pocket and Benjamin in the other.

"Spread yourselves, men," he cried, as he passed the ladies, with his heavy feet sounding along the street like the tread of a dozen; "spread yourselves; to the mountains; they'll be in the mountain in a quarter of an hour, and then look out for a long rifle."

His cries were echoed from twenty mouths, for not only the jail but the taverns had sent forth their numbers, some earnest in the pursuit, and others joining it as in sport.

As Elizabeth turned in at her father's gate, she saw the wood-chopper stop at the cart, when she gave Benjamin up for lost. While they were hurrying up the walk, two figures, stealing cautiously but quickly under the shades of the trees, met the eyes of the ladies, and in a moment Edwards and the hunter crossed their path.

"Miss Temple, I may never see you again," exclaimed the youth; "let me thank you for all your kindness; you do not, cannot know my motives."

"Fly! fly!" cried Elizabeth—"the village is alarmed. Do not be found conversing with me at such a moment, and in these grounds."

"Nay, I must speak, though detection were certain."

"Your retreat to the bridge is already cut off; before you can gain the wood your pursuers will be there.—If"——

"If what?" cried the youth. "Your advice has saved me once already; I will follow it to death."

"The street is now silent and vacant," said Elizabeth, after a pause; "cross it, and you will find my father's boat in the lake. It would be easy for you to land from it where you pleased in the hills."

"But Judge Temple might complain of the trespass."

"His daughter shall be accountable, sir."

The youth uttered something in a low voice, that was heard only by Elizabeth, and turned to execute what she had suggested. As they were separating, Natty approached the heiress, and said—

"You'll remember the canister of powder, children. Them beavers must be had, and I and the pups be getting old; we want the best of ammunition."

"Come, Natty," said Edwards, impatiently.

"Coming, lad, coming. God bless you, young ones, both of ye, for ye mean well and kindly to the old man."

The ladies paused until they lost sight of the retreating figures, when they immediately entered the Mansion-house.

While this scene was passing in the walk, Kirby had overtaken the cart, which was his own, and had been driven by Edwards without asking the owner, from the place where the patient oxen usually stood at evening, waiting the pleasure of their master.

"Woa—come hither, Golden," he cried; "why how come you off the end of the bridge, where I left you, dummies?"

"Heave ahead," muttered Benjamin, giving a random blow with his lash, that alighted on the shoulder of the other.

"Who the devil be you?" cried Billy, turning round in surprise, but unable to distinguish, in the dark, the hard visage that was just peering over the cart rails.

"Who be I! why I'm helmsman aboard of this here craft, d'ye see, and a straight wake I'm making of it. Ay! ay! I've got the bridge right ahead, and the bilboes dead-aft; I calls that good steerage, boy. Heave ahead."

"Lay your lash in the right spot, Mr. Benny Pump," said the wood-chopper, "or I'll put you in the palm of my hand, and box your ears. Where be you going with my team?"

"Team!"

"Ay, my cart and oxen."

"Why, you must know, Master Kirby, that the Leather-stocking and I—that's Benny Pump—you knows Ben?— well, Benny and I—no, me and Benny; dam'me if I know how 'tis; but some of us are bound after a cargo of beaver-skins, d'ye see, and so we've pressed the cart to ship them 'ome in. I say, Master Kirby, what a lubberly oar you pull! —you handle an oar, boy, pretty much as a cow would a musket, or a lady would a marling-spike."

Billy had discovered the state of the steward's mind, and he walked for some time alongside of the cart, musing with himself, when he took the goad from Benjamin, (who fell back on the hay, and was soon asleep,) and drove his cattle down the street, over the bridge, and up the mountain, towards a clearing in which he was to work the next day, without any other interruption than a few hasty questions from parties of the constables.

Elizabeth stood for an hour at the window of her room, and saw the torches of the pursuers gliding along the side of the mountain, and heard their shouts and alarms; but, at the end of that time, the last party returned, wear'ed and disappointed, and the village became again still as when she issued from the gate, on her mission to the jail.

Chapter XXXVI

"And I could weep'—th' Oneida chief
His descant wildly thus began—
'But that I may not stain with grief
The death-song of my father's son."
GERTRUDE OF WYOMING

It was yet early on the following morning; when Elizabeth and Louisa met by appointment, and proceeded to the store of Monsieur Le Quoi, in order to redeem the pledge that the former had given to the Leather-stocking. The people were again assembling for the business of the day, but the hour was too soon for a crowd, and the ladies found the place in possession only of its polite owner, Billy Kirby, one female customer, and the boy who did the duty of helper or clerk.

Monsieur Le Quoi was perusing a packet of letters, with manifest delight, while the wood-chopper, with one hand thrust into his bosom, and the other in the folds of his jacket, holding an axe under his right arm, stood sympathizing in the Frenchman's pleasure with a good-natured interest. The freedom of manners that prevailed in the new settlements, commonly leveled all difference in rank, and with it, frequently, all considerations of education and intelligence. At the time the ladies entered the store they were unseen by the owner, who was saying to Kirby—

"Ah! ha! Monsieur Beel, dis lettair mak-a-me de most happi of mans. Ah! ma chère France! I vill see you aga'n."

"I rejoice, Monsieur, at any thing that contributes to your happiness," cried Elizabeth, "but must hope we are not going to lose you entirely."

"Ah! Ma'mselle Templ'! vat honneur I feel to me; mais I 'ave lettair, dat mak-a mon coeur sautez de joie. Ah! Ma'mselle Templ', if you 'ave père, 'ave mère, 'ave leetl'—Jean-tone, vy you dont' and de ladi a pins, eh!—if you 'ave amis beeg and leetl' you voud be glad to go back. Attendez vous, Ma'mselle, si vous plais; je vous lirai. A Monsieur Monsieur Le Quoi, de Mersereau à Templetone, Noo Yorck, les Etats Unis d'Amerique. Très cher ami, je suis ravis"——

"I apprehend that my French is not equal to your letter, Monsieur," said Elizabeth, glancing her eye expressively at her companion; "will you favour us with its substance in English?"

"Oh! pardonnez moi—I 'ave been so long from Paris dat I do forget de—a—a—a pronounsasshong. You vill 'ave consideration pour moi, and vill excusez my read in France," returned the polite Gaul, bowing with deep humility, as if lamenting his ignorance of his own language; "mais I shall tell you en bon Anglois. I 'ave offeece à Paris, in Bureau, dans le temps du bon Louis; I fly; run avay to sav-a-my 'ead. I 'ave in Martinique von leetl' plantation pour sucre—ah! ha!—vat you call in dis countray—ah! ha! —Monsieur Beel, vat you call de place vere you vork-a? eh?"

"Clearing," said the wood-chopper, with a kind nod.

"No, no clear—vere you burn-a my troat, eh!"

Billy hitched up his shoulder, and turned his eyes askance at the ladies, with a broad grin on his face, as he answered—

"I guess 'tis a sugar-bush that the Mounsheer means;—but you musn't take that to heart, man; 'tis the law of the woods."

"Ah! coquin, I pardonne you," returned the Frenchman, placing his hand involuntarily on his throat—"diable! de law should be altair. Mais, I 'ave sucre-boosh in Martinique: I fly dere too;—I come ici;—votre père help-a me;—I grow reech—yais? I grow reech; mais I 'ave not France!—L'Assemblée Nationale pass von edict"——

"What's that?" interrupted Billy, who was endeavouring, with much interest, to comprehend the story.

"Eh! vat dat! vy vat you call, ven de Assemblee d'Alban' mak-a de law?"

"That's an act of the Legyslatoore," said Kirby, with the readiness of an American on such a subject.

"Vell! dis vas act of Legyslatoore, to restorer my land; my charactair, my sucre-boosh; and ma country. Ah! Ma'mselle Templ', je suis enchantíe! mais I 'ave grief to leav-a you; Oh! yais! I 'ave grief ver mooch."

The amount of all this was, that Mr. Le Quoi, who had fled from his own country more through terror than because he was offensive to the ruling powers in France, had succeeded at length, in getting an assurance that his return to the West Indies would be unnoticed; and the Frenchman, who had sunk into the character of a country shop-keeper, with so much grace, was about to emerge again from his obscurity into his proper level in society.

We need not repeat the civil things that passed between the parties on this occasion, nor recount the endless repetitions of sorrow that the delighted Frenchman expressed, at being compelled to quit the society of Miss Temple. Elizabeth took an opportunity during this expenditure of polite expressions, to purchase the powder privately of the boy, who bore the generic appellation of Jonathan. Before they parted, however, Mr. Le Quoi, who seemed to think that he had not said enough, solicited the honour of a private interview with the heiress, with a gravity in his air that announced the importance of the subject. After conceding the favour, and appointing a more favourable time for the meeting, Elizabeth succeeded in getting out of the store, into which the countrymen now began to enter, as usual, where they met with the same attention and bienséance as formerly.

Elizabeth and Louisa pursued their walk as far as the bridge in profound silence, but when they reached that place, the latter stopped, and appeared anxious to utter something that her feeling suppressed.

"Are you ill, Louisa?" exclaimed Miss Temple; "had we not better return, and seek another opportunity to meet the old man?"

"Not ill, but terrified. Oh! I never, never can go on that hill again with you only. I am not equal to it, indeed I am not."

This was an unexpected declaration to Elizabeth, who, although she experienced no idle apprehensions of a danger that no longer existed, felt most sensitively all the delicacies of maiden modesty. She stood for some time, deeply reflecting within herself, the colour gradually gathering over her features at her own thoughts; but, as if sensible that it was a time for action instead of reflection, she struggled to shake off her hesitation, and replied firmly—

"Well, then it must be done by me, and alone. There is no other than yourself to be trusted, or poor old Leather-stocking will be discovered. Wait for me in the edge of these woods, that at least I may not be seen strolling in the hills by myself just now. One would not wish to create remarks, Louisa—if—if. You will wait for me, dear girl?"

"A year, in sight of the village, Miss Temple," returned the agitated Louisa, "but do not, do not ask me to go on that hill."

Elizabeth found that her companion was really unable to proceed, and they completed their arrangement by posting Louisa out of the observation of the people who occasionally passed, but nigh to the road, and in plain view of the whole valley. Miss Temple then proceeded alone. She ascended the road which has been so often mentioned in our narrative, with an elastic and firm step, fearful that the delay in the store of Mr. Le Quoi, and the time necessary for reaching the summit, would prevent her being punctual to the appointment. Whenever she passed an opening in the bushes, she would pause for breath, or perhaps, drawn from her pursuits by the picture at her feet, would linger a moment to gaze at the beauties of the valley. The long drought had, however, changed its coat of verdure to a hue of brown, and though the same localities were there, the view wanted the lively and cheering aspect of early summer. Even the heavens seemed to share in the dried appearance of the earth, for the sun was concealed by a haziness in the atmosphere, which looked like a thin smoke without a particle of moisture, if such a thing were possible. The blue sky was scarcely to be seen, though now and then there was a faint lighting up in spots, through which masses of rolling vapour could be discerned gathering around the horizon, as if nature were struggling to collect her floods for the relief of man. The very atmosphere that Elizabeth inhaled was hot and dry, and by the time she reached the point where the course led her from the highway, she experienced a sensation like suffocation. But, disregarding her feelings, the heiress hastened to execute her mission, dwelling in her thoughts on nothing but the disappointment. and even the helplessness, the hunter would experience, without her aid.

On the summit of the mountain which Judge Temple had named the "Vision," a little spot had been cleared, in order that a better view might be obtained of the village and the valley. It was at this point that Elizabeth understood the hunter she was to meet him; and thither she urged her way, as expeditiously as the difficulty of the ascent and the impediments of a forest in a state of nature would admit. Numberless were the fragments of rocks, trunks of fallen trees, and branches, that she had to contend against; but every difficulty vanished before her resolution, and, by her own watch, she stood on the desired spot several minutes before the appointed hour.

After resting a moment on the end of a log, Miss Temple cast a scrutinizing glance about her in quest of her old friend, but he was evidently not in the clearing; when she arose and walked around its skirts, examining every place where she thought it probable Natty might deem it prudent to conceal himself. Her search was fruitless; and, after exhausting not only herself, but her thoughts, in efforts to discover or imagine his situation, she ventured to trust her voice in that solitary place.

"Natty! Leather-stocking! old man!" she called aloud, in every direction; but no answer was given, excepting the reverberations of her own clear tones, as they were echoed in the parched forest.

While calling, Elizabeth gradually approached the brow

of the mountain, where a faint cry, like the noise produced by striking the hand against the mouth, at the same time that the breath is strongly exhaled, was heard, answering to her own voice. Not doubting in the least that it was the Leather-stocking lying in wait for her, and who gave that signal to indicate the place where he was to be found, Elizabeth descended for near a hundred feet, until she gained a little natural terrace, thinly scattered with trees, that grew in the fissures of the rocks, which were covered by a scanty soil. She had advanced to the edge of this platform, and was gazing over the perpendicular precipice that formed its face, when a rustling among the dry leaves near her drew her eyes in another direction. Miss Temple certainly was startled by the object that she then saw, but a moment restored her self-possession, and she advanced firmly, and with some interest in her manner, to the spot.

On the trunk of a fallen oak Mohegan was seated, with his tawny visage turned towards her, and his glaring eyes fixed on her face with an expression of wildness and fire that would have terrified a less resolute female. His blanket had fallen from his shoulders, and was lying in folds around him, leaving his breast, arms, and most of his body bare. The medallion of Washington reposed on his chest, a badge of distinction that Elizabeth well knew he only produced on great and solemn occasions. But the whole appearance of the aged chief was more studied than common, and was in some particulars terrific. The long black hair was plaited on his head, falling either way so as to expose his high forehead and piercing eyes, without their usual shading. In the enormous incisions of his ears were entwined ornaments of silver, beads and porcupine's quills, mingled in a rude taste, and after the Indian fashions. A large drop, composed of similar materials, was suspended from the cartilage of his nose, and, falling below his lips, rested on his chin. Streaks of red paint crossed his wrinkled brow, and were traced down either cheek, with some variations in the lines as caprice or custom suggested. His body was also coloured in the same manner; the whole exhibiting an Indian warrior prepared for some event of more than usual moment.

"John! how fare you, worthy John?" said Elizabeth as she approached him; "you have long been a stranger in the village. You promised me a willow basket, and I have had a shirt of calico in readiness for you this month past."

The Indian looked steadily at her for some time without answering, and then shaking his head, he replied, in his low, guttural tones—

"John's hand can make baskets no more—he wants no shirt."

"But if he should, he will know where to come for it," returned Miss Temple. "Indeed, old John, I feel as if you had a natural right to order what you will from us."

"Daughter," said the Indian, "listen:—Six times ten hot summers have passed, since John was young; tall like a pine; straight like the bullet of Hawk-eye; strong as the buffalo; spry as the cat of the mountain. He was strong, and a warrior like the Young Eagle. If his tribe wanted to track the Maquas for many suns, the eye of Chingachgook found the print of their moccasins. If the people feasted and were glad as they counted the scalps of their enemies, it was on his pole they hung. If the squaws cried because there was no meat for their children, he was the first in the chase. His bullet was swifter than the deer.—Daughter, then Chingachgook struck his tomahawk into the trees; it was to tell the lazy ones where to find him and the Mingoes—but he made no baskets."

"Those times have gone by, old warrior," returned Elizabeth; "since then, your people have disappeared, and in place of chasing your enemies, you have learned to fear God and to live at peace."

"Stand here, daughter, where you can see the great spring, the wigwams of your father, and the land on the crooked-river. John was yet young, when his tribe gave away the country, in council, from where the blue mountain stands above the water, to where the Susquehanna is hid by the trees. All this, and all that grew in it, and all that walked over it, and all that fed there, they gave to the Fire-eater—for they loved him. He was strong, and they were women, and he helped them. No Delaware would kill a deer that ran in his woods, nor stop a bird that flew over his land; for it was his. Has John lived in peace! Daughter, since John was young, he has seen the white man from Frontinac come down on his white brothers at Albany, and fight. Did they fear God! He has seen his English and his American Fathers burying their tomahawks in each others' brains, for this very land. Did they fear God, and live in peace! He has seen the land pass away from the Fire-eater, and his children, and the child of his child, and a new chief set over the country. Did they live in peace who did this! did they fear God!"

"Such is the custom of the whites, John. Do not the Delawares fight, and trade their lands for powder, and blankets, and merchandize?"

The Indian turned his dark eyes on the heiress, and kept them there, with a scrutiny that alarmed her a little, as he replied, in a louder and more animated voice—

"Where are the blankets and merchandize that bought the right of the Fire-eater! are they with him in his wigwam? Did they say to him, brother, sell us your land, and take this gold, this silver, these blankets, these rifles, or even this rum, for it? No; they tore it from him, as a scalp is torn from an enemy; and they that did it looked not behind them, to see whether he lived or died. Do such men live in peace, and fear the Great Spirit?"

"But you hardly understand the circumstances," said Elizabeth, more embarrassed than she would own, even to herself. "If you knew our laws and customs better, you would judge differently of our acts. Do not believe evil of my father, old Mohegan, for he is just and good."

"The brother of Miquon is good, and he will do right. I have said it to Hawk-eye—I have said it to the Young Eagle, that the brother of Miquon would do justice."

"Whom call you the Young Eagle?" said Elizabeth, averting her face from the gaze of the Indian as she asked the question; "whence comes he, and what are his rights?"

"Has my daughter lived so long with him, to ask this question?" returned the Indian, warily. "Old age freezes up the blood, as the frosts cover the great spring in winter; but youth keeps the streams of the blood open, like a sun in the time of blossoms. The Young Eagle has eyes; had he no tongue?"

The loveliness to which the old warrior alluded was in no degree diminished by his allegorical speech; for the blushes of the maiden who listened, covered her burning cheeks, till her dark eyes seemed to glow with their reflection; but, after struggling a moment with her shame, she laughed, as if unwilling to understand him seriously, and replied in a tone of pleasantry—

"Not to make me the mistress of his secret. He is too much of a Delaware, to tell his secret thoughts to a woman."

"Daughter, the Great Spirit made your father with a white skin, and he made mine with a red; but he coloured both their hearts with blood. When young, it is swift and warm; but when old, it is still and cold. Is there difference below the skin? No. Once John had a woman. She was the mother of so many sons"—he raised his hand with three fingers elevated—"and she had daughters that would have made the young Delawares happy. She was kind, daughter, and what I said she did. You have different fashions; but do you think John did not love the wife of his youth—the mother of his children!"

"And what has become of your family, John, your wife and your children?" asked Elizabeth, touched by the melancholy of the Indian's manner.

"Where is the ice that covered the great spring? It is melted, and gone with the waters. John has lived till all his people have left him for the land of spirits; but his time has come, and he is ready."

Mohegan dropped his head in his blanket, and sat in silence. Miss Temple knew not what to say. She wished to draw the thoughts of the old warrior from his gloomy recollections, but there was a dignity in his sorrow, and in his fortitude, that repressed her efforts to speak again, for some time. After a long pause, however, she renewed the discourse, by asking—

"Where is the Leather-stocking, John? this canister of powder I have brought at his request; but he is nowhere to be seen. Will you take charge of it and see it delivered?"

The Indian raised his head slowly, and looked earnestly at the gift of the heiress, which she put in his hand.

"This is the great enemy of my nation. Without this, when could the white men drive the Delawares! Daughter, the Great Spirit gave your fathers to know how to make guns and powder, that they might sweep the Indians from the land. There will soon be no red-skin in the country. When John has gone, the last will leave these hills, and all his family will be dead." The aged warrior stretched his body forward, leaning his elbow on his knee, and appeared to be taking a parting look at the objects of the vale, which were still visible through the misty atmosphere; though the air seemed to thicken at each moment around Miss Temple, who became conscious of an increased difficulty of respiration. The eye of Mohegan changed gradually, from its sorrowful expression to a look of wildness, that might be supposed to border on the inspiration of a prophet, as he continued—"But he will go to the country where his fathers have met. The game shall be plenty as the fish in the lakes. No woman shall cry for meat. No Mingo can ever come. The chase shall be for children, and all just red-men shall live together as brothers."

"John! this is not the heaven of a Christian!" cried Miss Temple; "you deal now in the superstition of your forefathers."

"Fathers! sons!" said Mohegan with firmness—"all gone —all gone! I have no son but the Young Eagle, and he has the blood of a white man."

"Tell me, John," said Elizabeth, willing to draw his thoughts to other subjects, and at the same time yielding to her own secret interest in the youth; "who is this Mr. Edwards? Why are you so fond of him, and whence does he come?"

The Indian started at the question, which evidently recalled his recollection to the earth, and, taking her hand, he drew Miss Temple to a seat beside him, and pointed to the country beneath them, before he answered.

"See, daughter," he said, directing her looks towards the

north; "as far as your young eyes can see, was the land of his"——

But immense volumes of smoke at that moment rolled over their heads, and whirling in the eddies formed by the mountains, interposed a barrier to their sight, while he was speaking. Startled by the circumstance, Miss Temple sprung on her feet, and turning her eyes toward the summit of the mountain, she beheld it covered by a similar canopy, while a roaring sound was heard in the forest above her, like the rushing of furious winds.

"What means it, John!" she exclaimed; "we are enveloped in smoke, and I feel a heat like the glow of a furnace."

Before the Indian could reply, a voice was heard, crying in the woods, with a painful anxiety——

"John! where are you, old Mohegan! the woods are on fire, and you have but a few minutes for escape."

The chief put his hand before his mouth, and making it play on his lips, produced the kind of noise that had attracted Elizabeth to the place, when a quick and hurried step was heard dashing through the dried underbrush and bushes, and presently Edwards rushed to his side, with horror painted in every feature.

Chapter XXXVII

Love rules the court, the camp, the grove.
LAY OF THE LAST MINSTREL

"It would have been sad indeed, to lose you in such a manner, my old friend," said Oliver, catching his breath for utterance. "Up and away! even now we may be too late; the flames are circling round the point of the rock below, and unless we can pass there, our only chance must be over the precipice. Away! away! shake off your apathy, John, for now is the time of need."

Mohegan pointed towards Elizabeth, who, forgetting her danger, had shrunk back to a projection of the rock, soon as she recognised the sounds of Edward's voice, and said, with something like awakened animation—

"Save her—leave John to die."

"Her, whom mean you?" cried the youth, turning quickly to the place the other indicated;—but when he saw the figure of Elizabeth, bending toward him in an attitude that powerfully spoke her terror, blended with her reluctance to meet him in such a place, the shock, for a moment, deprived him of speech.

"Miss Temple!" he cried, when he found words; "you here! is such a death reserved for you!"

"No, no, no—no death, I hope, for any of us, Mr. Edwards," she replied, endeavouring to speak calmly, and rallying her thoughts for the emergency. "There is smoke, but still no fire to harm us. Let us endeavour to retire."

"Take my arm," said Edwards; "there must be an opening in some direction for your retreat. Are you equal to the effort?"

"Certainly. You surely magnify the danger, Mr. Edwards. Lead me out the way you came."

"I will—I will," cried the youth, with a kind of hysterical utterance. "No, no—there is no danger—I have alarmed you unnecessarily."

"But shall we leave the Indian—can we leave him here, as he says, to die?"

An expression of painful emotion crossed the face of the young man, who stopped, and cast a longing look at Mohegan; but, dragging his companion after him, even against her will, he pursued his way, with enormous strides, toward the pass by which he had just entered the circle of flame.

"Do not regard him," he said, in those horrid tones that denote a desperate calmness; "he is used to the woods, and such scenes; he will escape up the mountain—over the rock —or he can remain where he is in safety."

"You thought not so this moment, Edwards! Do not leave him there to meet with such a death," cried Elizabeth, fixing a look on the countenance of her conductor, that seemed to distrust his sanity.

"An Indian burn! who ever heard of an Indian dying by fire? an Indian cannot burn; the idea is ridiculous. Hasten, hasten, Miss Temple, or the smoke may incommode you."

"Edwards! your look, your eye terrifies me! tell me the danger; is it greater than it seems? I am equal to any trial."

"If we reach the point of yon rock before that sheet of fire, we are safe, Miss Temple!" exclaimed the young man, in a voice that burst without the bounds of his forced composure. "Fly! the struggle is for your life!"

The place of the interview between Miss Temple and the Indian has been already described as one of those platforms of rock which form a sort of terrace in the mountains of that country, and the face of it, we have said, was both high and perpendicular. Its shape was nearly a natural arc, the ends of which blended with the mountain, at points where its sides were less abrupt in their descent. It was round one of these terminations of the sweep of the rock that Edwards had ascended, and it was towards the same place that he urged Elizabeth to a desperate exertion of her speed.

Immense clouds of white smoke had been pouring over the summit of the mountain, and had concealed the ap-

proach and ravages of the element; but a crackling sound
drew the eyes of Miss Temple, as she flew over the ground,
supported by the young man, towards the outline of smoke,
where she already perceived the waving flames shooting
forward from the vapour, now flaring high in the air, and
then bending to the earth, seeming to light into combustion
every stick and shrub on which they breathed. The sight
aroused them both to redouble their efforts; but, unfortunately, there was a collection of the tops of trees, old and
dried, which lay directly across their course; and, at the
very moment when both had thought their safety ensured,
an eddying of the warm currents of the air swept a forked
tongue of flame across the pile, which lighted at the touch;
and when they reached the spot, the flying pair were opposed by the surly roaring of a body of fire, as if a furnace
were glowing in their path. They recoiled from the heat, and
stood on a point of the rock, gazing in a sort of stupor at
the flames, which were spreading rapidly down the mountain, whose side soon became a sheet of living fire. It was
dangerous for one clad in the light and airy dress of Elizabeth to approach even to the vicinity of the raging element;
and those flowing robes, that gave such softness and grace
to her form, seemed now to be formed for the instrument of
her destruction.

The villagers were accustomed to resort to that hill in
quest of timber and fuel; in procuring which, it was their
usage to take only the bodies of the trees, leaving the tops
and branches to decay under the operation of the weather.
Much of the hill was, consequently, covered with such light
fuel for the flames, which, having been scorching under the
sun for the last two months, ignited with a touch. Indeed,
in some cases, there did not appear to be any contact between the fire and these piles, but the flames seemed to dart
from heap to heap, as the fabulous fire of the temple is represented to relumine its neglected lamp.

There was beauty as well as terror in the sight, and
Elizabeth and the youth stood viewing the progress of the
desolation, with a strange mixture of horror and interest.
Edwards, however, shortly roused himself to new exertions,

and drawing his companion after him, they skirted the edge of the smoke, the young man penetrating frequently into its dense volumes in search of a passage, but in every instance without success. In this manner they proceeded in a semi-circle around the upper part of the terrace, until, arriving at the verge of the precipice, opposite to the point where Edwards had ascended, the horrid conviction burst on both in the same instant, that they were completely encircled by the fire. So long as a single pass up or down the mountain was unexplored, hope had invigourated them with her secret influence; but when retreat seemed to be absolutely impracticable, the horror of their situation broke upon Elizabeth as powerfully as if she had hitherto considered the danger nothing.

"This mountain is doomed to be fatal to me!" she whispered, rather than uttered aloud; "we shall find our graves on it!"

"Say not so, Miss Temple, there is yet hope," returned the youth, in the same tone, while the vacant, horrid expression of his eye, contradicted his words; "let us return to the point of the rock; there is, there must be, some place about it where we can descend."

"Lead me there," exclaimed Elizabeth; "let us leave no effort untried." She did not wait for his compliance, but turning, retraced her steps to the brow of the precipice, murmuring to herself, in suppressed hysterical sobs, "My father—my poor, distracted father!"

Edwards was by her side in an instant, and with aching eyes he examined into every fissue in the crags, in quest of some opening that might offer the facilities of flight. But the smooth, even surface of the rocks afforded hardly a resting place for a foot, much less those continued projections which would have been necessary for a descent of nearly a hundred feet. Edwards was not slow in feeling the conviction that this hope was also futile, and with a kind of feverish despair, that still urged him to action, he turned to some new expedient.

"There is nothing left, Miss Temple," he said, in a hollow accent, "but to lower you from this place to the rock beneath. If Natty were here, or even that Indian could be roused, their ingenuity and long practice would easily devise methods by which to do it; but I am a child, at this moment, in every thing but daring. Where shall I find means? This dress of mine is so light, and there is so little of it—then the blanket of Mohegan. We must try—we must try —any thing is better than to see you a victim to such a death!"

"And what shall become of you!" said Elizabeth. "Indeed, indeed, neither you nor John must be the sacrifice to my safety."

He heard her not, for he was already by the side of Mohegan, who yielded his blanket without a question, retaining his seat with Indian dignity and composure, though his own situation was even more critical than that of the others. The blanket was cut into shreds, and the fragments fastened together; the loose linen jacket of the youth, and the light muslin shawl of Elizabeth, were attached to them, and the whole thrown over the rocks, with the rapidity of lightning; but the united pieces did not reach half way to the bottom.

"It will not do—it will not do!" cried Elizabeth; "for me there is no hope! The fire comes slowly but certainly. See! it destroys the very earth before it!"

Had the flames spread on the rock with half the quickness with which they leaped from bush to tree, in other parts of the mountain, our painful task would have soon ended; for they would have swept off the victims, who were suffering doubly under the anticipations of their approaching fate. But the peculiarity of the situation afforded Elizabeth and her companion the respite, of which they availed themselves to make the efforts we have recorded.

The thin covering of earth over the rock on which they stood, supported but a scanty and faded herbage, and most of the trees that had found root in the fissures had already died, during the intense heats of previous summers. Those which still retained the appearance of life, bore a few dry and withered leaves, that were drained of their nourishment; while the others were merely the wrecks of pines, oaks, and maples. No better materials to feed the fire could be found, had there been a communication with the flames; but the ground was destitute of the leaves and boughs that led the destructive element like a torrent over the remainder of the hill. As auxiliary to this scarcity of fuel, there was one of the large springs which abound in that country, gushing out of the side of the ascent above, which, after creeping sluggishly along the level land, saturating the mossy covering of the rock with moisture, swept round the base of the little cone that formed the pinnacle of the mountain, and entering the canopy of smoke near one of the terminations of the terrace, found its way to the lake, not by dashing from rock to rock, but by the secret channels of the earth. It would rise to the surface, here and there, in the wet seasons, when it exhibited a mimic torrent, overflowing the ground for some distance; but in the droughts of summer, it was to be traced only by the bogs and moss that announced the proximity of water. When the fire reached this barrier, it was compelled to pause, until a concentration of its heat could overcome the moisture, like an army impatiently waiting the operations of a battering train, to open its way to death and desolation.

That fatal moment seemed now to have arrived; for the hissing streams of the spring appeared to be nearly exhausted, and the moss of the rocks was already curling under the intense heat that was thrown across the little spot of wet ground, while the fragments of bark that yet clung to the dead trees, began to separate from their trunks, and fall to the ground in crumbling masses. The air seemed quivering with rays of heat which might be seen playing along the parched stems of the trees. The excited imagination of Elizabeth, as she stood on the verge of the precipice, and gazed about her, viewing the approach of their powerful enemy, fancied every tree and herb near her on the point of ignition. There were moments when dark clouds of smoke would sweep along the little terrace, and as the eye lost its power, the other senses contributed to give effect to the fearful horror of the scene. At such moments, the roaring of the flames, the crackling of the furious element, with the tearing of falling branches, and occasionally, the thundering echoes of some prostrated tree, united to alarm the victims. Of the three, however, the youth appeared much the most agitated. Elizabeth, having relinquished entirely the idea of escape, was fast obtaining that resigned composure with which the most delicate of her sex are known to meet unavoidable evils; while Mohegan, who was much nearer to the danger, maintained his seat with the invincible resignation of the Indian warrior. Once or twice the eye of the aged chief, which was ordinarily fixed in the direction of the distant hills, turned towards the young pair, who seemed doomed to so early a death, with a slight indication of pity crossing his composed features, but it would immediately revert again to its former gaze, as if already looking into the womb of futurity. Much of the time he was chanting a kind of low dirge, in the Delaware tongue, using the deep and remarkably guttural tones of his people.

"At such a moment, Mr. Edwards, all earthly distinctions end," whispered Elizabeth; "persuade John to move nearer to us—let us die together."

"I cannot—he will not stir," returned the youth, in the same horridly still tones. "He considers this as the happiest moment of his life. He is past seventy; and has been decaying rapidly for some time; he received some injury in chasing that unlucky deer, too, on the lake. Oh! Miss Temple, that was an unlucky chase indeed! it has led, I fear, to this awful scene."

The smile that beamed on the lovely features of Elizabeth was celestial, as she answered, in a soft soothing voice, "Why name such a trifle now—at this moment the heart is dead to all earthly emotions!"

"If any thing could reconcile a man, in the vigour and pride of manhood, to this death," cried the youth with fervour, "it would be to meet it in such company!"

"Talk not so, Edwards, talk not so," interrupted Miss Temple, "I am unworthy of it; and it is unjust to yourself. We must die; yes—yes—we must die—it is the will of God, and let us endeavour to submit like his own children."

"Die!" the youth rather shrieked than exclaimed, "No— no—there must be hope yet—you must not, shall not die."

"In what way can we escape?" asked Elizabeth, pointing with a look of heavenly composure, towards the fire. "Observe! the flame is crossing the barrier of wet ground—it comes slowly, Edwards, but surely.—Ah! see! the tree! the tree is already lighted!"

Her words were too true. The heat of the conflagration had, at length, overcome the resistance of the spring, and the fire was slowly stealing along the half-dried moss; while a dead pine kindled with the touch of a forked flame, that, for a moment, wreathed around the stem of the tree, as it whirled, in one of its evolutions, under the influence of the air. The effect was instantaneous and magical. The flames danced along the parched trunk of the pine, like lightning quivering on a chain, and immediately a column of living fire was raging on the terrace. It soon spread from tree to tree, and the scene was evidently drawing to a close. The log on which Mohegan was seated lighted at its farther end, and the Indian appeared to be surrounded by the fire. Still he was unmoved. As his body was unprotected, his suffering must have been great, but his fortitude was superior to all. His voice could yet be heard, raising its tones, even in the midst of these horrors. Elizabeth turned her head from the sight, and faced the valley. Furious eddies of wind were created by the heat, and just at that moment, the canopy of fiery smoke that overhung the valley, was cleared away, leaving a distinct view of the peaceful village beneath them.

"My father!—My father!" shrieked Elizabeth. "Oh! this— this surely might have been spared me—but I submit."

The distance was not too great, for the figure of Judge Temple to be seen, standing in his own grounds, and, apparently, contemplating, in perfect unconsciousness of the danger of his child, the mountain in flames. This sight was still more painful than the approaching danger; and Elizabeth again faced the hill.

"My intemperate warmth has done this?" cried Edwards, in the accents of despair. "If I had possessed but a moiety of your heavenly resignation, Miss Temple, all might yet have been well."

"Name it not—name it not," she said. "It is now of no avail. We must die, Edwards, we must die—let us do so as Christians. But—no—you may yet escape, perhaps. Your dress is not so fatal as mine. Fly! leave me. An opening may yet be found for you, possibly—certainly it is worth the effort. Fly! leave me—but stay! You will see my father; my poor! my bereaved father! Say to him, then, Edwards, say to him, all that can appease his anguish. Tell him that I died happy and collected; that I have gone to my beloved mother; that the hours of this life are as nothing when balanced in the scales of eternity. Say how we shall meet again. And say," she continued, dropping her voice, that had risen with her feelings, as if conscious of her worldly weaknesses, "how dear, how very dear, was my love for him. That it was near, too near, to my love for God."

The youth listened to her touching accents, but moved not. In a moment he found utterance and replied:

"And is it me that you bid to leave you! me, to leave you on the edge of the grave! Oh! Miss Temple, how little have you known me," he cried, dropping on his knees at her feet, and gathering her flowing robes in his arms, as if to shield her from the flames. "I have been driven to the woods in despair; but your society has tamed the lion within me. If I have wasted my time in degradation, 'twas you that charmed me to it. If I have forgotten my name and family, your form supplied the place of memory. If I have forgotten my wrongs, 'twas you that taught me charity. No—no —dearest Elizabeth, I may die with you, but I can never leave you!"

Elizabeth moved not, nor answered. It was plain that her thoughts had been of heaven. The recollection of her father, and her regrets at their separation, had been mellowed by a holy sentiment, that lifted her above the level of earthly things, and she was fast losing the weakness of her sex, in the near view of eternity. But as the maiden, standing in her extremity, listened to these words, she became once more woman. The blood gathered slowly, again, in those cheeks, that had, in anticipation of the tyrant's triumph, assumed the livid appearance of death, until they glowed with the loveliness of her beauty. She struggled with herself against these feelings, and smiled, as she thought she was shaking off the last lingering feeling of her nature, when the world, and all its seductions, rushed again to her heart, with the sounds of a human voice, crying in piercing tones—

"Gal! where be ye, gal! gladden the heart of an old man, if ye yet belong to 'arth!"

"List!" said Elizabeth, "'tis the Leather-stocking; he seeks me!"

"'Tis Natty!" shouted Edwards, springing on his feet, "and we may yet be saved!"

A wide and circling flame glared on their eyes for a moment, even above the fire of the woods, and a loud report followed, that was succeeded by a comparative stillness.

"'Tis the canister! 'tis the powder," cried the same voice, evidently approaching them. "'Tis the canister, and the precious child is lost!"

At the next instant Natty rushed through the streams of the spring, and appeared on the terrace, without his deer-skin cap, his hair burnt to his head, his shirt of country check, black and filled with holes, and his red features of a deeper colour than ever, by the heat he had encountered.

Chapter XXXVIII

Even from the land of shadows, now,
My father's awful ghost appears.
GERTRUDE OF WYOMING

For an hour after Louisa Grant was left by Miss Temple, in
the situation already mentioned, she continued in feverish
anxiety, awaiting the return of her friend. But as the time
passed by without the re-appearance of Elizabeth, the ter-
rors of Louisa gradually increased, until her alarmed fancy
had conjured every species of danger that appertained to
the woods, excepting the one that really existed. The heavens had become obscured, by degrees, and vast volumes of
smoke were pouring over the valley; but the thoughts of
Louisa were still recurring to beasts, without dreaming of
the real cause for apprehension. She was stationed in the
edge of the low pines and chestnuts that succeeded the first
or large growth of the forest, and directly above the angle
where the highway turned from the straight course to the
village and ascended the mountain, laterally. Consequently she commanded a view not only of the valley, but
of the road beneath her. The few travellers that passed, she
observed, were engaged in earnest conversation, and frequently raised their eyes to the hill, and at length she saw
the people leaving the court-house, and gazing upward also.
While under the influence of the alarm excited by such unusual movements, reluctant to go, and yet fearful to remain,
Louisa was startled by the low cracking, but cautious treads
of some one approaching through the bushes. She was on the
eve of flight when Natty emerged from the cover and stood
at her side. The old man laughed, as he shook her kindly
by a hand that was passive with fear, and said—

"I am glad to meet you here, child, for the back of the mountain is a-fire, and it would be dangerous to go up it now, till it has been burnt over once, and the dead wood is gone. There's a foolish man, the comrade of that varmint, who has given me all this trouble, digging for ore, on the east side. I told him that the kearless fellows who thought to catch a practys'd hunter in the woods after dark, had thrown the lighted pine knots in the brush, and that 'twould kindle like tow and warned him to leave the hill. But he was set upon his business, and nothing short of Providence could move him. If he isn't burnt and buried in a grave of his own digging, he's made of salamanders. Why, what ails the child! you look as skeary as if you see'd more painters! I wish there was some to be found, they'd count up faster than the beaver. But where's the good child of a bad father? did she forget her promise to the old man?"

"The hill! the hill!" shrieked Louisa; "she seeks you on the hill, with the powder!"

Natty recoiled for several feet at this unexpected intelligence, and exclaimed—

"The Lord of Heaven have mercy on her! She's on the Vision, and that's a sheet of fire ag'in this. Child, if ye love the dear one and hope to find a friend when you need it most, to the village and give the alarm. The men be us'd to fighting fire, and there may be a chance left. Fly! I bid ye fly! nor stop even for breath."

The Leather-stocking had no sooner uttered this injunction than he disappeared in the bushes, and when last seen by Louisa, was rushing up the mountain with the activity of youth, and with a speed that none but those who were accustomed to the toil could attain.

"Have I found ye!" the old man exclaimed, when he burst out of the smoke; "God be praised, that I've found ye; but follow, there is no time left for talking."

"My dress!" said Elizabeth; "it would be fatal to trust myself nearer to the flames in it."

"I bethought me of your flimsy things," cried Natty, throwing loose the folds of a covering of buck-skin that he carried on his arm, and wrapping her form in it, in such a manner as to envelope her whole person; "now follow, for it's a matter of life and death to us all."

"But John! what will become of John," cried Edwards; "can we leave the old warrior here to perish?"

The eyes of Natty followed the direction of Edward's finger, when he beheld the Indian, still seated as before, with the very earth under his feet consuming with fire. Without delay the hunter approached the spot and cried in Delaware—

"Up and away, Chingachgook! will ye stay here to burn, like a tortured Mingo, at the stake! The Moravians have teached ye better, I hope; the Lord preserve me if the powder hasn't flashed atween his legs, and the skin of his back is roasting. Will ye come, I say? will ye follow?"

"Why should Mohegan go?" returned the Indian, gloomily. "He has seen the days of an eagle, and his eye grows dim. He looks on the valley; he looks on the water; he looks in the hunting-grounds—but he sees no Delawares. Every one has a white skin. My fathers say, from the far-off land, come. My women, my young warriors, my tribe, say, come. The Great Spirit says, come. No—let Mohegan die."

"But you forget your friend," cried Edwards.

" 'Tis useless to talk to an Indian with the death-fit on him, lad," interrupted Natty, who seized the strips of the blanket, and with wonderful dexterity strapped the passive chieftain to his own back; when he turned, and with a strength that seemed to bid defiance, not only to his years, but to his load, he led the way to the point whence he had issued. Even as they crossed the little terrace of rock, one of the dead trees, that had been tottering for several minutes, fell on the spot where they had stood, and filled the air with its cinders.

Such an event quickened the steps of the party, who followed the Leather-stocking with the urgency required by the occasion.

"Tread on the soft ground," he cried, when they were in a gloom where sight availed them but little, "and keep in the white smoke; keep the skin close on her, lad; she's a precious one, I tell you, sich another will be hard to be found."

Obedient to the hunter's directions, they followed his steps and his advice implicitly, and although the narrow passage along the winding of the spring led amid burning logs and falling branches, yet they happily achieved it in safety. No one but a man long accustomed to the woods could have traced his route through a smoke, in which respiration was difficult, and sight nearly useless; but the experience of Natty conducted them to an opening through the rocks, where, with a little difficulty, they soon descended to another terrace, and emerged at once into a tolerably clear atmosphere.

The feelings of Edwards and Elizabeth, at reaching this spot, may be imagined, though not easily described. No one seemed to exult more than their guide, who turned, with Mohegan still lashed to his back, and laughing in his own manner, said—

"I know'd 'twas the Frechman's powder, gal; it went so altogether like; your coarse grains will squib for a minute. The Iroquois had none of the best powder when I went ag'in the Canada tribes, under Sir William. Did I ever tell you the story, lad, concerning the skrimmage with"——

"For God's sake, tell me nothing now, Natty, until we are entirely safe. Where shall we go next?"

"Why, on the platform of rock over the cave, to be sure; you will be safe enough there, or we'll go into it, if you be so minded."

The young man started, and appeared agitated with a strong emotion, but looking around him with an anxious eye, said quickly—

"Shall we be safe on the rock? cannot the fire reach us there, too?"

"Can't the boy see?" said Natty, with the coolness of one who was accustomed to the kind of danger he had just encountered. "Had ye staid in the place above ten minutes longer, you would both have been in ashes, but here you may stay for ever, and no fire can touch you, until they burn the rocks as well as the woods."

With this assurance, which was obviously true, they proceeded to the spot, and Natty deposited his load, placing the Indian on the ground with his back against a fragment of the rocks. Elizabeth sunk on the ground and buried her face in her hands, while her heart was swelling with a variety of conflicting emotions.

"Let me urge you to take a restorative, Miss Temple," said Edwards respectfully; "your frame will sink else."

"Leave, leave me," she said, raising her beaming eyes for a moment to his; "I feel too much for words! I am grateful, Oliver, for this miraculous escape; and next to my God to you."

Edwards withdrew to the edge of the rock, and shouted —"Benjamin! where are you, Benjamin?"

A hoarse voice replied, as if from the bowels of the earth, "Here away, master; stow'd in this here bit of a hole, which is all the same as hot as the cook's coppers. I'm tired of my birth, d'ye see, and if-so-be that Leather-stocking has got much overhauling to do before he sails after them said beaver, I'll go into dock again, and ride out my quarantine 'till I can get prottick from the law, and so hold on upon the rest of my 'spaniolas."

"Bring up a glass of water from the spring," continued Edwards, "and throw a little wine in it; hasten, I entreat you."

"I knows but little of your small drink, master Oliver," returned the steward, his voice issuing out of the cave into the open air, "and the Jamaiky held out no longer than to take a parting kiss with Billy Kirby, when he anchored me alongside the highway last night, where you run me down in the chase. But here's sum'mat of a red colour that may suit a weak stomach, mayhap. That master Kirby is no first-rate in a boat, but he'll tack a cart among the stumps, all the same as a Lon'on pilot will back and fill through the colliers in the Pool."

As the steward ascended while talking, by the time he had ended his speech, he appeared on the rock, with the desired restoratives, exhibiting the worn-out and bloated features of a man who had run deep in a debauch, and that lately.

Elizabeth took from the hand of Edwards the liquor which he offered, and then motioned to be left again to herself.

The youth turned at her bidding, and observed Natty kindly assiduous around the person of Mohegan. When their eyes met, the hunter said sorrowfully—

"His time has come, lad; I see it in his eye;—when an Indian fixes his eye, he means to go but to one place; and what the wilful creaters put their minds on, they're sure to do."

A quick tread diverted the reply of the youth, and in a few moments, to the amazement of the whole party, Mr. Grant was seen clinging to the side of the mountain, and striving to reach the place where they stood. Oliver sprang to his assistance, and by their united efforts, the worthy divine was soon placed safely among them.

"How came you added to our number?" cried Edwards; "Is the hill alive with people at a time like this?"

The hasty but pious thanksgivings of the clergy-man were soon ejaculated; and when he succeeded in collecting his bewildered senses, he replied—

"I heard that my child was seen coming to the mountain; and when the fire broke over its summit, my uneasiness drew me up the road, where I found Louisa, in terror for Miss Temple. It was to seek her that I came into this danger-ous place; and I think but for God's mercy, through the dogs of Natty, I should have perished in the flames myself."

"Ay! follow the hounds, and if there's an opening they'll scent it out," said Natty; "their noses be given to them the same as man's reason."

"I did so, and they led me to this place; but praise be to God that I see you all safe and well."

"No, no," returned the hunter, "safe we be, but as for well, John can't be called in a good way, unless you'll say that for a man that's taking his last look at the 'arth."

"He speaks the truth!" said the divine, with the holy awe with which he ever approached the dying;—I have been by too many death-beds, not to see that the hand of the tyrant is laid on this old warrior. Oh! how consoling it is, to know that he has not rejected the offered mercy, in the hour of his strength and worldly temptations! The offspring of a race of heathens, he has in truth been 'as a brand plucked from the burning.' "

"No, no," returned Natty, who alone stood with him by the side of the dying warrior, "it's no burning that ails him, though his Indian feelings made him scorn to move, unless it be the burning of man's wicked thoughts for near four-score years; but it's nater giving out in a chase that's run too long.—Down with ye, Hector! down, I say!—Flesh isn't iron, that a man can live for ever, and see his kith and kin driven to a far country, and he left to mourn, with none to keep him company."

"John," said the divine, tenderly, "do you hear me? do you wish the prayers appointed by the church, at this trying moment?"

The Indian turned his ghastly face to the speaker, and fastened his dark eyes on him, steadily, but vacantly. No sign of recognition was made; and in a moment he moved his head again slowly towards the vale, and began to sing, using his own language, in those low, guttural tones, that have been so often mentioned, his notes rising with his theme, till they swelled to fulness, if not to harmony:—

"I will come! I will come! to the land of the just I will come! No Delaware fears his end; no Mohican shrinks from death; for the Great Spirit calls, and he goes. My father I have honoured; I have cherished my mother; to my tribe I've been faithful and true. The Maquas I have slain!—I have slain the Maquas! and the Great Spirit calls to his son. I will come! I will come! to the land of the just I will come!"

"What says he, Leather-stocking?" inquired the priest, with tender interest; "sings he the Redeemer's praise?"

"No, no—'tis his own praise that he speaks now," said Natty, turning in a melancholy manner from the sight of his dying friend; "and a good right he has to say it all, for I know every word of it to be true."

"May Heaven avert such self-righteousness from his heart!" exclaimed the divine. "Humility and penitence are the seals of Christianity; and without feeling them deeply seated in the soul, all hope is delusive, and leads to vain expectations. Praise himself! when his whole soul and body should unite to praise his Maker! John! you have enjoyed the blessings of a gospel ministry, and have been called from out a multitude of sinners and pagans, and I trust, for a wise and gracious purpose. Do you now feel what it is to be justified by our Saviour's death, and reject all weak and idle dependence on good works, that spring from man's pride and vainglory?"

The Indian did not regard his interrogator, but he raised his head again, and said, in a low, distinct voice—

"Who can say that the Maquas know the back of Mohegan! What enemy that trusted in him did not see the morning? What Mingo that he chased ever sang the song of triumph? Did Mohegan ever lie? No; for the truth lived in him, and none else could come out of him. In his youth, he was a warrior and his moccasins left the stain of blood. In his age, he was wise; and his words at the council fire did not blow away with the winds."

"Ah! he has abandoned that vain relic of paganism, his songs," cried the good divine;—"what says he now? is he sensible of his lost state?"

"Lord! man," said Natty, "he knows his ind is at hand as well as you or I, but, so far from thinking it a loss to him, he believes it to be a great gain. He is now old and stiff, and you've made the game so scarce and shy, that better shots than him find it hard to get a livelihood. Now he thinks he shall travel where it will always be good hunting; where no wicked or unjust Indians can go; and where he shall meet all his tribe together ag'in. There's not much loss in that, to a man whose hands be hardly fit for basket-making. Loss! if there be any loss, 'twill be to me. I'm sure, after he's gone, there will be but little left for me to do but to follow."

"His example and end, which, I humbly trust, shall yet be made glorious," returned Mr. Grant, "should lead your mind to dwell on the things of another life. But I feel it to be my duty to smooth the way for the parting spirit. This is the moment, John, when the reflection that you did not reject the mediation of the Redeemer, will bring balm to your soul.

Trust not to any act of former days, but lay the burthen of your sins at his feet, and you have his own blessed assurance that he will not desert you."

"Though all you say be true, and you have scripter gospels for it, too," said Natty, "you will make nothing of the Indian. He hasn't seen a Moravian priest sin' the war; and it's hard to keep them from going back to their native ways. I should think 'twould be as well to let the old man pass in peace. He's happy now; I know it by his eye; and that's more than I would say for the chief, sin' the time the Delawares broke up from the head-waters of their river, and went west. Ah's me! 'tis a grievous long time that, and many dark days have we both seen together sin' it."

"Hawk-eye!" said Mohegan, rousing with the last glimmering of life. "Hawk-eye! listen to the words of your brother."

"Yes, John," said the hunter, in English, strongly affected by the appeal, and drawing to his side; "we have been brothers; and more so than it means in the Indian tongue. What would ye have with me, Chingachgook?"

"Hawk-eye! my fathers call me to the happy hunting-grounds. The path is clear, and the eyes of Mohegan grow young. I look—but I see no white-skins; there are none to be seen but just and brave Indians. Farewell, Hawk-eye—you shall go with the Fire-eater and the Young Eagle, to the white man's heaven; but I go after my fathers. Let the bow, and the tomahawk, and pipe, and the wampum of Mohegan, be laid in his grave; for when he starts 'twill be in the night, like a warrior on a war-party, and he cannot stop to seek them."

"What says he, Nathaniel?" cried Mr. Grant, earnestly, and with obvious anxiety; "does he recall the promises of the mediation? and trust his salvation to the Rock of ages?"

Although the faith of the hunter was by no means clear, yet the fruits of early instruction had not entirely fallen in the wilderness. He believed in one God, and one heaven; and when the strong feeling excited by the leave-taking of his old companion, which was exhibited by the powerful

working of every muscle in his weather-beaten face, suffered
from him to speak, he replied—

"No—no—he trusts only to the Great Spirit of the savages,
and to his own good deeds. He thinks, like all his people, that
he is to be young ag'in, and to hunt, and be happy to the
ind of etarnity. It's pretty much the same with all colours,
parson. I could never bring myself to think that I shall meet
with these hounds, or my piece, in another world; though
the thoughts of leaving them for ever, sometimes brings
hard feelings over me, and makes me cling to life with a
greater craving then beseems threescore-and-ten."

"The Lord in his mercy avert such a death from one who
has been sealed with the sign of the cross!" cried the minister, in holy fervour. "John—"

He paused; for the scene, and the elements, seemed to
conspire to oppress the powers of humanity. During the
period occupied by the events which we have related, the
dark clouds in the horizon had continued to increase in
numbers and magnitude; and the awful stillness that now
pervaded the air, announced a crisis in the state of the atmosphere. The flames, which yet continued to rage along
the sides of the mountain, no longer whirled in the uncertain currents of their own eddies, but blazed high and
steadily towards the heavens. There was even a quietude in
the ravages of the destructive element, as if it foresaw that
a hand, greater than even its own desolating power, was
about to stay its progress. The piles of smoke which lay
above the valley began to rise, and were dispelling rapidly;
and streaks of vivid lightning were dancing through the
masses of clouds that impended over the western hills.
While Mr. Grant was speaking, a flash, which sent its quivering light through the gloom, laying bare the whole opposite
horizon, was followed by a loud crash of thunder, that rolled
away among the hills, seeming to shake the foundations of
the earth to their centre. Mohegan raised himself, as if in
obedience to a signal for his departure, and stretched forth
his wasted arm towards the west. His dark face lighted with
a look of joy; which with all other expression, gradually disappeared; the muscles stiffening as they retreated to a state

of rest; a slight convulsion played, for a single instant, about his lips; and his arm slowly dropped, rigid and motionless, by his side; leaving the frame of the dead warrior reposing against the rock, with its glassy eyes open, and fixed on the distant hills, as if the deserted shell were tracing the flight of the spirit to its new abode.

All this Mr. Grant witnessed in silent awe; but when the last echoes of the thunder died away, he clasped his hands together, with pious energy, and repeated, in the full rich tones of assured faith—

"O Lord! how unsearchable are thy judgments; and thy ways past finding out! 'I know that my Redeemer liveth, and that he shall stand at the latter day upon the earth: And though after my skin, worms destroy this body, yet in my flesh shall I see God; whom I shall see for myself, and mine eyes shall behold, and not another.' "

As the divine closed this burst of devotion, he bowed his head meekly to his bosom, and looked all the dependence and humility that the inspired language expressed.

When Mr. Grant retired from the body, the hunter approached, and taking the rigid hand of his friend, looked him wistfully in the face for some time without speaking; when he gave vent to his feelings by saying, in the mournful voice of one who felt deeply—

"Red skin, or white, it's all over now! He's to be judged by a righteous Judge, and by no laws that's made to suit times, and new ways. Well there's only one more death, and the world will be left to me and the hounds. Ahs! me! a man must wait the time of God's pleasure, but I begin to weary of my Life. There is scearcely a tree standing that I know, and it's hard to find a face that I was acquainted with in my younger days."

Large drops of rain began now to fall, and diffuse themselves over the dry rock, while the approach of the thunder shower was rapid and certain. The body of the Indian was hastily removed into the cave beneath, followed by the whining hounds, who missed, and moaned for, the look of intelligence that had always met their salutations to the chief.

Edwards made some hasty and confused excuse for not

taking Elizabeth into the same place, which was now completely closed in front with logs and bark, saying something that she hardly understood about its darkness, and the unpleasantness of being with the dead body. Miss Temple, however, found a sufficient shelter against the torrent of rain that fell, under the projection of a rock which overhung them. But long before the shower was over, the sounds of voices were heard below them, crying aloud for Elizabeth, and men soon appeared, beating the dying embers of the bushes, as they worked their way cautiously among the unextinguished brands.

At the first short cessation in the rain, Oliver conducted the heiress to the road, where he left her. Before parting, however, he found time to say, in a fervent manner, that his companion was now at no loss to interpret—

"The moment of concealment is over, Miss Temple. By this time tomorrow, I shall remove a veil that perhaps it has been weakness to keep around me and my affairs so long. But I have had romantic and foolish wishes and weaknesses; and who has not, that is young and torn by conflicting passions? God bless you! I hear your father's voice; he is coming up the road, and I would not, just now, subject myself to detention. Thank heaven, you are safe again, and that alone removes the weight of a world from my spirit!"

He waited for no answer, but sprang into the woods. Elizabeth, notwithstanding she heard the piercing cries of her father as he called upon her name, paused until he was concealed among the smoking trees, when she turned, and in a moment rushed into the arms of her half-distracted parent.

A carriage had been provided, to remove her body, living or dead as Heaven had directed her fate, into which Miss Temple hastily entered; when the cry was passed along the hill, that the lost one was found, and the people returned to the village, wet and dirty, but elated with the thought that the daughter of their landlord had escaped from so horrid and untimely an end.

· *Chapter XXXIX* ·

Selictar! unsheath then our chief's simetar;
Tambourgi! thy 'larum gives promise of war;
Ye mountains! that see us descend to the shore,
Shall view us victors, or view us no more.

BYRON

The heavy showers that prevailed during the remainder of the day, completely stopped the progress of the flames; though glimmering fires were observed during the night, on different parts of the hill, wherever there was a collection of fuel to feed the element. The next day the woods, for many miles, were black and smoking, and were stript of every vestige of brush and dead wood; but the pines and hemlocks still reared their heads proudly along the hills, and even the smaller trees of the forest retained a feeble appearance of life and vegetation.

The many tongues of rumour were busy in exaggerating the miraculous escape of Elizabeth, and a report was generally credited, that Mohegan had actually perished in the flames. This belief became confirmed, and was indeed rendered probable, when the direful intelligence reached the village, that Jotham Riddel, the miner, was found in his hole, nearly dead with suffocation, and burnt to such a degree that no hopes were entertained of his life.

The public attention became much alive to the events of the last few days, and just at this crisis, the convicted counterfeiters took the hint from Natty, and, on the night succeeding the fire, found means to cut through their log prison also, and to escape unpunished. When this news began to circulate through the village, blended with the fate of Jotham, and the exaggerated and tortured reports of the events on the hill, the popular opinion was freely expressed, as to the propriety of seizing such of the fugitives as re-mained within reach. Men talked of the cave, as a secret receptacle of guilt; and, as the rumour of ores and metals found its way into the confused medley of conjectures, counterfeiting, and every thing else that was wicked and dangerous to the peace of society, suggested themselves to the busy fancies of the populace.

While the public mind was in this feverish state, it was hinted that the wood had been set on fire by Edwards and the Leather-stocking, and that, consequently, they alone were responsible for the damages. This opinion soon gained ground, being most circulated by those who, by their own heedlessness, had caused the evil; and there was one irre-sistible burst of the common sentiment, that an attempt should be made to punish the offenders. Richard was by no means deaf to this appeal, and by noon he set about in ear-nest, to see the laws executed.

Several stout young men were selected, and taken apart with an appearance of secrecy, where they received some im-portant charge from the Sheriff, immediately under the eyes, but far removed from the ears, of all in the village. Possessed with a knowledge of their duty, these youths hurried into the hills, with a bustling manner, as if the fate of the world depended on their diligence, and, at the same time, with an air of mystery, as great as if they were engaged on secret matters of the state.

At twelve precisely, a drum beat the "long roll" before the "Bold Dragoon," and Richard appeared, accompanied by Captain Hollister, who was clad in his vestments as com-mander of the "Templeton Light-Infantry," when the former demanded of the latter the aid of the posse comitatus, in enforcing the laws of the country. We have not room to re-cord the speeches of the two gentlemen on this occasion, but they are preserved in the columns of the little blue news-paper, which is yet to be found on file, and are said to be highly creditable to the legal formula of one of the parties, and to the military precision of the other. Every thing had been previously arranged, and as the red-coated drummer continued to roll out his clattering notes, some five-and-

twenty privates appeared in the ranks, and arranged themselves in order of battle.

As this corps was composed of volunteers, and was commanded by a man who had passed the first five-and-thirty
years of his life in camps and garrisons, it was the nonpareil
of military science in that country, and was confidently pronounced, by the judicious part of the Templeton community, to be equal in skill and appearance to any troops in
the known world; in physical endowments they were, certainly, much superior. To this assertion there were but three
dissenting voices, and one dissenting opinion. The opinion
belonged to Marmaduke, who, however, saw no necessity
for its promulgation. Of the voices, one, and that a pretty
loud one, came from the spouse of the commander himself,
who frequently reproached her husband for condescending
to lead such an irregular band of warriors, after he had filled
the honourable station of sergeant-major to a dashing
corps of Virginian cavalry through much of the recent war.

Another of these skeptical sentiments was invariably expressed by Mr. Pump, whenever the company paraded, generally in some such terms as these, which were uttered with
that sort of meekness that a native of the island of our fore-
fathers is apt to assume, when he condescends to praise the
customs or characters of her truant progeny—

"It's mayhap that they knows sum'mat about loading and
firing, d'ye see; but as for working ship! why a corporal's
guard of the Boadishey's marines would back and fill on
their quarters in such a manner as to surround and capti-
vate them all in half a glass." As there was no one to deny
this assertion, the marines of the Boadicea were held in a
corresponding degree of estimation.

The third unbeliever was Monsieur Le Quoi, who merely
whispered to the sheriff, that the corps was one of the finest
he had ever seen, second only to the Mousquetaires of Le
Bon Louis! However, as Mrs. Hollister thought there was
something like actual service in the present appearances,
and was, in consequence, too busily engaged with certain
preparations of her own, to make her comments; as Benjamin was absent, and Monsieur Le Quoi too happy to find

fault with any thing, the corps escaped criticism and comparison altogether on this momentous day, when they certainly had greater need of self-confidence, than on any other previous occasion. Marmaduke was said to be again closeted with Mr. Van der School, and no interruption was offered to the movements of the troops. At two o'clock precisely the corps shouldered arms, beginning on the right wing, next to the veteran, and carrying the motion through to the left with great regularity. When each musket was quietly fixed in its proper situation, the order was given to wheel to the left, and march. As this was bringing raw troops, at once, to face their enemy, it is not to be supposed that the manoeuvre was executed with their usual accuracy, but as the music struck up the inspiring air of Yankee-doodle, and Richard, accompanied by Mr. Doolittle, preceded the troops boldly down the street, Captain Hollister led on, with his head elevated to forty-five degrees, with a little, low cocked hat, perched on its crown, carrying a tremendous dragoon sabre at a poise, and trailing at his heels a huge steel scabbard, that had war in its very clattering. There was a good deal of difficulty in getting all the platoons (there were six) to look the same way; but, by the time they reached the defile of the bridge, the troops were in excellent order. In this manner they marched up the hill to the summit of the mountain, no other alteration taking place in the disposition of the forces, excepting that a mutual complaint was made by the sheriff and the magistrate, of a failure in wind, which gradually brought these gentlemen to the rear. It will be unnecessary to detail the minute movements that succeeded. We shall briefly say, that the scouts came in and reported, that, so far from retreating, as had been anticipated, the fugitives had evidently gained a knowledge of the attack, and were fortifying for a desperate resistance. This intelligence certainly made a material change, not only in the plans of the leaders, but in the countenances of the soldiery also. The men looked at one another with serious faces, and Hiram and Richard began to consult together, apart.

At this juncture, they were joined by Billy Kirby, who

came along the highway, with his axe under his arm, as much in advance of his team as Captain Hollister had been of his troops in the ascent. The wood-chopper was amazed at the military array, but the sheriff eagerly availed himself of this powerful reinforcement, and commanded his assistance in putting the laws in force. Billy held Mr. Jones in too much deference to object; and it was finally arranged that he should be the bearer of a summons to the garrison to surrender, before they proceeded to extremities. The troops now divided, one party being led by the captain, over the Vision, and were brought in on the left of the cave, while the remainder advanced upon its right, under the orders of the lieutenant. Mr. Jones and Dr. Todd, for the surgeon was in attendance also, appeared on the platform of rock, immediately over the heads of the garrison, though out of their sight. Hiram thought this approaching too near, and he therefore accompanied Kirby along the side of the hill, to within a safe distance of the fortifications, where he took shelter behind a tree. Most of the men discovered a wonderful accuracy of eye in bringing some object in range between them and their enemy, and the only two of the besiegers, who were left in plain sight of the besieged, were Captain Hollister on one side, and the wood-chopper on the other. The veteran stood up boldly to the front, supporting his heavy sword, in one undeviating position, with his eye fixed firmly on his enemy, while the huge form of Billy was placed in that kind of quiet repose, with either hand thrust into his bosom, bearing his axe under his right arm, which permitted him, like his own oxen, to rest standing. So far, not a word had been exchanged between the belligerents. The besieged had drawn together a pile of black logs and branches of trees which they had formed into a chevaux-de-frize, making a little circular abbatis in front of the entrance to the cave. As the ground was steep and slippery in every direction around the place, and Benjamin appeared behind the works on one side, and Natty on the other, the arrangement was no means contemptible, especially as the front was sufficiently guarded by the difficulty of the approach.

By this time, Kirby had received his orders, and he advanced cooly along the mountain, picking his way with the same indifference as if he were pursuing his ordinary business. When he was within a hundred feet of the works, the long and much dreaded rifle of the Leather-stocking was seen issuing from the parapet, and his voice cried aloud—

"Keep off! Billy Kirby, keep off! I wish ye no harm; but if a man of ye all comes a step nigher, there'll be blood spilt a-twixt us. God forgive the one that draws it first; but so it must be."

"Come, old chap," said Billy, good naturedly, "Don't be crabbed, but hear what a man has got to say. I've no consarn in the business, only to see right 'twixt man and man; and I don't kear the valie of a beetle-ring which gets the better; but there's Squire Doolittle, out yonder behind the beech sapling, he has invited me to come in and ask you to give up to the law—that's all."

"I see the varmint! I see his clothes!" cried the indignant Natty; "and if he'll only show so much flesh as will bury a rifle bullet, thirty to the pound, I'll make him feel me. Go away, Billy, I bid ye; you know my aim, and I bear you no malice."

"You over calkilate your aim, Natty," said the other, as he stepped behind a pine that stood near him, "If you think to shoot a man through a tree with a three foot but. I can lay this tree right across you, in ten minutes, by any man's watch, and in less time, too; so be civil—I want no more than what's right."

There was a simple seriousness in the countenance of Natty, that showed he was much in earnest; but it was, also, evident that he was reluctant to shed human blood. He answered the vaunt of the wood-chopper, by saying—

"I know you drop a tree where you will, Billy Kirby; but if you show a hand, or an arm, in doing it, there'll be bones to be set, and blood to stanch, I tell you. If it's only to get into the cave that ye want, wait till a two hour's sun, and you may enter it in welcome; but come in now you shall not. There's one dead body, already, lying on the cold rocks, and there's another in which the life can hardly be said to stay. If you will come in, there'll be dead without as well as within."

The wood-chopper stept out fearlessly from his cover, and cried—

"That's fair; and what's fair is right. He wants you to stop till it's two hours to sun-down; and I see reason in the thing. A man can give up when he's wrong, if you don't crowd him too hard; but you crowd a man, and he gets to be like a stubborn ox—the more you beat, the worse he kicks."

The sturdy notions of independence maintained by Billy, neither suited the emergency, nor the impatience of Mr. Jones, who was burning with a desire to examine the hidden mysteries of the cave. He therefore interrupted this amicable dialogue with his own voice.

"I command you, Nathaniel Bumppo, by my authority, to surrender your person to the law," he cried. "And I command you, gentlemen, to aid me in performing my duty. Benjamin Penguillan, I arrest you, and order you to follow me to the jail of the county, by virtue of this warrant."

"I'd follow ye, Squire Dickens," said Benjamin, removing the pipe from his mouth, (for during the whole scene the ex major-domo had been very composedly smoking,) "Ay! I'd sail in your wake, sir, to the end of the world, if-so-be that there was such a place, which there isn't, seeing that it's round. Now mayhap, Master Hollister, having lived all your life on shore, you isn't acquainted that the world, d'ye-see—"

"Surrender!" interrupted the veteran, in a voice that startled his hearers, and which actually caused his own forces to recoil several paces; "Surrender, Benjamin Pengullum, or expect no quarter."

"Damn your quarter," said Benjamin, rising from the log on which he was seated, and taking a squint along the barrel of the swivel, which had been brought on the hill, during the night, and now formed the means of defence on his side of the works. "Look you, Master, or Captain thof I questions if ye know the name of a rope, except the one that's to hang ye, there's no need of singing out, just as if ye was hailing a deaf man on a top-gallant-yard. Mayhap you think you've got my true name in your sheepskin; but what British sailor finds it worth while to sail in these seas, without a sham on his stern, in case of need, d'ye-see. If you call me Penguillan, you calls me by the name of the man on whose land, d'ye-see, I hove into daylight; and he was a gentleman and that's more than my worst enemy will say of any of the family of Benjamin Stubbs."

"Send the warrant round to me, and I'll put in an alias," cried Hiram, from behind his cover.

"Put in a jackass, and you'll put in yourself, Mister Doobut-little," shouted Benjamin, who kept squinting along his little iron tube, with great steadiness.

"I give you but one moment to yield in," cried Richard. "Benjamin! Benjamin! This is not the gratitude I expected from you."

"I tell you, Richard Jones," said Natty, who dreaded the sheriff's influence over his comrade; "though the canister the gal brought, be lost, there's powder enough in the cave to lift the rock you stand on. I'll take off my roof, if you don't hold your peace."

"I think it beneath the dignity of my office to parley further with the prisoners," the sheriff observed to his companion, while they both retired with a precipitancy that Captain Hollister mistook for the signal to advance.

"Charge baggonet!" shouted the veteran; "march!"

Although this signal was certainly expected, it took the assailed a little by surprise, and the veteran approached the works, crying, "courage, my brave lads! give them no quarter unless they surrender," and struck a furious blow upwards with his sabre that would have divided the steward in moieties, by subjecting him to the process of decapitation, but for the fortunate interference of the muzzle of the swivel. As it was, the gun was dismounted at the critical moment that Benjamin was applying his pipe to the priming, and in consequence, some five or six dozen of rifle bullets were projected into the air, in, nearly, a perpendicular line. Philosophy teaches us that the atmosphere will not retain lead; and two pounds of the metal moulded into bullets, of thirty to the pound, after describing an ellipsis in their journey, returned to the earth, rattling among the branches of the trees directly over the heads of the troops stationed in the rear of their captain. Much of the success of an attack made by irregular soldiers, depends on which way they are first got in motion. In the present instance, it was retrograde, and in less than a minute after the loud bellowing report of the swivel among the rocks and caverns, the whole weight of the attack, from the left, rested on the prowess of the single arm of the veteran. Benjamin received a severe contusion from the recoil of his gun, which produced a short stupor, during which period the ex-steward was prostrate on the ground. Capt. Hollister availed himself of this circumstance to scramble over the breast-work and obtain a footing in the bastion—for such was the nature of the fortress, as connected with the cave. The moment the veteran found himself within the works of his enemy, he rushed to the edge of the fortification, and waving his sabre over his head, shouted—

"Victory! come on, my brave boys, the work's our own!"

All this was perfectly military, and was such an example as a gallant officer was in some measure bound to exhibit to his men; but the outcry was the unlucky cause of turning the tide of success. Natty, who had been keeping a vigilant eye on the wood-chopper, and the enemy immediately before him, wheeled at this alarm, and was appalled at beholding his comrade on the ground, and the veteran standing on his own bulwark, giving forth the cry of victory! The muzzle of the long rifle was turned instantly towards the captain. There was a moment when the life of the old soldier was in great jeopardy; but the object to shoot at was both too large and too near for the Leather-stocking, who, instead of pulling his trigger, applied the gun to the rear of his enemy, and by a powerful shove, sent him outside of the works with much greater rapidity than he had entered them. The spot on which Capt. Hollister alighted was directly in front, where, as his feet touched the ground, so steep and slippery was the side of the mountain, it seemed to recede from under them. His motion was wonderfully swift, and so irregular, as utterly to confuse the faculties of the old soldier. During its continuance, he supposed himself to be mounted and charging through the ranks of his enemy. At every tree he made a blow, of course, as at a foot-soldier; and just as he was making the cut "St. George" at a half-burnt sapling, he landed in the highway, and, to his utter amazement, at the feet of his own spouse. When Mrs. Hollister, who was toiling up the hill, followed by at least twenty curious boys, leaning with one hand on the staff with which she ordinarily walked, and bearing in the other an empty bag, witnessed this exploit of her husband, indignation immediately got the better not only of her religion, but of her philosophy.

"Why, Sargeant! is it flying ye are?" she cried—"That I should live to see a husband of mine turn his back to the inimy! and sich a one! Here have I been telling the b'ys as we come along, all about the saige of Yorrektown, and how ye was hurted; and how ye'd be acting the same ag'in the day; and I mate ye retrating jist as the first gun is fired. Och! I may trow away the bag! for if there's plunder 'twill not be the wife of sich as yeerself that will be privileged to be getting the same. They do say too, there is a power of goold and silver in the place—the Lord forgive me for setting my heart on sich worreldly things; but what falls in the battle, there's Scripter for believing it the just property of the victor."

"Retreating!" exclaimed the amazed veteran; "where's my horse? he has been shot under me—I—"

"Is the man mad!" interrupted his wife—"divil the horse do ye own, sargeant, and yee're nothing but a shabby captain of malaishy. Och! if the ra'al captain was here, 'tis the other way ye'd be riding, dear, or you would not follow your lader!"

While this worthy couple were thus discussing events, the battle began to rage more violently than ever, above them. When the Leather-stocking saw his enemy fairly under head-way, as Benjamin would express it, he gave his attention again to the right wing of the assailants. It would have been easy for Kirby, with his powerful frame, to have seized the moment to scale the bastion, and with his great strength, to have sent both its defenders in pursuit of the veteran; but hostility appeared to be the passion that the wood-chopper indulged the least in, at that moment, for, in a voice that was heard even by the retreating left wing, he shouted,

"Hurrah! well done, captain! keep it up! how he handles his bush hook! he makes nothing of a sapling!" and such other encouraging exclamations to the flying veteran, until, overcome by his mirth, the good-natured fellow seated himself on the ground, kicking the earth with delight, and giving vent to peal after peal of laughter.

Natty stood all this time in a menacing attitude, with his rifle pointed over his breast-work, watching with a quick and cautious eye the least movement of the assailants. The outcry unfortunately tempted the ungovernable curiosity of Hiram to take a peep from behind his cover at the state of the battle. Though this evolution was performed with great caution, in protecting his front, he left, like many a better commander, his rear exposed to the attacks of his enemy. Mr. Doolittle belonged physically to a class of his countrymen, to whom nature has denied, in their formation, the use of curved lines. Every thing about him was either straight or angular. But his tailor was a woman who worked like a regimental contractor, by a set of rules that gave the same configuration to the whole human species. Consequently, when Mr. Doolittle leaned forward in the manner described, a loose drapery appeared behind the tree, at which the rifle of Natty was pointed with the quickness of lightning. A less experienced man would have aimed at the flowing robe, which hung like a festoon half way to the earth; but the Leather-stocking knew both the man and his female tailor better, and when the smart report of the rifle was heard, Kirby, who watched the whole manoeuvre in breathless expectation, saw the bark fly from the beech, and the cloth at some distance above the loose folds, wave at the same instant. No battery was ever unmasked with more promptitude than Hiram advanced, from behind the tree at this summons.

He made two or three steps, with great precision, to the front, and, placing one hand on the afflicted part stretched forth the other, with a menacing air, towards Natty, and cried aloud—

"Gawl darn ye! this shan't be settled so easy; I'll follow it up from the 'common pleas' to the 'court of errors.'"

Such a shocking imprecation, from the mouth of so orderly a man as Squire Doolittle, with the fearless manner in which he exposed himself, together with, perhaps, the knowledge that Natty's rifle was unloaded, encouraged the troops in the rear, who gave a loud shout, and fired a volley into the tree-tops, after the contents of the swivel. Animated by their own noise, the men now rushed on in earnest, and Billy Kirby, who thought the joke, good as it was, had gone far enough, was in the act of scaling the works, when Judge Temple appeared on the opposite side, exclaiming—

"Silence and peace! why do I see murder and bloodshed attempted! is not the law sufficient to protect itself, that armed bands must be gathered, as in rebellion and war, to see justice performed!"

"'Tis the posse comitatus," shouted the Sheriff, from a distant rock, "who"—

"Say rather a posse of demons. I command the peace."—

"Hold! shed not blood!" cried a voice from the top of the Vision—"Hold! For the sake of Heaven, fire no more! all shall be yielded! you shall enter the cave!"

Amazement produced the desired effect. Natty, who had reloaded his piece, quietly seated himself on the logs, and rested his head on his hand, while the "Light Infantry" ceased their military movements, and waited the issue in mute suspense.

In less than a minute Edwards came rushing down the hill, followed by Major Hartmann with a velocity that was surprising for his years. They reached the terrace in an instant, from which the youth led the way, by the hollow in the rock, to the mouth of the cave, into which they both entered; leaving all without silent and gazing after them with astonishment.

· Chapter XL ·

I am dumb.
Were you the Doctor, and I knew you not!
SHAKSPEARE

During the five or six minutes that elapsed before the youth and Major reappeared, Judge Temple and the Sheriff, together with most of the volunteers, ascended to the terrace, where the latter began to express their conjectures of the result, and to recount their individual services in the conflict. But the sight of the peace-makers, ascending the ravine, shut every mouth.

On a rude chair, covered with undressed deer-skins, they supported a human being, whom they seated carefully and respectfully in the midst of the assembly. His head was covered by long, smooth locks, of the colour of snow. His dress, which was studiously neat and clean, was composed of such fabrics as none but the wealthiest classes wear, but was threadbare and patched; and on his feet were placed a pair of moccasins, ornamented in the best manner of Indian ingenuity. The outlines of his face were grave and dignified, though his vacant eye, which opened and turned slowly to the faces of those around him in unmeaning looks, too surely announced that the period had arrived, when age brings the mental imbecility of childhood.

Natty had followed the supporters of this unexpected object to the top of the cave, and took his station at a little distance behind him, leaning on his rifle, in the midst of his pursuers, with a fearlessness which showed that heavier interest than those which affected himself were to be decided. Major Hartmann placed himself beside the aged man, uncovered, with his whole soul beaming through those eyes which so commonly danced with frolic and humour. Edwards rested with one hand familiarly, but affectionately, on the chair, though his heart was swelling with emotions that denied him utterance.

All eyes were gazing intently; but each tongue continued mute. At length the decrepit stranger, turning his vacant looks from face to face, made a feeble attempt to rise, while a faint smile crossed his wasted face, like an habitual effort at courtesy, as he said, in a hollow, tremulous voice—

"Be pleased to be seated, gentlemen. The council will open immediately. Each one who loves a good and virtuous king, will wish to see these colonies continue loyal. Be seated—I pray you, be seated, gentlemen. The troops shall halt for the night."

"This is the wandering of insanity!" said Marmaduke; "who will explain this scene?"

"No sir," said Edwards, firmly, " 'tis only the decay of nature; who is answerable for its pitiful condition, remains to be shown."

"Will the gentlemen dine with us, my son?" said the old stranger, turning to a voice that he both knew and loved. "Order a repast suitable for his Majesty's officers. You know we have the best of game always at our command."

"Who is this man?" asked Marmaduke, in a hurried voice, in which the dawnings of conjecture united with interest to put the question.

"This man!" returned Edwards calmly, his voice, however, gradually rising as he proceeded; "this man, sir, whom you behold hid in caverns, and deprived of every thing that can make life desirable, was once the companion and counsellor of those who ruled your country. This man, whom you see, helpless and feeble, was once a warrior, so brave and fearless, that even the intrepid natives gave him the name of the Fire-eater. This man, whom you now see destitute of even the ordinary comfort of a cabin in which to shelter his head, was once the owner of great riches; and, Judge Temple, he was the rightful proprietor of this very soil on which we stand. This man was the father of"—

"This, then," cried Marmaduke, with powerful emotion, "this, then, is the lost Major Effingham!"

"Emphatically so," said the youth, fixing a piercing eye on the other.

"And you! and you!" continued the Judge articulating with difficulty.

"I am his grandson."

A minute passed in profound silence. All eyes were fixed on the speakers, and even the old German appeared to wait the issue in deep anxiety. But the moment of agitation soon passed. Marmaduke raised his head from his bosom, where it had sunk, not in shame, but in devout mental thanksgivings, and, as large tears fell over his fine manly face, he grasped the hand of the youth warmly, and said—

"Oliver, I forgive all thy harshness—all thy suspicions. I now see it all. I forgive thee every thing, but suffering this aged man to dwell in such a place, when not only my habitation, but my fortune, were at his and thy command."

"He's true as ter steel!" shouted Major Hartmann; "titn't I tell't you, lat, dat Marmaduke Temple vast a friend dat woult never fail in ter dime as of neet!"

"It is true, Judge Temple, that my opinions of your conduct have been staggered by what this worthy gentleman has told me. When I found it impossible to convey my grandfather back whence the enduring love of this old man brought him, without detection and exposure, I went to the Mohawk in quest of one of his former comrades, in whose justice I had dependence. He is your friend, Judge Temple, but if what he says be true, both my father and myself may have judged you harshly."

"You name your father!" said Marmaduke, tenderly— "Was he, indeed, lost in the packet?"

"He was. He had left me, after several years of fruitless application and comparative poverty, in Nova-Scotia, to obtain the compensation for his losses, which the British commissioners had at length awarded. After spending a year in England, he was returned to Halifax, on his way to a government, to which he had been appointed, in the West-Indies, intending to go to the place where my grandfather had sojourned during and since the war, and take him with us."

"But, thou!" said Marmaduke, with powerful interest; "I had thought that thou hadst perished with him."

A flush passed over the cheeks of the young man, who gazed about him at the wondering faces of the volunteers, and continued silent. Marmaduke turned to the veteran captain, who just then rejoined his command, and said—

"March thy soldiers back again, and dismiss them; the zeal of the sheriff has much mistaken his duty. Dr. Todd, I will thank you to attend to the injury which Hiram Doolittle has received in this untoward affair. Richard, you will oblige me by sending up the carriage to the top of the hill. Benjamin, return to your duty in my family."

Unwelcome as these orders were to most of the auditors, the suspicion that they had somewhat exceeded the wholesome restraints of the law, and the habitual respect with which all the commands of the Judge were received, induced a prompt compliance.

When they were gone, and the rock was left to the parties most interested in an explanation, Marmaduke, pointing to the aged Major Effingham, said to his grandson—

"Had we not better remove thy parent from this open place, until my carriage can arrive?"

"Pardon me, sir, the air does him good, and he has taken it whenever there was no dread of a discovery. I know not how to act, Judge Temple; ought I, can I, suffer Major Effingham to become an inmate of your family?"

"Thou shalt be thyself the judge," said Marmaduke. "Thy father was my early friend. He intrusted his fortune to my care. When we separated, he had such confidence in me, that he wished no security, no evidence of the trust, even had there been time or convenience for exacting it.—This thou hast heard?"

"Most truly, sir," said Edwards, or rather Effingham, as we must now call him, with a bitter smile.

"We divided in politics. If the cause of this country was successful, the trust was sacred with me, for none knew of thy father's interest. If the crown still held its sway, it would be easy to restore the property of so loyal a subject as Col. Effingham.—Is not this plain?"

"The premises are good, sir," continued the youth, with the same incredulous look as before.

"Listen—listen, poy," said the German. "Dere is not a hair as of ter rogue in ter het of ter Tchooge."

"We all know the issue of the struggle," continued Marmaduke, disregarding both; "Thy grandfather was left in Connecticut, regularly supplied by thy father with the means of such a subsistence as suited his wants. This I well knew, though I never had intercourse with him, even in our happiest days. Thy father retired with the troops to prosecute his claims on England. At all events, his losses must be great, for his real estates were sold, and I became the lawful purchaser. It was not unnatural to wish that he might have no bar to his just recovery?"

"There was none, but the difficulty of providing for so many claimants."

"But there would have been one, and an insuperable one, had I announced to the world that I held these estates, multiplied, by the times and my industry, a hundred fold in value, only as his trustee. Thou knowest that I supplied him with considerable sums, immediately after the war."

"You did, until"—

"My letters were returned unopened. Thy father had much of thy own spirit, Oliver; he was sometimes hasty and rash." The Judge continued, in a self-condemning manner—"Perhaps my fault lies the other way; I may possibly look too far ahead, and calculate too deeply. It certainly was a severe trial to allow the man, whom I most loved, to think ill of me for seven years, in order that he might honestly apply for his just remunerations. But had he opened my last letters, thou wouldst have learnt the whole truth. Those I sent him to England, by what my agent writes me, he did read. He died, Oliver, knowing all. He died my friend, and I thought thou hadst died with him."

"Our poverty would not permit us to pay for two passages," said the youth, with the extraordinary emotion with which he ever alluded to the degraded state of his family; "I was left in the Province to wait for his return, and when the sad news of his loss reached me, I was nearly pennyless."

"And what didst thou, boy?" asked Marmaduke, in a faltering voice.

"I took my passage here in search of my grandfather; for I well knew that his resources were gone, with the half-pay of my father. On reaching his abode, I learnt that he had left it in secret; though the reluctant hireling, who deserted him in his poverty, owned to my urgent entreaties, that he believed he had been carried away by an old man, who had formerly been his servant. I knew at once it was Natty, for my father often"——

"Was Natty a servant to thy grandfather?" exclaimed the Judge.

"Of that too were you ignorant!" said the youth, in evident surprise.

"How should I know it? I never met the Major, nor was the name of Bumppo ever mentioned to me. I knew him only as a man of the woods, and one who lived by hunting. Such men are too common to excite surprise."

"He was reared in the family of my grandfather; served him for many years during their campaigns at the west, where he became attached to the woods; and he was left here as a kind of locum tenens on the lands that old Mohegan (whose life my grandfather once saved) induced the Delawares to grant him, when they admitted him as an honorary member of their tribe."

"This, then, is thy Indian blood?"

"I have no other," said Edwards, smiling;—"Major Effingham was adopted as the son of Mohegan, who at that time was the greatest man in his nation; and my father, who visited those people when a boy, received the name of the Eagle from them, on account of the shape of his face, as I understand. They have extended his title to me. I have no other Indian blood or breeding; though I have seen the hour, Judge Temple, when I could wish that such had been my lineage and education."

"Proceed with thy tale," said Marmaduke.

"I have but little more to say, sir. I followed to the lake where I had so often been told that Natty dwelt, and found him maintaining his old master in secret; for even he could not bear to exhibit to the world, in his poverty and dotage, a man whom a whole people once looked up to with respect."

"And what did you?"

"What did I! I spent my last penny in purchasing a rifle, clad myself in a coarse garb, and learned to be a hunter by the side of Leather-stocking. You know the rest, Judge Temple."

"Ant vere vast olt Fritz Hartmann!" said the German, reproachfully; "didst never hear a name as of olt Fritz Hartmann from ter mout of ter fader, lat?"

"I may have been mistaken, gentlemen," returned the youth; "but I had pride, and could not submit to such an exposure as this day even has reluctantly brought to light. I had plans that might have been visionary; but, should my parent survive till autumn, I purposed taking him with me to the city, where we have distant relatives, who must have learnt to forget the Tory by this time. He decays rapidly," he continued, mournfully, "and must soon lie by the side of old Mohegan."

The air being pure, and the day fine, the party continued conversing on the rock, until the wheels of Judge Temple's carriage were heard clattering up the side of the mountain, during which time the conversation was maintained with deep interest, each moment clearing up some doubtful action, and lessening the antipathy of the youth to Marmaduke. He no longer objected to the removal of his grandfather, who displayed a childish pleasure when he found himself seated once more in a carriage. When placed in the ample hall of the Mansion-house, the eyes of the aged veteran turned slowly to the objects in the apartment, and a look like the dawn of intellect would, for moments, flit across his features, when he invariably offered some useless courtesies to those near him, wandering, painfully, in his subjects. The exercise and the change soon produced an exhaustion, that caused them to remove him to his bed, where he lay for hours evidently sensible of the change in his comforts, and exhibiting that mortifying picture of human nature, which too plainly shows that the propensities of the animal continu even after the nobler part of the creature appears to have vanished.

Until his parent was placed comfortably in bed, with Natty seated at his side, Effingham did not quit him. He then obeyed a summons to the library of the Judge, where he found the latter, with Major Hartmann, waiting for him.

"Read this paper, Oliver," said Marmaduke to him, as he entered, "and thou wilt find that, so far from intending thy family wrong during life, it has been my care to provide that justice should be done at even a later day."

The youth took the paper, which his first glance told him was the will of the Judge. Hurried and agitated as he was, he discovered that the date corresponded with the time of the unusual depression of Marmaduke. As he proceeded, his eyes began to moisten, and the hand which held the instrument shook violently.

The will commenced with the usual forms, spun out by the ingenuity of Mr. Van der School; but after this subject was fairly exhausted, the pen of Marmaduke became plainly visible. In clear, distinct, manly, and even eloquent language, he recounted his obligations to Colonel Effingham, the nature of their connexion, and the circumstances in which they separated. He then proceeded to relate the motives for his long silence, mentioning, however, large sums that he had forwarded to his friend, which had been returned, with the letters unopened. After this, he spoke of his search for the grandfather, who had unaccountably disappeared, and his fears that the direct heir of the trust was buried in the ocean with his father.

After, in short, recounting in a clear narrative, the events which our readers must now be able to connect, he proceeded to make a fair and exact statement of the sums left in his care by Col. Effingham. A devise of his whole estate to certain responsible trustees followed; to hold the same for the benefit, in equal moieties, of his daughter, on one part, and of Oliver Effingham, formerly a major in the army of Great Britain, and of his son Edward Effingham, and of his son Edward Oliver Effingham, or to the survivor of them, and the descendants of such survivor, for ever, on the other part. The trust was to endure until 1810, when, if no person appeared, or could be found, after sufficient notice, to claim the moiety so devised, then a certain sum, calculating the principal and interest of his debt to Col. Effingham, was to be paid to the heirs at law of the Effingham family, and the bulk of his estate was to be conveyed in fee to his daughter, or her heirs.

The tears fell from the eyes of the young man, as he read this undeniable testimony of the good faith of Marmaduke, and his bewildered gaze was still fastened on the paper, when a sweet voice, that thrilled on every nerve, spoke, near him, saying,

"Do you yet doubt us, Oliver?"

"I have never doubted *you!*" cried the youth, recovering his recollection and his voice, as he sprung to seize the hand of Elizabeth; "no, not one moment has my faith in you wavered."

"And my father—"

"God bless him!"

"I thank thee, my son," said the Judge, exchanging a warm pressure of the hand with the youth; "but we have both erred; thou hast been too hasty, and I have been too slow. One half of my estates shall be thine as soon as they can be conveyed to thee; and if what my suspicions tell me, be true, I suppose the other must follow speedily." He took the hand which he held, and united it with that of his daughter, and motioned towards the door to the Major.

"I telt you vat, gal!" said the old German, good humouredly; "if I vast, ast I vast, ven I servit mit his grantfader on ter lakes, ter lazy tog shouldn't vin ter prize as for nottin."

"Come, come, old Fritz," cried the Judge; "you are seventy, not seventeen; Richard waits for you with a bowl o: egg-nog, in the hall."

"Richart! ter duyvel!" exclaimed the other, hastening ou of the room; "he makes ter nog ast for ter horse. I vilt shov ter sheriff mit my own hants! Ter duyvel! I pelieve he sweet ens mit ter yankee melasses!"

Marmaduke smiled and nodded affectionately at the young couple, and closed the door after him. If any of our readers expect that we are going to open it again, for their gratification, they will soon find themselves in a mistake.

The tête-à-tête continued for a very unreasonable time; how long we shall not say; but it was ended by six o'clock in the evening, for at that hour Monsieur Le Quoi made his appearance, agreeably to the appointment of the preceding day, and claimed the ear of Miss Temple. He was admitted; when he made an offer of his hand, with much suavity, together with his "amis beeg and leet', his père, his mère, and his sucre-boosh." Elizabeth might, possibly, have previously entered into some embarrassing and binding engagements with Oliver, for she declined the tender of all, in terms as polite, though perhaps a little more decided, than those in which they were made.

The Frenchman soon joined the German and the Sheriff in the hall, who compelled him to take a seat with them at the table, where, by the aid of punch, wine, and egg-nog, they soon extracted from the complaisant Mr. Le Quoi the nature of his visit. It was evident that he had made the offer, as a duty which a well-bred man owed to a lady in such a retired place, before he left the country, and that his feelings were but very little, if at all, interested in the matter. After a few potations, the waggish pair persuaded the exhilarated Frenchman that there was an inexcusable partiality in offering to one lady, and not extending a similar courtesy to another. Consequently, about nine, Monsieur Le Quoi sallied forth to the Rectory, on a similar mission to Miss Grant, which proved as successful as his first effort in love.

When he returned to the Mansion-house, at ten, Richard and the Major were still seated at the table. They attempted to persuade the Gaul that he should next try Remarkable Pettibone. But, though he was stimulated by mental excitement and wine, two hours of abstruse logic were thrown away on this subject; for he declined their advice, with a pertinacity truly astonishing in so polite a man.

When Benjamin lighted Monsieur Le Quoi from the door, he said, at parting—

"If-so-be, Mounsheer, you'd run alongside Mistress Pretty-bones, as the Squire Dickens was bidding ye, 'tis my notion you'd have been grappled; in which case, d'ye see, you mought have been troubled in swinging clear again in a handsome manner; for thof Miss 'Lizzy and the parson's young'un be tidy little vessels, that shoot by a body on a wind, Mistress Remarkable is sum'mat of a galliot fashion; when you once takes 'em in tow, they doesn't like to be cast off again."

Chapter XLI

Yes, sweep ye on!—We will not leave,
For them who triumph, those who grieve.
With that armada gay
Be laughter loud, and jocund shout—
——But with that skiff
Abides the minstrel tale.

LORD OF THE ISLES

The events of our tale carry us through the summer; and, after making nearly the circle of the year, we must conclude our labours in the delightful month of October. Many important incidents had, however, occurred in the intervening period; a few of which it may be necessary to recount.

The two principal were, the marriage of Oliver and Elizabeth, and the death of Major Effingham. They both took place early in September; and the former preceded the latter only by a few days. The old man passed away like the last glimmering of a taper; and though his death cast a melancholy over the family, grief could not follow such an end.

One of the chief concerns of Marmaduke was to reconcile the even conduct of a magistrate, with the course that his feelings dictated to the criminals. The day succeeding the discovery at the cave, however, Natty and Benjamin re-entered the jail peaceably, where they continued, well fed and comfortable, until the return of an express to Albany, who brought the Governor's pardon to the Leather-stocking. In the mean time, proper means were employed to satisfy Hiram for the assaults on his person; and on the same day, the two comrades issued together into society again, with their characters not at all affected by their imprisonment.

Mr. Doolittle began to discover that neither his architec

ture, nor his law, was quite suitable to the growing wealth and intelligence of the settlement; and, after exacting the last cent that was attainable in his compromises, to use the language of the country, he "pulled up stakes," and proceeded further west, scattering his professional science and legal learning through the land; vestiges of both of which are to be discovered there even to the present hour.

Poor Jotham, whose life paid the forfeiture of his folly, acknowledged before he died, that his reasons for believing in a mine, were extracted from the lips of a sybil, who, by looking in a magic glass, was enabled to discover the hidden treasures of the earth. Such superstition was frequent in the new settlements; and after the first surprise was over, the better part of the community forgot the subject. But at the same time that it removed from the breast of Richard a lingering suspicion of the acts of the three hunters, it conveyed a mortifying lesson to him, which brought many quiet hours, in future, to his cousin Marmaduke. It may be remembered that the Sheriff confidently pronounced this to be no 'visionary' scheme, and that word was enough to shut his lips, at any time within the next ten years.

Monsieur Le Quoi, who has been introduced to our readers, because no picture of that country would be faithful without such a Gaul, found the island of Martinique, and his "sucre-boosh," in possession of the English; but Marmaduke, and his family, were much gratified in soon hearing that he had returned to his bureau, in Paris; where he afterwards issued yearly bulletins of his happiness, and of his gratitude to his friends in America.

With this brief explanation we must return to our narrative. Let the American reader imagine one of our mildest October mornings, when the sun seems a ball of silvery fire, and the elasticity of the air is felt while it is inhaled; imparting vigour and life to the whole system. The weather, neither too warm, nor too cold, but of that happy temperature which stirs the blood, without bringing the lassitude of spring.

It was on such a morning, about the middle of the month, that Oliver entered the hall, where Elizabeth was issuing her usual orders for the day, and requested her to join him in a short excursion to the lake-side. The tender melancholy in the manner of her husband, caught the attention of Elizabeth, who instantly abandoned her concerns, threw a light shawl across her shoulders, and concealing her raven hair under her gypsey, she took his arm, and submitted herself, without a question, to his guidance. They crossed the bridge, and had turned from the highway, along the margin of the lake, before a word was exchanged. Elizabeth well knew, by the direction they took, the object of their walk, and respected the feelings of her companion too much to indulge in untimely conversation. But when they gained the open fields, and her eye roamed over the placid lake, covered with wild fowl, already journeying from the great northern waters, to seek a warmer sun, but lingering to play in the limpid sheet of the Otsego, and to the sides of the mountain, which were gay with the thousand dies of autumn, as if to grace their bridal, the swelling heart of the young wife burst out in speech.

"This is not a time for silence, Oliver!" she said, clinging more fondly to his arm; "every thing in nature seems to speak the praises of the Creator; why should we, who have so much to be grateful for, be silent."

"Speak on," said her husband, smiling; "I love the sounds of your voice. You must anticipate our errand hither; I have told you my plans, how do you like them?"

"I must first see them," returned his wife. "But I have had my plans, too; it is time I should begin to divulge them."

"You! It is something for the comfort of my old friend Natty, I know."

"Certainly of Natty; but we have other friends besides the Leather-stocking, to serve. Do you forget Louisa, and her father?"

"No, surely; have I not given one of the best farms in the county to the good divine. As for Louisa, I should wish you to keep her always near us."

"You do," said Elizabeth, slightly compressing her lips; "but poor Louise may have other views for herself; she may wish to follow my example, and marry."

"I don't think it," said Effingham, musing a moment; "I really don't know any one hereabouts good enough for her."

"Perhaps not here; but there are other places besides Templeton, and other churches besides 'New St. Paul's.' "

"Churches, Elizabeth! you would not wish to lose Mr. Grant, surely! though simple, he is an excellent man. I shall never find another who has half the veneration for my orthodoxy. You would humble me from a saint to a very common sinner."

"It must be done, sir," returned the lady, with a half-concealed smile, "though it degrades you from an angel to a man."

"But you forget the farm."

"He can lease it, as others do. Besides, would you have a clergyman toil in the fields!"

"Where can he go? you forget Louisa."

"No, I do not forget Louisa," said Elizabeth, again compressing her beautiful lips. "You know, Effingham, that my father has told you that I ruled him, and that I should rule you. I am now about to exert my power."

"Any thing, any thing, dear Elizabeth, but not at the expense of us all; not at the expense of your friend."

"How do you know, sir, that it will be so much at the expense of my friend?" said the lady, fixing her eyes with a searching look on his countenance, where they met only the unsuspecting expression of manly regret.

"How do I know it! why, it is natural that she should regret us."

"It is our duty to struggle with our natural feelings," returned the lady; "and there is but little cause to fear that such a spirit as Louisa's will not effect it."

"But what is your plan?"

"Listen, and you shall know. My father has procured a call for Mr. Grant to one of the towns on the Hudson, where he can live more at his ease than in journeying through these woods; where he can spend the evening of his life in comfort and quiet; and where his daughter may meet with such society, and form such a connexion, as may be proper for one of her years and character."

"Why, Bess! you amaze me! I did not think you had been such a manager!"

"Oh! I manage more deeply than you imagine, sir," said the wife, archly smiling, again; "but it is my will, and it is your duty to submit,—for a time at least."

Effingham laughed; but as they approached the end of their walk, the subject was changed by common consent.

The place at which they arrived was the little spot of level ground where the cabin of the Leather-stocking had so long stood. Elizabeth found it entirely cleared of rubbish, and beautifully laid down in turf, by the removal of sods, which, in common with the surrounding country, had grown gay, under the influence of profuse showers, as if a second spring had passed over the land. This little place was surrounded by a circle of mason-work, and they entered by a small gate, near which, to the surprise of both, the rifle of Natty was leaning against the wall. Hector and the slut reposed on the grass by its side, as if conscious that, however altered, they were lying on ground, and were surrounded by objects, with which they were familiar. The hunter himself was stretched on the earth, before a head-stone of white marble, pushing aside with his fingers the long grass that had already sprung up from the luxuriant soil around its base, apparently to lay bare the inscription that was there engraven. By the side of this stone, which was a simple slab at the head of a grave, stood a rich monument, decorated with an urn, and ornamented tastefully with the chisel.

Oliver and Elizabeth approached the graves, with a light tread, unheard by the old hunter, whose sunburnt face was working with his feelings, and whose eyes twinkled as if something impeded their vision. After some little time, Natty raised himself slowly from the ground, and said aloud—

"Well, well—I'm bold to say it's all right! There's something that I suppose is reading; but I can't make any thing of it; though the pipe, and the tomahawk, and the moccasins, be pretty well—pretty well, for a man that, I dares to say, never seed 'ither of the things. Ah's me! there they lie, side by side, happy enough! Who will there be to put me in the 'arth, when my time comes!"

"When that unfortunate hour arrives, Natty, friends shall not be wanting to perform the last offices for you," said Oliver, a little touched at the hunter's soliloquy.

The old man turned, without manifesting any surprise, for he had got the Indian habits in this particular, and running his hand under the bottom of his nose, seemed to wipe away his sorrow with the action.

"You've come out to see the graves, children, have ye?" he said; "well, well, they're wholesome sights to young as well as old."

"I hope they are fitted to your liking," said Effingham; "no one has a better right than yourself to be consulted in the matter."

"Why, seeing that I an't used to fine graves," returned the old man, "it is but little matter consarning my taste. Ye laid the Major's head to the west, and Mohegan's to the east, did ye, lad?"

"At your request it was done."

"It's so best," said the hunter; "they thought they had to journey different ways, children; though there is One greater than all, who'll bring the just togeether ag'in at his own time, and who'll whiten the skin of a black-moor, and place him on a footing with princes."

"There is but little reason to doubt that," said Elizabeth, whose decided tones were changed to a soft, melancholy voice; "I trust we shall all meet again, and be happy together."

"Shall we, child! shall we!" exclaimed the hunter, with unusual fervour; "there's comfort in that thought, too. But before I go, I should like to know what 'tis you tell these people, that be flocking into the country like pigeons in the spring, of the old Delaware, and of the bravest white man that ever trod the hills."

Effingham and Elizabeth were surprised at the manner of the Leather-stocking, which was unusually impressive and solemn; but attributing it to the scene, the young man turned to the monument, and read aloud—

"Sacred to the memory of Oliver Effingham, Esquire, for-

merly a Major in his B. Majesty's 60th Foot; a soldier of tried
valour; a subject of chivalric loyalty; and a man of honesty.
To these virtues, he added the graces of a Christian. The
morning of his life was spent in honour, wealth, and power;
but its evening was obscured by poverty, neglect, and disease, which were alleviated only by the tender care of his
old, faithful, and upright friend and attendant, Nathaniel
Bumppo. His descendants rear this stone of the virtues of
the master, and to the enduring gratitude of the servant."

The Leather-stocking stared at the sound of his own name,
and a smile of joy illumined his wrinkled features, as he
said—

"And did ye say it, lad? have you then got the old man's
name cut in stone, by the side of his master's? God bless ye,
children! 'twas a kind thought, and kindness goes to the
heart as life shortens."

Elizabeth turned her back to the speakers, but the pure
cambric, that, contrasted to her dark eyes, attested the feelings of the youthful bride. Effingham made a fruitless effort
to speak before he succeeded in saying—

"It is there cut in plain marble; but it should have been
written in letters of gold!"

"Show me the name, boy," said Natty, with simple eagerness; "let me see my own name placed in such honour. 'Tis
a gin'rous gift to a man who leaves none of his name and family behind him in a country, where he has tarried so long."

Effingham guided his finger to the spot, and Natty followed the windings of the letters to the end, with deep interest, when he raised himself from the tomb, and said—

"I suppose it's all right, and it's kindly thought, and
kindly done! But what have ye put over the Red-skin?"

"You shall hear"—

"This stone is raised to the memory of an Indian Chief, of
the Delaware tribe, who was known by the several names of
John Mohegan; Mohican"—

"Mo-hee-can, lad; they call theirselves! 'he-can."

"Mohican; and Chingagook"—

" 'Gach, boy;—'gach-gook: Chingachgook; which, intarpreted, means Big-sarpent. The name should be set down right, for an Indian's name has always some meaning in it."

"I will see it altered," said Edwards. "He was the last of his people who continued to inhabit this country; and it may be said of him, emphatically, that his faults were those of an Indian, and his virtues those of a man."

"You never said a truer word, Mr. Oliver; ah's me! if you had know'd him as I did, in his prime, in that very battle, where, the old gentleman who sleeps by his side, sav'd his life, when them thieves, the Iriquois, had him at the stake, you'd have said all of that, and more too. I cut the thongs with this very hand, and gave him my own tomahawk and knife, seeing that the rifle was always my fav'rite weapon. He did lay about him like a man! I met him as I was coming home from the trail, with eleven Mingo scalps on his pole. You needn't shudder, Madam Effingham, for they was all from shav'd heads and warriors. When I look about me at these hills, where I used-to could count, sometimes twenty smokes, curling over the tree-tops, from the Delaware camps, it raises mournful thoughts, to think, that not a Red-skin is left of them all; unless it may be a drunken vagabond from the Oneida's, or them Yankee Indians, who, they say, be moving up from the sea-shore; and who belong to none of God's creaters, to my seeming; being, as it were, neither fish nor flesh; neither white-man, nor savage. Well! well! the time has come at last, and I must go"—

"Go!" echoed Edwards, "whither do you go?"

The Leather-stocking, who had imbibed, unconsciously, many of the Indian qualities, though he always thought of himself, as of a civilized being, compared with even the Delawares, averted his face to conceal the workings of his muscles, as he stooped to lift a large pack from behind the tomb, which he placed deliberately on his shoulders.

"Go!" exclaimed Elizabeth, approaching him, with a hurried step; "you should not venture so far in the woods alone, at your time of life, Natty; indeed, it is imprudent. He is bent, Effingham, on some distant hunting."

"What Mrs. Effingham tells you, is true, Leather-stock-

ing," said Edwards; there can be no necessity for your submitting to such hardships now! So throw aside your pack,
and confine your hunt to the mountains near us, if you will
go."

"Hardship! 'tis a pleasure, children, and the greatest that
is left me on this side of the grave."

"No, no; you shall not go to such a distance," cried
Elizabeth, smiling and laying her white hand on his deer-
skin pack; "I am right! I feel his camp-kettle and a canister
of powder! he must not be suffered to wander so far from us,
Oliver; remember how suddenly Mohegan dropp'd away."

"I know'd the parting would come hard, children; I know'd
it would!" said Natty, "and so I got aside to look at the
graves by myself, and thought if I left ye the keep-sake
which the Major gave me, when we first parted in the woods,
ye wouldn't take it unkind, but would know, that let the old
man's body go where it might, his feelings staid behind him."

"This means something more than common!" exclaimed
the youth; "where is it, Natty, that you purpose going?"

The hunter drew nigh him with a confident reasoning air,
as if what he had to say would silence all objections, and
replied—

"Why, lad, they tell me, that on the Big-Lakes, there's the
best of hunting, and a great range, without a white man on it,
unless it may be one like myself. I'm weary of living in clearings, and where the hammer is sounding in my ears from sun-
rise to sundown. And though I'm much bound to ye both,
children; I wouldn't say it if it was not true; I crave to go
into the woods ag'in, I do."

"Woods!" echoed Elizabeth, trembling with her feelings;
"do you not call these endless forests woods?"

"Ah! child, these be nothing to a man that's used to the
wilderness. I have took but little comfort sin' your father
come on with his settlers; but I wouldn't go far, while the
life was in the body that lies under the sod there. But now
he's gone, and Chingachgook is gone; and you be both
young and happy. Yes! the big-house has rung with merriment this month past! And now, I thought, was the time, to

try to get a little comfort, in the close of my days. Woods!
indeed! I doesn't call these woods, Madam Effingham, where
I lose myself every day of my life, in the clearings."

"If there be any thing wanting to your comfort," cried Oliver, "name it, Leather-stocking; and if it be attainable it is
yours."

"You mean all for the best, lad; I knew it; and so does
Madam, too; but your ways isn't my ways. 'Tis like the dead
there, who thought, when the breath was in them, that one
went east and one went west to find their heavens; but
they'll meet at last; and so shall we, children.—Yes, ind as
you've begun, and we shall meet in the land of the just, at
last."

"This is so new! so unexpected!" said Elizabeth, in almost
breathless excitement; "I had thought you meant to live
with us, and die with us, Natty."

"Words are of no avail!" exclaimed her husband; "the
habits of forty years are not to be dispossessed by the ties
of a day. I know you too well to urge you further, Natty;
unless you will let me build you a hut, on one of the distant hills, where we can sometimes see you, and know that
you are comfortable."

"Don't fear the Leather-stocking, children; God will see
that his days be provided for, and his ind happy. I know
you mean all for the best, but our ways doesn't agree: I love
the woods, and ye relish the face of man; I eat when hungry
and drink when a-dry, and ye keep stated hours and rules;
nay, nay, you even over-feed the dogs, lad, from pure kindness; and hounds should be gaunty to run well. The meanest of God's creaters be made for some use, and I'm form'd
for the wilderness; and, if ye love me, let me go where my
soul craves to be ag'in!"

The appeal was decisive; not another word of entreaty,
for him to remain, was then uttered; but Elizabeth bent her
head to her bosom and wept, while her husband dashed away
the tears from his eyes, and, with hands that almost refused
to perform their office, he produced his pocket-book, and extended a parcel of bank-notes to the hunter.

"Take these," he said, "at least, take these; secure them

about your person, and, in the hour of need, they will do you good service."

The old man took the notes, and examined them with a curious eye, when he said—

"This, then, is some of the new-fashioned money that they've been making at Albany, out of paper! It can't be worth much to they that hasn't larning! No, no, lad—take back the stuff; it will do me no sarvice. I took kear to get all the Frenchman's powder, afore he broke up, and they say lead grows where I'm going. It isn't even fit for wads, seeing that I use none but leather!—Madam Effingham, let an old man kiss your hand, and wish God's choicest blessings on you and your'n."

"Once more let me beseech you, stay!" cried Elizabeth. "Do not, Leather-stocking, leave me to grieve for the man who has twice rescued me from death, and who has served those I love so faithfully. For my sake, if not for your own, stay. I shall see you in those frightful dreams that still haunt my nights, dying in poverty and age, by the side of those terrific beasts you slew. There will be no evil that sickness, want, and solitude can inflict, that my fancy will not conjure as your fate. Stay with us, old man; if not for your own sake, at least for ours."

"Such thoughts and bitter dreams, Madam Effingham," returned the hunter, solemnly, "will never haunt an innocent parson long. They'll pass away with God's pleasure. And if the cat-a-mounts be yet brought to your eyes in sleep, 'tis not for my sake, but to show you the power of him that led me there to save you. Trust in God, Madam, and your honourable husband, and the thoughts for an old man like me can never be long nor bitter. I pray that the Lord will keep you in mind—the Lord that lives in clearings as well as in the wilderness—and bless you, and all that belong to you, from this time, till the great day when the whites shall meet the red-skins in judgment, and justice shall be the law, and not power."

Elizabeth raised her head, and offered her colourless cheek to his salute, when he lifted his cap, and touched it respectfully. His hand was grasped with convulsive fervour by the youth, who continued silent. The hunter prepared himself for the journey, drawing his belt tighter, and wasting his moments in the little reluctant movements of a sorrowful departure. Once or twice he essayed to speak, but a rising in his throat prevented it. At length he shouldered his rifle, and cried, with a clear huntsman's call, that echoed through the woods—

"He-e-e-re, he-e-e-re, pups—away, dogs, away;—ye'll be foot-sore afore ye see the ind of the journey!"

The hounds leaped from the earth at his cry, and, scenting around the graves and the silent pair, as if conscious of their own destination, they followed humbly at the heels of their master. A short pause succeeded, during which even the youth concealed his face on his grandfather's tomb. When the pride of manhood, however, suppressed the feelings of nature, he turned to renew his entreaties, but saw that the cemetery was occupied only by himself and his wife.

"He is gone!" cried Effingham.

Elizabeth raised her face, and saw the old hunter standing, looking back for a moment, on the verge of the woods. As he caught their glances, he drew his hard hand hastily across his eyes again, waved it on high for an adieu, and, uttering a forced cry to his dogs, who were crouching at his feet, he entered the forest.

This was the last that they ever saw of the Leatherstocking, whose rapid movements preceded the pursuit which Judge Temple both ordered and conducted. He had gone far towards the setting sun,—the foremost in that band of Pioneers, who are opening the way for the march of our nation across the continent.

FINIS.

Rinehart Editions